With an insatiable appetite for other people's business, Erica James will readily strike up conversation with strangers in the hope of unearthing a useful gem for her writing. She finds it the best way to write authentic characters for her novels, although her two grown-up sons claim they will never recover from a childhood spent in a perpetual state of embarrassment at their mother's compulsion.

The author of several bestselling novels, including *Gardens of Delight* which won the Romantic Novel of the Year Award, Erica divides her time between Cheshire and Lake Como in Italy, where she now strikes up conversation with unsuspecting Italians.

THE QUEEN OF NEW BEGINNINGS

Clayton Miller's life is a mess. One of the country's best comedy scriptwriters, his career has stalled. His girlfriend has left him for his ex-best friend and ex-writing partner. When he commits a spectacularly public fall from grace and is hounded by the press, his agent banishes him to a remote country house until the dust settles . . . Alice Shoemaker is a voiceover artist who habitually avoids telling the truth. She's agreed to help a friend, by shopping and cleaning for the unknown man staying at Cuckoo House. She suspects that Clayton has something to hide. But equally, so does she . . . As they discover the truth about each other, an unlikely friendship is formed and secrets are revealed, until Alice discovers the worst kind of betrayal.

Books by Erica James
Published by The House of Ulverscroft:

A BREATH OF FRESH AIR
A SENSE OF BELONGING
ACT OF FAITH
THE HOLIDAY
PRECIOUS TIME
HIDDEN TALENTS
PARADISE HOUSE
LOVE AND DEVOTION
GARDENS OF DELIGHT
TELL IT TO THE SKIES

ERICA JAMES

THE QUEEN OF NEW BEGINNINGS

Complete and Unabridged

CHARNWOOD
Leicester

First published in Great Britain in 2010 by
Orion Books
an imprint of
The Orion Publishing Group Ltd.
London

First Charnwood Edition
published 2011
by arrangement with
The Orion Publishing Group Ltd.
London

British Library CIP Data

James, Erica, *1960 –*
   The queen of new beginnings.
   1. Authors, English- -Fiction.
   2. Voice actors and actresses- -Fiction.
   3. Large type books.
   I. Title
   823.9′2–dc22

ISBN 978–1–44480–578–9

Published by
F. A. Thorpe (Publishing)
Anstey, Leicestershire

Set by Words & Graphics Ltd.
Anstey, Leicestershire
Printed and bound in Great Britain by
T. J. International Ltd., Padstow, Cornwall

This book is printed on acid-free paper

To Edward and Samuel who are unquestionably the best.

Acknowledgements

I'm grateful to a great number of people who directly or indirectly made this book possible.

Thank you to new friends and old at Orion, especially Susan Lamb, Kate Mills, Jade Chandler, Genevieve Pegg, Juliet Ewers, Lord Anthony Beardy-Keates of Luton, Andrew Taylor, Jo Carpenter, Ian Diment, Lisa Milton, Sophie Mitchell, Helen Richardson, Lisa Ginanne, Peter Roche, Dallas Manderson, Malcolm Edwards, Mark Streatfield and Pandora White. And not forgetting the ever-supportive reps who like to lunch and gossip with me: Jon Small, David Asquith and Judy King.

Thanks, of course, to Jonathan Lloyd — Agent of the Year. *Way to go!*

A colossal amount of thanks to my wonderful friend and comedy scriptwriter extraordinaire, Ray Allen, who never fails to make me laugh. One day I just know he's going to pull himself together.

Thanks also to the nice people at White House Sound Ltd and the wonderfully gifted Maggie Mash who gave me an invaluable insight into the world of voiceover work. As did Teresa Gallagher.

Thanks to all my lovely new friends in Italy: Rita Annunziata, Sara Cilia, and Harold Lubberdink, Mikael Mammen, Massimo, Tony and Vicki Monaco, Anne and Ian, and Anna and Simon Carden.

'All happy families resemble one another, each unhappy family is unhappy in its own way.'

Anna Karenina — Leo Tolstoy

1

Clayton Miller had a new hobby. Some might argue it was more of an obsession than a hobby and certainly he knew Stacey wouldn't hesitate to use the word obsession. She would probably say that it was yet another example of his rampant self-absorption.

Maybe she was right. Either way, he didn't care. So what if he now spent what Stacey would describe as an unnatural amount of time writing his obituary? It served the purpose of keeping his mind active whilst distracting it at the same time. Not that he went along with the Use It Or Lose It evangelists. On the contrary. He believed in using his brain as little as he could get away with in the hope that it wouldn't be worn out when he needed it most. Look at Iris Murdoch. One of the sharpest minds of the last century and she still went ga-ga. Why? Because she wore her brain out. Case closed.

The obituary page was often what he read first in a newspaper; he enjoyed peering in through the gap in the curtains of a stranger's life. Frequently, though, he found himself speculating just how accurate the descriptions were. The question he was facing with his own obituary was just how truthful he should be. The lure to embellish his life with a flourish of colour here and there was proving strong.

Clayton Miller, aged only forty-four and undoubtedly one of the most prolific and best comedy scriptwriters this country has produced, tragically died on his way home to his weekend retreat in the country from an award ceremony during which he'd been given a much-deserved lifetime achievement award for his contribution to the world of comedy; the standing ovation he received went on for a record twelve minutes and fifty-two seconds. An hour later his Bentley Continental GTC Convertible was involved in a head-on collision with a Vauxhall Astra driven by an unknown man. The unknown man survived the crash, but will spend the rest of his life with the death of a truly exceptional writer on his conscience.

A private funeral service will take place for the much-missed Clayton Miller, followed later by a memorial service at Westminster Abbey where his legion of fans can pay their last respects.

In a bizarre twist of fate it would later be revealed that the unknown man was none other than Barry Osborne, Clayton's one-time best friend and writing partner.

He was not a vindictive man by nature, but circumstances had altered Clayton's thinking when it came to Barry — or Lucky Bazza as he thought of him. He couldn't go so far as to kill him off in his imagination or wish a gruesome life-threatening illness on him, but he did think it appropriate that if Clayton should be unfortunate enough to meet an untimely end, Lucky Bazza should suffer for it. If only with a guilty conscience. A fair exchange in Clayton's opinion, given that Bazza had robbed Clayton not only of his writing career, but his long-term partner as well.

But so much for embellishment. A truthful obituary would sadly fall well short of the glowing tribute Clayton had in mind for himself. All that would stand up to a lie detector would be Clayton's age. By no stretch of the imagination could he now be described as prolific. Nor did he own a Bentley. Or a house in the country. And since he hadn't written anything more coherent than a shopping list or his obituary in the last three years, there would be some people who would call him a has-been. A failure.

If it hadn't been for recent events — he squeezed his eyes shut at the memory — he would be lucky to get more than a couple of lines in the papers: *Clayton Miller, co-writer and creator of the hit series* Joking Aside *died today aged forty-four. Separated from his long-term girlfriend six months ago, he lived alone with only his writer's block for company.*

But if he were to die right now, as a consequence of recent events he would garner quite a few column inches. Though God knew what they would write about him. Probably they would point the finger at his mental balance and say he'd been off his rocker. Crazier than Britney Spears. Or more out of control than Messrs

Brand and Ross. They might even hint that his death was not from natural causes, that he had engineered it as a way out.

He opened his eyes. Another five minutes trapped in this rattling, airtight Nissan taxi and engineering his suicide would look remarkably appealing. The car's suspension made it seem like taking a ride on a jelly — not that he'd ever taken a ride on a jelly; who had? — and its lurching motion was causing his stomach to pitch and heave. He was sure that his face was as green as the toxic, pine tree-shaped air freshener dangling from the rear-view mirror. The driver had the heater switched to hot-enough-to-melt-the-dashboard and worse, the man kept coughing and sneezing. Bubonic plague was probably in the offing.

Clayton blamed his current predicament on Glen, his agent.

It had been Glen's idea for him to hide out in some off-the-beaten-track place where the press wouldn't find him. Doubtless it would prove to be one of those places where there were road names like Lower Bottom Lane, Big Bottom Lane, and Up Your Bottom.

Whatever hellish place he was destined to take refuge in, he hoped the driver knew the way, that he hadn't been lying when he'd looked at the address Clayton had given him at the station. There was no sign of any satnav equipment on the dashboard, which Clayton took to be a good sign. It ruled out the possibility of a bossy-voiced woman misdirecting them down a one-way track to a ravine and their certain death.

4

Death. There it was again. It kept popping into his thoughts at the slightest provocation. Was he suicidal?

Murderous, more like it. He could happily take out all those journalists who had written about him lately and never experience a moment's regret. It wouldn't solve a damned thing, but since when had revenge been about solving anything?

He wiped at the steamed up window and looked out. Nothing. Zilch. Just miles of empty fields and drystone walls. Wherever he was, with the light fading, it looked suspiciously like the end of the world. He closed his eyes once more and tried to picture himself in happier times when he had been at the height of his creativity.

★ ★ ★

It was dark when the Nissan finally came to a stop. The ratcheting sound of the handbrake being yanked on woke Clayton. He stepped out of the car and stretched. Weary and dishevelled, he was in need of a long hot shower.

He looked up at the house and didn't like what he saw. It was huge. Huge and unwelcoming. It seemed to glower down at him with the kind of I'm-bigger-than-you attitude that had terrorized many a school playground since time immemorial. It made him want to run and hide.

'It's some place you've got yourself here,' the driver said as he hauled Clayton's luggage out of the boot.

'It's not mine,' Clayton answered him.

5

'Just visiting, then?'

Eager not to part with any information about himself — Glen had warned him to keep his mouth shut — he shrugged and nodded evasively. He paid the man and watched the tail lights of the Nissan disappear down the lengthy, straight drive and into the night.

Alone, he sought out the large flowerpot he had been instructed to locate, and rummaged around in the dark until he found what he was looking for. What kind of a neighbourhood was it that you could leave a key under a flowerpot in this day and age?

He let himself in and at once experienced a pang of longing for the toxic warmth of the Nissan taxi. The house was icy-cold. Was this his punishment? To freeze in hell?

How Stacey and Lucky Bazza would love that.

2

'OK, Alice, we're all done here. That last bit works perfectly now. Thanks for doing it again. You're a star.'

Alice looked through the glass to where Josie and the sound engineer were sitting; she nodded at the thumbs up sign they were both giving her. She took off her headphones and stretched. It had been a tiring day. Eight hours of speaking like a chipmunk; it would wear anyone out.

Alice first discovered she had a talent for mimicry when she was eleven years old. Her mother had been away in London and her father, in a frenzy of creativity, had locked himself in his darkroom at the top of the house. Which meant Alice was left to her own devices, a state of affairs she was more than used to. On this particular Monday morning, being between au pairs, she had knocked on her father's door to ask him to drive her to school. Getting no response, and being a resourceful child, she had taken matters into her own hands. She had gone back downstairs and dialled the number for the school secretary's office. She could have walked but it would have taken for ever, and it would also have drawn attention to her father's somewhat casual attitude to parenting. And anyway, Alice hadn't felt like school that day. 'I'm very sorry,' she had said in her mother's low velvet-smooth voice — the voice that millions were familiar with both on radio and television — 'This is Mrs Barrett and I'm calling to say that Alice is suffering from a horrible stomach bug and will be staying at home today.'

She had spent most of the day lying on the sofa in toast and peanut butter heaven watching corny old movies, happily dreaming one day of being an actress herself. Of being a star. Her father appeared in the middle of the afternoon and didn't bat an eyelid at the sight of her still in her dressing gown. 'You're home early,' he remarked, helping himself to her last piece of toast.

From mimicking her mother, she moved on to impersonating her teachers. This raised her stock amongst her peers — if not her teachers — and further fuelled her ambition to be an actress.

Five years ago she might have believed that there was still a chance of that dream coming true. But now, at the age of thirty-one, she had accepted that things hadn't turned out quite as she'd hoped; a corner had been turned and stardom had passed her by on the other side of the road.

Instead she did voiceovers, along with reading for audio books. She was doing rather well with children's books right now and the author James Montgomery — be still her beating heart — was, as her agent told her, her number one fan and would have no one else read his books. His sales were growing but experience told Alice this was a double-edged sword. If his books became massively successful, she would be out of a job; a big named actor would be brought in to take her place. Some years back she had been the original voice of This Little Piggy — a porcine version of My Little Pony. Her voice, so she had been told, was perfect when the television advertisement was first aired, but six months later, when sales for This Little Piggy had gone through the roof of the pig-sty and were expected to soar higher still with a worldwide market, her agent telephoned with the bad news that Zoë Wanamaker had been signed up in her place.

So yes, Alice was pragmatic enough to know that James Montgomery might well be her number one fan now, but things had a nasty habit of changing. Whatever the future held, she was quite used to taking disappointment on the chin and convincing herself something better — a new beginning — was just around the corner.

She left the recording studio thirty minutes later and drove home. Whenever she told people what she did for a living, they always assumed that she was up and down to London to some kind of glamorous Media Land studio, mixing with the rich and famous. When she explained that the bulk of her work was done in a converted coach house on the outskirts of Nottingham, she saw the disappointment in their faces. Suddenly her work didn't seem so thrilling. And nor was it: it could be painstaking and exhausting. But at least the work her agent found her was plentiful and varied. She could be in a studio in Manchester one day doing an advert for a commercial radio station, the next she could be down in London providing the voice for a major bank and its telephone-operated accounts, and another she could be the calm, reassuring voice advising airline passengers how to avoid a DVT and what to do in an emergency. The first time she had worked for an airline company, midway through the recording of what to do in the event of a crash she had been overcome with the urge to say in a quiet matter-of-fact voice, 'Never in the history of aviation has an aircraft survived an impact with the ocean at great speed, so if I were you, I wouldn't bother with the life jackets.' She would have loved then to scream into the microphone in a terrified voice, 'You're all going to die!'

It took her longer than usual to complete the journey home to Stonebridge and before she had got the key in the door of her cottage, she heard footsteps behind her. She turned, hoping it wasn't who she thought it might be. She really wasn't in the mood.

Another wish denied her: sure enough it was Bob the Body Builder. 'Hello, Bob,' she said. 'What are you doing there lurking like a mugger in the shadows?'

'Hey, no one who looks as good as this lurks in the shadows.' To prove his point, he flexed his biceps and thrust out his colossal chest. Goodness only knew how many hours of weightlifting he was doing now or what quantity of steroids he was consuming. Despite the cold November weather, he was dressed in his customary bursting-at-the-seams T-shirt and baggy tracksuit bottoms. His exposed flesh was sun-bed tanned and as hairless as a baby's bottom. He was buffed to within an inch of his life. 'This is a package that stands out,' he said. 'Trust me when I say it amazes and astonishes.'

'As does your modesty.'

'I've told you before, Alice, all that modesty claptrap is for losers.'

'So what can I do for you?'

'Mum needs a favour. She said to ask you to come round the moment you got home.' Suddenly Bob the Body Builder sounded like a six-year-old boy. Sweet.

'Tell her I'll be there in five minutes.'

He puffed out his chest again. 'How about that drink you're just dying to have with me tonight?'

Ah, not so sweet. 'Sorry, Bob, it's been a long day.'

He shrugged. 'Your loss.'

'I'll do my best to try and get over it,' she said. She turned the key in the lock of her door and stepped inside.

Ever since Bob and his mother had moved in next door last year, Ronnetta Tanner had been trying to fix Alice up with her beloved son. 'He'd be perfect for you,' Ronnetta had said. In what way exactly, Alice wasn't entirely sure. The only thing they had in common was their age.

* * *

Whenever Ronnetta Tanner opened the doors of her 1960s drinks cabinet, Alice always expected to hear the tinkling music-box sound of Greensleeves, accompanied by a mechanical ballerina pirouetting stiffly amongst the glasses

11

and bottles. In the absence of these two things, there was a light that illuminated the interior of the cabinet as well as the two flamingos etched into the glass panels on the inside of the doors. Kitsch didn't do it justice.

'What'll it be, then?' Ronnetta asked Alice in her gravelly voice that had only recently seen the back of a fifty-a-day habit following a course of hypnotherapy. It was a gift of a voice for Alice to copy and she had used it several times in her voiceover work.

'I'll have my usual, but make it a small one, please, Ronnetta. Go easy on the gin. What was it you wanted to ask me? Bob mentioned something about a favour.'

Their drinks poured and ice added with tongs from a plastic ice bucket, Ronnetta handed Alice her tumbler and settled herself in the chair opposite. Ten years older than her drinks cabinet, Ronnetta was just as showy and unrestrained. She was dressed in black leggings with an oversized red mohair sweater belted at her waist. Black high-heeled shoes were trimmed with two red bows. Alice had never seen her in flat shoes. Even for cutting the small patch of lawn at the back of her house, Ronnetta wore high-heeled slingbacks. The style Nazis would claim that for her age she wore too much jewellery and too much make-up. Her long nails — her pride and joy — were the real thing and were carefully manicured and varnished every other day, and by Ronnetta herself. As she repeatedly told Alice, she wasn't about to entrust her precious nails to some gum-chewing, clueless girl who would cover them with plastic monstrosities quick as a flash. In the year that Alice had known her neighbour, she had never once seen those nails unpainted. Today they were red, in keeping with her outfit. Her real name was Veronica but it had been shortened to Ronnie as a child and then later in life she became Ronnetta. The name certainly suited her.

'I've been let down by one of my girls,' Ronnetta said after Alice had taken a sip of her gin and tonic, 'and I was wondering if you could help me out. I need someone tomorrow. Sorry it's such short notice.' She crossed her thin legs, got herself even more comfortable. 'How're you fixed?'

'What kind of a job is it this time?'

'Cleaner, but there's a possibility that there could be a bit of housekeeping thrown in.'

'And how many times a week would I be needed?'

'That's up to the client really. I said to the chap who's organized it all on behalf of the client that we'd play it by ear, see how things go. I only saw the house for the first time yesterday after I'd been sent the key, but I can tell you it's big. The poor man will be rattling around in it like a pea in a drum. At least that means the cleaning should be minimal. You'll have to do his shopping, though. He doesn't drive.'

'What about cooking?'

'I don't think you'll be expected to do that.'

Alice considered Ronnetta's request. Since Ronnetta had started her cleaning agency, going from just two women from the village who worked for her to having a team of more than twenty to handle the extra services offered, Alice had often helped her neighbour out when she'd been let down. It wasn't that she needed the money; it was more a matter of enjoying the opportunity to poke about in someone else's life. 'How long will you need me for?' she asked.

'The job itself is open-ended at the moment. But I'd only need you for the next week or two. By then I'll have found a replacement for the girl who's messed me about. Usual wages apply.' She added these last words with a crinkly-eyed smile and a jangle of bangles as she raised her glass to her lips.

'Go on then, why not? It looks like I'm in for a quiet fortnight anyway. What time do I have to be on parade tomorrow?'

'Eleven o'clock.'

'Is it here in the village?'

'On the outskirts, on the Matlock road. It's very remote. Real back of beyond stuff, half a mile from the main road. Not a single neighbour on the doorstep. I'll get the address for you.'

While Ronnetta was out of the room, Alice took a long, thoughtful sip of her drink. Outskirts of Stonebridge. On the Matlock road. What were the chances? A huge place with not a single neighbour? It sounded very like Cuckoo House.

'Here you are,' Ronnetta said when she returned and handed over a slip of paper to Alice. 'The client is a Mr Shannon and he's staying at Cuckoo House. Have you heard of it? You always seem to know everyone and everything round here.'

'It certainly rings a bell.'

3

Clayton had a thing about splashy taps.

He disliked the sudden hostility of them. There they sat, as innocent as you like, just waiting for their moment when they could take the uninitiated by surprise. Strange houses always had more than their fair share of such taps. Along with toilets that had their own mysterious way of flushing. Fail to unlock the secret code and you could be in there for hours frantically pumping the handle trying to get rid of the evidence of your visit.

This house in particular had some viciously splashy taps, the sort that knew no half measures; they were either off or gushing like a geyser in all directions. The tap he'd just encountered had produced a force of water that was so powerful it had bounced off the basin and soaked him comprehensively.

One day he would get to the bottom of why. Was it all about water pressure? Or plain old ineptitude on the part of plumbers the world over? It was a mystery. But then so much of life was, to him. Never more so than now when everything felt like a monumental uphill struggle. No matter what he did, nothing seemed to go right for him these days. He was tired of it. Tired of the black cloud hanging over him. When would it ever end?

He dried his hands and gave his sweater, scarf

and jeans a half-hearted pat, then went back into the bedroom. Out of a choice of seven bedrooms, he'd picked one that wasn't the largest, but it had an interesting windowed turret in the furthest corner of the room. It also had a panoramic view of the garden and a more extensive view of a whole lot of nothing. The nothingness was green, hilly and sodden. Wet and depressingly dreary, it was pure hillbilly country. He could understand why Glen had said it would be the perfect place to lie low.

Glen had phoned him late last night, just as Clayton had given up ever figuring out how to switch on the boiler and inject some warmth into the place. 'You've arrived, then?' Glen had said. 'Everything all right?'

'No! Everything is not all right! The boiler doesn't work, I'm dying of cold and there's nothing to eat. Other than what I picked up on the train. And I ate that last night.'

'Don't complain, Clay. With only twenty-four hours' notice I've found you a house with furniture, electricity, water, even the internet. So yes, feel free to go ahead and call me Mr Wonderful. Just don't expect me to throw in room service as well.'

'Tell me again about these friends of yours. What kind of people are they that want to live in this back of beyond place? I swear my nearest neighbour must be at least ten miles away.'

'I've known Craig and Anthea for years. In fact I was at school with Craig. He used to be in financial services, had his own business here in London, sold it for a killing and moved up there

16

for a change of lifestyle.'

'And presumably they came to their senses and hightailed it out of here. Where've they gone?'

'They spend the winter months in warmer climes; they've bought a place in the Caribbean. As I said to you before, be glad they have. Stonebridge will be the perfect place for you to lie low. And remember, they're letting you stay there as a favour to me. Don't let me down. You've trashed your career; please don't trash their home in a fit of pique as well. Oh, and don't forget, the cleaning agency I've arranged to take care of things for you is sending someone round in the morning. About eleven, I think. Be nice to whoever it is. You'll be totally dependent on the person they send.'

'So that's two things I have to remember. One: I must not trash the house, and two: I must be nice to the cleaner. Anything else?'

'Yes. Sort your head out. And when you've done that, try doing some writing. After all, what else are you going to do up there?'

Good bloody question, Clayton had thought. 'Is there anything happening down there I should know about?'

'There's nothing.'

'What does that mean?'

'What do you mean, what does that mean?'

'I mean, is there something that you think I shouldn't know about?'

'What, like trivial stuff? Like I've been given tickets for the premiere of the new Colin Farrell and Daniel Craig movie?'

'Why would I want to know that?'

'I don't know. You started this.'

'Look, just tell me, is there anything being said about me that I should or shouldn't know about?'

'But if I think you shouldn't know about it, I'd hardly tell you, would I?'

'JUST TELL ME!'

'There's stuff. Yes. But I really don't think you should know about it.'

He'd ended the call exhausted.

* * *

At twenty minutes past eleven, Clayton gave up waiting for the sound of the doorbell and decided to make himself a cup of coffee. He turned on the tap and water immediately bounced off the rim of the kettle and shot up into his face and down his dried-out front.

That was when he heard the doorbell. Two loud, demanding rings. Not a polite little ring — *yoo-hoo, I'm here!* — but two bossy intrusive rings — *Oi, you in there, get your sorry arse to the door!* He banged the kettle down and traversed the mile to the front foor.

'You're late,' he said, wiping his face with his scarf. 'Timekeeping not your speciality, I take it?'

For a moment the girl, swamped in a thick padded jacket with the hood up, didn't say anything. She just stood there in the porch, sheltering from the rain with her lips pursed tightly shut. Her eyes, though, were darting about, looking beyond and around him, as if she were casing the joint.

'I sorry for late,' she said eventually. 'I lose myself. You going to keep me here on doorstep all day, mister? Why you covered in water? You been out in rain?'

He frowned at the foreign accent. That was all he needed, a lippy Polish cleaner. There again, she didn't look Polish. Romanian or Bulgarian perhaps. Now that she'd pushed back the hood of her jacket, he could see her hair was long and wavy and very dark brown. As dark as her eyes which, now they had stopped darting about, he realized were assessing him. Her stare was disconcertingly direct. 'I was making some coffee,' he said. 'The tap, it — ' He stopped short. Why in hell's name was he explaining himself to a complete stranger? She was here to keep house for him, not to interrogate him.

She shrugged and, armed with a plethora of cleaning equipment, she stepped inside. 'Thank you. A cup of coffee before I start working very hard for you. Thank you, mister.'

He closed the door, wishing she was on the other side of it. 'Are you Polish?' he asked.

The dark assessing eyes leapt to his. 'How many languages you speak?'

He silently groaned. Great. Her English wasn't up to much. 'I asked if you were Polish,' he said, this time more loudly, his words clearly and slowly enunciated.

'And I said, how many languages you speak?'

'Just English.'

'Oh, so mister who no speak anything but English thinks I am speaking Polish. Well, clean out ears, mister.'

Stunned at her rudeness, his jaw dropped. The cheeky little strumpet! He said, 'I didn't say that. All I meant was that you *sound* Polish.'

'Well, I not Polish. Not Polish at all. You insult me. This way to kitchen?'

He chased after her down the stone-flagged corridor. This wouldn't do. Glen would have to ring the agency and arrange for someone else to come. He wasn't going to stand for this sort of behaviour. He caught up with her. 'I think there's been a mistake,' he tried. 'The agency must have sent you to the wrong house.'

She turned and stared at him. 'No mistake, mister. This is Cuckoo House. I am Katya. All is correct.'

He searched again for a way out. 'And you're here in the UK legally? I don't want any trouble.'

She skewered him with a fierce look. 'You read too much newspaper shit.'

He scoffed. 'I assure you I do no such thing. I wouldn't wipe my arse with a single one of those rags.'

'And don't get no funny ideas about me doing that for you, mister.' She wagged a finger at him. 'You go to toilet on your own.'

She turned her back on him, shook off her coat and began sorting noisily through her collection of cloths and cleaning products, setting them out on the table where the remains of his supper from last night still lay — several plastic sandwich packets and two cans of Red Bull.

He walked round to the other side of the table, using it as a barrier. 'So if you're not from

Poland, where are you from? Romania?'

'Does it matter where I from?'

'I'm just trying to be polite.'

'Well, you not polite. You rude. You very rude man.'

'You think it's an insult for someone to enquire about your cultural background? And if you don't mind me saying, your reaction to me thinking you were Polish smacks of racism.'

She looked up sharply. 'What's that you say? You want to smack me? Let me tell you, mister. One smack from you and I report you to police! I have my rights.'

He put his hands up. '*Whoa!* That's not what I said.' Choosing his words with extra care, he added, 'I think it might be better if the agency sends someone who can speak English properly. It would be easier all round. Don't you agree?'

'Now you accuse me of being stupid. Mister, I plenty smart enough. You will have job keeping up with me.'

'Really?'

'Yes, really. I am very clever. My brain goes whir, whir, all day long.'

Clayton could believe it. Her tongue, too. 'Tell me,' he said, no longer caring whether he offended her, 'does your great big yapper ever stop?'

She looked at him blankly. She had a quirky face, he decided, wide cheekbones and a small pointy chin. Almost pixie-like. 'Do you ever stop talking, is what I asked,' he said.

Her lips curved into a faint smile. 'I know what you ask. I was proving you wrong.'

'How so?'

'Mister, you really are as stupid as you look. I was proving I can stop my big yapper any time I choose. And please, I like my coffee with milk. No sugar.'

Clayton gave up. *Stupid!* She had actually called him stupid. Didn't she know who was paying her wages? He went over to the kettle. 'And when does the mothership come back for you?' he muttered under his breath as he risked the tap again.

'Nothing wrong with my hearing, mister. I no alien. And if you want the truth, I am from Latvia. You even hear of my country?'

★ ★ ★

It was his appalling rudeness that had set Alice off. That and her apprehension about being back at Cuckoo House. She had come close to telling Ronnetta she had changed her mind about taking on the job, and the reason why, but curiosity had got the better of her. Why not go back? What harm could it do? More to the point, if she were honest, wasn't it what she'd always wanted to do one day?

But undoubtedly she had caused quite a lot of harm by the looks of things. Ronnetta was due a massive apology. She had messed up this job in grand style. She had given the client — Mr Shannon — every reason to complain and demand someone else to take her place, preferably one with a civil tongue in her head.

It wasn't the first time she had adopted a

different persona when she helped Ronnetta out — not that Ronnetta knew that. It was the actress in her. Occasionally she dressed for the part. Sometimes she wore a blonde wig and pretended she was Astrid from Dusseldorf, here in England to learn zee goot English. She'd had some fun with Astrid. But Katya was new. She had been devised very much on the spur of the moment. In fact, Alice was rather pleased with her latest creation.

It had been fun putting such a rude man in his place and she would make no apology for that. As though it was a major task he had been set, she had watched him clatter ineptly about the kitchen making the coffee. Tall and thin, he seemed all angles. She wondered if he always looked so crumpled and angry. Interestingly his eyes looked younger than the rest of him. The coffee finally made, he had taken himself off, leaving her, he'd said pointedly, to get on with her work.

If the kitchen — which was nothing like she remembered — was anything to go by, excluding the isolated mess on the table, the house appeared clean enough. She hoped he wasn't going to prove to be one of those mucky types, incapable of doing anything without making a mess.

It was difficult to pin an exact age on him; he could be mid forties or early fifties. But oddly, there was something familiar about him. Maybe he just reminded her of someone. He'd look a lot better if he tidied himself up, though. A shave and a brush through his thick unruly hair would

23

be a good start. He could also do with losing the attitude and lightening up. And while he was about it, sorting out his dress sense wouldn't go amiss either. The tatty old pullover he was wearing was fraying at the cuffs; it had definitely seen better days. As had his jeans — one of the back pockets was ripped and hanging off. And the scarf around his neck was distinctly moth-eaten. Overall he cut an eccentric and shambolic figure. She could almost feel sorry for him.

Almost.

She took a sip of the coffee he'd made, winced at the sweetness of it — damn the man, he'd added sugar — and dismissed him from her mind. She had more important things to think of. Like having a good snoop round. To establish, after all this time, exactly how she really felt being back where she had grown up.

And where better to start than upstairs in her bedroom?

But first, how about some heat? The house was bone-numbingly cold. She went over to the nearest radiator and touched it. Mm . . . if she was going to spend any amount of time here, there would have to be some changes. Mr Shannon might like the idea of freezing to death, but she did not.

*　*　*

As he warmed his hands on his mug of coffee, Clayton considered his latest attempt at his obituary on his laptop. This time it revolved around being found frozen to death by a crazy Latvian housekeeper.

The room he had retreated to was directly beneath the bedroom he had chosen and he was sitting at an antique writing desk in the window of the turret. He gazed disconsolately out of the window. It was still raining. The sky was still grey. It still depressed the hell out of him. If Glen had thought this was a suitable place for him to get his head sorted while lying low, he'd made a big mistake. It only added to his problems. It compacted the realization just how pathetic his life had become.

Somewhere in the faraway distance, he could hear Katya moving about upstairs. He'd got his own back on her. Using the sachet of sugar he had pinched on the train yesterday — he never could resist helping himself to those perfectly shaped little packets, even though he never took sugar in his own drinks — he had added it to her coffee. Served her right. Small victories. They were not to be knocked.

He had made up his mind. Just as soon as she had gone shopping and stocked the cupboards and fridge with food, he'd call Glen and insist he speak to the agency and demand someone else to shop and clean for him. He could just imagine Glen's response. He'd probably say having a foreigner as his only point of contact with the outside world was ideal. It meant she wouldn't have a clue who he was.

A scratching noise behind him had him spinning round in his chair.

Mice?

He cocked his head and listened hard. There it was again. Not mice, he concluded. And not a scratching noise as he'd thought, but a ticking.

Seconds passed.

Tick . . . tick . . . gurgle . . . tick.

It was the gurgle that did it. He knew then what the sound was. It was the sound of trapped air.

Was it possible?

Had Katya succeeded where he had failed?

He went over to one of the two radiators in the room. *Yes!* Heat. Glorious heat. The girl was a miracle worker. He wasn't going to die of hypothermia after all.

4

Of all the bedrooms he could have picked, Mr Shannon had chosen Alice's old bedroom. But like the kitchen downstairs, which was sleek and showroom-smart with shiny granite work surfaces and state-of-the-art appliances, it bore very little resemblance to the bedroom of Alice's childhood.

When it had been Alice's room, it had contained an eclectic mix of rugs and cumbersome furniture, including her great aunt Eliza's rocking chair. Alice had spent hours rocking in it, either lost in a book or simply daydreaming while gazing out of the windows. Thanks to her father, who had never been short on whimsical ideas when it came to presents, she had had a small wooden stool and a spinning wheel and she used to sit at it in the turret and pretend that she was Rapunzel waiting for her prince to appear.

As an only child she had learned from a young age to lose herself in her imagination and would often write, direct and star in her own one-woman shows. Just occasionally she would perform for her parents or the au pair, but her regular audience consisted of her collection of spellbound dolls and teddy bears.

At the end of her bed there had been a large wooden trunk that had travelled the world with Great Aunt Eliza. It had ended its life as Alice's

dressing-up box and most of its contents —
tailored dress suits, floaty evening dresses,
scarves, beads, brooches, hats, shoes and
handbags — had belonged to a woman that Alice
only remembered from photographs. She couldn't
have been very big because when Alice was only
ten years old, Great Aunt Eliza's shoes fitted her
perfectly.

As well as a dressing-up box, Alice also had an
intriguing store of props to use in her
one-woman shows. This was mostly down to her
father, who had an obsessive eye for anything of
a fanciful or theatrical nature. 'I came across this
the other day and thought you might like it,
Alice,' he would say. One day he presented her
with an ornate birdcage with a stuffed mynah
bird inside. It was a week before Alice discovered
there was a key under the base of the cage and
that when she turned it, the mynah bird moved
its head, opened its beak and sang. Other 'finds'
had included the spinning wheel and stool, a top
hat, a Russian copy of Leo Tolstoy's *Anna
Karenina*, a false beard, an old-fashioned
telephone, a Sherlock Holmes-style pipe, a
battered dinner gong, and a scruffy pair of red
tap shoes, which her father soon regretted giving
her.

To Alice's disappointment the tap shoes only
fitted her for a few months. But during those
months she drove her parents to distraction by
endlessly tap-tap-tapping her way round the
house. She loved the noise the metal taps made,
especially on the wooden floorboards in her
bedroom. She would roll back the threadbare

28

rugs and dance and dance. If her parents were away she would seize her opportunity and dance until her legs ached and she was doubled over with a stitch. But if her father was home, he would crash into her room after only a few minutes, throw her over his shoulder and threaten to chuck her down the stairs if she made any more noise. She never actually thought he would, but on one occasion, the au pair — a quiet, studious girl from Stockholm who had only been with them a few days — thought he was serious. At the sight of Alice being dangled over the banisters, she burst into tears with fright. She packed her bags and left that very evening in a taxi, saying she couldn't stay in such a mad house a moment longer.

Untidiness was a sign of a creative mind, so Alice's mother maintained. Which seemed to be the family excuse for the chaotic state of the house, a chaos that guaranteed nothing could ever be found when it was needed. Her parents would frequently drive themselves wild looking for their car keys or a pen. Shrieking at the top of their voices, they would accuse each other of moving whatever it was they couldn't find. Invariably it was Alice who would find what they were looking for. Instead of thanking her, they would suspect that she had been playing a game with them, of hiding the kitchen scissors or the TV licence that urgently needed paying, merely to gain their attention.

So much for Cuckoo House when she was growing up, when it had been a casual, messy and informal environment.

Under its current ownership, it looked and felt a very different house. Alice couldn't imagine anyone threatening to throw a nuisance tap-dancing child down the stairs in these immaculate surroundings.

The walls of her old bedroom were decorated with a subtly patterned cream and blue wallpaper and the pale-blue carpet was fitted and invitingly soft underfoot. The furniture was antique, elegant and highly polished; it reeked of good taste and sophistication, and of order. Most striking of all was the enormous bed with its intricately carved headboard. Not so striking was that Mr Shannon hadn't bothered to cover the duvet or pillows.

After a brief search, she found what she was looking for in a large chest of drawers: fresh bedlinen. She began making up the bed, allowing herself once again to explore her secret store of memories.

One of her earliest memories was when her father had returned home from one of his many trips abroad. He had tiptoed into her room and woken her with a scratchy kiss. At first she hadn't recognized him because of his beard, and she'd let out a startled cry and buried herself deep beneath the bedclothes. He'd laughed and tugged her out and when she'd looked at him closely she could see that he wasn't a stranger come to steal her after all. He'd given her a toy koala and a wooden snake that moved like the real thing.

As a naturalist photographer of some repute, Bruce Barrett was frequently away for months at a time. His work was always being featured in the *National Geographic* magazine as well as the Sunday supplements. When he was home he was more often than not at the top of the house in his darkroom. There was no guessing what kind of mood he'd be in when he opened the door and emerged blinking mole-like into the light. He could be sulky and withdrawn, or waging war on anything or anyone who was unfortunate enough to get in his way. Other times he had a ridiculous sense of the dramatic and would dress up as a pirate, complete with wooden peg leg and eye patch. Waving a fake cutlass he would chase Alice round the house until her giddy excitement tipped over into high-pitched squealing terror and she'd be shaking and screaming for him to stop. He never knew when enough was enough, that a small child could only take so much. There were other times, though, when he would sit for hours at a time quietly reading to her. She often fell asleep in his arms.

A typical way for him to emerge from his darkroom was to slide down the banisters and bellow at the top of his voice, 'What's a man to do round here to get anything to eat?'

'Oh, do stop crashing around like a five-year-old,' Alice's mother would say when he burst into her study. 'I'm trying to write my column. Now go away.'

'But I'm hungry,' he would complain. 'I haven't eaten for twenty-four hours.'

'You have no one to blame but yourself. I'm sure if you asked Thalia nicely she would rustle

31

something up for you. Now go away and leave me in peace.'

Thalia, a Greek girl from Athens, had been one of many young au pairs who came to Cuckoo House. They rarely stayed long. Some said they couldn't cope with the isolation, or the unconventional way the household was run. Others, the prettier ones, had a different reason for leaving.

Alice's mother, Dr Barbara Barrett, was a psychiatrist and in her husband's opinion — an opinion he loved to taunt her with — she had turned her back on a respectable profession to pursue the dark arts of popular psychology in the name of slapstick fame.

Her change of career happened quite by accident. After one of her patients, a man who worked for the BBC, put in a good word for her, she became a media family and relationship expert. By the time Alice was ten, Dr Barbara Barrett was writing a weekly column for a national newspaper and appeared regularly on the television and radio. She was also an agony aunt for a monthly women's magazine. Yet for all her so-called professional expertise, Barbara Barrett had no handle on her own domestic situation. She regularly forgot Alice's birthday and left most of her care to whichever au pair was currently employed. Her husband was beyond her comprehension, or control, and too often when she was preoccupied with work she left him dangerously to his own devices.

Whilst it was true that two such larger than life characters had a volatile love-hate relationship and couldn't cope with each other on a full-time basis, it was also true that they couldn't live without each other. Any agony aunt worth her salt would have told them to take greater care of each other. Had they done so, who knew how differently life would have been at Cuckoo House in the years that followed?

5

Another day, another dollar.

As the saying goes. Who first said it and when, Clayton didn't have a clue. Or the slightest care. All that was of interest to him was that he'd eaten well last night, he'd slept the sleep of the dead, he was warm, it had stopped raining, the sun was shining and the coffee was made. The only dilemma to the day was whether to have two fried eggs with his sausages and bacon, or one. He tossed an egg in the air as if flipping a coin for his answer and caught it deftly with one hand. Oh, what the hell, he'd have two.

He cracked the eggs into the crowded sizzling pan then spooned hot oil over them. Ooh, yeah, life was good. 'What's that you say?' he asked himself aloud. 'Clayton my man, I said life was kickassing *GOOD!*'

Clayton often held conversations with himself. He used to quip that it was the only way he could participate in an intelligent discussion. If that was a sign of madness, well, he'd crossed that line a long time ago. Truth was, he couldn't remember a time when he hadn't talked to himself.

When Stacey used to walk into his office and found him chuntering away to himself, she would say he was madder than a box of monkeys. That was in the days when she said it as an endearment and with a smile on her face.

When she accused him of lunacy towards the end of their relationship, the smile had been replaced with an expression of disgust and loathing. 'You need help, Clayton,' she had said on more than one occasion. 'Professional help.'

He switched off the gas, tipped the frying pan with well-practised precision and slid his breakfast onto a warmed plate. 'There, the perfect breakfast.' He took the plate over to the table and sat down. He was a man transformed. A man who was happy to know that for the next thirty minutes of his life, all was right in the world.

He tucked into his breakfast with relish. A piece of sausage poised on the prongs of his fork, he held it an inch or two from his mouth. He smiled. 'Come to Daddy.' In it went. He chewed on it slowly, savouring the texture — crumbly yet reassuringly meaty. 'Yeah baby! That's what I'm talking about! *Dee*-licious.' Next he tried a piece of bacon. It was as good as the sausage. 'My compliments to the chef. And to the lippy Katya for doing my shopping.'

'Local food,' she had explained when she had returned from the shops. 'Organic meat. From Mr Butcher in village. I no buy you rubbish.'

For all their getting off on the wrong foot yesterday, he was grateful for what Katya had done for him. She had shown him how the heating system worked and had bought him everything he'd put on his shopping list, plus other things he hadn't given a thought to, such as toilet paper and tissues. She had suggested that for the time being he should use the

Armstrongs' washing powder, dishwasher tablets and washing up liquid and replace them when required. He had given her a wad of cash and convinced that she would try to con him, he'd checked all the items off against the till receipts when she'd left. But everything was just as it should be.

He had decided not to make that call to Glen. For now, the girl could stay. Her next scheduled visit was for the day after tomorrow. She had offered to cook for him, but not wanting the bother of having to make conversation with her for longer than was necessary, he'd said he was quite capable of cooking for himself.

Stacey would have sneered at that. 'You, cook?' she would have said. 'Don't make me laugh.'

How he had ever got sucked into Stacey's gravitational force-field, he didn't know. He used to say that they were such opposites that they'd met at their polar parts coming in the opposite direction. Thinking this now, it somehow didn't make the same sense it had then. If any.

Actually, he knew exactly how they had been drawn together and who was responsible: Lucky Bazza. Bazza had got himself a new date lined up and had suggested Clayton and the date's best friend join them at the pub to make a foursome. This was back in 1994, in the days when they were sharing a flat in Clapham and were struggling to make ends meet. To supplement their meagre earnings from their writing, Bazza was working in a bar and Clayton had a job in a seedy hotel as a night porter. He spent most of those nights — when he wasn't turning a blind eye to questionable women coming and going — working on a script. They were both twenty-nine and beginning to think they had hit a dead end, when suddenly things were finally looking up for them: their script had been accepted by the BBC.

They had been writing together since their days at university, mostly gags and sketches for up and coming comedians. They had never felt the lure of the stage or screen themselves, preferring to write for others. Their goal was to write situation comedy, but not just any old sitcom; they wanted to claim the crown of Best Ever Sitcom. Which they did. They racked up record ratings and made stars of the actors who, until the pilot show had gone out, had been unknowns. Now they were household names with two of the central characters currently making films in Hollywood. Clayton didn't believe those writers, actors or programme makers who claimed retrospectively that they had no idea they'd had a potential hit on their hands. He and Bazza had *known*. They had known right from the outset that what they'd written was bloody good.

The fourth and final series of *Joking Aside* had been broadcast five years ago and yet only last year it had come out top again in a poll conducted by the *Radio Times* to establish the best ever sitcom. Holding the hefty piece of glassware aloft at the award ceremony at the Grosvenor Hotel in London, Clayton had mumbled drunkenly into the microphone, 'How

37

do you like them bananas, Ricky Gervais?'

Bazza hadn't been able to attend; he'd been over in Los Angeles sucking up to some big studio boss, but doubtless he would have made a far more eloquent and self-effacing acceptance speech. But then, had Bazza been around to accept the award, Clayton wouldn't have gone within a mile of the place. He and Bazza hadn't spoken for more than two years. Their relationship, as Bazza repeatedly referred to their writing partnership in the countless interviews he gave, had lost its creative spark. That wasn't all it had lost.

Normally only too quick to attend a lavish do of celebrity back-patting, Stacey hadn't accompanied Clayton to the Grosvenor; she had stayed at home, saying she didn't want to be seen in public with him when, once again, he would make an idiot of himself. But Glen had been there. Through thick and thin, his agent had always been there for Clayton.

It had meant a lot to him that when Bazza made the unilateral decision to end their writing partnership — claiming he felt stifled and needed to spread his creative wings, no hard feelings, blah, blah — Glen, who had represented them both, stuck with Clayton. It was a decision he must have regretted at least a million times a day ever since. Had he chosen Bazza, he would have earned much more than he did with Clayton. Not that Clayton was hard up. Far from it. He had more than enough money. The royalties from *Joking Aside* showed no sign of drying up. He had lost count how many countries the series was shown in around the world and with DVD sales continually on the up, even if he never wrote another successful script again, he would be comfortable for the rest of his life.

But he wanted to write. He missed the buzz that writing used to give him. His life felt meaningless without a script in front of him. It was his identity. And it was thanks to Bazza that he couldn't write. He had taken it badly when Bazza had ended the partnership. At first he had thought it was a joke; that his old mate was playing a number on him. He had even checked their office for hidden cameras, certain that Bazza was setting him up for some kind of funny-ha-ha candid TV moment. When the truth finally hit Clayton, that Bazza wasn't mucking about, he was gutted. To his eternal shame, he had resorted to begging Bazza to reconsider. 'But we're the golden ticket,' he'd said. 'We've got a licence to print money right now. Why would you give that up?'

'It's not about the money,' Bazza had said. 'I want to write new things.'

'Then let's do it together. Just as we've always done.'

'No, I want to write on my own. It's something I've wanted to do for some time. I'm sorry, Clayton, it's over. We've gone as far as we can together. We had a good run, but let's look to the future now.'

In the days, weeks and months that followed, Clayton swung from high optimism that he was free to write the best stuff he'd ever written

— now that he wasn't carrying such a useless co-writer — to feeling adrift and incapable of writing a single line of dialogue. It wasn't long before he ran dry of optimism and all he had left was a debilitating fear that he would never be able to write again.

Then his parents died, one after the other in obscenely quick succession. One minute they were both alive and nagging him to visit more often; the next his father died of a heart attack and two months later his mother suffered a massive stroke and died a week later. It was then that he discovered that while they had both been supremely proud of what he had achieved, they hadn't trusted it. To them, it hadn't seemed like a proper job. After his mother's funeral, while he'd been staying at the house where he'd grown up, he had found a building society book. It was a joint account and it had over four hundred and fifty thousand pounds in it. Every month, regular as clockwork, a cheque had been paid into the account. It was the exact same amount Clayton had sent his parents every month to provide them with a bit of luxury, holidays, a new car, new clothes, that kind of thing. But here was the evidence that they hadn't spent a penny of his success. Many times he had offered to buy them a new house, somewhere in the country or by the sea, but they'd refused, saying there was nothing wrong with the house they had. There had been a handwritten note contained within the pages of the account book — written by his mother — and it said that when they died, the money they had saved was for Clayton, just in case things hadn't worked out for him.

If there had been any uncertainty before that he was experiencing a phase of writer's block, losing his parents and squaring up to his own mortality ensured there was not a shred of doubt from then on.

Meanwhile, Lucky Bazza's writing career went from strength to strength. If they had once been the crowned kings of comedy writing, Lucky Bazza was now the golden boy who couldn't put a foot wrong. While Clayton was deeply mired in a state of inertia, Bazza had written a film script for a major box-office hit and had thrown himself into trying to save Africa, along with just about every other comedian, actor, writer and musician in the country.

Never mind saving Africa, Clayton had his work cut out saving himself!

There was no getting away from it; one person's success is another person's failure. Clayton had tried hard to pretend that Lucky Bazza's success didn't bother him, but the truth was it hurt like hell. He had believed it to be the bitterest pill of all to swallow. But then Stacey left him for Bazza.

Throughout this dark, depressing period of his life, and presumably in an effort to raise his flagging spirits, Stacey had kept up a steady onslaught of derogatory comments. 'You're not funny at all,' she complained to him one day. 'I can't remember the last time you made me laugh.'

He couldn't remember ever telling her that he was funny. Why would he? Why would he go around saying he was funny? *Who, me? Oh, I'm the funniest man on the planet. Wind me up and watch me go. I'll have you in stitches for hours.* Comedy doesn't work that way. Everyone knows that. Everyone except for Stacey, maybe.

The way he saw it, being funny was a disability. It dragged a person down with the sheer weight of expectation that it fostered. 'Go on, then, make me laugh,' was the expectation of anyone who met him for the first time. It was a hell of a weight to lug around.

When it became obvious that Clayton was not going to earn his agent any money from fresh writing, Glen began getting him appearances on panel shows for TV and radio. He rapidly made a name for himself as the grumpy, dry-witted, mordant guest. Then one week when he was appearing on a topical news show, he let rip with a vociferous attack on the guest host, a sickening man with a squeaky-clean image and an ego the size of Texas. Clayton couldn't abide him. Off camera, the squeaky-clean image was anything but squeaky-clean. 'Let me stop you right there, Baby Doll,' Clayton had said when the host, grinning from squeaky-clean ear to squeaky-clean ear, had started to describe Clayton as a one-hit wonder who couldn't write without his co-writer, the much more talented Barry Osborne.

Clayton's diatribe made the headlines the next day and, ever since, when an example of a truly excruciating on-screen moment was called for, the clip of him outing the host as a cokehead with a penchant for dressing up in baby-doll nightdresses whilst indulging in sex with men twenty years his junior was shown. The man's proclivities were well known in certain showbiz circles, and Clayton didn't regret his outburst, or the man's subsequent downfall from primetime television.

For weeks afterwards Clayton was hot property. Every newspaper and chat show host wanted to interview him, probably in the hope that he would let rip with some other salacious exposé. He was glad when the circus left town and the telephone stopped ringing.

Stacey wasn't so happy. He had never been interested in being Mr Showbiz, but Stacey had loved the razzamatazz of an opening night or the chance of being snapped by the paparazzi coming out of a restaurant or a club late at night. He'd played along initially, knowing that it pleased her, but when they'd reached the sniping Heather versus Macca stage of their relationship, he told her he would sooner stay at home playing Scrabble while having his toenails systematically ripped out at the roots. Stacey's response was to accuse him of being small-minded.

Later, when she announced that she was leaving him for Bazza, she said his small-mindedness wasn't his only area of deficiency. Small in the trouser department? That was news to him. But apparently, Lucky Bazza was gloriously endowed. Funny, because as far as Clayton could recall from the many side-by-side urinal situations they'd shared, Lucky Bazza hadn't shown any outstanding tendencies.

When he thought about it, gravitational

forcefields were odd things. He had been sucked into Bazza's life, then Stacey's, and now here he was, drawn into the unlikeliest of situations; holed up miles from anywhere pretending his name was Shannon, and with only a cheeky Latvian housekeeper for intermittent company.

Once again he was hot property, but this time it was because he'd made a spectacularly stupid mistake. This time the press was baying for his blood. He was a hated man. He was a national disgrace. Probably right now there were MPs demanding for capital punishment to be brought back for people like him.

6

'You're not cross with me, then?'

Ronnetta laughed. 'Cross with you? I wish I'd been there to witness your performance! As well as all your previous ones. I really had no idea what you'd been getting up to behind my back. Certainly no clients have ever said anything to me in the past. Although when I come to think about it, there was one woman who mentioned something about how efficient you'd been; that it was typical of where you were from. I didn't give it another thought.'

'But what if Mr Shannon complains to you?' Alice pressed. 'What if he says I didn't know my place, that I was rude to him? Which I was. Take my word for it; I was breathtakingly rude to him.'

'Stop beating yourself up. If he was going to complain, don't you think he would have done so by now?'

It was a good point. Most people who have a beef about something usually complain straight away. They like nothing better than to make a huge fuss while they're still steamed up. But twenty-four hours had passed since Alice's encounter with Mr Shannon, so maybe Ronnetta was right and he'd decided not to make a fuss. Was he a classic example of having a bark worse than his bite? He had seemed happy enough yesterday when she'd left him. She'd known, however, just absolutely known, that the first thing he would have done after she'd driven off was to check the till receipts she had given him, to see whether a bolshy Latvian had had the nerve to rob him.

'What interests me more,' Ronnetta said, leaning across her desk with a rattle of bangles and poking the air with a biro, 'is what Mr Shannon is doing here all on his own in a great big place like Cuckoo House. And why, I want to know, has someone else down in London made all the arrangements for his stay? What's that all about? You don't suppose he's some kind of criminal, do you? Or how about an informant who's in hiding? Maybe MI6 is behind this and Cuckoo House is a safe house for him.'

Alice laughed. 'You've been watching too many episodes of *Spooks*. If he was being hidden because he was in danger, do you suppose for one minute they'd allow a stranger to come in and clean for him?'

'Mm . . . perhaps not. So what was he like? Good-looking bloke? Single?' Ronnetta wiggled her eyebrows. 'If yes to either of those last two questions, do you think he'd like some company? I'm sure I could make myself available.'

In her own words Ronnetta had been divorced since the Crimean War and whilst there had been many a romantic entanglement in the intervening years she had not yet found that special person to be Husband Number Two. The search was ongoing. 'I'm not sure about his marital status or that he's your type,' Alice said. 'To be honest, I don't see him as being anybody's type. He's got an attitude that could etch glass.'

46

'Haven't we all at times? How old do you reckon?'

'That's a tricky one.' Alice didn't want to say outright that she thought Mr Shannon was too young for Ronnetta, so instead she described him, scruffy clothes and all.

'He sounds like he needs someone to take him in hand,' Ronnetta said, slipping the biro between her lips and sucking on it — despite the hypnotherapy, she had yet to lose certain urges and habits. 'I'm intrigued,' she added. 'Keep me posted.'

The mobile on her desk rang; she picked it up to take the call. Alice took it as her cue to leave. They both had work to do. She quietly closed the door of Ronnetta's office — a 1999 Swift Corniche three-berth caravan parked in her back garden — and went home. A manuscript had arrived in the post that morning and Alice was eager to make a start on reading it.

She let herself in at the back door, put the kettle on and opened the jiffy bag that contained the manuscript for a new children's book. The title of it was: *Liar, Liar, Pants on Fire*. It made her think of the conversation she'd just had with Ronnetta.

Alice hadn't actually lied to her neighbour, but then nor had she been exactly fulsome with her confession regarding Katya. At no stage had she mentioned that she knew Cuckoo House, let alone admitted that she had grown up there. If for some reason that was now to come out, it would be rather embarrassing to say the least.

The trouble with telling lies, even small ones,

or lies by omission, is that once you start, there seems no way to stop and it rapidly becomes an unbreakable habit. One way or another, Alice had been telling lies nearly all her adult life. She wasn't a pathological liar — a crazy fantasist who couldn't open her mouth without lying — it was more a matter of creating edited versions of the truth, of constructing separate universes within her own world in order to compartmentalize her life. She firmly believed there was a distinction between good and bad untruths and the ones she told were not designed to hurt anyone, merely to keep people out.

She had learned the art of crafting slight truths at the feet of two of the greatest technicians: her parents. Although it was always possible that there had been no learning process involved, it could be that the liar gene had been passed down to her. Just as she had inherited her mother's wide cheekbones and small chin, perhaps she had been born with the gift of embroidering the truth to suit.

Typical untruths for Alice's mother had been to lie about her age or to give the public the impression that her home life was other than it really was. As for Alice's father, a man who had never seemed to have a real grasp on reality, anything went for truth as far as he was concerned.

As a child Alice had lost herself in colourful landscapes of make-believe where anything was possible, so what could be more natural than to do the same as an adult? This wasn't as bad as it sounded; she only did it as a means to reinvent herself. Even then, not to the point that she was unrecognizable to herself. All she had done over the years was apply a light dusting of reinterpretation here and there.

Really, it was extraordinary how easy it was to make people think what you wanted them to think merely by glossing over the bits you didn't want them to know. Another trick was to deflect any unwanted questions by inviting people to talk about themselves. In her experience people would much rather talk about themselves than listen to someone else droning on. Yes, she would say if she was pushed to explain herself, she had spent her childhood living in the area . . . Oh, you know, I did the usual thing of leaving home just as soon as I was old enough . . . no, no brothers or sisters . . . and sadly both parents now dead . . . but tell me about you; where did you grow up?

Keeping people at arm's length was the easiest thing in the world to do. Allowing herself to be close to anyone was not so easy for Alice. Closeness meant being honest. It meant she would have to open herself up to another and allow that person to poke and pry. People were like that. If they sensed something out of the ordinary, they nibbled away at it until they had devoured the whole story. Of course, she could have saved herself a lot of bother by not coming back to the area. But what did they say about criminals always returning to the scene of the crime?

Two and a half years ago, when she was approaching her twenty-eighth birthday and yet another relationship had unravelled, she had felt alone and aimless. Sitting in her London flat in Earls Court, listening to the noisy party that was going on in the flat below her, life had suddenly seemed very bleak. Her non-stop party-loving Aussie neighbours had invited her to the party but seeing as her ex-boyfriend, a software designer from Sydney, was going to be there, she had declined. There had been a brief moment of fantasy during her relationship with Austin when she had imagined being whisked off to Sydney to start a new life with him. She had liked the idea of that. Living somewhere completely new. But Austin had pulled out of the relationship, saying he found her impossible to live with. He said he'd given up trying to understand whether she was joking or being straight with him. He had known her for more than a year, and other than locating her G-spot, he didn't think he knew any more about her than when they'd first met. He said he was tired of searching for the key to unlock the real her. She'd told him he'd been reading too many women's magazines. He'd told her he was moving out.

So that was that. A nice straightforward break-up. It seemed to be her forte.

In this aimless state, she began to dream of the scenery of her childhood, the wide open spaces, the vast empty skies, the undulating hills and the sweeping stretches of moorland. She would find herself lingering over the dreams when she woke in the morning and would feel haunted for the rest of the day. She almost succeeded in resisting the beckoning call, and then she learned that her father was dead. That he had been dead for some years. The beckoning call became a screaming siren.

There was nothing else for it. She packed an overnight bag and headed north. Her plan was simple. She would visit Stonebridge safe in the knowledge that one look at it would be enough to convince her that her subconscious had been playing tricks on her. She would realize in an instant that it was the last place on earth she should move back to. She also believed that the visit would help resolve her feelings for her father.

It was a silly plan; there was only ever going to be one outcome. Sure enough, nine weeks later she moved into Dragonfly Cottage just five miles away from Cuckoo House. Her agent, Hazel, said that Alice couldn't have made a smarter move as a new recording studio had just started operating on the outskirts of Nottingham and it would be an easy journey to undertake on a regular basis. What was more, if the owners were to be believed, it looked like the work would be plentiful.

Ha, ha! The Queen of New Beginnings triumphs again!

7

Clayton had been busy.

In readiness for Katya's visit he had been swotting up. She had accused him of knowing nothing about her country; well, today he'd show her. Unable to sleep last night, he'd gone online and read all he could about Latvia. He'd also looked up a few key words of vocabulary and using a language site and in response to a robotic woman's voice, he had been practising his pronunciation. Nobody got away with making out he was a jackass by implying he was ignorant. No siree!

Perversely he was now looking forward to Katya's arrival. His hands clasped behind his head, he leaned back in the chair and stared out of the window. He liked this room. If this was his house, this would be where he'd choose to write; it would be his den. It was home to nearly as many books as he possessed in his house down in London, so perhaps the owners, Glen's friends, used it as a study. Or maybe they called it something grander: a library. Dotted about the room were framed photographs of the Armstrongs; it didn't matter whether they were dressed for the ski slopes, a race course meeting, a tropical beach or an occasion that warranted a dinner jacket and a ball gown, they looked smug with happiness. It was enough to make Clayton feel ill.

Where he was sitting in the turreted area of the room, the windows looked directly out onto the front garden and in the distance, at the end of the long, straight drive he could see the white-painted metal gate and the trees that flanked it. The trees had lost nearly all of their leaves but the thick impenetrable hedge that ran the perimeter of the land to the front showed no sign of doing the same. It must be an evergreen hedge of some sort. Laurel? Rhododendron? He racked his brain to think what else it could be. It didn't look coniferous. Holly? Beech? No, beech was deciduous. Any fool knew that. He scratched his chin and once again took himself by surprise at the feel of it. Two weeks without shaving and he had developed quite a beard. Apart from when he'd been a student, when it was obligatory to sport a pretentiously goatee affair, he had never grown a proper beard before. Stacey wouldn't have stood for it. He had only to go two days without shaving and she would turn her cheek away from him when he tried to kiss her. 'Horrible,' she would say with a shudder, 'go and shave.' He stroked his beard with exaggerated pleasure. 'This is for you, Stacey!'

It was raining again. Perhaps that was how it was going to be; whenever it was a Katya day it would rain. Certainly there was something of the storm cloud about her.

So far he hadn't put a foot outside of his prison walls. Not even yesterday when it was dry and sunny. Instead, he had explored the house spending time in each room, as if trying them for size. Every room was large and high-ceilinged and starting from the ridiculously over-sized entrance hall complete with chandelier was the room he was currently in and opposite was a dining room. Beyond were two sitting rooms — possibly one for relaxing in and the other, the larger of the two, for not relaxing in, for pretending to be something other than one's natural self. At the back of the house was the kitchen and a collection of associated rooms — laundry, pantry and larder — and a general dumping area where a selection of outdoor coats hung on old-fashioned, black-painted metal pegs with an assortment of leather walking boots and green wellingtons below. A wide staircase led up to four bedrooms and three bathrooms on the first floor and a smaller staircase gave access to a further three bedrooms and two more bathrooms.

His mother would have been hopelessly overawed by it. She would have crept about the house as if she had no right to be there. Dad, too, would have felt out of place and had one of his chippy turns. The pair of them had been bad enough when they used to come and stay with him and Stacey. 'My, this is fancy,' Mum had said when she'd stepped over the threshold of the house in Fulham which he'd bought on the success of the first series of *Joking Aside*. 'Is it all yours?' she'd asked. 'All of it? That's never a cream carpet, is it? Oh, you'll regret that.'

Stacey had seen to all the decorating and furnishing and for some obscure reason she had taken great pleasure in telling his parents just how much everything had cost. 'All that on curtains?' Dad had exploded. 'That's how much I earn in a year!' Clayton had very nearly exploded as well. He'd had no idea curtains could cost so much. The only room Stacey hadn't decorated or furnished was his office-cum-den. She had wanted to but he'd put his foot down. One of the few times he had.

At the end of the drive, he saw what looked like a red toy car stop at the gate. He checked his watch. Eleven o'clock. Katya was on time today. She got out of the car and he watched her open the gate, get back in her car, drive forward, get out, shut the gate, get back in the car, then drive slowly up the drive.

He drew a piece of paper towards him and quickly read through the vocabulary he'd been learning. No worries, he was word perfect. He pushed back his chair and stood up. 'Prepare to be amazed and astonished, Katya,' he said aloud.

* * *

'*Sveiki!*' he greeted her at the door. '*Ka jums klajas?*'

From the expression on her face, he could see she really was amazed and astonished. Who wouldn't be? He'd not only said hi, but had enquired after her health. He stood back to let her in. '*Paldies par palidzibu,*' he continued. He was showing off now, thanking her for coming.

She still had the same look on her face.

'I've been learning Latvian,' he said. 'Aren't you impressed?' Of course she was. He could see it in her eyes, and by the way she had put a finger to her top lip and her face was reddening. She was obviously touched that he'd gone to so much trouble. For some unaccountable reason, he felt touched that she was touched. But then her expression changed. She began to smile. Next thing she was giggling, a hand covering her mouth. 'What?' he said. 'What's so funny?'

'Sorry, mister. Sorry for rude. But you just say big funny thing. You say you have sexy goat in bath.'

His jaw dropped.

She laughed some more. 'I tell you for sure, I no clean bath if goat in it.'

'But I couldn't have got it so wrong. I've . . . I've been practising.' He felt embarrassed at the admission. Far from impressing her he'd just made a fool of himself. *No change there, then*, he heard the irritating voice of Captain Sensible mutter inside his head. *That's what you get for showing off*.

'Is good for you to learn new language but bad for me. I here to learn English. I no want to speak Latvian.'

'Oh,' he said, feeling flattened.

'English. Only English. You must speak good English to me so I learn well. One day I speak like Queen. Right, mister?'

'Oh,' he said again.

'Now I roll up sleeves and start work.' She sped off towards the kitchen. 'Ooh,' she let out, 'look at big mess mister has made here. You make much work for me.'

Clayton left her to it. He closed the door on the room he'd claimed as his study, took out his list of vocabulary and switched on his laptop. Where had he gone wrong?

★ ★ ★

That, Alice told herself, had been a close-run thing. She hadn't seen that coming. Fancy him trying to learn Latvian. Given that she knew next to nothing about her supposed country of birth, she had to hope that his next step wasn't to start badgering her about it. If he did that she would have to read up on the subject; the last thing she wanted to do was to let Ronnetta down. After discussing the matter, they had both decided that it would be better for Alice to continue as Katya. Understandably, Ronnetta didn't think it would be a good idea for a client to think he'd been made a monkey of, not when he was paying top dollar for Alice's services.

When she had finished cleaning the kitchen, Alice went upstairs to see how big a mess Mr Shannon had made up there. It wasn't too bad. Despite what she'd said about the kitchen, on the whole he wasn't an untidy man. As far as she could see his impact on the house was minimal. He'd brought just the one case with him, along with a laptop bag and his clothes took up hardly any space in the wardrobe and chest of drawers.

She wondered what he did to pass the time. Was he lonely? Bored? Was that why he had been teaching himself a few choice Latvian expressions? The fact that he had, amused her and, to a degree, raised him in her estimation. Had she really been Latvian, she would have been pleased that he'd gone to so much trouble.

She finished cleaning his bathroom — giving his toiletries a quick inspection — straightened the curtains in his bedroom, then went downstairs for the vacuum cleaner. Passing his door, she knocked on it, waited politely for him to respond then went inside. 'Sorry to disturb, mister,' she said. 'You make list for shopping?'

'Not yet,' he said, not bothering to turn round and look at her. His attention was focused on his laptop in front of him. She was reminded of all the occasions her mother had sat in the very same spot. Clattering away on her typewriter, she would barely notice if anyone came into the room. Unless, of course, it had been her father, who, like a cyclone, had been impossible not to notice. But many times Alice had stood on the threshold of her mother's study waiting for her to turn round. She once timed how long it took for her mother to stop what she was doing and to answer Alice's question: ten whole minutes. She had been a patient and determined child.

'I make busy with vacuum,' Alice said, 'and then I go shopping for you. You want me to clean in here?' She stepped further into the room, peered to see what was of such interest to him on his laptop. She made out just one word — *OBITUARY*.

As if sensing what she was doing, he snapped the lid shut and turned to face her. He then looked about the room. 'It doesn't look like it needs cleaning to me. Does it to you?'

She shrugged. 'Perhaps no. You very tidy in here.'

He raised an eyebrow. 'Unlike the kitchen?'

'Much grease everywhere in kitchen. You fry too much, mister. Try grill or oven. Healthier for you.'

'I'll bear that in mind.'

'Maybe you like me to cook you one day.'

He cracked a smile. 'Trust me; I've been well and truly cooked.'

'Well, mister, I leave you to write list.' She closed the door after her. Interesting, she thought. What exactly did he mean by being cooked?

She lugged the vacuum cleaner upstairs. When she reached the landing, instead of turning right to go to her old bedroom, which Mr Shannon was using, she turned left.

She pushed open the door of her parents' old bedroom. She had grabbed her chance to have a quick look at it the other day, but today she wanted to linger. She had dreamed of it last night, or more precisely, she had dreamed of her parents in this room.

It was like all the other rooms in the house, beautifully furnished and tastefully decorated. If Alice was honest, the decor was beginning to grate on her. It was as if the heart and soul character of the house had been stripped away in the name of good taste. That was something her parents would never have been guilty of.

She went over to the window seat, sat down and closed her eyes. In her mind's eye she could see the room as it had once been. Clothes strewn everywhere, rugs rucked up, the paintings hanging lopsided on the walls, lampshades dusty and dented and the chest of drawers and dressing table covered with all manner of objects — Great Aunt Eliza's silver-backed hairbrush set, strings of beads, safety pins, an old china teapot with a spider plant growing out of it, a framed picture of her father when he'd been at university, and teetering piles of books.

Alice had been twelve when her mother died. Dr Barbara Barrett's sudden death had been perfectly in keeping with the way her parents lived their lives. Why go quietly when you could go with a bang? And her mother had died with a bang. She had managed to electrocute herself by watching television in the bath. Alice's father had repeatedly warned her to be careful, but she would roll her eyes at him, saying that if anyone needed to be careful it was him with all those chemicals he stored in his darkroom. Watching herself on television while soaking in the bath with a glass of wine became a happy eight o'clock weekly ritual for her. The programme she took part in was always pre-recorded and she said it was her duty to scrutinize her performance in order to appear at her best. 'One has to be professional,' she would claim. Then stop talking about sex all the time when you're on the telly! Alice had wanted to say.

It was so embarrassing to be known at school as the daughter of a sex and relationship expert. She was regularly teased for it and girls were always coming up to her and asking her questions about something her mother had said on TV. It was a wonder she had been able to walk, her toes had been so constantly curled.

Her mother's death was reported in the newspapers and while nobody could ever be sure exactly what had happened, the coroner's verdict was that Dr Barbara Barrett must have slipped whilst getting into the bath and had accidentally knocked the portable TV set in with her. She wasn't found for two days, not until Alice's father returned from a trip photographing Emperor penguins. Alice was informed of her death at school by the headmistress. The news was bluntly delivered; no attempt was made to soften the blow.

Her father came to fetch her home from the boarding school she had recently started attending and the only words he uttered whilst driving her back to Cuckoo House were: 'Thank God I was out of the country when it happened. At least no one can accuse me of finishing her off!' The day of the funeral, with tears in his eyes, he admitted to Alice that they'd had a terrible row before he'd left for Antarctica and he just wished they'd had a chance to make up before she'd died. For years afterwards, Alice could never think kindly of Emperor penguins. If her father hadn't gone rushing off to photograph them her mother might not have died.

There were many things about her parents that Alice had never understood, but two things she could say of them with absolute certainty: her father was a powerfully charismatic man and her mother was impervious to his tantrums, wrapped as she was in her own self-absorption. There was an intense rivalry between them, each believing that their own area of expertise was superior to the other and it was probably this that made their relationship so volatile.

The simplest thing could set them off, such as a disagreement over who was the greatest living artist. 'Hockney?' Alice's father would roar with incredulity as if his wife had suggested Donald Duck. 'You can't be serious!' They would hurl themselves into a screaming match, sometimes throwing things at each other, not caring what they were smashing or what physical injury they might inflict. During one argument, Alice's father caught a hardback edition of *Roget's Thesaurus* full in the face and ended up with a bag of frozen peas pressed to his swelling eye. An hour later they were laughing and joking in each other's arms and skulking upstairs to their bedroom for a kiss and make up session.

Less than a year later, the same headmistress who had informed Alice that her mother was dead informed her that she now had a stepmother.

Her father had by now established a habit of delivering good and bad news by proxy.

8

At first, Clayton thought it was his mobile. But the ringtone — the sound of an old-fashioned telephone ringing — wasn't coming from his phone, but from the one on the kitchen table next to Katya's bag. He decided to be helpful. He took the mobile and went to look for her, following the noise of the vacuum cleaner.

By the time he'd tracked her down to his bedroom — he couldn't think what she'd found in there to hoover up — she'd only done it a few days ago — the mobile had stopped ringing. She looked surprised that he'd gone to so much trouble. 'Thank you, mister,' she said, taking it from him.

'Sorry I wasn't fast enough,' he said.

He watched her check to see who had called and saw her trying but failing to suppress a smile. It was a smile of undisguised delight. The mobile started to ring again. He left her to answer it.

But something made him hover halfway down the stairs. It was the fact that the phone was still ringing, that she hadn't answered it straight away. And then the bedroom door closed.

It was wrong what he did next. Wholly wrong. But he was curious. He wanted to know what or who had made her smile in the way she had. He crept back up the stair and went and listened at the door. Initially he couldn't make sense of what he was hearing. Katya was speaking perfect English. *Proper* English. Queen's English. There wasn't a trace of foreign accent to her voice.

Holy hell, she was no more Latvian than he was! What the devil was she up to?

* * *

Alice switched off her mobile. She punched the air and danced a little jig. James Montgomery had called to invite her to have lunch with him. Oh, yes! The girl was hot. Hot, hot, *hot!*

* * *

Downstairs, Clayton debated with himself what to do next. Challenge Katya the moment she finished cleaning upstairs — was Katya even her real name? — or wait and see just how much further she would take this charade?

Agitated, he paced the length of the room. Something strange was going on here. But what exactly? Why would she pretend to be foreign, go to such lengths to conceal her true identity?

Then it hit him. And the thought chilled him to the bone. She was a journalist! She was pretending to be a Latvian cleaner just so that she could get some kind of a scoop on him.

Now it was his turn to close the door and talk in private. He called Glen. But Glen wasn't answering his mobile.

What should he do? He raked his hands through his hair. Should he call the police? And say what? If he did get the police involved, it would come out who he was and then he'd have God only knew how many other journalists banging on the door. That was going to happen anyway. Whatever he did he was screwed. Either way — whether he challenged the girl or continued to play along — she was going to write a humiliating piece about him. That was a dead cert.

All he could be grateful for was that he had sussed her before she'd got anything out of him. As things stood, what did she have so far? That he was calling himself Mr Shannon and was staying in a house in the middle of nowhere. It wasn't much of a story, was it? But that could be worse for him. No story meant the newspaper would make one up.

One thing was for sure: he had to get rid of her. He would have to do it with good grace. He would have to say something like, 'No hard feelings, but I've sussed what you're up to; the show's over. Please leave me alone.' If he displayed any kind of anger, he would be portrayed as unbalanced. A nut job.

Well guess what, right now, this very minute, he did feel unbalanced!

A knock at the door made him jump. He steadied himself with a deep breath, went to the door and opened it.

There she was staring back at him. As cool as you like. 'I go for shopping now,' she said, hitching her bag onto her shoulder. 'You have list? I see you have only little shampoo. You want me get you some?'

The sound of her fake bad English was too

much. 'No,' he said, 'I don't have a list for you and I don't want any shampoo. But I'll tell you what I do want, and that's for you to go.'

'I sorry,' she said, a startled look on her face. 'I no understand.'

'I think you understand all too well,' he replied, 'so do us both a favour and drop the act. I know you're no more from Latvia than I am.'

Her face blushed crimson and her gaze wavered. He could see the uncertainty in her eyes; she was weighing up how best to proceed. She readjusted the bag on her shoulder.

'Let me help you,' he said. 'I know exactly what you're really doing here. How about you just get your things and go? I'm sure you're disappointed you haven't got the story you hoped for, but I'm equally sure you'll fill in the blanks where necessary. For the record, which newspaper are you from?'

'Newspaper?' she repeated, her gaze back on his again. 'Why do you say that?' But at least she had dropped the fake accent.

'You know what? I'm surprising myself here at just how calm I'm being, but please don't test my patience any further. I'll ask you again: which newspaper do you write for?'

She shook her head. 'I'm sorry, I don't have any idea what you're talking about. I don't write for a newspaper.'

'I'm using the term 'write' loosely. You put words one after the other and sometimes they even make sense. Sound familiar to you?'

'Um . . . look, this is getting a bit weird. Do you think we could sit down so I can apologize properly and try and explain why I did what I did?'

'An apology from a journalist? That's a first.'

'You think I'm a journalist?'

'I think you're a lot of things, but the word journalist will suffice for now.' He stepped away from the door. 'Be my guest. Come on in and make yourself at home. You'll have to excuse me if I don't sit down; I may need to rush to the nearest loo to be violently sick if your apology is too much to take.'

He watched her go over to the sofa, but she seemed to change her mind, and skirting round the back of it, she went to the fireplace. Perched on the worn green leather of the club fender, she looked up at him. 'Usually I don't get found out. What gave me away?'

'I heard you talking on your mobile.'

'You eavesdropped on me? That's outrageous.'

'Hey, you're in no position to try and take the moral high ground.'

She sighed. 'You're right. The thing is, I used to be an actress, now I do voiceover work, and sometimes I can't help myself; I just love slipping into a character. I hadn't intended to do it when I turned up here to work for you, but it was . . . ' she hesitated. 'Well, can we just say extenuating circumstances made me do it?'

'No we cannot!' he snapped. 'And frankly, you're going to have to do a lot better than that load of bull before I accept your apology.'

'I'm telling you the truth. And if you hadn't been so rude to me when you opened the door I might not have got myself into this mess.'

'Oh, this gets better and better. Now it's my fault.' He laughed bitterly. 'Where have I heard that before?'

'You're not a very happy man, are you?'

'My happiness has got nothing to do with you.'

She shrugged. 'Just making conversation.'

'No you weren't. You were looking for a way to make me open up to you. Well, forget it. I'm not that stupid. Confide in a journalist? I'd sooner stick a wasp up my arse!'

She shrugged again. 'Each to his own. Can I ask you something?'

'I don't think you've figured how this works. I'm the one asking the questions.'

Ignoring him, she said, 'Why do you think I'm a journalist?'

'Because what else could you be? Certainly not an actress.'

She sat up straight. 'Don't you go disparaging my acting skills. Not when I convinced you every step of the way that I was Katya from Latvia. I was acting my socks off there. But you know what intrigues me?'

He rolled his eyes. 'I can't begin to think.'

'The question I keep asking myself is why you think a journalist would be so interested in you, to the extent she would adopt a false identity while shopping and cleaning for you. Who are you? Or more to the point, what have you done that makes you so incredibly newsworthy?'

9

'Who said anything about me being newsworthy?'

'You with your paranoia, thinking I was a journalist. Which I'm not. I swear it. Hand on heart.'

'Hand on heart,' he mimicked. 'You expect me to believe that you're telling the truth when you've done nothing but lie since you showed up here? Don't make me laugh. By the way, you were breathtakingly rude to me.'

'Yes, I was. Sorry about that. But once I got into the character of Katya, I couldn't stop myself. She just seemed naturally bossy.'

'Does that mean in the real world you're nothing like her?'

She smiled. 'I spend as little time in the real world as I possibly can.'

'Meaning what exactly? That you're crazy?'

'Aren't we all from time to time?'

He faltered in his response as the image of a rabbit's head — all ten feet of its monstrous circumference grotesquely illuminated — popped into his mind. He blinked and chased the image away. 'What's your real name?' He asked. 'In the *real* world?'

'Alice,' she replied. 'Alice Shoemaker.'

'Yeah, right, and I'm Michael Shumacher. I've never heard a more made up name.'

'All names are made up,' she said indignantly.

'True, but Alice Shoemaker sounds like it was snatched from the ether fifteen seconds ago.'

She rooted in her bag, pulled out a wallet, opened it and crossed the room to him. 'See, there's my driving licence. It clearly states my name.'

It did. And her address. 'You're local? You're not from London?'

'I'm as local as it's possible to be. In fact — ' She broke off.

'In fact what?'

'I was born in this very house. Upstairs in my parents' bedroom. I arrived two weeks early in the middle of the night and there wasn't time to get my mother to the hospital. I grew up here.'

Clayton raked a hand through his hair. It was all becoming too much for him. 'Have I got this right? Your name is Alice Shoemaker, you used to live here and you're an actress. So why, then, are you keeping house for me? Are times that hard that you clean while you're 'resting''?

'Sorry to correct you, but as I said earlier, it's voiceover work that I do, not acting per se. And not that it's any of your business, but times are far from hard for me; I'm doing this job as a favour for my neighbour who runs the cleaning agency.'

'Can you prove it?'

'Prove what? That I'm not strapped for cash?'

'That it's voiceover work you do and you're not a journalist.'

'You really are paranoid, aren't you?' Once more she rooted around inside her bag, pulled out her wallet again. 'There,' she said, 'my equity card. Satisfied now? Or would you like to speak to Ronnetta who runs the cleaning agency? She'll corroborate everything I've told you. Well, except the bit about me having grown up here. She doesn't know that.'

'And the reason why not?'

'It's complicated and nothing to do with you,' she said.

'Excuse me, but I think it's got everything to do with me. You've been working here under false pretences.'

She stuck out her chin. 'So shoot me!'

'Please don't tempt me!'

Shoulders squared, they glared at each other, the atmosphere between them suddenly scorched with hostility.

Then Clayton lost it. For no real reason he could think of, he began to laugh. He laughed and laughed. He laughed so much his sides and jaw ached and he had to collapse onto the sofa.

★ ★ ★

Unnerved, Alice didn't know what to make of this strange man now sprawled on the sofa. 'Are you all right?' she asked when his manic laughter finally subsided. *All right?* What was she saying? The man was deranged! He was probably a raging psycho! She had to be a few screws loose herself still to be in the same room as him. Especially as she'd just invited him to shoot her.

'Couldn't be better,' he said. He wiped his eyes with the backs of his hands.

71

Dear God, was he crying? 'Look,' Alice said, inching away from him and towards the door and safety. 'I'd better be going.'

'No!' he said, snapping forward.

She stepped further away from him. 'I've caused enough trouble here for you. I'll get my things and go.'

'No,' he said, 'don't go.'

Now he really was creeping her out. 'You were very clear about wanting me to go a short while ago.'

'I've changed my mind.' He sat up, wiped his eyes again. 'I'm sorry,' he said, hauling himself to his feet. 'I lost it there for a moment. I've . . . I've been under a lot of stress recently. I think I need a drink. Have one with me.'

★ ★ ★

This was insane! How had she got herself into a situation whereby she was being held hostage by a mad man insisting that she have coffee with him? She had to be glad that it hadn't been an alcoholic drink he'd had in mind; at least she was spared the prospect of having to fend off a drunken mad man.

As she sat apprehensively at the kitchen table, Alice waited for him to finish fossicking around with the coffee machine. It was one of those complicated-looking machines with buttons and levers that made cappuccino and espresso coffee. It seemed to be taking for ever. She wished he'd opted to use the kettle as he had before.

Eventually he brought two goldfish bowl-sized

cups of frothy coffee to the table. 'Biscuit?' he asked.

'No thank you.'

'Mind if I do?'

I don't care what you do, she thought, so long as I get out of here alive. And so long as it isn't in ten years' time when I'm found chained and emaciated in the cellar.

Once he was settled at the table and had managed to wrestle open a packet of Jaffa Cakes, she started the process of negotiating her freedom by engaging him in conversation. 'Um . . . you mentioned something about being under a lot of stress recently. Problems at work?'

'Problems with everything would be a more accurate description,' he said glumly. 'My life's hit the skids and there doesn't seem to be a damn thing I can do about it. I'm a cliché in my own lifetime.'

'Oh, we've all been there,' she said airily. If he was looking for a sympathetic hostage, he was out of luck.

'But did you have your every misfortune, failure and cock-up written about in the newspapers? Did you have journalists door-stepping you all hours of the day and night?'

Alice thought of her mother's death and then of the events that took place some years later. There had been a brief flurry of press interest and speculation, but not on the level he appeared to be talking about. 'No,' she said, 'I can't say that I have.'

'Then count yourself lucky.'

His tone was morose and it made her wonder. There was something going on here. She had been right to think there was more to him than met the eye. What's more, she sensed the only hostage sitting round this table was the one opposite her. She took a sip of her coffee. It was surprisingly good. Feeling that she was now the one in control of the situation, she helped herself to a Jaffa Cake. 'Having established *my* true identity,' she said, 'how about we do the same with you?'

'I don't know what you're talking about.'

She smiled her best winsomely enticing smile, the same smile she would be putting to good use during lunch with James Montgomery tomorrow.

He looked at her strangely. 'You've got — ' He flapped his hand vaguely across his top lip, 'coffee froth on your . . . ' His voice trailed away.

She wiped her mouth. So much for winsome and enticing. 'What did you find so hysterically funny earlier?' she asked.

He shifted awkwardly in his seat, closed his eyes. They stayed closed for some moments as if he were in pain. When he opened them, he said, 'I think it was the absurdity of it all. That and remembering something Beckett once said, that there's nothing funnier than unhappiness. Haven't you ever thought how futile and ludicrous life is sometimes, and that if you don't take refuge in laughter you'll end up in a far worse place?'

'That's quite profound.'

'What can I say? I'm a profound kind of guy.'

A profoundly unhappy guy, she thought. 'Shall I tell Ronnetta that she needs to find a replacement for me? I don't know how long it will take — she's short-staffed at the moment. Which is why you landed up with me. She scraped the barrel and there I was.'

A silence fell between them.

'I'd rather not have anyone else,' he said after a lengthy and uncomfortable pause.

'Will you be able to manage on your own?' she asked, surprised. 'What about your shopping? How will you do that without a car? You could walk, I suppose. It's over three miles to the nearest shops, though. You could always use a taxi. I can recommend a good firm to you.'

He picked up his coffee cup and looked at her uneasily over its rim. 'I thought maybe you could keep coming.'

'Even though I lied to you and you think I'm untrustworthy?'

'Who's to say the next person won't lie to me? But at least I know you.'

'Now that's where you're wrong. You know my name, my profession, that I grew up here, and that I live locally. But that's all. You don't know *me* from a bar of soap.'

'Wrong. I know that you take your coffee without sugar — sorry, by the way, about the sugar I put in it the other day. I know that a certain man called James makes you smile and turns you pink at the edges, and that you're probably unhappy with your life the way it is. Maybe you never have been happy with it. Oh, and I also know that you're thirty-one years old.'

'That's nothing but a load of supposition and guesswork.'

'You think so? How old are you, then?'

She frowned. 'OK, you got that right. But how?'

'Your driving licence.'

'Mm . . . you're sharper than you look.'

'I certainly hope so.'

'The beard — it's a new thing for you, isn't it?'

'It could be.'

'I think you probably look better without it. Maybe even younger. Are you hiding behind it? Just as you're hiding here at Cuckoo House?'

'Have another biscuit and be quiet.'

'You are, aren't you?'

He didn't say anything.

'I won't tell anyone. I'm very good with secrets. Just as long as I'm in on them.' She gave him what she hoped was a deep, dark, penetrating look.

'That sounds suspiciously like a threat.'

'In the nicest possible way.' She leaned across the table and smiled. 'Tell me who you are. Please.' Back to being winsome and enticing. Good cop, bad cop all rolled into one; how good was she?

'And if I don't?'

'You'll have to manage on your own.'

His face twitched with something that could have very nearly passed for a smile. 'I think I preferred it when you were Katya. She wasn't half so manipulative.'

'You only saw the good side of her.'

'And which side of you am I currently seeing?'

76

'Oh, definitely my good side. Believe me, you don't want to see my bad side. Why did you say you thought I was unhappy with my life the way it is?'

'You ask a lot of questions for someone who isn't a journalist.'

She drummed her fingers on the table. 'Waiting for your answer.'

'It's obvious: why else would you choose, and I quote, *to spend as little time in the real world as possible*, if you were happy with it?'

Ouch, thought Alice. 'And what about you? Are you happy with your lot as you sit here in a strange house wearing a strange comedy beard?'

'Don't forget the strange girl I'm sitting with.'

She drummed her fingers again. 'And waiting once more.'

'I've been happier,' he admitted.

It would be difficult not to have been, she thought. 'Well,' she said, 'this has been tremendous fun but I really ought to be going.' She stood up, took her cup and saucer over to the dishwasher.

'What about my shopping?' he asked.

She closed the dishwasher and looked at him, determined to try one last shot at reeling him in. There was a mystery here and by hook or by crook she wanted to get to the bottom of it. 'You know deal, mister. You tell Katya the truth, then she shop for you.'

He let out a short bark of a laugh. 'Not even in the game, kid. I'll walk.'

She switched back to Alice again. 'Sure you will. All three and a half miles there and all three and a half miles back. With those big heavy bags. In the rain. In the wind. And the snow. We often get snow here in November.'

'I'll ring for a taxi.'

'And he or she will help to keep the house clean for you? Come on, let me help you. Tell me who you really are.'

'We seem to be stuck in a rut here. Backwards and forwards we go but never getting anywhere.'

'I hate to break the bad news to you but that well of cynicism will dry up one day.'

'But it's working a treat for me now; it's what makes me so cute and adorable.'

'If you say so. If there isn't anything else I can do for you, I'll be going. Enjoy your stay here.' She pulled on her coat and began gathering together her cleaning things.

'How does it feel?' he said.

She stopped what she was doing. 'How does what feel?'

'Being back in this house, where you grew up?'

'You have no idea.'

*   *   *

From the window of the room he'd claimed as his den, Clayton watched the small red car drive away. Well, he thought. That's that, then.

He retraced his steps to the kitchen. Lunch. He needed something to eat. A sandwich. A nice cheese and pickle sandwich. He opened the breadbin and found a solitary crust.

10

It wasn't often that an author came into the studio, not unless a bonus author interview was being added to the CDs and cassettes, but James Montgomery always came into the studio for the first day of recording; he said he liked to be a part of the process.

Alice had a real fondness for his spirited protagonist, a twelve-year-old girl called Mattie Munroe. To all intents and purposes, Mattie was a perfectly normal girl who lived in a perfectly normal house with a perfectly normal mother and father and two perfectly normal older brothers. She wasn't a posh, clever child like Hermione from Harry Potter, nor was she one of those angsty troubled types coping with a dysfunctional family, playground bullies or teenage gangsters. But as with most children, she had a secret world into which she disappeared. Her secret world just happened to be a bit different from the usual level of make-believe children created for themselves. Hers was real, for a start. Whenever she opened a magic umbrella in her bedroom she and the family pet — an African grey parrot called Eric — would be transferred to faraway lands where they would be caught up in all manner of hair-raising adventures. During these adventures, Eric had to act as Mattie's interpreter for the many strange languages they encountered, but on their return to her bedroom — the umbrella neatly furled and put away in the wardrobe — Eric reverted to his usual level of who's-a-pretty-boy? communication. Just occasionally, though, he let slip a word or two regarding their escapades, ensuring that both the reader and Mattie knew that what took place was real and not a figment of Mattie's imagination.

As a child Alice would have loved James's books; she would have read and re-read them. She enjoyed them as an adult, too. But then she was biased. She would love anything James wrote. He once told her that Mattie was based on a girl he had a crush on when he was a young boy. 'It was the freckles that did it,' he'd confided. 'They made her look so charmingly kooky. I've never forgotten her.' As a child Alice had had plenty of freckles but she had never dreamed that anyone might find them charming, least of all a boy who would one day grow into a man as divine as James. Looking through the glass to where James was sitting with Josie, she regretted having grown out of those freckles. Was it possible nowadays to have them painted on with the aid of cosmetic surgery?

It was probably seriously uncool to have a crush on someone at her age, but Alice couldn't help herself. Nor was she alone in her adoration. Josie always came over all of a dither whenever James came to the studio, and she was way, *way* older than Alice. More than a decade older, practically menopausal and at an age when she should be thinking about grandchildren, never mind making disgraceful eyes at James. It wasn't just the females at the studio who batted their eyelashes at him. In his own words, Chris, the sound engineer, considered him as majorly droolworthy. Only when James came into the studio did Chris wear his best Dolce & Gabbana T-shirt with indecently tight white jeans and diamond stud earrings. Any other day and it was skanky khaki from head to toe and boring silver hoops through his ears.

This morning James was indeed looking majorly droolworthy. His trademark lopsided fringe of dark-brown hair was flopping sexily across his wide intelligent forehead and brushing his sapphire-blue eyes. His publicity photographs didn't do him justice; in the flesh he was sinfully good-looking.

He was chatting with Josie on the other side of the glass. They were taking a break while Chris twiddled the knobs — the noise of an aeroplane flying overhead had been picked up and they would have to redo the last page. Alice took a long, thirsty swig of water from her bottle on the desk, got up and stretched. Her shoulders ached from sitting still for so long. She imagined James offering to rub her neck and shoulders and instantly felt the tension drain out of her.

She had once read that the greater part of any relationship was carried out inside one's head. The hopes, the longing, the erotic fantasy of desire, in short, the best of a relationship, was all acted out in the mind. Alice couldn't disagree with the theory. In her own head (putting aside all the great sex they'd had — it went without saying that they were a perfect match in bed) she had been on countless dates with James. They had been on romantic dinners, enjoyed long weekends away in country retreats with roaring log fires and expensive Frette bedlinen, and strolled along the Champs Élysées in Paris. And naturally, they had lain on sun-drenched beaches in exotic locations.

The life she led inside her head was far more interesting than the one she really lived. The most excitement she'd had this last week was to clean for a strange man whilst fooling him she was Latvian.

She had to concede, however, that as strange as Laughing Boy clearly was, he was not unobservant. He had sussed her feelings for James with disturbing alacrity. Was is possible that others had picked up on the effect James had on her? Had James himself? Was that why he had invited her out for lunch today? To put her gently right, to explain that whilst he was enormously flattered, there could never be anything other than a working relationship between them? He'd probably be very apologetic, push a rueful hand through that fringe of his, and say that he hoped he hadn't given out any misleading signals.

Well, it wouldn't be the first time that had happened to her. Given the crumpled road map of her failed relationships, misleading signs were par for the course.

Following her last visit to Cuckoo House, she had told Ronnetta what had happened, that her Katya act had been rumbled, and in her typical come-what-may fashion Ronnetta had told Alice

82

not to lose any sleep over it. She had said she would ring the contact number she had and see if the agency's services were still required.

She might have known that she had got the wrong end of the stick. Lunch was not the cosy intimate affair Alice had imagined, or hoped for. Instead, James had invited Josie and Chris as well. What on earth had made her think that James would single her out for lunch?

A stonking great dose of wishful thinking, that's what! Funny, though, that neither Josie nor Chris had mentioned anything earlier about having lunch with James. Perhaps they had also leapt to the mistaken hope that they had been chosen for special treatment and hadn't wanted to let on.

Oh, well, another misread sign.

They were sitting at a corner table in the Fox and Barrel, a drab pub within walking distance of the studio. Snow Patrol's latest dreary offering was playing in the background, adding to the dismal mood. The middle of Alice's pizza was stone cold — judging from its rubbery outer ring, it probably hadn't spent long enough in the microwave — and she was struggling to rally any enthusiasm to eat it. In fact, such was her disappointment, she was struggling to join in with the conversation around the table. Chris was telling them a supposedly hysterically funny story about how he'd locked himself out of his house wearing only a towel and a smile. What a tart he was, thought Alice. Chris was only telling the story so that James was obliged to picture his body naked.

It wasn't like Alice to feel so petulant, but really, why couldn't Josie and Chris have done the decent thing and declined James's suggestion for them all to have lunch together? Why did they have to be so selfish? She mentally kicked herself. Great! Why not add irrational paranoia to petulance?

At this rate she'd soon be as nuts as Laughing Boy.

'Aren't you going to eat that?'

Alice looked up. Josie's fork was pointing at her barely touched pizza. 'I'm not really hungry,' Alice responded.

'Waste not want not,' Josie said with a cheerful laugh.

This from the thirteen-stone woman who claimed that she ate no more than a sparrow. Yeah right, a sparrow the size of an ostrich! 'Be my guest,' Alice said. She pushed the plate nearer to Josie.

'Eu-ew!' said Josie, after she'd taken a mouthful. 'That's disgusting. It's barely cooked.'

'Really? asked James, putting down his knife and fork. Concern was written all over his handsome face.

'I think it may need a minute or two longer in the oven,' Alice murmured.

'It needs binning, more like,' asserted Josie. 'Take it back, Alice, and demand they give you something else.'

The perfect gentleman, James was up on his

feet, the offending plate of pizza in his hands. 'Come on Alice, let's go and order you something that's edible.'

Alice didn't need asking twice. In a flash she was out of her seat and at James's side. Hurrah, alone with him at last!

The young girl behind the bar was working solo and had her hands full with a sudden influx of customers. 'Looks like we could be here for a while,' Alice said, adding, but not meaning it, 'You'd better go back and eat your lunch.'

James smiled. 'No rush. My Caesar salad won't spoil. In fact, I'm pleased that we've got this chance to be alone. There's something I want to talk to you about.'

She was just thinking how grateful she was that James was the kind of man who ate salad for lunch, and how his smile was the most devastating smile she had ever been on the receiving end of, when her thoughts came to a crashing stop. Oh God, was this going to be the I'm-flattered-but-there-can-never-be-anything-between-us pep talk? 'Something you wanted to discuss with me?' she said casually. 'What's that then?'

'The thing is — ' His words hung in the air, his attention diverted by a messily folded newspaper to the left of him. He reached for it, opened it and smoothed out the pages. 'What do you make of this story?'

'What story's that?' she asked, moving closer to James, her shoulder ever so slightly pressing against his arm.

'I was at school with him. Well, actually that's stretching the truth a bit. We were at the same school; he was in the sixth form when I joined aged eleven.'

'Who?'

James laughed and pointed at one of the photographs in the newspaper. 'You're obviously above sullying yourself with grubby tabloid tittle-tattle, aren't you?'

'I wouldn't say that exactly. Who is he?' she repeated.

'Only one of the greatest comedy writers this country's ever produced.'

'Really? What's he known for?'

'Latterly for all the wrong reasons. But you must have heard of him. His name's Clayton Miller and he and his writing partner, Barry Osborne, wrote *Joking Aside*. They were right up there with the greats in double-act comedy writing: Perry and Croft, Galton and Simpson, Gervais and Merchant — '

'*Joking Aside*?' Alice interrupted. 'I loved that; I never missed an episode. It was brilliant.'

'It still is. Which is more than can be said for Clayton Miller. He's disappeared, apparently. Gone crackers maracas if the papers are to be believed.'

Alice looked at the double-page spread. There was a small photo of a man wearing a tuxedo minus the bow tie and holding up an award. He had a wide grin on his face; he looked nothing short of ecstatic, like a man on top of the world. Below it was another picture of a very different-looking man, dishevelled, shoulders hunched, and a hand partially covering a scowling face. On the opposite page was a picture of a man and a woman sitting on a sofa; they were holding hands and looking adoringly into each other's eyes. They looked very staged, like one of those couples who'd just undergone a makeover. They were both immaculately dressed in what appeared to be matching straw-coloured linen suits and their hair was coiffured to perfection. Alice had the feeling she had seen them before, on the television or maybe in a magazine. Yes, that was it; she'd seen them in a copy of Ronnetta's preferred choice of reading material, *Hello!*. It had been something about a big charity event.

'Sorry to keep you waiting. What can I get you?'

Alice looked up to see the young girl behind the bar wilting beneath the strength of James's devastating smile. 'I think your chef must be having an off day,' he said good-naturedly whilst handing her the plate.

'My pizza wasn't cooked properly,' explained Alice. James or no James, she was quite capable of fighting her own battles.

'No problem,' the girl said brightly. 'Shall I put it back in the oven for you? Or would you prefer to choose something else?'

Her gaze was fixed on James; Alice was as good as invisible by his side. James turned to Alice. 'I'll have a sandwich,' she said. 'Cheese and pickle.'

'No problem. I'll bring it over to your table. Where are you sitting?'

'Over in the corner,' James said.

'No problem.'

Wondering if the girl lived a permanently problem-free life, Alice turned to go. James put a hand on her arm. 'Alice,' he said, 'before we join the others, can I just — ' But he got no further. He delved into his trouser pocket and pulled out his ringing mobile. 'Sorry about this,' he said.

Alice stayed where she was, fighting the urge to snatch the mobile out of his hands and tell whoever was calling him to call back later because right now James had something important to say to her, and that something was clearly meant for her ears only. Doing her best to convince herself it was something nice he wanted to share with her, she allowed her mind to race with happy speculation while she pretended to be fascinated by the newspaper article they'd been looking at.

James's call seemed set to go on and on. In between making apologetic faces, he kept giving her twinkly looks with his mesmerizing blue eyes. The sensible thing to do would be to leave him to it and go back to Chris and Josie, but no way was she going to do that.

By now she was no longer pretending to read the newspaper article but reading it properly. She was halfway through it when she began to get a funny feeling. She stared at the photographs closely. Not the large one of the couple whose names she now knew were Barry Osborne and Stacey Cook, but the two smaller pictures; the ones of the two very different-looking men. She now knew that it was the same man in the photographs, a classic comparison of before and after pictures. There was something distinctly familiar about the 'after' shot.

But did you have your every misfortune, failure and cock-up written about in the newspapers? Did you have journalists door-stepping you all hours of the day and night?

If this particular newspaper was to be believed, Alice knew the exact whereabouts of a dangerously vindictive man who, according to Stacey Cook, was in urgent need of medical help. 'To have done what he did, he's clearly sick in the head,' she was reported as saying. 'If Barry and I weren't suffering to the extent we are, we'd pity him.'

11

Clayton was not going to be beaten. Well, no more beaten than he already was. If food was required, then he would go in search of it.

For his intrepid expedition he had helped himself to a selection of outdoor clothing from the room off the kitchen — boots, thick socks, a full-length green raincoat that had several bulky and heavy layers to it, and a hat with a wide brim so large a family of four could take shelter beneath it. He looked and felt ridiculous. Everything was too big for him; Glen's friend had to be some kind of colossus. He had seen stuff like this advertised in the back of magazines but never thought people actually wore it. Funny what people got up to in the country. But at least there wasn't a chance of anyone recognizing him in this get-up. He didn't recognize himself, come to that.

He had been walking for what felt like several days, but was in actual fact only three quarters of an hour, and still there was no sign of any shops. Had that wretched girl Alice deliberately lied to him? Were the shops further away than she'd made out?

She hadn't lied about how dreadful the weather could be, that much he knew. It had rained solidly all day. He'd been tempted to go online and arrange for a supermarket to deliver the things he needed, but after nearly a week of being cooped up, cabin fever had kicked in. He needed a change of scene. It was a simple choice between venturing out into the great unknown and going stir crazy. Knowing his luck, if he did try ordering anything online, given the remoteness of where he was staying, the chances of his order arriving would be slim. So tramping the wilderness it was. Because the sharp pointy end of the stick was, deny a man the essential sustenance of his existence — bread, milk, eggs, bacon, sausages, coffee, wine — and who knew what kind of a monster he might turn into?

He'd also acquired a fixation for peanut butter. He hadn't eaten it for years but suddenly it was all he could think of. Peanut butter on hot buttered toast. Peanut butter on hot buttered crumpets. Smooth peanut butter. Crunchy peanut butter. Organic peanut butter. Peanut butter with every known noxious additive and deadly preservative added to it. He didn't care how it came, so long as he could get his hands on a jar to satisfy his craving.

As a young child he used to eat masses of it, usually in front of the television on a Sunday evening whilst waiting for his hair to dry before going to bed. His mother had been a belt, buckle and braces kind of mother, the sort who believed he would catch pneumonia if he went to bed with so much as a single strand of hair that was damp. He had been eight years old when he'd finally convinced her that he didn't need to take a spare pair of underpants to school with him every day. She had claimed she was only trying to save him the shame of embarrassing himself in front of his friends if he had what she coyly referred to as a 'little accident'. Never mind that the humiliation of his peers discovering the underpants in his bag one day and chucking them from the window of the school bus damn near killed him.

When *Joking Aside* took off and he and Bazza were regularly pitching up at award ceremonies, Clayton's mother was constantly on the phone warning him of the perils of not having an extra pair of trousers to hand for such a special occasion. 'What if you trip on the way and rip your trousers? What if you spill a drink over yourself? There'll be all those cameras. Everyone will *see*. What will they *think* of you?' She had never fully accepted that he had outgrown the worst of his childhood clumsiness. He had been a hopelessly uncoordinated child, incapable of catching or kicking a ball, but a world-class athlete in tripping over his own shadow.

God only knew how his mother would have coped with the shame of the last few weeks. In contrast, he knew exactly how his father would have handled it. He would have been tight-lipped and assumed his normal position of regarding his only son as the oddity he'd always believed him to be. Death had at least spared them both the ignominy of having to face the neighbours.

He stomped through a puddle and hoped he wasn't making the mistake of reliving his childhood to avoid the here and now. He had never been in favour of staring up his backside in search of an answer to the meaning of life. His life in particular. He had done many futile things in his time, but esoteric journeys of navel gazing weren't about to be added to the list. He'd had enough of that with Stacey.

In the last year of their relationship she had taken to sitting up in bed preaching to him from the latest book of life-enhancing flim-flam she was currently swallowing whole. 'You need to hug and touch more,' she had informed him one night.

'I tried that earlier and you said you weren't interested.'

'That was sex, Clayton. I'm talking about embracing your inner child and inviting others to touch that child.'

'Whoa! What the hell are you reading? *The Paedophile's Getting to Know You Handbook?*'

'That's so typical of you,' she'd said, slapping the book shut and slamming it down on the bedside table. 'You purposely misunderstand things so you don't have to admit you need to change. Why do you always have to be so aggressively anal? Would it kill you to consider there's another way to be? That hugging a stranger might just make you less of a stranger to yourself?'

It was all part of the litany of You-know-what's-wrong-with-you-don't-you? Would hugging people he didn't know have saved his career or his relationship with Stacey? Was that what Lucky Bazza was so good at? And when, he wanted to know, had it become a crime not to want to be hugged and kissed by a total stranger?

It seemed to Clayton that an ever increasing

number of people were obsessed with change. Why couldn't they accept that not everyone needed to change the way they were, that maybe they were even happy with the status quo? Could it be that the Staceys of this world were only capable of being happy when changing others to suit their needs? It also meant they were doing a canny job in avoiding holding up the mirror to themselves.

He felt his mobile vibrating in his jeans pocket and after fumbling under the layers of his coat for it, Caller ID told him it was Glen. About time too!

'Sorry I didn't get back to you yesterday, Clay,' Glen said. 'I had wall-to-wall meetings then a dinner to attend in the evening. I'm just on my way back to the office after a long lunch with the new Head of Light Entertainment at the Beeb. I'm having a busy week.' Clayton could hear voices and the rumble of traffic in the background. It was music to his ears: civilization! 'So how's it going?' Glen asked.

'Glad you could find the time to ask,' Clayton replied. 'Two words: bloody and awful.'

'That's three.'

'Your perspicacity astounds me at times.'

'I've told you before, if it's love you're after, there are plenty of women out there only a credit card away.'

'Something you'd know all about.'

'Is that the sound of righteous self-pity I hear?'

'Hey, if I don't feel sorry for myself, who will?' Clayton then recounted his discovery, regarding Alice pretending to be Katya.

94

He'd just got as far as saying how she'd admitted that she'd grown up at Cuckoo House when Glen said, 'Yes, I got a call from the cleaning agency this morning. I must say, that girl sounds nearly as off-kilter as you. But what did I say about keeping a low profile? There was to be no engaging in any conversation. You were to keep your head down and avoid trouble. Which bit of my advice did you not understand?'

'I tried but believe me, she was a force of nature. She would sweep in and just start yapping on and on.'

'Do you think she knows who you are?'

Never mind the girl, Clayton suddenly wanted to shout at his agent. What about me, forced now to scavenge for food in the pouring rain? Was this what his life had come to? 'She'd latched onto the idea that I was hiding here,' he said, attempting to get a grip on his exasperation, 'but from the way she was interrogating me, I'm pretty sure she doesn't know who I am. She even tried to blackmail me.'

'*What?*'

'She said she would continue to shop and clean for me if I told her who I really was.'

'I don't like the sound of that. You be careful. Maybe it wasn't such a good idea of mine to pack you off up there. Have you seen a newspaper recently?'

'I've seen zilch. I'm not even looking at the stuff online. Why do you ask?'

'You're back in a few of the red tops today. Stacey and Bazza are whoring themselves around the neighbourhood again. I heard they're making another television appearance in the coming week.'

'You'd think they'd be bored of it by now. Or at least the public would be. What do you think they're trying to gain by it?'

'Sympathy? Higher profile? You tell me.'

'At this rate I'll never be able to come home.'

'We need an angle, Clay. Something with which to fight back. Got any ideas?'

'I could try committing suicide.'

'Mmm . . . you know, that might just work.'

'I was joking!'

'Oh, right. Yes. Of course. Ha, ha, funny one.'

'Yeah, bloody hilarious.'

'It's good you haven't lost your sense of humour. No chance that you've had a creative urge and written anything, have you?'

'St Glen the Patron Saint of the Bottom Line. You're all heart, Glen.'

'It's just a thought. Besides, what else have you got to do up there?'

After the sound of a siren blaring in Clayton's ear had passed, he said, 'Is there any point in me writing anything ever again? Who's going to want it?'

'Have faith, my old mate. You write something good, I'll find a home for it. That's a promise. Did I tell you I've just taken on a new client?'

'Wow! Like I'm really interested to hear that.'

'He reminds me of you. In the old days when you used to produce some of the best stuff ever written.'

'Go to hell!'

'Be nice to me, Clay.'

'Just remind me how you're able to drive around in an Aston Martin?'

'I work my butt off for you. Always have. Always will.'

'What's ten per cent of an Aston Martin these days? Because that's how nice I am to you.'

'Sorry to burst that balloon of self-sacrifice but it's not enough for the amount of grief you put me through. Now what do you want me to tell that woman at the cleaning agency? Do you want someone else? Although if you do, you'll have to wait a while as apparently she's — '

'Short-staffed,' Clayton cut in impatiently. 'Yes, I know all about that. For now I'll manage on my own.'

'It'll probably be safer that way. Just don't make a mess of the house. Meanwhile, stay out of trouble.'

Clayton rang off, shoved his mobile into one of the many pockets the coat had and trudged on in the rain.

Stay out of trouble.

Glen made it sound as if he deliberately went around looking for trouble. It was the other way around. Trouble came looking for him. It always had.

He thought of his agent's new client and idly wondered what kind of money was involved. The thing about the industry was that no matter how much an individual was paid to come up with a hit show, there was always someone else coming up on the rails with a potentially bigger and better hit show and being paid more for it. It was what made it the bitchy, ego-crushing world it was. Sometimes he thought he was well out of it. Other times he thought he'd sell his own liver and kidneys to get back in the game.

Having slogged to the crest of a hill, he was now peering through the rain and misty gloom at a stretch of long and winding tarmac road; it was completely deserted, not a car or person in sight. It crossed his mind that he might be lost. He had assumed that if he kept walking in a straight line, he would sooner or later end up where he needed to be. Had he missed a vital turning? If he had, he'd probably done it when he was talking to Glen. What should he do? Continue on, or retrace his steps?

If he retraced his steps he might well find himself back at Cuckoo House, and what would he have achieved then? No eggs. No bacon. No peanut butter.

He had to have that peanut butter.

No matter what else, he was not going to return to Cuckoo House without a jar of peanut butter.

The answer was to press on and hope for the —

He froze.

Gunfire? What was this, bandit country? Another gunshot going off had him looking around for something to take cover behind. Then through the gloom, coming from the direction he'd just walked, he saw what was causing the noise: it was a car. Deliverance! It was the first car he had seen. No way was he going to let it pass.

He stepped into the middle of the road as the

car slowly approached. It was an ancient Morris Minor, with . . . with no one at the wheel. How was that possible? Had he slipped through a portal into a weirdly surreal world where cars drove themselves? Whatever was driving it, the car appeared to have no intention of stopping. He held his ground. It was almost upon him when through the windscreen he saw a small, beaky face peering over the steering wheel. A hand was waving furiously at him to get out of the way. Clayton held his breath and stayed where he was. He wanted that jar of peanut butter and nothing on this earth was going to stop him.

Just inches from the toes of his borrowed boots, the car backfired to a stop. The engine wheezed, spluttered, rattled and then died. His heart banging with fear and relief inside his chest, Clayton swallowed. He went round to the driver's side of the car. The small, beaky face belonged to a hobgoblin wearing a plastic rain-hood. He hadn't seen a rain-hood in years. Not since the days when his mother had worn one to protect her hair when she came home from the hairdressers. Come to think of it, when was the last time he'd seen a hobgoblin?

On closer inspection the hobgoblin was in actual fact a wizened old woman. She was staring implacably at him through the steamed up side window. The ferocious hostility in her face made him take a step back. 'I seem to have lost my way,' he said loudly. 'Can you help me?'

She made no attempt to wind down the window.

'I'm looking for the shops?' he shouted. 'Can. You. Help. Me?'

Still nothing.

He leaned down and tapped on the window. He would not be denied his peanut butter. Very slowly, the window was lowered and a grudging three-inch gap appeared at the top.

Through which the barrel of a handgun appeared.

12

'OK, sonny, I'm warning you now, any funny business and I'll blow your head off.'

Rooted to the spot, Clayton knew that he should be backing away, and fast. But he couldn't move. His body had locked tight. He was rigid with mind-numbing terror. Even his life was too scared to flash before him. The only part of him that appeared to have ability to move was the bit that Glen maintained he'd never been able to control: his mouth. 'And a good day to you, madam,' he heard himself say. *Stay out of trouble*, Glen had said . . .

'Oh, fancy yourself a smart aleck, do you? Well, let's see how smart you are with half your ugly mug missing!'

Clayton Miller, aged just forty-four and the nation's favourite comedy writer, was brutally murdered by a mad woman. What has the world come to when an innocent and much-loved genius is gunned down simply for asking directions so that he could buy himself a jar of peanut butter?

'Are you listening to me?'

'I'm sorry,' he said, 'I'd drifted off there for a moment.'

'Drifted off?' Her beady eyes looked at him incredulously. 'Are you on drugs?'

'Never touch the stuff. So don't waste your time trying to sell me any.'

She pursed her thin lips. There was a hint of a moustache on her top lip and her face, creased and severely weather-beaten, looked like it had been given a regular coating of creosote for the last fifty years. 'You've escaped from somewhere, haven't you?' she said. 'You're not the full shilling.'

'Do you suppose we could hold this delightful conversation without that gun being pointed at me?'

'Not until I'm sure about you. What do you want?'

'Directions. I'm trying to get to the nearest shops.'

'Where've you come from?'

He hesitated. *Stay out of trouble . . .*

The beady eyes tightened their grip on him. 'You're obviously not local. Where are you staying? Come on, out with it. I haven't got all day.' She had one of those terrifyingly superior voices, the sort of voice that had been born to boss people about.

'Cuckoo House,' he said obediently.

'Oh, there.'

'You know it?'

She snorted. 'I've lived here all my life; of course I know it. You're a friend of the Armstrongs, then?'

'Yes,' he lied. 'They're letting me stay there until I've got myself sorted.'

'If you'd said that at the outset, it would have saved us both a lot of bother.' She withdrew the gun. 'Saddle up and get in. I'm on my way to the shops; I'll give you a lift. I'll give you a lift back if you behave yourself.'

102

* * *

At about ten miles an hour the Morris Minor rattled, juddered and backfired its way along the winding road. Its driver seemed happily oblivious to the deafening racket of the car. She was too busy wiping the steamed up windscreen with the back of her hand and crashing the gears to worry about a little thing like hearing loss.

'Sorry about the gun,' she shouted at him. 'But one can never be too careful. What was I supposed to do? I see a strange man standing in the middle of the road — you could have been anyone. What's your name?'

'Ralph Shannon,' Clayton said.

'Well, Shannon, you can call me George.'

'Is that Miss, Ms or Mrs?'

'Just George. And that's Percy in the back.'

Percy? Who the hell was Percy? Clayton spun round. On the back seat was a large, murderous-looking rooster. His head was tilted and his eyes were as beady as those of the mad woman driving the car. A choice between death by rooster or a single gunshot; Clayton knew which he'd take any day of the week. The rooster glared threateningly at Clayton, then jerked his head and began scratching and pecking at the tattered seat. 'Stop that at once, Percy!' the woman roared, making Clayton jump. 'Or Shannon and I will have you for supper!' She turned to Clayton. 'I had to bring him with me. He's turned into a frightful sex pest and won't leave the poor hens alone. He's at them day and night.'

'Right,' said Clayton as though they were

having a perfectly normal conversation. He stared intently ahead, despite being unable to see anything out of the windscreen. There was only one windscreen wiper and it was on the driver's side.

'So where's home?' she demanded. 'London, I'm guessing. Am I right?'

'You might be.' She thought he looked like a Londoner in this garb? Or maybe that was the point; no local in his right mind would dress so preposterously.

'Of course I'm right. You have that worn-down manner only Londoners have. Had some kind of a breakdown, have you?'

'Why do you ask that?'

'You're as jumpy as hell.'

'So would you be if you'd just had a gun shoved in your face.'

She thumped the steering with both hands and laughed out loud as though he'd said the funniest thing. He had to find a way to stop the old biddy asking so many questions. A thought occurred to him. 'You said you've lived here all your life?'

'That's right.'

'Do you know a girl called Alice Shoemaker? I believe she grew up here.'

'Shoemaker, you say. No, that name doesn't ring a bell. I knew an Alice Barrett. The Barretts owned Cuckoo House years ago.'

'How many years ago was that?'

With a bloodcurdling scream of resistance from the engine, she changed gear and shot him a look. 'Why do you want to know?'

'I'm interested.'

'Evidently. But *why* are you interested?'

'I . . . I met a girl the other day called Alice Shoemaker and she said she grew up at Cuckoo House.'

'Really? How old was she?'

'I'm not very good at guessing ages. Especially when it comes to women.'

'Don't be pathetic. I'm looking for a rough ball-park figure. Imagine I have my gun to your head, and your life depends upon an answer. Was she in her twenties? Thirties? Fifties?'

Imagining all too well the gun pressed to his head, Clayton suddenly remembered exactly how old Alice was. 'She's thirty-one,' he said.

'That's a very precise ball-park figure, but in that case I'd say you met Alice Barrett, as was. Where did you meet her? London? I always suspected that's where she ran off to.'

'I met her at Cuckoo House.'

'Well, I never. Alice back at Cuckoo House. Mind you, I thought she'd show up one day.'

After another gear change and a thunderous explosion from the rear of the car, they juddered to an abrupt stop. Clayton's seat belt did little to prevent him from very nearly slamming against the windscreen. Surely the car would never pass an MOT? But then its owner didn't strike him as being the sort of person who would worry over such a minor detail.

'Right, Shannon, here we are. There's a Co-op over there. A butcher's next door, a grocer's shop across the road and a baker's right here where we're parked.'

105

'Is there a bank?'

'In between the outdoor clothing shop and the Penny-Farthing cafe. Be back here in an hour. Any later and I'll be gone and you'll have to walk.'

★ ★ ★

The good news was that the rain had let up. Clayton was about to dispense with his hat and stuff it in a pocket when he thought better of it. The hat gave him something to hide beneath. Although, as he caught sight of his reflection in a shop window, he had to acknowledge that overall he stuck out like a very sore thumb. He wasn't exactly blending in, was he? Most other people were sensibly dressed in ordinary coats and carried umbrellas.

It was mid afternoon and the light was fading; illuminated shop windows shone invitingly. His first port of call was the bank. He needed some cash. This he acquired from a hole in the wall since the bank itself had closed for the day. He then progressed to the butcher's. He wanted some more of those sausages Alice had bought him. There was a choice of three different varieties, so he bought two pounds of each. He could use the freezer back at Cuckoo House to store a fortnight's worth of them. He did the same with bacon. And since the butcher also sold eggs, he bought a dozen of those, too.

Next it was on to the Co-op.

Peanut butter, peanut butter, he silently chanted to himself as he grabbed a trolley. He found it next to the pots of jam and marmalade and stripped the shelf of its entire stock, all three jars. He then worked methodically round the store, slinging items into the trolley. He was joining the queue for the checkout when he noticed the depleted racks of newspapers. He couldn't stop himself. He added three tabloids to the basket and joined the queue.

It took an age to pay and, heavily laden with six bags of shopping, he hurried outside. He crossed the street to where he'd been instructed to meet the old woman.

But there was no sign of her. Or of the Morris Minor. He checked his watch. He was two minutes late.

★　★　★

Alice's headlights picked out the lumbering figure ahead of her. Even before he turned round, she knew who it was and what she was going to do and say. After all, this was no accidental meeting; curiosity in all its grubby glory had drawn her here.

She slowed the car, pulled alongside him and lowered her window. 'You're lucky it's stopped raining,' she said. 'Want a lift?'

A grimace of tired relief passed across his face. 'I'll give you anything you want,' he groaned, 'just so long as you get me back to Cuckoo House, preferably alive.'

She got out of the car, went round to the boot and opened it. She helped him to load the shopping inside, and noticed the newspapers protruding from one of the carrier bags.

He slumped in the passenger seat next to her. 'You're not used to exercise, are you?' she said, managing to stifle a smile at the sight of him in such a ridiculous get-up.

Ignoring her question, he said, 'What brings you to this neck of the woods? The desire to gloat?'

'Oh, don't be like that. Not when I'm doing such a splendid job of being your very own angel of mercy. Would 'thank you' be so very difficult for you to say?'

'Thank you.'

'With a little more feeling would be nice.'

'What do you want? Blood squeezed drop by drop from me?'

She smiled to herself and drove the rest of the journey in silence. When they reached the gate at Cuckoo House, she said, 'You left it open; I wouldn't have thought a man in your position would do that.'

He said nothing.

She drove through the gate, then stopped the car. She turned and looked at him. 'Yes, that's right, I'm waiting for you to get out and close it.'

Scowling, he did as she instructed.

When he was back in the car, he said, 'What did you mean, a man in my position?'

'You tell me.' She saw a flicker of unease darken his eyes.

Up at the house, she helped him carry his shopping inside. 'That's a lot of peanut butter you've bought,' she remarked as she automatically started to unpack the bags for him while he shrugged off the enormous coat he'd been wearing.

'I thought I'd stockpile a few jars since I've developed an unaccountable craving for it.'

'I know what you mean; I was addicted to it as a child. I still slip back into my bad old ways now and then. It has to be the ultimate in comfort food, don't you think?'

'Are you suggesting I'm in need of comfort?'

She held up her hands. 'I'm suggesting nothing. Merely making polite conversation.'

When he made no effort to reply, she said, 'Since I'm here, is there anything you'd like me to do for you?'

'I've dispensed with the agency.'

'I know. I was offering my services for free.'

'Free? There's no such thing.'

'Not in your world maybe, but in mine there is.' She reached into the last remaining bag to unpack and pulled out the newspapers. The one she'd read at lunchtime was on the top. 'Would you mind if I checked the television programmes for tonight, please?' Without waiting for him to respond, she opened the paper, but seeing the undisguised alarm in his face, she stopped what she was doing. It was unnecessarily cruel to tease him this way. She had no idea how much truth had been written about him in the papers, if any, but one thing she knew with unquestionable certainty, from first-hand experience, was that things were rarely as they first appeared. During her drive home from the studio she had wondered about his comment the other day that he'd been under a lot of stress lately. Had that been before his spectacular fall from grace or as a result of it? Stress was guaranteed to make a person act out of character and for all she knew his inability to write — as mentioned in the newspaper — might be the cause of his problems.

'I have a confession to make,' she said, deciding to come clean. 'I found out earlier today who you really are. You're Clayton Miller.'

He could not have looked more shocked.

'I read about you in the paper,' she explained, experiencing a rush of compassion for him. Seeing him like this, she couldn't believe the worst of what she'd read. It just didn't square up. He seemed no madder or more malicious than her. 'It took me a while to make the connection,' she said, 'but I eventually recognized you from the pictures.' She sounded as if she was apologizing for having recognized him.

He came over to her, held out his hand for the newspaper. 'May I?'

She gave it to him, then watched him sink into the nearest chair. He flicked through the pages until he found what he was looking for. His hand flat on the table as if steadying himself, he began reading. Not knowing what else to do, Alice made herself useful. She filled the kettle, put it on the hob, then opened one of the packets of crumpets on the table. She slotted four into the Dualit toaster, found some plates and knives, a dish of butter in the fridge and lastly a jar of newly bought crunchy peanut butter. She then cleared the table of the shopping, taking care not to knock the paper that was being read so intently. The poor man now had his head in his hands.

The kettle began to whistle. She made the tea, the crumpets popped up and seconds later they were oozing a trillion calories a piece. She slid one of the plates in front of the man whose spirit she appeared to have broken. For the first time since he'd sat down, he looked up at her. 'How do you like your tea?' she asked.

'Milk, no sugar,' he murmured.

She poured out two mugs, gave him one. Her hand resting on the back of a chair opposite, she said, 'May I?'

He nodded.

'Is *any* of it true?' she asked, inclining her head towards the newspaper.

'They've got my name right and the fact that I haven't managed to write anything since Barry ended our partnership.'

'And the bit about you being responsible for them losing their baby?'

He raked his hands through his hair. 'Stacey and Bazza say I'm responsible, so I must be.'

'But if you're not, you're just going to take what's been written about you?'

'What would you do?'

She sighed. 'I hate to admit it, but I'd run away and hide, just like you.'

'You would? You don't strike me as the run-and-hide sort. Far from it.'

'My track record says otherwise. The circumstances weren't entirely the same, but years ago, I ran and hid from — ' she hesitated, searching for the right words. 'Let's just call it a difficult situation.'

'Was it something to do with living here?'

She took a bite of crumpet and chewed on it slowly and thoughtfully. 'What makes you think that?' she said at length.

'Whilst you were putting two and two together about me today, I found out something about you. Your surname used to be Barrett, didn't it?'

'How did you come across that?'

'I met a crazy old woman called George this afternoon.'

'Good God! She's not still alive is she? She was a hundred and ten when I was a child.'

'She was very much alive. I stopped her car to ask for directions to the shops and she pulled a gun on me.'

Alice laughed. 'A small handgun?'

'It didn't look that small to me.'

'It's a fake. She always used to ride around with it. She wasn't by any chance still driving her beloved Morris Minor?'

'She was certainly driving a clapped out Morris Minor. Whether it was beloved I couldn't say.'

'How extraordinary,' Alice pondered. 'Georgina Harrington-Smythe still alive and kicking. Who'd have thought it?'

'Is that her real name?'

'Yes. But she only used to use it with people she didn't like. If she'd introduced herself as George it means she took a shine to you.'

'I'm not sure she took that much of a shine to me. She didn't hang around to give me a lift back.'

'I wouldn't take that personally. How did she seem to you?'

'One word covers it: indomitable. Not unlike the friend she had with her. A sex pest of a rooster who goes by the name of Percy.'

Again Alice laughed. 'That sounds exactly the kind of friend George would have.'

'They did seem ideally suited,' he agreed with an unexpected flash of lightness to his voice. 'Can I ask you what you're going to do now that you know who I am?' he added.

'What would you like me to do?'

'To keep quiet. To tell no one that I'm here.'

'Then that's exactly what I shall do. You have my word on it.'

A shadow of wary doubt covered his face. 'I haven't cut any corners to get to this level of neurosis,' he said, 'so I have to tell you that I'm obliged to ask why you would do that. Why would you keep schtum for me?'

'What can I say? I like to think I'm adept at reading between the lines and you seem the epitome of a man in need of a break in life. Plus, there's something about you I like.' She felt her cheeks redden at the admission.

'You have a weakness for failures?'

'Now you're just fishing for sympathy. You're not a failure. You created one of the best sitcoms ever. One of my absolute favourites.'

He didn't look especially flattered.

'I give you my word,' she said. 'I won't tell a soul. Who else knows you're here?'

'Only my agent.'

'And his connection with the house?'

'He knows the Armstrongs, the current owners. He asked them if a friend of his could stay here for a while. Is the house very different from how you remembered it?'

'Yes,' she said simply. 'You can't imagine how different.' Or how it makes me feel being back here, she thought. So many memories. So many emotions. It was almost too much to take in, as if she couldn't bring herself to acknowledge that she was really here. But then she had always been good at blocking out anything that was too painful to deal with. When her mother had died, she had hardly cried at all. She had taken her lead from the headmistress who had delivered the news — bluntly and to the point — assuming that was the way it had to be done. What tears she had shed, she had done so in private. Even when she had seen her father visibly upset she hadn't shared her true feelings with him. One of them had to be strong, she had decided, and who else was there to support her father? It never occurred to her that anyone should have supported her. Nor had it occurred to her that she could admit how much she missed her mother. And anyway, apart from her father, who could she have talked to?

'Will you tell me how it happened?' she asked Clayton.

'How what happened?'

'What the papers are calling your *spectacular fall from grace*.'

'Maybe. But first, I want to know more about you. Tell me about those circumstances that made you run and hide.'

She ran a finger round her buttery plate, then licked her finger. 'It's a very long story.'

'I've got time,' he said. 'I'm not due anywhere for the foreseeable future, certainly not for the next few hours. How about you?'

Alice thought of what was waiting for her back at Dragonfly Cottage. Probably only another irresistible offer from Bob to turn down. But there was the slimmest of chances that James might call. He never had got around to saying whatever it was he'd wanted to share with her, and his parting words were that he'd give her a ring. He hadn't said when.

'No,' she said, 'I'm not busy this evening.'

'Then let's have another cup of tea and some more crumpets and you can tell me your story. If nothing else, it'll take my mind off my predicament.'

They both got to their feet at the same time. Alice took charge of the toast and he poured the tea. And all the while she kidded herself that what she was about to tell Clayton was for his benefit, to help him escape his problems for a few hours, but deep down she knew that what she was about to embark upon was for her own benefit. Being back at Cuckoo House had done exactly what she had known it would. It had crystallized the past and awakened an ache deep inside of her.

They sat down again at the table.

'It was the cherry liqueurs that did it,' she said quietly, surprising herself that this should be her starting point.

13

Alice's stepmother, Julia Raphael-Barrett, had a vague, spacey manner. She drifted aimlessly about Cuckoo House as if she were lost. With hindsight, she probably was.

When her father brought his new bride to live at Cuckoo House, it was the first sighting Alice had of the woman who had replaced her mother. The wedding had taken place in London at Kensington Register Office while Alice was at school writing an essay about Charles I and his belief in the Divine Right of Kings.

Julia didn't arrive alone. With her came her two children — Rufus and Natasha — and two items of furniture: a delicate antique dressing table and a matching stool with a pretty silk-covered seat. The furniture had been ineptly wrapped and tied to the roof of Bruce Barrett's Jaguar and for Alice there had been something pitiful about the arrival of the upside-down dressing table and stool. With their elegant legs poking through the plastic wrapping, Alice could imagine the disgrace at being forced to travel all the way from London in such humiliating circumstances.

While the three strangers had stepped cautiously out of the car and looked guardedly about them at their new home, Alice's father had made a great drama of hefting the furniture down from the roof, cursing loudly at one of the straps which threatened to get the better of him. He had then led the way with an embarrassing excess of enthusiasm and when he threw his arms around Alice and kissed her, she almost expected him to say, 'Darling, I went to the pet shop and look what I came home with for you!' Laughing and joking, he ushered everyone into the house, issuing instructions as he went: introduce yourselves . . . make yourselves at home . . . put the kettle on, Alice. In an effort to calm things down, Alice had shyly offered to take Natasha and Rufus upstairs and show them their rooms.

It soon became apparent that, not unlike her predecessor, Julia had no interest in anything of a domestic nature and encouraged Alice, along with her own children, to do whatever they wanted rather than bother her. She didn't mind if they left their clothes strewn on the floor of their bedrooms, or played music so loud the windows rattled, or made bonfires that got out of hand, or broke a window as a result of an energetic game of Ker-Plunk, or left trails of muddy footprints through the house.

In many ways, Alice had always had a free rein to do as she pleased, but sharing that freedom with Natasha and Rufus made it all the more enjoyable. Tasha, as she insisted Alice call her, was the same age as Alice — thirteen — and Rufus was three years older. Whereas Tasha was open and direct, Rufus was quiet and withdrawn. He scowled a lot and was often astonishingly rude. Alice developed an instant crush on him.

It was her first real crush and she kept it

hidden; he was her stepbrother, after all. He was easily the best-looking boy she had ever set eyes on. He was tall — almost as tall as Alice's father — broad-shouldered and he had the most amazing blue eyes. His skin had an olive hue, as did Tasha's, and his hair was very dark. His hand was constantly pushing his dangly fringe out of his eyes. He excelled at whatever he put his mind to, particularly sport, and the windowsills in his bedroom at Cuckoo House were devoted to his collection of cups, shields and awards for all his achievements — tennis, cross country, high jump, long jump and cricket. He had an enormous appetite, yet never gained any weight, and Alice frequently found herself in the kitchen late at night making him a sandwich.

Tasha idolized her brother, but that didn't stop her from teasing him or sneaking into his room to 'borrow' his things. Rufus would rant and rave that he couldn't find his calculator or the CD he'd just bought and Alice would be torn between wanting to be the one who 'found' the missing object and therefore rewarded by being in Rufus's good books, or being in cahoots with Tasha.

Alice had no idea why her father had married Julia, or how they'd met, but she was glad he had because for the first time in her life, she had a proper best friend and a sister all rolled into one. 'We'll be like twins,' Tasha announced one day. 'We'll even pretend we are to anyone who hasn't met us before.'

'But we don't look anything alike. We might both have dark hair,' Alice had conceded, 'but

I'm pale and freckly and you're . . . you're beautiful.'

There was no denying the disparity. According to Julia, who was a redhead with skin paler than Alice's, Tasha and Rufus had inherited their looks from their father, who had been half French. Tasha's skin was a fraction darker than her brother's but her eyes were the same extraordinary blue. Her nearly black hair was long and silky and Alice loved to brush and comb it. No matter how hard she tried, she could never get her own hair to fall in the same sleek way that Tasha's did; it was much too thick and wavy. Tasha had shown Alice photographs of her father and explained that he had died two years ago in a skiing accident in Switzerland. Rarely did Alice hear Rufus talk about his father, but then seldom did she refer to her mother.

That summer was one of the happiest times for Alice. There were no arguments between her father and Julia, no screaming matches and no plates or ornaments thrown. She was not a voluble or argumentative woman, but somehow Julia managed to get her way on most things. It was only later that Alice came to realize that this was more to do with her father being on his best behaviour for his new wife than Julia having an easygoing temperament.

At Julia's insistence they acquired a cook. Mrs Randall came in five days a week and her arrival at Cuckoo House transformed Alice's eating habits. Used to her mother's cack-handed attempts, or those of a teenage au pair, she had been a picky eater and often ate nothing but toast and peanut butter. But the delicious meals that Mrs Randall produced were a revelation. Melt-in-the-mouth cakes and pastries appeared, as did wonderful soups, pies and casseroles. Herbs were used, and not just from dusty little glass jars that were years old. These were real herbs that Mrs Randall grew in pots on the windowsill. Everything was homemade — Alice's mother had once made an inedible cake using a shop-bought cake mix — and Alice enjoyed watching Mrs Randall at work. She found it comforting to watch the magical process happen before her eyes, breathing in the tantalizing smells, enjoying the warm steamy environment. She would sit in rapt attention as Mrs Randall weighed ingredients, chopped, mixed and rolled, sending little puffs of flour or icing sugar into the air. If Alice was lucky, she would be allowed to use the shaped pastry cutters, or better still, given a spoon to lick clean the mixing bowl. Tasha, who didn't know what all the fuss was about and considered herself too grown up for such things, left Alice to it.

The summer passed and in September Tasha switched schools to the boarding school that Alice attended. For a while they convinced everyone that Tasha was Alice's long-lost sister who had been kidnapped at birth. When they started to over-exaggerate the story — Tasha had spent several years being brought up in a Bedouin tent in the desert — the other girls smelt a rat and refused to believe anything they said. Tasha had said it was a relief; she'd grown tired of trying to remember their story. But Alice had been disappointed; she'd had all sorts of further embellishments planned.

Rufus had refused point blank to consider moving schools and with ten grade A GCSEs under his belt, he stayed at his current boarding school in Somerset and moved up into the lower sixth. His subjects were all science based; he was going to be a doctor. Alice would often daydream about him examining her. The thought of him doing so caused a slow thud in her chest and a sudden awareness of her body. In particular its many shortcomings. Why couldn't she have a chest more like Tasha's? Why did hers have to be so flat? And her nose too snubbed. And her chin too pointy. And why, oh why, did she have to have freckles? Rufus was always teasing her about them. She had got so upset on one occasion, she had taken a nail brush to the bridge of her nose to rid herself of the horrible things.

'What the hell have you done to your face?' demanded Rufus when she finally emerged from the bathroom and sat down to supper.

'Yes,' chimed in Tasha, 'you're very red. Is that blood on your nose?'

Oh, the shame!

The next morning she awoke to find that her nose looked like it had been pebbledashed during the night; it was a mass of pin-prick scabs.

As well as Mrs Randall, they now had her husband to keep the garden looking more like a garden and less like a wilderness. He mended the old greenhouse and, at his wife's suggestion, he created two large fruit and vegetable plots.

Alice's father's level of interest in the running of the house was as insignificant as it had always been, and once Julia was sure that all responsibility for the house and the children lay securely in the hands of others — an au pair would materialize during the school holidays — she washed her hands of them. It was then that she picked out a room for her own private use upstairs and turned it into what she called her sanctuary. It was where she could go to escape the hurly-burly of three children. She read in there, took naps late in the afternoon and listened to music. Mostly classical and more often than not operas by Puccini. Her favourite books all seemed to revolve around tragic heroines such as Anna Karenina and Madame Bovary.

There were times when Tasha could be openly critical of her mother. 'I'm never going to be like her when I grow up,' she would say. 'She's so pathetically useless. I'm going to do something with my life. I don't want to be just a wife and mother.' Rufus, on the other hand, had a much closer relationship with their mother and if he ever heard his sister criticizing Julia, he would rebuke her severely.

It was following one of Tasha's declarations that she was going to do something worthwhile with her life, that Alice shared with her her dream to be an actress. 'An actress,' repeated Tasha, her eyes wide. 'What a brilliant idea! Why don't we both be actresses?'

So it was agreed, she and Tasha would both be

big stars. They rushed to tell Rufus the news. He scoffed at their excitement. But even so, the following term he accompanied Julia to see them both in their school production of *A Midsummer Night's Dream* — Alice's father couldn't make it; he was away on a photographic trip. Rufus had been surprisingly generous with his praise and had actually said they were the two best things about the production. Alice had basked in his words but Tasha had ruined it by saying that what he'd meant was that it was all relative, that they were only marginally better than the awfulness of the play. It was true that the girl playing Puck kept muddling up her lines and that the scenery had wobbled and the lights hadn't worked properly, but the play hadn't been that bad.

Rufus's appearance at their school caused a massive stir. For weeks afterwards, Tasha and Alice were pestered by girls wanting to know all about the heart-achingly good-looking Rufus Raphael-Barrett. Tasha was a mixture of nonchalance ('oh, that's just my silly old brother') and shining pride. Alice, on the other hand, felt a faint stirring of jealousy. It was a new phenomenon for her and she wasn't at all sure she liked it.

Exactly a year after they'd come to live at Cuckoo House, Tasha confided in Alice that Rufus hadn't approved of his mother marrying Alice's father. In his opinion, Bruce Barrett wasn't good enough for his mother. What's more, he believed Bruce wasn't right in the head. Ever quick to defend her father, Alice had said,

'But he's a brilliant photographer,' as if this explained everything. But Tasha sided with her brother and said that surely Alice had to admit that he wasn't normal.

From then on, Alice observed her father through new eyes. Suddenly she could see that his behaviour was far from normal. She was so used to his wildness and unpredictable ways that she had never thought anything of it. Now she began to cringe whenever he stamped about the house and yelled uncontrollably at the top of his voice, declaring that he was living with a houseful of idiots. She cringed too when Julia was out and he offered to show the au pair his darkroom. It was obvious to Alice that the honeymoon period of her father's good behaviour had passed.

For the first time in her life, Alice was ashamed of her father and she hated herself for it. Never had she felt more confused or upset.

14

It was a mortifying realization to discover that your father wasn't normal.

Nothing could have proved Rufus and Natasha's point more than when Alice's father woke them early one morning during the Christmas holiday and announced that he was taking them on a mystery outing. 'I'm not going anywhere,' Rufus muttered crossly. He caved in when Alice and Tasha, unaccountably consumed with excitement, bounced on his bed and begged him to come with them.

'It won't be any fun without you,' Tasha pleaded.

'No dice,' he mumbled in a muffled voice from beneath his pillow. 'I've got revision to do for my mocks.'

'Please come,' Alice tried, 'you know how silly my father can be. He'll behave himself if you're with us.'

His hair sticking up all over his head, Rufus emerged from his pillow. 'God you're right, Alice. Who knows what danger he'll put you both in without a responsible adult around?'

Alice was shocked that she'd resorted to such a tactic, reinforcing Rufus's view that her father was a dangerous lunatic, but at the same time she was delighted that Rufus would be joining them.

Julia declined to come, claiming she wasn't

feeling well; a headache. She suffered from a lot of headaches these days. The kind that meant she had to spend hours and hours alone in her sanctuary. She waved them off with a fluttery hand.

Alice had been on many mystery outings with her father. There were two that stuck in her mind. The day after her sixth birthday he had driven her to London. Except, of course, she hadn't had a clue where they were going because that was all part of the game. On this particular trip, when excitement had eventually given way to tiredness, she had fallen asleep on the back seat of the car. When she woke up her father was pointing out of the window and saying, 'Look, Alice, there's Big Ben and the Houses of Parliament.' London. She was in *London!* Her father often visited with his work, as did her mother, but it was her father who had promised to bring her one day. And now he had.

They had driven round and round. She saw Buckingham Palace, the Royal Albert Hall, Trafalgar Square, Nelson's Column, Downing Street, and a man peeing in the gutter. That was her abiding memory. It was what she rushed to tell her mother when, gone midnight, they arrived home. 'Mummy, Mummy,' she blurted out, 'I saw a man doing a number one in the street!'

'It wasn't your father, was it?' her mother had asked. Then in a hissy voice that Alice knew she wasn't supposed to hear and which immediately took the shine off the day, her mother had said to her father, 'Why the hell didn't you tell me you were taking off for the day? I didn't have a clue where you were. I was worried.'

A long time later, Alice couldn't remember precisely when or exactly where they had gone, but her father had taken her to Scotland. They had driven for what seemed like for ever and all she could really remember of the trip was that her father had stopped for petrol on the motorway and bought two cans of Coke, a large box of Quality Street and some egg and cress sandwiches which were gritty with eggshell. He had thrown them out of the window in disgust only to have a car overtake, driven by a woman who was gesticulating angrily at him — one of the sandwiches had glued itself to her bonnet. Alice and her father had laughed collusively; her father had even waved back at the irate woman. He had also bought a cassette at the motorway service station and played it on a continuous loop throughout the long journey there and back. Alice's head had been spinning with songs by the Bee Gees when they eventually arrived home.

They never got out of the car when they reached their destination; they just cruised around, leaning out of the car window whenever there was something of interest to look at. Her father said the point of the outing had nothing to do with their final destination; it was all about the journey.

In the car now, on a bitterly cold December morning, Rufus in the front with her father — he'd bought a biology textbook with him to revise from — and Alice and Tasha in the back with a picnic hamper, Alice wasn't feeling as excited as she had been earlier when she'd been bouncing on Rufus's bed. She was feeling nauseous with anxiety. What if Tasha and Rufus didn't enjoy the outing? What if they didn't understand?

Then a worse thought occurred to her. What if *she* didn't understand any more? What if it would prove to be just a boring long drive somewhere? She realized then that it could never be like it used to be. She wasn't a young child any more; she and Tasha were fourteen and Rufus was seventeen. Why hadn't she tried to stop her father? It was all going to go horribly wrong. The day would turn out to be a disaster.

She closed her eyes and willed her father somehow to make the trip special.

Fifteen minutes into the journey and the day really was destined to be a disaster.

It started when Rufus's Nirvana cassette jammed in the tape player, just as 'Smells Like Teen Spirit' started. He tried to eject it and when it got stuck — half in, half out — he yanked on it only to end up with the cassette in his hand and the tape unwinding inside the machine. He swore loudly, left the cassette dangling and threw himself back in his seat. He kicked at the dashboard. Not once, but twice.

'Hey, watch the car!' The Jaguar, like the one Inspector Morse drove around in, was Dad's pride and joy. Yet as much as he loved driving it, he never cleaned or polished it; his love didn't stretch that far. Instead, once a month he took it to a garage where it was cleaned inside and out. Occasionally, he'd just go and sit in it. It was where he liked to think, he said.

'Why should I?' retaliated Rufus. 'It's a bloody wreck, this car. It should be crushed for scrap metal. My father wouldn't have been seen dead in a heap like this.'

'Then it's a good thing he's been spared the ignominy by dying so conveniently.'

'You bastard!'

Alice's father laughed nastily. 'Takes one to know one.' He then wound down his window and chucked out Rufus's Nirvana cassette. But, of course, it was still attached to the tape machine and wasn't going anywhere far. It clattered noisily against the outside of the car.

'You mad crazy bastard!' yelled Rufus. He gave the dashboard another vicious kick and the glove compartment popped open. Out fell a magazine. Rufus leaned forward to pick it up. From where she was sitting in the back, Alice saw exactly what kind of magazine it was. Her face turned the colour of beetroot.

Quick as a flash, her father snatched the magazine out of Rufus's hands and threw that the way of the cassette. The cassette was still clattering frantically against the side of the car, somewhere near the back of it now. It sounded like someone knocking desperately to get in with them. *Let me in! Let me in!*

Let me out, thought Alice miserably.

Rufus smirked. 'Anything else you want to throw out of the window, my pervy stepdad?'

'Yeah, you!'

'You realize, don't you, that my silence will cost you?'

'Rufus, dear boy, just so as you know, on the outside I might look the picture of cool composure but on the inside you're making me shake with fear.'

'Oh, go to hell!'

Fraught with the need to intervene, to make the awful atmosphere go away, Alice leaned forward. 'Dad, can we stop please?'

'Why?' he snapped.

'We need to rescue Rufus's cassette or it will ruin the paintwork on your car.'

Her father looked at her in the rear-view mirror. 'Good thought, Alice. At least someone cares about my car.'

Luckily Tasha had missed the entire exchange — she was listening to Take That on her Walkman with her eyes closed — and only opened them when the car came to a stop. 'Are we here, then?' she asked, removing the headphones from her ears.

'No such bloody luck,' Rufus muttered.

Alice got out of the car and retrieved the tangled mess of tape. She bundled it up and passed it to her father, who then shoved it unceremoniously onto Rufus's lap.

'What happened to that?' asked Tasha.

'Mr Temper-Temper here happened, that's what!' Rufus said through gritted teeth.

★ ★ ★

They had been driving for an hour when they ran out of petrol and ground to a halt in a deserted country lane.

130

An empty tank wasn't Alice's father's immediate thought. Cursing and swearing, he marched round to the front of the car and threw open the bonnet.

Nobody inside the car moved.

'It's turning out to be quite a day, isn't it?' Rufus said. His voice was heavy with sarcasm. 'Does your father have the first idea about engines, Alice?'

'Um . . . I'm not really sure.'

'I'll take that as a no.'

Five minutes later and the reason for the breakdown became clear: they were out of petrol — or gas, as Alice's father, for some strange reason, liked to call it.

'And naturally you've got an emergency can of petrol in the boot?' Rufus enquired. He managed to make his question sound both helpful and mockingly sceptical.

'Why don't we have our picnic now?' Alice intervened once more. She knew very well there was about as much chance of there being an emergency can of petrol in the boot as there was of Rufus ever thinking well of her father. Or of Rufus ever loving her in the way she desperately wanted him to.

Wiping his oily hands on the front of his jeans, her father smiled. 'As a matter of fact, Rufus, I do have an emergency supply of gas. Yeah, I thought that would wipe the smirk off your pretty-boy face.'

Bowled over with surprise, Alice felt like hugging her father. She stepped out of the car and went round to the boot with him to see if she could help.

Under a tatty, oil-stained tartan blanket, there was a red metal can. 'Thank goodness for that,' she said.

'Don't tell me you doubted me, Alice?'

'Of course not, Dad.'

He grinned and unscrewed the black cap. He peered inside the can, then shook it. 'Oh, shit!' he said. 'It's empty.'

'No!' she cried. 'It can't be!' She snatched it from him and shook it herself.

'Sorry, Alice. Looks like I've ruined the day.'

She swallowed back something that felt like tearful anger. 'Couldn't you walk to the nearest garage and get it filled?'

He scratched his head, looked about him vaguely. 'I could, I suppose.' Frowning and surveying the deserted road to his right and to his left, he scratched his head some more as if weighing up the pros and cons of her suggestion. Then: 'Can you cover for me?'

'How do you mean?'

'Tell smart arse Rufus that . . . that there was a dead mouse in the can and we couldn't use it. You're good with stories; you'll easily convince him.'

'He's not a smart arse, Dad.' Her tone was tight and defensive.

Her father looked at her doubtfully and shrugged. 'If you say so. Right, I'll be off.'

'Haven't you brought a coat?'

He wrinkled his nose. 'Didn't think I'd need one.'

'But it's freezing.' It was; the sky was grey and low with the threat of snow. Two minutes out of the car and she was shivering with cold.

'I'll be fine. Toodle-pip!'

Alice watched him saunter off, the empty can swinging from his arm. She then got back into the relative warmth of the Jag.

'So,' Rufus said with weighty emphasis. 'Just as I suspected, we have a zero fuel situation.'

'There was a dead mouse in the can,' Alice replied without hesitation. 'It would have been dangerous to use the petrol when it was contaminated. It would have ruined the engine.'

Rufus slowly turned round to face her. His face was dark and hopelessly handsome. 'And just how did the mouse get into the can in the first place?' he asked. 'Was the lid not screwed on properly?'

Stop it! Stop it! Stop it! She wanted to shout at him. Stop making me choose between you and my father! To her horror and shame she burst into tears.

'Now see what you've done!' Tasha said. She put her arm around Alice, which made her cry all the more.

'I'm sorry, Alice,' Rufus said. 'Really I am. Don't make the day any worse for me than it already is by crying. I couldn't stand that.'

'Shut up, Rufus!'

'I'm ... I'm sorry,' Alice blubbed with confused embarrassment. She couldn't recall ever crying in front of anyone. 'I don't ... I don't even know why I'm crying.'

'I expect it's just that time of the month for you,' Rufus said matter of factly. 'It's well known that women lose all sense of proportion when — '

133

'*RUFUS!*' said Tasha. 'If you don't shut up, I swear to God, I will personally throttle you.' Then more gently, she said, 'Alice, how about something to eat from the picnic? That'll make you feel better, won't it?'

Calmer now, Alice managed a small nod. She found a tissue tucked inside her sleeve and blew her nose loudly. 'Sorry,' she said again. 'I don't know what came over me.'

'I do,' Tasha said with a laugh. 'My brother did. He can be a right pain at times. Isn't that true, Rufus?'

Rufus snorted a laugh and smiled wickedly. 'Me, oh, I'm a total tosser. Take no notice, Alice. Here, come and sit in the front with me. Tasha can act as waitress and serve us from the back, which is, of course, just where she belongs. And since there's no heat, perhaps it would be a good idea if we put on our coats, girls.'

Alice did as Rufus said; she put on her coat and slipped into the driver's seat. Just as Tasha had done moments before, Rufus put his arm around her. 'There, that's better, isn't it?'

She didn't know what he was really referring to, but everything did indeed now feel better. 'I'm sorry about your cassette,' she said.

He cast a casual glance in the direction of the footwell where his Nirvana cassette now lay in a tangled mess. 'No worries, I can easily replace it. It's no big deal.'

'And I'm sorry about my father. He doesn't mean half the things he says.'

'I'm not so sure about that. But you have to admit, his behaviour is not that of a normal sane man, is it? He's a destructive force if you want my honest opinion. I'm just glad he's not my real father. But none of that's your fault, Alice, so no more apologizing.' He put a finger to her chin and turned her face towards him. He stared intently at her, his gaze piercing right through her. 'OK?'

Lost in the depths of his extraordinary blue eyes, and thinking that she could never love anyone else as much as she loved Rufus, she whispered, 'OK.'

He smiled and she felt something well up inside her. Then her heart exploded. She had never seen him smile at her quite that way before. Was she imagining it, or was it possible that she'd got it wrong, that he could love her?

'Pork pie, anyone?'

Alice started at Tasha's voice. She'd forgotten that they weren't alone. She'd forgotten everything, that they were miles from anywhere, stuck in a freezing cold car, waiting for her father to return. She'd even forgotten all that had gone before. All that was important was the way Rufus had smiled at her.

And the way he was still smiling at her.

15

Money was a peculiar thing. Some people never referred to it, while others, like Tasha, were always going on about it.

George gave the impression of not having a bean to her name but the rumour was she was loaded. She had lived at Well House since time began and whenever something went wrong with the place, she fixed the problem herself. It was patched up like a ragged patchwork cushion and inside it was even untidier than Cuckoo House.

She grew most of what she ate, and occasionally kept pigs and sheep. For as long as Alice could remember, George had supplied her family with eggs and when she was home from school and the weather was fine, it had been Alice's job to fetch them. When it rained George would make the delivery herself in her Morris Minor.

Tasha didn't always go with Alice to fetch the eggs; she said she didn't like the smell of George's house. The chickens the old woman kept were given free rein to roam wherever they pleased and that included the house. It seemed perfectly normal to Alice to share a chair with a fluffy bantam but Tasha thought it was anything but normal. She also doubted that George had any money. 'If she really was sitting on a pile of money, don't you think she'd use it to do something about the hovel she lives in?' she argued. 'Not to mention do something about her awful appearance.'

'Her priorities aren't the same as other people's,' Alice tried to explain. She rather liked the way George lived. The woman didn't seem to give a damn about anything. She just quietly got on with enjoying her life. She never bothered anyone else and in return expected others not to bother her.

In contrast, Tasha had always given the impression that there was plenty of money in her family — there were aunts, uncles and grandparents who, in Tasha's own words, were all amazingly well off. Alice had met a number of these relatives in the three years since her father had married Julia, and their lives did indeed appear quite glamorous compared to theirs; they regularly jetted off on exotic holidays to the Caribbean and the ski slopes of France and Switzerland. Sometimes they invited Julia and Tasha and Rufus to join them. One aunt had extended an invitation to include Alice but two days before they were due to go away, Alice had developed an ear infection and the doctor had banned her from flying for fear of her perforating her eardrum.

When Alice's mother had been alive, family holidays had been non-existent. Her parents hadn't cared for the concept; they were perfectly happy to stay at home. They had encouraged Alice to go on the various trips school offered but as far as they were concerned they already spent enough time away from Cuckoo House — her father travelling the world taking photographs and her mother travelling backwards and forwards to London every week. It was a way of life Alice had never once questioned. After all, she was quite happy with how things were. Tasha said she was too easygoing for her own good. Maybe she was. Maybe that was why she hadn't questioned Tasha's assertion that her mother was as wealthy as the rest of her family. Once or twice Rufus had even hinted that Alice's father had married Julia for her money.

But yesterday afternoon, when Alice had overheard a conversation between Rufus and his mother, that assertion was proved wrong.

Home from university for the Easter holidays — he was now studying medicine in London — Rufus had been asking his mother for money to buy a car now that he'd passed his driving test. Alice hadn't intended to listen in on the conversation but there was something in Julia's tone that made her hover behind the slightly open door.

'I can't, Rufus,' Alice had heard his mother say. 'I simply don't have the money to buy you a car.'

'What do you mean you don't have the money? What about Dad's money?'

'It really wasn't that much, and what there was has gone.'

'Gone where?'

'Please don't badger me. And you must promise not to tell Natasha anything about this. I don't want her upset.'

'But Mum, you're not seriously telling me

there's nothing of what Dad left us?'

'I've already told you, there wasn't that much, what with death duties and — '

'To hell with death duties! Dad wouldn't have done this to us. I know he wouldn't.'

'Rufus, please, just leave things be.'

'No! No I won't! Tell me exactly where the money has gone. Oh my God, you're not saying that fool of a man you married, the man who has as much financial acumen as a racoon, has taken it from you, are you? Because if that's the case, I'll bloody well — '

'Calm down, Rufus. Bruce hasn't done anything. But darling, these things are complicated. Why can't you just accept that our life is very different from how it used to be?'

'Please don't patronize me, Mum. Just tell me the truth.'

There was a sigh, a rustle, and then: 'Rufus, the truth of the matter is, your father left us barely any money at all. I'm sorry, but he just wasn't the successful businessman you thought he was. In fact, he should never have gone into business; he really wasn't suited to it. He was too quick to think well of people and in turn, sadly those people were only too quick to take advantage of his good will.'

'Why didn't you tell me this before?'

'Because you adored your father and I didn't want you to think badly of him.'

There was a long pause and then Rufus said, 'Why did you marry Bruce?'

'Why do you think? I wanted a secure future for you and Natasha.'

'But your family . . . Dad's family, they would have helped us. Surely, you only had to ask and they would have — '

'I didn't want them to know the truth,' Julia interrupted. 'I don't want them treating us as the poor branch of the family. Can you honestly say you would have welcomed them looking down on us?'

'So what you're saying is that you married a raving lunatic to save face?'

'Yes.'

'In that case, I'll ask Bruce to buy me a car.' Rufus's voice was flat.

At the sound of a long silence and then crying — Julia crying — Alice had crept silently away to her bedroom. She had lain on the bed, her hands clasped behind her head as she stared up at the ceiling. Had her father any inkling of what he'd got himself into?

★ ★ ★

It was the first warm and sunny day of April, and Alice and Tasha were walking to Well House to fetch some eggs for Mrs Randall, who had promised to make Alice her favourite lemon drizzle cake. Having kept what she knew to herself for two whole days, Alice was bursting with the need to tell Tasha what she'd overheard. But on a sudden whim to accompany her, Tasha was talking nineteen to the dozen and there wasn't a hope of getting a word in edgeways. Perhaps it was just as well. Better to let Tasha believe in a lie than know the truth. Besides, they

140

had more important things to think about.

When she and Natasha returned to school after the Easter break they would have their GCSEs to get through. If all went to plan, they were planning on taking the same A-level subjects and then going on to university together to study English Literature. After they graduated they would then get a place at drama school in London — Guildhall was their first choice. They had sent off for all the relevant information and whenever Alice looked at the prospectus for Guildhall, she experienced a shivery thrill.

Tasha had been all for skipping university and going straight to drama school, but Rufus had stepped in and advised against it. 'What if you don't make it in the acting world?' he'd asked. 'What then? A degree will be a great fallback option.'

Alice suspected that the reason Tasha had suggested what she had was because exams didn't come easily to her. 'I'm not like you,' she often grumbled to Alice. 'You have a photographic memory.'

This wasn't strictly true. Yes, Alice had a good memory, but the way she learned things was by reading them to herself in a voice inside her head other than her own. For maths she had her father's megaphone voice booming inside her head; for biology and chemistry it was Rufus's voice, and for all the remaining subjects she mimicked her teachers' voices.

Her skill for mimicry was better than ever and Rufus loved her impersonations. She could do a great Princess of Wales and her Margaret

Thatcher always made him laugh. As a joke, and at Tasha's suggestion, she had once phoned him when he was away at university and pretended to be his mother. She had totally fooled him and it was only when he heard Tasha giggling in the background that he had realized he'd been set up. He'd seen the funny side of it, thank goodness.

She loved being able to make him laugh. When that happened, for that brief moment, it was as if she was at the centre of his world. When she acted in one of the school productions, in her mind she was acting solely for him. It wasn't always possible for him to get away from London to come and see her and Tasha perform, but when he did, he was always generous with his praise and encouragement. He still attracted a huge amount of interest when he showed up at their school and Tasha teased him mercilessly for it. She also teased him because he didn't have a girlfriend. He'd retaliated once by saying, 'Of course I have a girlfriend; Alice is my girlfriend, isn't that right, Alice?'

She had known that he was joking, but blushing from head to toe, she hadn't been able to answer him. Tasha had pulled a face. '*Ee-uw*, that's sick! Alice can't be your girlfriend, she's your stepsister.'

'We're not blood related so there's nothing sick about it,' he'd said, putting his arm around Alice and holding her tight.

Alice had no idea if Rufus knew how she felt about him, but she was determined not to reveal her feelings until she was at least eighteen. If she did it now, he'd dismiss her love out of hand. He would accuse her of childish infatuation. There were several girls in their year at school who had boyfriends three years older than they were, but as they said themselves, they were hardly serious about the relationships they were involved in. It was just a bit of fun, they said, easy come, easy go.

But Alice wanted more than that. So much more. She wanted Rufus to love her. A long time ago she had sneaked into his room while he'd been away in London and had helped herself to one of his T-shirts. She slept with it every night, breathing in the musky scent of him.

It was a two-mile walk across the fields to Well House and after a long and dreary winter, the land was showing signs of slowly coming to life. All along the hillside, gorse bushes were pinpricked with yellow and gold and in the distance newborn lambs bleated and gambolled in the sunshine.

When they reached their destination they found George at the front of the house at the top of a ladder painting a window frame. 'Be with you in a tick,' she shouted down to them. 'Why don't you go inside and make yourself at home. Oh, and put the kettle on while you're about it.'

Standing in the kitchen where haphazard piles of books, tools, pots of paint and crockery vied for space, Tasha wrinkled her nose. 'How does she put up with the stink? It can't be healthy.'

'It's not that bad,' Alice said absently from the sink where she was filling the kettle. Through the open window, a hen that was perched on the sill outside poked its head in. 'Hello,' Alice said. 'And what's your name?'

Tasha tutted. 'You're as crazy as she is.'

'Crazy as who?' asked George, coming into the kitchen. She was wearing a pair of mud-caked wellington boots and tucked into them were the baggy legs of scruffy workman's overalls. Her short, mannish hair was partially covered by a scarf tied around her head. This was standard attire for her and it reminded Alice of those Land Girls she had seen in a history book at school. It was always possible that George had actually been a Land Girl. A very small one, at that. The top of her head was on a level with Alice's shoulder.

'As nuts as a girl in our class at school,' Alice ad-libbed diplomatically.

George put the paintbrush she'd been using into a jam jar of murky-coloured liquid on the kitchen table. 'You're the least crazy person I know, Alice,' she said. 'I'd go so far as to say you're the sanest person I know. How's that father of yours? Home or away?'

'Just back from a trip to Iceland.'

'Be sure to give him my regards. Now then, who's for a cup of coffee? I have some shortbread knocking around somewhere.'

'We can't really stop for long,' Tasha said. 'We just came for the eggs.'

George swivelled round to look at Tasha, as if she had only just noticed she was in the room. 'In that case, don't let me keep you. The eggs are in the box in the usual place.'

'I'm sure we could stay for a few minutes,'

Alice placated. She was fond of George. She had the uneasy feeling, though, that George didn't care for Tasha too much.

'All right,' Tasha conceded grudgingly and threw Alice one of her looks — the look that said, *What on earth were you thinking?* 'But we can't stay too long; we've got revision to do.'

George muttered something Alice didn't catch and went over to the kettle that was now boiling.

⋆ ⋆ ⋆

Tasha was in a tetchy mood when they left to go home. 'There's no excuse for that woman allowing herself to live in such squalor. The crime of it is, that house could actually be turned into something half decent. If it was mine, I'd spend a fortune on it and make it really special.'

'It's her house,' Alice said quietly. 'She can live how she wants to.'

'I could understand it if she really was poor,' Tasha carried on. 'But you said yourself, she's got money. Lots of it.'

'What? Like your family?'

Tasha turned her head sharply. 'What's up with you?'

'Nothing's up with me.'

'Yes there is. You're in a foul mood.'

'No I'm not. I just don't like you criticizing George. What harm has she ever done to you?'

'Well, if that's how you feel, I shan't bother to come with you again. To be honest, it will be a massive relief. Mum's never been happy about me going inside that house. She reckons it has more germs than a public lavatory.'

'But she's happy enough to eat George's eggs,' Alice muttered.

'What's got into you? You're being a right bitch!'

On the verge of saying something she knew she would regret, Alice clamped her lips tightly shut and walked on fast. Until now she hadn't realized just how angry Julia and Rufus's conversation had made her feel. Her father was being used. He was nothing but a source of money to Julia. OK, he had his faults, Alice would be the first to admit that, but did he deserve to be conned?

Stomping across the fields, Alice experienced a sudden longing for her mother. Her parents may have fought like mad, but there had been a predictable and honest madness to their relationship. Neither one of them had pretended to be anything other than the person they were.

* * *

Alice wasn't the only one to be in a bad mood. Back at Cuckoo House, Rufus was in a furious temper and was refusing to say why. What was more, he was leaving. He was in his room, packing to go and stay with a friend.

Alice climbed the stairs to the top of the house and knocked on the door of her father's darkroom. When he let her in and she'd adjusted her eyes to the darkness, she asked him if he knew what had upset Rufus.

He laughed. 'Cheeky sod demanded I bought

146

him a car. He even tried to blackmail me. I told him to get lost and buy himself a bike. Does he think I'm made of money? Nobody bought me a car when I was that age.'

'What did he try to blackmail you about?'

'Nothing you need to concern yourself with.' He returned his attention to what he must have been doing before she had disturbed him. Scrutinizing the photographs that were pegged above his head, he said, 'What do you think of these, Alice?'

'Are they from Iceland?' she asked, looking at a photograph of what could have been the surface of the moon.

'They certainly are. I haven't lost my touch, have I? Am I a genius, or what?'

She forced herself to smile. 'You're a genius, Dad.'

'Right, that's enough flattery. Off you go and play.'

'Dad, I'm sixteen. I don't *play* any more.'

'Oh, Alice, that's the saddest thing I ever heard. We're never too old to play. Now bugger off and let me get on.'

★ ★ ★

Tasha was upset her brother was leaving so suddenly and she kept asking him why he was going. He wouldn't say.

When it was almost time for Rufus to go — he'd called for a taxi to take him to the station, refusing his mother's offer to drive him — he knocked on Alice's door. She let him in,

147

but couldn't look him in the eye. She was angry with her father for being the cause of Rufus's departure, but she was also angry with Rufus for behaving like a spoiled child. She wanted to bang their heads together.

'I know why you're going,' she said, going over to the turret and sitting in her great aunt Eliza's rocking chair. 'Dad told me.'

He came and stood in the window in front of her. Sunlight poured in on him, making his black hair shine iridescently like the feathers of a raven. He stared out at the view, then turned to face her. 'I know he's your father and you'll always take his side, but have you ever thought how difficult it must be for me? He hates me.'

'Don't exaggerate. He doesn't hate you. He doesn't hate anyone.'

'You're wrong. He hates me because . . . because he knows how I really feel about you.'

Alice stopped rocking and held her breath. 'What do you mean?'

He knelt in front of her, tipped the chair towards him and took her face in his hands. 'Your father doesn't think I'm good enough for his only daughter. It's possible he could be right.' Brushing the hair from her face, Rufus closed the gap between them and kissed her. Alice kept her eyes open, not wanting to miss a second of the single most important moment of her life.

He pulled away, his eyes lowered. 'I promised myself I wouldn't do that.'

She breathed out. 'Why?'

'I didn't want to risk ruining things between us. We've always had . . . ' he broke off as if searching for the right words and reached for her hands on her lap. He raised his gaze to hers. 'We've always had such a close relationship,' he said finally. 'You understand me, Alice. In a way no one else does. Have I ruined everything by kissing you?'

Mesmerized, she shook her head.

'May I kiss you again?'

She nodded. The power of speech had deserted her.

He lifted her to her feet and wrapped his arms around her. He kissed her for the longest time, her head spinning, her heart bursting. She had got her wish, at long last.

'I have to go now,' he whispered in her ear. 'Come and see me in London. But don't tell anyone. Especially not your father. Promise me that.'

16

'I'm sorry, I must be boring you to death with my rambling on.'

Clayton shook his head. 'Not at all.'

'There's no need to be polite.'

'I've been accused of many things, but politeness is not one of them.'

'Even so, I ought to be going.'

They both looked at their watches. It was gone ten.

'I had no idea it was so late,' she said, rising from her chair.

Clayton was out of his chair, too. He was disappointed she was leaving. He'd not only enjoyed the novelty of having some company for the evening, he was fascinated by her story. 'You can't leave me on such a cliff-hanging moment,' he said. 'You have to tell me what happened next. I insist.'

'You really want to know?'

'I shan't sleep a wink.'

She smiled faintly. 'Got any theories on how it works out?'

'I have the feeling there's not going to be a happy ending between you and Rufus. Doubtless, he proves to be less than a perfect gentleman?'

'Not even close.' She hooked her bag over her shoulder. 'I'll be seeing you, then.'

'When exactly?'

★ ★ ★

Clayton woke several times in the night. Something was nagging away at him inside. It was a sensation he hadn't experienced in a long, long time. He almost didn't recognize it. But when he did, he sat up and switched on the bedside lamp. He was breathing hard. He felt a little shaky. A little panicky. He pushed back the bedclothes, slipped out of bed and steadying his breath, he stood for a moment, very still, very quiet. He waited to see if something else would happen.

It did.

The nagging turned to a flutter of exhilaration that caused a low, resonating buzz in his head. He shook his head, testing to see if it was really there.

It was.

He smiled.

But then the smile slipped from his face.

Too soon, the voice of Captain Sensible warned him. *You've been here before. And on more than one occasion.*

He got back into bed. He lay down. He closed his eyes. The buzzing receded.

There, Captain Sensible said smugly. *I told you it wasn't to be trusted.*

An hour later Clayton stirred. 'Cherry liqueurs,' he mumbled sleepily. 'What about the cherry liqueurs?'

★ ★ ★

151

The next morning, Alice was having trouble concentrating.

'Anything wrong?' Josie asked her.

At Alice's request, they had stopped for a short break. She had made mistake after mistake, misreading lines, stumbling over words, mispronouncing names or getting the intonation wrong. Her stomach was rumbling as well, despite the two bananas she had eaten earlier, and with every slightest sound picked up by the microphone, poor Chris had had his work cut out. She was glad James wasn't here to witness her making such a hash of the closing stages of Mattie's latest adventure.

'I'm sorry,' Alice said to Josie as they stood in the small kitchen with their drinks, 'I didn't sleep very well last night. I've got a fuggy head.'

'I wasn't going to say anything, but you do look a bit rough.'

'Thanks!'

'You know what I mean. You're not — ' Josie leaned away from Alice ' — coming down with something, are you?'

'I'm fine. Really.' In her line of work, a cold, a sore throat, or a bunged up nose caused no end of problems. She took out a jar of her favourite honey from her bag and helped herself to a spoon from the cutlery drawer. She placed a spoonful of the honey on her tongue and let it slowly slide down her throat. It was just one of the many things she had to do to keep her voice in tip top condition. She had a whole armoury of herbal remedies at home that she relied upon to take care of her one and only asset.

Forever the taskmaster — time was money — Josie checked her watch. 'OK to carry on, now?'

Alice nodded and went back to her side of the studio. Watching Josie and Chris resume their positions the other side of the glass, she put her headphones back on and tried to focus her thoughts. But she couldn't. She was here in body, but her mind was elsewhere; it was with Rufus and Tasha, her father and Julia. And Isabel. After all, it was all down to Isabel what happened in the end.

Alice hadn't been lying when she had told Josie that she hadn't slept well last night. But what else could she expect after spending the entire evening reliving the past? And reliving it with such poignant clarity by being back at Cuckoo House. For hour after hour she had lain awake in bed haunted by painful memories of those she had once loved. What little sleep she had finally snatched had been disrupted with myriad dreams. Most of them had revolved around Rufus. She had loved him so very much, to the point of misery. She could still vividly remember how when he'd kissed her, her ribs had felt too tight and she had thought she would pass out for lack of oxygen. She had believed that Rufus was the only man she would ever love and to her shame, so far that had been true. All of her relationships had come undone for the same reason — she simply couldn't commit herself enough. Rufus had ensured she had never been able to trust anyone again.

She hadn't intended to tell Clayton her story

in such detail last night, but once she had started she had been like a moth drawn to the light and had become totally caught up in reliving those past events. More surprising was that the man on the receiving end of her tale, a relative stranger, had been such an attentive listener, to the extent of wanting to know what happened next.

In exchange for him cooking her supper this evening — heaven only knew what he would give her! — she had promised to conclude her story. She could have offered him the no-frills-cut-a-long-story-short version last night before she had left, but she had chosen not to. She had wanted to squeeze another evening out of him in the hope that she could try and get to know him better. Well, it wasn't every day you stumbled across a man like Clayton Miller. She had loved *Joking Aside* from the very first episode and had been a dedicated fan right through to the final series, so naturally she was keen to know more about one of the show's creators. He struck her as being a one off.

Then, of course, there was all that stuff written about him in the newspapers. Could any of it be believed? The question they were all obsessed with was whether Clayton Miller was mad or just plain old malicious, desperate to get back at his ex-partner and ex-girlfriend? He struck Alice as being neither mad nor malicious. Above average cranky was how she would describe him.

Mad was how she would describe her behaviour last night. After she had left Cuckoo House, she had tried ringing James. She had promised herself faithfully that she wouldn't do

154

anything silly — like ring James — but ring him she did. She simply *had* to know what it was he had wanted to say to her. When she'd got no reply — his mobile must have been switched off — she had been relieved. Especially so when she realized just how late it was. Any sane person would have accepted that if James had had anything of importance to say, such as 'Alice, I can't live without you!', he could have called her by now. It was probably safe to assume that all he had had in mind to ask her was something so inconsequential that he'd forgotten all about it since yesterday.

Work, she reminded herself when Josie's voice came through her headphones asking if she was ready to continue. 'Ready,' she replied.

*   *   *

Clayton was pulling out all the stops. He was cooking. Not just frying or grilling, but the real thing. Actual hot-diggity, death-defying, back-against-the-wall cooking! And all, drum roll if you please, without a safety net. *Ta-daar!*

He had the Armstrongs' CD player on — music was piped through the ground floor of the house, just as he had at home in London — and having raided their CD collection, Leonard Cohen was singing 'First We Take Manhattan'. Accompanying the great man, Clayton shimmied his way across the kitchen, juggling a couple of eggs, tossing them deftly higher and higher, then lower, then one behind his back. Oh yeah, look at him go! He had taught himself to juggle

155

during the early stages of his writer's block. He had read somewhere that it could unblock and free up the mind. Just went to show that you couldn't believe a damn word you read.

He placed the eggs carefully on the worktop beside the bag of flour he'd found in one of the cupboards and rolled up his sleeves. 'Right,' he said, flattening the pages of the cookery book he'd helped himself to from the shelf above the wine rack. 'Toad in the hole. First catch your toad. Ha, ha! Nothing like an old gag. What's that you say, Leonard? There ain't no cure for love? Sure there is. It's right there, where it always is, at the bottom of a bottle of Jack Daniel's! You just gotta keep on digging for it, Lennie my old mate.'

A loud rapping at the window made him jump. 'What the hell!' he exclaimed.

It was dark now so all he could see as he tried to peer through the window was his startled reflection looking back at him. That and the rain lashing against the glass. He bent forward to see better. But then he leapt away from the window. What if Alice had lied to him? What if she had called one of the newspapers and told them where he was? So much for giving him her word!

Another sharp, insistent rap at the window had him jumping again.

'Shannon!' yelled a voice. 'What are you playing at in there? Hurry up and let me in. I'm getting soaked to the skin out here.'

He recognized the haughty voice as belonging to the gun-toting old crone from yesterday. He went to let her in. As rude and as batty as she was, she was a better prospect than some scuzzy journalist dropping by in the hope of getting an exclusive.

'You looked scared to death through the window,' she said, stripping off her dripping wet coat and shoving it at him. 'You'd best put that near the boiler to dry.'

'You're stopping, then?'

'Looks that way to me. I've bought you a present.' She brandished a bottle which worryingly bore all the hallmarks of something homemade.

'What is it?' he asked.

She smiled. 'Wait and see. Go on, hang up my coat. The last time I was here, the boiler room was second door on the left.'

He did as she said then found that she'd disappeared. He went through to the kitchen and found her poking about inside a cupboard.

'Bingo! I've found the glasses,' she said. 'Come on, sit yourself down and have a sip of this. It'll put the colour back into your cheeks.'

'You seem very at home here.'

'If you're referring to me using the back door as opposed to the front, that's what I've always done. As for helping myself to a glass, I was merely being helpful.' She cocked an eye at the open cookery book. 'What are you cooking?'

'Roast neighbour. I haven't measured her yet, but I reckon she'll just about fit in the oven.'

She laughed throatily and passed him a shot glass. 'Here's mud in your eye!' She chinked her glass against his.

'It's not the mud I'm concerned about,' he said, regarding the urine-coloured liquid warily. He took a cautious sip. It seemed innocuous enough. Nothing too . . . *Whoa!* He opened his mouth, half expecting flames to leap out and scorch the table in front of him. He caught his breath. 'What the hell is that?' he gasped.

'Just a little something I like to throw together. Top up?'

'You've got to be kidding!' He slammed a hand over his glass.

'Get on with you.' She downed her glass in one then poured herself another shot.

OK, she was a total show-off! 'I hope you're not planning to get drunk and take advantage of me,' he said.

She roared with laughter. 'What a splendid idea! Bottoms up!'

He watched in amazement as she downed yet more of her devil's brew. 'Why didn't you wait for me yesterday?' he asked.

'I told you to be there on time.'

'I was two minutes late.'

She shrugged. 'You may have time to squander but I don't. At my age, every minute counts. So what's cooking chez Cuckoo House? If I like the sound of it I might stay.' She frowned and cupped a hand behind her ear. 'Who's the crooner? He doesn't sound very happy. Wouldn't have thought a man in your state should be listening to something as grim as this.'

'Oh, really? What do you recommend? 'The Birdie Song'? And what do you mean, a man in my *state*?'

'Your breakdown. The reason you're here. Taking it easy. Although in my opinion, some good old-fashioned hard work would sort you out a lot quicker. Tidying yourself up would help, too. Who wouldn't be depressed seeing that reflection in the mirror every day? You look like a train wreck.'

'Speak your mind, why don't you?'

'I will when we've got to know one another better.'

'I look forward to it.'

'So what caused your breakdown?'

Good God, she was obsessed with the idea! 'How can I say this in terms that you'll actually understand?' he said. 'I. Have. Not. Had. A. Breakdown.'

'Really? You do surprise me. Oh, well, never mind. What time's supper?'

He shook his head. 'Sorry, but I have someone coming.'

'Oh?' She made a great play of tipping her head back and sniffing. She looked ridiculous, like a Pekinese dog twitching its nose. 'Is there love in the air?' she asked. 'And would it have anything to do with Alice Barrett?'

'Shoemaker,' he corrected her. He immediately regretted opening his mouth. Now he'd as good as admitted he and Alice had something going. 'Not that she and I — ' he started to say in an attempt to refute any conclusion she might have leapt to.

The old woman held up a gnarled hand. 'Please, spare me the details,' she interrupted him. 'Another person's love life is their own affair.'

'I'm glad you consider some subjects to be off limits, but Alice has nothing to do with my love life. Such as it is.'

'What? A dearth of nooky? None at all? A fine specimen like you. Heavens! What has the world come to? There again, you've obviously let things slide. That would be a contributing factor to your current dry patch.'

'And what's your excuse?'

She chortled. 'Who says I'm not getting my share? A catch like me, I have them queuing at the door.'

'Surprise me: has there ever been a Mr George in your life?'

'Don't be a complete idiot, Shannon. As if I'd make that kind of a mistake. So how's Alice these days? What is she up to? I remember she wanted to become an actress.'

'From what she's told me, the actress thing didn't come off for her. She does voiceovers. Not that I know that much about her.' Which was an odd thing to say, given how much he'd learned about Alice as a teenager last night. 'When was the last time you saw her?' he asked, curious now to see what information he could extract from his unforeseen guest.

George topped up her glass. 'She must have been about eighteen when I last saw her. Maybe older. I've lost track. I was sad to see her go. But I quite understood why she had to do what she did. If she'd stayed, folk round here would have gone on talking for ever. She would have been the focus of an endless stream of tittle-tattle. Worse, they would have poured sympathy on her. Who in their right mind wants that? Certainly not a young girl with her whole life before her.' She paused, then once more tossed back the contents of her glass. 'Well, Shannon,' she said, pushing the empty shot glass away from her, 'this fancy dinner of yours won't cook itself. It's time to stop your idle gossiping and drinking and get stuck in.' With a creak of bones, she rose from her chair.

His curiosity lured out into the open only to be left exposed and unsatisfied, Clayton felt perversely cheated she was leaving as unexpectedly as she had arrived. He wanted to know more. What had gone on here all those years ago? Could he rely upon Alice to tell him the whole story? Or would she skip over the really interesting bits?

'I'll see myself out,' George said when Clayton had made no attempt to move from his seat.

'No chance,' he said, jumping up. 'I want to make sure you've really gone. I don't want any nasty surprises, like stumbling over you in the middle of the night and giving myself a heart attack.'

'And they say chivalry is dead. By the way, you haven't said where Alice is now living. Do you have her address?'

'Sorry, I don't. All I know is that she's somewhere local.'

'Telephone number?'

'Only a mobile number.'

'Excellent. Give it to me the next time we meet.'

He walked her to the boiler room, helped her

into her coat, which swallowed her up whole, then opened the back door. He pulled a face. 'It's a foul night,' he said.

'I've seen worse.' She buttoned her coat up to her chin. 'Give Alice my best wishes. Tell her to call in on me. Tell her that I'm furious she hasn't done so before now. And — ' She broke off and put a hand on his arm.

'And what?' he asked, nervous at what might be coming next.

'I've decided you need keeping an eye on, young fella m'lad. I'll call in again soon. Take care.'

17

Clayton had never cooked Toad in the Hole before and now that the situation seemed thoroughly out of his control, he was wondering why he had ever thought of cooking it in the first place. How difficult could it be? The batter was just eggs, flour, milk and water. Basic ingredients. Nothing tricky. And surely, doubling the quantities involved so he could make a really big Toad in the Hole couldn't have affected anything, could it?

He had followed the recipe to the letter, even sieving the flour, but the trouble had started the moment an electric whisk was called for. He had never used one before. Could that have been his mistake? Had the jug-like container not been the right bit of kit to use? Whatever it was, it was an instrument of the devil and had just sent the mixture flying at supersonic speed, splattering everything within range, including him. Now, as he tried to mop his face clean, two things occurred to him: should he have put a lid on the instrument of the devil before switching it on, and what had possessed him to say he'd cook for Alice? Unless a grill or a frying pan was involved, he was a rubbish cook. What had he been thinking? Had he been trying to prove himself? If so, was this yet another level of pitiable behaviour he had been reduced to? Middle-aged man trying to impress young girl? Was that what this was about? He groaned and pushed a hand through his hair.

He checked the time. Forty-five minutes and Alice would be here. OK, plenty of time yet to put this mess right. He would dispense with any complicated machinery. Clearly he and electrical kitchen appliances of a whirring nature weren't compatible. He'd weigh yet more ingredients out and do things the old-fashioned way. He couldn't recall his mother ever using a mixer to make Toad in the Hole. When he thought about it, she had used a hand-held whisk. A balloon whisk, that's what it was called. He rummaged around in the drawers and came up with just the thing.

'Right. Six ounces of flour.' No, that wasn't right. He had to double the amount. 'OK. Twelve ounces of flour.' He tipped the bag and poured. It seemed a hell of a lot. Well, all the better. More for him to eat.

He found a larger mixing bowl, transferred the flour to it, added the eggs, then some milk. He began whisking. Except the mixture wasn't working with him. Like just about everything in his life these days, it was working against him. It was too stiff. He added more milk. Whisked again. Oh, what the hell. He added all the milk. And the water.

'Right,' he said with determined resolve. 'Here we go.' A puff of flour flew up into his face. He wiped at his cheek with the back of his hand. It was then that he realized something important: he had quadrupled the ingredients, hadn't he? He'd doubled up on the doubling up. Oh, shit!

This was going to be the mother of all Toad in the Holes!

He lost track of how long he'd been trying to whisk some sense into the bowl of lumpy gloop when he heard the doorbell.

Here already? She couldn't be. Why did she have to be so early? He looked at his watch. She was bang on time. Why couldn't she be more like Stacey? Stacey had taken so long to get ready to go out she had turned being late into an art form. It used to drive him mad. Really mad. So mad on one occasion he had pulled off the clothes he'd just put on, changed into his pyjamas, cancelled the taxi and restaurant he'd booked, ordered a takeaway pizza, poured himself a drink, and switched on the television. When she had finally appeared downstairs — looking a million dollars, it had to be said — she'd found him a third of the way through his favourite sausage and chilli pizza. 'Congratulations,' he'd said, 'I think that might be a record for you, darling. A spectacular two hours and thirty-seven minutes.'

The use of the word 'darling' was enough to alert her to the fact that he was being far from sincere. Although, if he was honest, he couldn't remember the last time he had been sincere with her.

★ ★ ★

It wasn't often that he was greeted with such a wide smile. 'What happened to you?' his guest asked when he opened the door.

165

He caught sight of himself in the large gilt-framed mirror on the wall to his right. Oh, smooth, he thought. His hair, face and beard were covered in a powdery, patchy white coating. He looked like he'd had his head in a trough of cocaine. Or he'd been Artexed. 'I was trying out a new face pack,' he said.

'Hmm . . . I think you may have overdone it.'

'That's me. One day I'll learn that less is more. Come through to the kitchen. But I have to warn you, there's been a hitch with supper. Basically, I'm wearing it.'

She laughed and carried on laughing when she saw the state of the kitchen. 'What happened?' she asked, her eyes sweeping round the scene of devastation, finally homing in on the instrument of the devil on the draining board. 'Oh, don't tell me,' she said. 'You forgot to put the lid on?'

'Don't be ridiculous,' he said, 'of course I put the lid on. Only a blithering fool would forget to do that.'

Her eyes then took in the table. 'Holy moley! Is that what I think it is? A bottle of George's grog? Tell me you didn't drink any.'

'I stopped after four,' he said, deadpan.

She raised an eyebrow. 'And you're still on your feet? You still know what day of the week it is?'

He shrugged and spread out his hands. 'Oh, all right, I admit it, I'm nothing but a big wuss; I managed one solitary, pathetic sip. But believe me, the stuff inside that bottle is firewater in its most evil form.'

'If it's as bad as I remember, you did the right

thing in avoiding it. She used to give us a bottle every year for Christmas. My father developed a taste for it in the end, but I never did. It's probably what's preserved her all these years.'

'Pickled on the inside and creosoted on the outside,' he agreed. 'Before I forget, I'm charged with passing on her best wishes to you and to instruct you to call in and see her. She was adamant on that point.'

'Did she . . . did she say anything about my family whilst she was here?'

Clayton noted the change in Alice's voice. Gone was the sure, light-hearted tone of before and in its place there was hesitancy. 'Nothing specifically about your family,' he said, 'only that had you not left Cuckoo House when you did you would have been on the receiving end of a certain amount of tittle-tattle.'

'How very discreet of her,' Alice murmured. Then looking about her again, she said, 'Would you like me to straighten things out here while you see to . . . ' she turned and looked directly at him, 'your face pack?'

'Please don't make me feel any more hopeless than I already do.'

She smiled. 'Just trying to help, that's all. What exactly is it that you're covered in?'

'Batter mix. I was trying to make Toad in the Hole. But the toad was a wriggly swine and wouldn't hold still.'

'In that case, I'd really recommend you wash it off quickly before it sets like concrete.'

'But I can't leave you down here tidying this lot up on your own. Even I can see that that would be pushing the boundaries of extreme bad manners.'

'I honestly don't mind.'

'You're sure?'

'I wouldn't offer if I didn't mean it.'

★ ★ ★

Left alone, Alice took a moment to take stock. Where to start? Hot water. And lots of it. She ran the hot tap, filled the sink and squirted in a long squeeze of Fairy Liquid.

The damage was fairly localized but still there was the stretch of worktop to scrub, the cabinet doors, the window, the tiles on the wall and an area of the floor. What was it with men and machinery? They made out that only a man could operate anything that came with a manual and an electrical supply, and yet they couldn't manage the simplest of things in the kitchen. Her father had once done exactly the same thing. The damage had been worse in his case since he'd been attempting to make carrot soup. The stains had been indelible; nothing had ever shifted them. Or her father's unshakeable conviction that of course he'd screwed the lid on firmly — what did people take him for, a raving imbecile?

As she recalled yet another poignantly vivid memory in the actual place where it had happened, Alice felt that if she looked hard enough she would come across those very same carrot soup stains . . . or if she listened hard enough she would hear the bellowing roar of her father's voice as he slid down the banisters. It didn't make her feel happy, though.

When she had everything in order, she looked at the abandoned bowl of greying, lumpy batter mix, put it to one side and started making a fresh batch. Next she found the sausages in the fridge, put them in a roasting tin with a heavy base and into the oven on a high heat. Some mashed potato would be nice, she thought. But after a thorough search, she couldn't find any potatoes. She did find a bag of peas in the freezer, however. And some stock cubes in one of the cupboards. Toad in the Hole with peas and gravy: perfect.

She was opening a stock cube when her mobile rang. It was her agent and at once she knew that Hazel had bad news to deliver. Hazel only ever asked Alice how she was when she was prevaricating. When there was good news to report, she was straight to it, no shilly-shallying.

'What is it, Hazel?'

'I'm sorry, Alice, and I can't tell you how angry this makes me, but you and I both know how this business works. The thing is, James Montgomery has just signed a new contract to write another five books and because his popularity is growing, his publishers want — '

'Let me guess. They want someone else to read his books. Someone else with a bigger profile. A name. A *big* name.'

'As I said, you and I know all too well how this industry works. If I could change it, Alice, I would. You know that.'

So that's what James had wanted to discuss

with her. That's what he didn't have the nerve to go through with. What a fool she had been! A bloody stupid fool. Would she never learn? Would she never learn to read the signs?

'Alice? Are you still there?'

'Yes,' she said tiredly. 'I'm still here.'

'You're upset; that's quite understandable. *I'm* upset. We're in this together, Alice. Don't ever forget that. Although I sometimes wonder why I do this job. It doesn't get any easier.'

Alice smiled to herself. You do it for your cut, she wanted to say. 'I shall miss Mattie,' she said.

'Mattie? Who's Mattie?'

Hazel was a good agent when it came to finding Alice work, whether it was audio books or voiceover, but her interest in the actual product was minimal. 'It doesn't matter,' she said. 'Thanks for letting me know.'

'I'll be chasing the next big thing for you, Alice. Trust me on that. Speak to you soon.'

Alice ended the call as cheerfully as she could manage. *The next big thing.* When it came down to it, that's what it was all about. From one day to the next, it was living in hope of the next big job. The next big relationship. The next big moment of happiness. The next new beginning.

James must have known for some time about his new contract and that she wouldn't be reading any more of his books. He had waited for her to finish work on her last Mattie adventure, then he had skedaddled. Yet as much as Alice wanted to blame him for the way she was feeling, she knew she was deluding herself. James owed her nothing. In fairness, he had very nearly plucked up the courage to talk to her, hadn't he? The mistake she had made was to read too much into his input at the studio, his occasional emails and his charming manner. She had allowed herself to create a make-believe world in which she and James were the two main characters. Again, in fairness to him, he had never once given her cause to think that they had anything more than a professional relationship. It was her overactive imagination that had got the better of her. Everything was fantasy for her. It always had been.

'Mm . . . something smells good.'

She turned at the sound of Clayton's voice.

Except it wasn't Clayton. It was a very different man. He was a clean-shaven stranger. His hair, still wet from the shower, was neatly combed into place and his shirt and jeans were less rumpled than she was used to seeing. He looked altogether less rumpled. Younger too, just as she had thought he would without the beard.

'You've wrought a miracle here,' he said, observing the tidy-up operation she had carried out.

'I have magical powers,' she said, adding 'and so have you by the looks of things.'

He smiled ruefully and rubbed his smooth chin. 'You were right about that stuff setting like concrete. I gave up trying to wash it out of my beard; it was easier to hack the lot off. I haven't done a brilliant job, though. It feels strange being me again.'

It was going to take some getting used to, Alice thought as she looked at him with new eyes. She had to fight the urge to gawp at him from all angles. The transformation was really quite something. 'Aren't you worried about someone recognizing you?' she asked.

'Round here? I don't think so. Would you have recognized me if you'd passed me in the street?'

'Perhaps not.'

'There you go. Paranoia had me kidding myself that I had made that big an impression on the world. Better to believe in one's smallness than one's greatness, don't you think?'

Aware that she still had her mobile in her hand, she said, 'Funny you should say that. I've just received a call from my agent that's made me realize how insignificant I am.'

'Sounds like you need to change your agent.'

She put the mobile away in her bag. 'It wasn't Hazel's fault; she was merely the messenger of bad news.'

'I'm sorry.'

'Me too. I've been replaced by a bigger name. It often happens in my line of work. If the product I've been helping to get off the ground hits the big time, the money men step in and demand a well-known actor to be used. It happened to me a few years ago. I was the original voice of *This Little Piggy* but when it took off, I was history.'

'And what's the product in this particular instance?'

'A series of children's books by James Montgomery.' She could see him thinking. The cogs literally grinding. 'I'll save you the trouble of asking your next question,' she said. 'He was the one who phoned me here that day. The one you said made me go pink at the edges.'

'That wasn't very gallant of me. I'm sorry. Does it muddy the waters, then, as far as your relationship goes, that this guy's ditched you, professionally speaking, in favour of a big name?'

Without answering him, she went over to the oven. She slipped on a pair of oven gloves and opened the door. She pulled out the roasting tin of cooked sausages. 'Pass me the bowl of batter mix, please,' she said. 'No, not your attempt. Mine.' When he'd passed her the correct bowl, she gave the mixture a stir then poured it over the sausages and returned them to the oven. 'Thirty-five minutes and we'll be ready,' she said. She removed the oven gloves and found that she was being stared at. She suddenly felt irritated. What right did he have to ask her such an intrusive question? 'Are you going to keep staring at me until I've answered you, is that it?'

He took a moment to reply. 'Actually, I was just thinking how annoyed I was with myself for upsetting you. Especially when you've gone to so much trouble to salvage the evening. I'm sorry.'

'You've done a lot of apologizing this evening.'

'What can I say? It's new to me. I'm trying to get the hang of it.'

She smiled. 'I'd say you've almost got it licked. And the answer to your question is that I had nothing but a work relationship with James. Typically for me, I misread the situation and thought there was more to it.'

173

'Ah, I see. Well, I'm doubly sorry in that case. Does that mean we get to spend part of the evening bitching about chummy-boy to make you feel better? We could go online and write some creatively cruel reviews about his books if you like.'

She laughed. 'That won't be necessary. I feel better already. By the way, he told me the other day that he had gone to the same school as you. He was several years below you.'

'What can I say? The school obviously turns out a nice line in bastards. How did my name crop up in the conversation?'

'It was him who pointed you out to me in the newspaper. In case you're wondering, I didn't let on that you were staying here.'

'Thank you for that. Right then, what can I do to help? Because so far, I've done nothing but my best to sabotage the evening.'

'I noticed a bottle of white wine in the fridge. How about you open that? If that's not too presumptuous of me — I am only a guest, after all. Pass me that small pan, please.'

'A bossy guest,' he said with a small smile.

She took the pan from him. 'You know, you're a much nicer man to be around without the beard. The beard was definitely a bad influence on you. Now all you need is a decent haircut.'

'That's the thing about women. They meet a man and all they want to do is change him.'

'But always for the better.'

'That's what they always say.'

★ ★ ★

Clayton sat back in his chair. He raised his glass to his dining companion. 'Alice, I can honestly say that was the best Toad in the Hole I've ever eaten. Thank you. Can I hire you to come and cook for me every day?'

She wagged a finger at him. 'You had your opportunity when I was Katya, but you turned me down flat.'

'Oh, how I miss Katya!'

'Liar. You hated her.'

'No I didn't. I was terrified of her!'

Alice laughed.

Clayton tipped his head back and closed his eyes. He had forgotten how much he enjoyed making someone laugh. He'd also forgotten how infectious laughter could be. He hadn't felt this relaxed in someone else's company in a very long while. He couldn't remember the last time when he'd found anything remotely amusing or experienced an emotion other than bitter regret. He and Bazza used to receive sack loads of letters from fans of *Joking Aside*, many of them from people who claimed the humour in the show had got them through a bad period in their lives. A shame that same humour hadn't been able to do the same for him.

'Can I ask you something?'

Clayton opened his eyes. 'Depends what it is.'

'Don't look so alarmed. I was just wondering what it must be like to be such a hugely popular writer.'

'The first thing you have to understand is that writing is a compulsion. Maybe like acting is for you. The second thing is that as strong as that compulsion is, there's no security in it. You're living off your wits and if those wits pack up and leave home, you're a goner. The compulsion then is to disappear into a great big black hole of nothing.'

'Is that what happened to you?'

'Yes,' he said simply.

'Will you write again, do you think? Do you even want to?'

He thought of last night, how his brain had felt as if it had momentarily rewired itself. 'Tell me about the cherry liqueurs,' he said.

18

'Oh, yes, the cherry liqueurs. Well, how about we move to the sitting room so I can tell you the rest of the story in comfort?'

'I've discovered a wood pile in one of the outhouses; why don't we make a fire, but in the room with the turret? I like that room.' Clayton's face was suddenly animated, his voice eager.

Alice smiled. 'A bedtime story round the camp fire? Is that what you want?'

'It's what everyone wants, isn't it?'

★ ★ ★

Ten minutes later and Clayton was clearly in his element. Give a man the opportunity to play with a fire and he was transformed. Alice's mother used to say that you could take the caveman out of the cave, but you couldn't take the cave out of the man. Alice's father had never been able to resist the lure of a log fire.

Sitting cross-legged on the floor, Alice watched Clayton, fascinated and amused. All his concentration was focused on building the perfectly constructed fire. How different he was from the dishevelled, bad-tempered, grumpy man she had met just a short time ago. He had mellowed beyond belief. She couldn't put her finger on it exactly, but there was certainly something about his character that she was warming to. Now that the beard was gone and she could see his face properly, she could discern his features more clearly. To her surprise, she liked what she saw.

He probably wouldn't ever be described as classically good looking, but his eyes were a soft hazel colour, and his mouth had an appealing lopsided curve to it. Unlike her, he hadn't been forced to wear a brace when he had been a child and two of his front teeth were slightly crooked. It seemed to reinforce her view of him, that somewhere along the line he had got bent out of shape. He had a tall, rangy build with broad shoulders; she doubted he was the kind of man who favoured working out at the gym. Maybe he burned the calories off with nervous energy.

Still observing him in profile, she watched him strike a match and hold it carefully against a screwed up ball of newspaper and kindling. She wondered if he'd picked out the pages of the paper in which he had featured. As the flames flickered and grew and his expression became even more absorbed, his face was illuminated with a golden light and his eyes turned to amber. He seemed so contentedly untroubled now and she found herself hoping that the crisis he was currently going through would soon be over, that he would be able to find a way to be happy again.

During supper, and although she was itching to know more, she had deliberately not pressed him on the exact details of his winding up here at Cuckoo House. He in turn hadn't asked her anything about her childhood, not until they'd finished eating and he'd raised the matter of the cherry liqueurs. Prior to that, he'd told her some anecdotes about working with the American studio that had made the US version of *Joking Aside*, how, before they'd flown over to meet everyone, Clayton, who had gone down with a bug the night before, had been sick during a conference call. The Americans had been too polite to say anything and had carried on with the conversation while Clayton had retched into a wastepaper bin. Only when Barry had started to sing 'Everything's Coming up Roses' did anyone break stride and enquire whether everything was all right.

He hadn't only spoken about himself, he had also asked her about her work and she had enjoyed showing off her catalogue of voices — Marge and Lisa Simpson, Victoria Beckham, Cheryl Cole, Davina McCall, Katie Price, Anne Robinson, and some of the absolute stock in trade Hollywood greats such as Zsa Zsa Gabor, Katharine Hepburn and Bette Davis. He had particularly liked her imitation of Sharon Osbourne as a foul-mouthed flight attendant. 'I swear she served me on the last internal flight I took in the States,' he'd said. He was a good audience and that was something she had never been able to resist.

'There,' he said, swinging round to her and wiping his hands on his trousers. 'Now we're all set for story time.'

'Not quite,' she said. She passed him his glass of wine from the tray she'd brought in with her. '*Now* we're ready.'

179

19

Alice had kept her promise to Rufus not to tell anyone about them. She hadn't even told Tasha. But in truth, there wasn't an awful lot to tell. Very little had actually changed since that day he had kissed her and walked out of Cuckoo House, vowing never to return, not unless her father apologized to him. Alice knew her father would never do that. Just as she knew Rufus would never admit that he had overreacted.

Once he was back in London he wrote to her, but the letters were always a disappointment. Whereas she couldn't stop herself from opening her heart to him, he never spoke of his feelings for her. 'I'm no good with putting my emotions down on paper,' he'd written in one letter, 'but you know in your heart how I feel about you.' She hung onto that and veered from euphoric delight whenever she recalled their first kiss to desperate misery that she couldn't see him. Every time she mentioned in a letter that maybe they could meet in London, as he'd suggested, he would write back saying he didn't think that was a good idea, not with him sharing a house with two other medical students. 'If you come and stay with me, I know we'll end up in bed together and I don't want our first time to be like that, not with Neil and Andy listening to our every move. I want it to be special for us, a moment we'll both remember for the rest of our lives.'

At Cuckoo House things were becoming increasingly difficult between Alice's father and Julia. Upset that Rufus was refusing to come home, Julia begged Bruce to make good the damage he had done. 'The damage *I've* done,' Alice and Tasha heard him shout incredulously at Julia. 'You have to be joking! Your son is nothing but a spoilt brat. It's time he woke up to the fact that money doesn't grow on trees. It has to be earned.'

The arguments escalated until they were no longer conducted behind closed doors. Alice was reminded of the days when her mother had been alive and she and he had rowed at the top of their voices, both deriving some kind of perverse pleasure from the exchange. But Julia was nothing like Alice's mother. She was no match for Bruce's vociferous outbursts; she would break down in tears and accuse him of bullying her. Alice knew that tears were anathema to her father. He simply couldn't tolerate them. He saw them as an easy way out for a woman. He would walk away from Julia in disgust whenever she cried. Something that was happening more and more.

The worst of it was that this newfound hostility put a strain on Alice and Tasha's friendship. Predictably Tasha took her mother's side and described her stepfather as a heartless tyrant. When Tasha did that, Alice would rush to defend her father. One day she blurted out that Tasha should be grateful for having such a generous stepfather, that if it hadn't been for him, they wouldn't have anything. 'What do you mean by that?' Tasha had demanded.

'Nothing,' Alice had said, snapping her mouth shut. She had promised herself she would never let on to Tasha that she and her family were as poor as the proverbial church mouse, that all those stories Tasha proudly told of her father — what a clever and successful man he'd been — were untrue. As the days and weeks passed, and Bruce made himself yet more unpopular in Tasha's eyes, she began to mention her dead father more frequently and would proudly show Alice the many photographs she had of him, pointing out how alike she was to him. Knowing how she felt about her own father, Alice couldn't bring herself to tell Tasha the truth about the man she clearly idolized. Instead she had to put up with Tasha complaining how unfairly her brother had been treated and how he'd bravely taken a stand against their horrible stepfather.

Alice had never kidded herself that things had been perfect at Cuckoo House, but for the first time in her life she didn't look forward to going home for the school holidays. Everyone who mattered most to her — her father, Tasha and Rufus, especially Rufus — was drifting away from her and there seemed nothing she could do about it.

One day, during the summer holidays, she pleaded with her father to write to Rufus and say he was sorry and that he'd reconsidered. 'Nothing doing, Alice,' her father had said, 'and do you really want to know why I'm not going to reconsider?'

'You want to teach Rufus a lesson?' she said.

'There is that, but more crucially, the truth of the matter is that, since your mother died, money has not been as plentiful as it once was. I'm not getting as many photographs published these days and those overseas trips don't come cheap. The bottom line is, I don't have enough to go splashing around on smart cars for a spoilt brat.'

'Rufus isn't a spoilt brat,' Alice said, quick as always to defend the man she loved. 'And I'm sure an ordinary car is all he wants.'

Her father scoffed. 'Yeah, and I'm the Queen of Sheba! Look, Alice, I think it's time I told you something important. I was going to wait until your birthday, but now is as good a time as any. Most of the money we have came from your mother's side of the family. It was your great aunt Eliza who had all the dosh. She left it in a trust to your mother when she died and when your mother died, a new trust was invoked which meant I would be paid a regular allowance to take care of you, but the bulk of the trust will pass to you when you turn eighteen. You see, your great aunt Eliza never trusted me when it came to money; she thought it would slip through my fingers like water. She also wanted to safe-guard it, in the eventuality of me surviving your mother and remarrying. She was determined that you would inherit the bulk of everything she had, which is why this house isn't in my name. When your mother died, it became yours. Well, strictly speaking it does when you turn eighteen. For now, it's wrapped up in a complicated trust, of which I have little understanding.'

Alice was astonished. 'Why didn't you tell me this before?'

He waved a tired hand around his head as if ridding himself of a tiresome fly. 'It all seemed such a bore to me. Plus I didn't want you growing up with the burden of it. Because these things can become a burden. And I'd strongly advise you not to tell anyone about this conversation. Especially not any young men you might become entangled with.'

Wondering if her father was thinking of a young man in particular, she said, 'Would I be right in saying that Julia has no money?'

He nodded. 'Of course, I've known all along that that was why she agreed to marry me. She thought I was the answer to all her problems.' He smiled. 'She had a nasty shock when she realized her mistake.'

'Why did you marry her, Dad?'

'Good question, Alice. Maybe I was lonely. Maybe I thought she'd make a good mother to you. Has Julia been a good mother to you?'

'I don't really know. She's not like Mum was.'

He smiled ruefully at this. 'Your mother was your mother. She was unique.'

'Do you miss her?'

'God, yes. It's not till you lose someone that you realize how important they were to you. Life was hell at times with Barbara, but it was never boring. A day doesn't go by when I don't miss her wit and her scathing put-downs. Julia has none of the qualities your mother had.'

'If Mum meant so much to you, why did you . . . ' Alice faltered but then forced herself to ask the question she had always wanted to ask her father. 'Why did you mess about with all those au pairs?'

Without a flicker of hesitation or embarrassment, he said, 'Neither your mother nor I were saints, Alice, but no matter what we got up to, we always felt connected to each other. We always came back to each other. Some relationships are made that way. But let's not dwell on any of that. There's something else I want to discuss with you. In September, you'll be eighteen; I want you to have a party. A real do. A marquee on the lawn affair. A disco. The full works. Invite all your friends from school.'

She looked at him doubtfully. 'Can we afford it?'

He rolled his eyes. 'Now you see, that's exactly why I never told you any of this nonsense about money before. You're going to waste time and energy worrying about it.'

'You can't protect me for ever, Dad.'

'I will if I can,' he replied, his expression suddenly stern.

★   ★   ★

On the day of the party, Cuckoo House was crammed to the rafters with guests. Most of them were staying for the weekend. Brooking no argument, her father had laid down the ground rules — the girls got to sleep in a bed (if they were lucky) or had to make do with a sleeping bag on the floor, and the boys, mostly brothers of the girls from school, were relegated to sleep

185

in the marquee in the garden when the party was over. Mrs Randall, whose services were now only required during the school holidays, had supervised the caterers and waitresses and her nephew was providing the disco. Mr Randall would be in charge of the bar. It was going to be the perfect party, so Tasha kept telling Alice.

The two of them were alone in Alice's bedroom getting dressed. For some weeks now there had been a truce in place between them; this was mostly down to Alice — forever the mediator searching for a way to keep the peace — who had suggested that she and Tasha have a combined eighteenth birthday party.

Tasha was wearing a strapless, ankle-length dress that had a ruched bodice. It was white and showed off her flawless olive skin. She looked stunning with her hair cascading down her back like a sheer black waterfall. Alice had chosen not to smoothe out her hair as she usually did, and had decided to go with the natural curl and wave of it. She had spent the last hour fiddling with a pair of curling tongs and was pleased with the results. She was pleased with her dress, too. Made of red silk, it was long and strapless like Tasha's. She had never worn silk before and it felt as sheer as a whisper against her skin. Tasha had done her make-up for her, making her eyes look dark and sultry. She had insisted Alice should wear lipstick the same colour as her dress and despite having worn red lipstick many times before on stage, worn like this, Alice felt quite different. She couldn't make up her mind whether it made her look sexily alluring or just plain tarty.

'Here, have some of this,' Tasha said. She passed Alice a bottle of vodka.

Alice put it carefully to her mouth, not wanting to ruin her make-up. She took a sip. Then another. And another. She wasn't planning on getting drunk, but she did want to drink enough to take away the pain and disappointment that Rufus wouldn't be at the party. She had begged him in numerous letters to put aside his differences with her father and to come home for the weekend. 'If you really care about me, you'll do this one small thing for me,' she had written two weeks ago. She knew she was taking a risk — emotionally blackmailing him — but she was desperate to see him. The risk had backfired; he hadn't replied to her letter. He hadn't even sent her a birthday card. She was devastated. She had pushed him too far. She had lost him. In the days that followed she had tried to be angry with him, to convince herself that he wasn't worth loving, but it hadn't worked. She loved him and that was all there was to it. Perhaps they had the same kind of relationship as her mother and father had had. No matter how many ups and downs they went through, their love would always pull them back to each other.

★　★　★

Alice was dancing with Jessica Lawton's brother. His name was Magnus and he was studying politics up in Edinburgh. He looked good in black tie. Very James Bond with his top button undone and his bow tie hanging loosely around his neck. A shame his breath smelled of champagne and cigarettes. He wasn't a bad dancer, if a little forceful, and as he spun her round to the music on the springy dance floor, Alice's vision blurred with a swirl of silk and taffeta like sheets flapping on the washing line. When he stopped spinning her round, she saw her father and Julia helping themselves to plates of food over at the buffet table. She hoped they were having a good time. Over by the bar, she spotted Tasha snogging Emma Carter's brother.

'The question I've been asking myself all evening,' Magnus yelled in her ear, his hands creeping around her waist and towards her chest, 'is why a girl as beautiful as you doesn't have a boyfriend.' His thumbs had almost made contact with her breasts. She shrugged and reached out for a glass of champagne from one of the waitresses circling the marquee. She took a gulp and nearly sneezed as the bubbles shot straight to her nose. Flirting didn't come easily to her, but she'd had sufficient to drink and now thought what the hell? Rufus didn't love her; why shouldn't she have some fun? It was her eighteenth birthday party; if she couldn't have fun tonight, when could she? She owed Rufus no loyalty. None whatsoever. She leaned into Magnus and said, 'Maybe I was waiting for the right person to come along.' She gave him what he hoped was a meaningful look.

He grinned. 'In that case, how about we put that to the test?' He took the glass from her hand, put it to his lips then kissed her.

Champagne flooded into Alice's mouth and because she hadn't been expecting it, her reflexes kicked in and she gagged, spluttering champagne back at him. 'Oh, my God,' she shouted above the music, 'I'm so sorry.'

He wiped his face and laughed. 'I can see I've got a lot to teach you.' He drained her glass in one long gulp, ditched the glass on a nearby chair and took her in his arms again. 'Come on,' he said, 'let's go somewhere quiet so I can give you my full attention.'

She allowed him to lead her outside into the dark and round to one side of the marquee. 'Now then,' he said, 'here's your first lesson of the night.'

'And what lesson would that be?' said a voice directly behind Alice. She spun round.

'Rufus!'

He smiled. 'Looks like I got here in the nick of time. Whoever you are,' he said to Magnus, the smile gone from his face, 'hands off. This one's mine. Go on, piss off before I get really mad with you.'

Magnus dissolved into the night.

'Rufus,' she said again, her voice full of disbelief as she took in how wonderful he looked dressed in black tie. 'What are you doing here?'

'It's your birthday; did you really think I wouldn't come?'

'But I asked you . . . I wrote . . . and when you didn't reply. I thought — ' her voice trailed away.

He stepped in closer to her. 'You thought what?'

'That I'd pushed you too hard, that you didn't

care about me anymore.'

'Alice, how could you think that?' He encircled her waist with his hands, pulled her to him and kissed her fiercely. She kissed him back, long and hard, wanting to make up for all the kisses she had been denied. She pressed her body close to his, wanting to melt right into him.

When they finally pulled apart, he said, 'I'd say that was definitely worth coming back for.'

Suddenly light headed, she could feel herself swaying, as if she was about to fall off a cliff. Or was it the sky that was falling in? There was an ocean of blood pounding inside her head. 'I think I'm going to faint,' she murmured.

He held her firmly. 'I've got you, Alice, and I'll never let you go.' She looked into his face. His dark eyes glittered like the twinkling fairy lights that were strung through the trees around them.

'Rufus? Is that you?'

They both turned to see Tasha standing a few feet away.

'Oh, my God, it is you, Rufus!' But then the expression of delight at seeing her brother slipped and was replaced with an expression of confusion. 'Why are you holding Alice like that? What's going on, Alice?'

Alice didn't know what to say.

But Rufus did. Still keeping an arm around her, he said, 'I couldn't *not* come to my girlfriend's eighteenth birthday party.'

Tasha laughed. 'Rufus, you say the stupidest things sometimes.'

Rufus tightened his hold on Alice. 'I'm being serious, Tasha.' As if to convince his sister, he bent his head and kissed Alice, his tongue exploring her mouth in a way that made her knees go weak and her heart thump wildly.

'Stop it, Rufus!' Tasha shrieked.

Embarrassed, Alice wriggled out of Rufus's arms. 'It's true,' she said shyly.

'Since when?' Tasha looked horrified.

'Since Easter,' Alice said. 'We've kept it a secret, though.'

'Why?' Tasha demanded.

Alice's mind went blank. Suddenly she couldn't remember why it had been so important to keep their relationship a secret.

'Because of Alice's father,' Rufus said matter of factly. 'He's hardly likely to approve, is he? But I've decided he can stick his disapproval.'

'What about you, Tasha?' Alice said, nervously. 'Do you approve?'

'Of course she approves,' Rufus said.

Tasha looked uncertainly between Rufus and Alice. 'I don't know,' she said. 'It's weird. I mean, it's practically incest.'

Rufus suddenly laughed. 'Hey, if I didn't know better I'd say my little sister is jealous.'

'I'm not! Don't be ridiculous.'

'Only joking, Tasha,' he said, 'but can't you be happy for us?'

Not answering the question, Tasha said, 'Since you're here, you'd better come and say hello to Mum. She'll be furious if you slip away without seeing her.'

'I'm not slipping away anywhere,' Rufus said. 'Didn't you hear me when I said that I've decided dear old Bruce can stick his disapproval?'

20

Rufus was all for marching straight off to find Bruce and Julia. But not wanting anything to spoil the moment, least of all an angry exchange between her father and Rufus, Alice tugged at his sleeve and held him back. 'Let's go and see them later,' she whispered in his ear. 'For now I want some time on my own with you.'

Smiling, Rufus grabbed her hand. 'I know the perfect place.'

The perfect place turned out to be his bedroom. As soon as he had the door shut, and not bothering to switch on the light, he pressed her to the wall and kissed her hard, his teeth crashing against hers. Their mouths locked tight, he somehow managed to fling off his jacket, then his bow tie. When he started to unbutton his shirt, she suddenly realized what he was planning to do. She panicked. How would she know what to do? Oh, God, what if she got pregnant? He was kicking off his shoes now. She broke the seal of their mouths. 'Rufus,' she murmured anxiously. 'I — '

'Oh, Alice,' he said gruffly, misunderstanding her. 'I want you too.' One of his hands slipped round to the back of her dress. He found the zip and pulled on it. She felt the silk fall away from her body. She shivered. She wasn't sure if it was from the sudden cold, or desire for him. He stared at her in her underwear. She withered under his gaze, grateful for the shadowy darkness. He smiled, picked her up and carried her over to his bed. He stood over her and ripped off his trousers.

I want this, Alice told herself. Wasn't it what she'd fantasized all this time? Hadn't she imagined this very moment? He lay on top of her, then as if by magic, her underwear was gone. She felt the hardness of him against her. Another wave of panic assailed her. How on earth would it fit inside her? And how would she not cry out if it hurt? His mouth and hands were exploring her body. His hands seemed to be everywhere. She tried not to think of what he was doing. She imagined herself on a beach, the hot sun blazing down on her, waves gently caressing her body. Her panic began to fade. She moved against him, enjoying the touch of his skin on hers. Maybe it would be all right, after all.

Abruptly he leaned over her and yanked open a drawer on the bedside table. 'I'm sorry, Alice,' he said, 'but I can't hold on any longer.' Next she heard him tearing something open. Her nervousness returned in an instant. She closed her eyes and waited. She felt something hard nudging against her. She braced herself. 'Relax,' he said.

Relax, she told herself. He pushed gently at first, then as if losing patience he pushed harder still and forced his way in. She pictured a large battering ram and gritted her teeth. She wrapped her arms around him, trying to ignore the burning sensation. He started to move, his hips working slowly against hers. He picked up speed, his breath quickening. She lay there not knowing quite what to do. Nothing much, it seemed. With his eyes closed, Rufus seemed in a world of his own. She couldn't even tell if he was enjoying himself. One of her legs was beginning to cramp. She badly wanted to change positions but sensed Rufus wouldn't welcome the interruption. How long would it go on for? She wondered. Oh, God, why was she even thinking that? Why wasn't she enjoying herself? Why wasn't she making the kind of noises women in films did? Why wasn't she crying out with rapturous ecstasy? She and Tasha had often competed with each other to see who could make the most convincing sound of a woman having an orgasm. *Oh, yes, yes, YES!* they would pant, then fall about laughing hysterically. Why wasn't that happening to her now? Well, not the hysterical laughter, but the glazed over eyes, the head thrown back, the breathlessness.

Above her, Rufus groaned and suddenly reared up, his back arched. He let out a long, shuddering moan then collapsed against her, his body hot and sweaty. Was that it? Was it over? A part of her was relieved. She stroked his clammy back. 'There,' he murmured into her messed-up hair. 'I've claimed you now, Alice. Now you're mine. Happy birthday.' He lay there heavily in her arms and just as she was about to shift position so she could stop her leg from cramping, the door flew open and the light flashed on.

Now she did cry out.

Perfectly framed in the doorway was her father and there was nowhere to hide; both lying on top of the duvet, their nakedness was fully exposed. Alice tried to get behind Rufus, but he rolled away from her. He sat up and casually dealt with the condom. 'Hey, Bruce,' he said, 'a little privacy if you don't mind. How would you feel if I burst in on you and my mother?'

Alice trembled.

Her father made a low grumbling sound. He came into the room and bent down to where her discarded dress lay puddled on the floor like a pool of blood. He scooped it up and flung it at Alice. She clutched it to her. 'When you've got a moment, Alice,' he said, 'we're ready to cut your cake.' He turned and left, slamming the door after him.

Mortified and close to tears, Alice held her head in shame. This wasn't how it was supposed to be.

Rufus rested a hand on her leg. 'Please don't cry. You'll spoil your party face and that would never do.' He moved his hand to her chin and lifted her face to his. 'You're eighteen now. You're not a child. You're going to have to learn to stand up to him.'

* * *

Nothing was said the next day until their guests had all left.

At Rufus's insistence, Alice had spent the

night in his room. 'You're a grown woman,' he'd said. 'You can sleep with whom you want and where you want.'

She hadn't said what was in her mind, that actually she wanted to sleep in her own bed. Alone. But she'd gone along with him. She had hardly slept, though. Within minutes of being in bed together, he was opening his bedside drawer. 'You'll enjoy it more this time,' he'd said. She must have been doing something wrong because she didn't enjoy it any more than the first time. She had been tense, horribly aware that her father, as well as all the guests, might hear what they were doing. Frankly, she couldn't see how they could miss it. Throughout it all Rufus had made loud grunting noises and had as good as yelled out her name at the top of his voice in a crescendo of — *Oh, oh, oh, Alice!* — when he'd exploded inside her. The bed had played its part, too. The headboard had thumped against the wall and the bed itself had creaked and squeaked so loudly she wouldn't have been surprised if George had heard the commotion, never mind anyone in the house.

To make matters worse, Rufus had wanted a repeat performance in the morning. 'Practice makes perfect,' he'd joked as his hands and mouth had started work again on her sore and aching body.

When they finally emerged downstairs for breakfast, everyone had stared at Alice. The girls sniggered and smirked, with the exception of Tasha who looked at her as though she was smeared in something unspeakable, and the

196

boys, with the exception of Magnus, gave Rufus lewd winks and thumbs up gestures. Some even slapped him on the back. It was all so embarrassing.

She had wondered how her father had known where to find her last night — why, of all the places he could have searched for her, he had chosen Rufus's bedroom. It turned out that Tasha, annoyed that they had given her the slip — when they were supposed to be finding her father and Julia to tell them that Rufus had shown up unexpectedly — had seen them sneaking off inside the house and had put two and two together and had helpfully pointed Alice's father in that direction when he'd asked her if she knew where Alice was.

She was glad when the last of the guests had left. Now all she had to cope with was her father. Leaving Rufus to talk with his mother, she went to look for him, wanting to get the inevitable over and done with.

She found him sitting in his car. She went round to the front passenger's side of the Jaguar and climbed in. For a long moment they sat in silence. Alice thought of all the journeys they'd taken together. The destination wasn't important, he used to say, it's the journey that counts. Was there a chance, just the merest chance, he would think the same about the journey she was currently embarking upon?

'I forbid you to see him again, Alice,' he said.

'I don't think you can do that, Dad,' she said quietly.

'He's not good enough for you.'

'He said you'd say that.'

'He's . . . he's only doing this to get at me.'

'Oh, Dad, not everything's about you.'

'Is that something else he's filled your head with?'

She turned and looked at her father. Really looked at him. When was the last time she had done that? She let her eyes travel the familiar, yet at the same time unfamiliar track of his profile. His nose was a bit on the beaky side, but as her friends had teased her yesterday, he wasn't a bad-looking man for forty-five. His hair needed cutting — Mum always used to do it for him, but since he'd married Julia, and when he remembered, he went to a barber. He hadn't gone grey yet and his hair was still the same dirty blonde it had always been. She'd been proud of him last night, all dressed up in his ancient dinner jacket, even if he had annoyed Julia by refusing to wear a bow tie. Sitting beside Alice now, he was dressed in faded jeans and a woollen sweater over a pale-blue denim shirt that matched the blue of his eyes. The collar of his shirt was askew: she could see he hadn't buttoned it correctly. She remembered how Mum used to say he couldn't be trusted to get himself dressed of a morning. She thought of him dressed as a pirate when she'd been little — the moustache he'd glued to his top lip, the peg leg he'd strapped on, the eye patch. He'd gone to so much trouble. And all for her. She felt her throat tighten. 'I love him, Dad,' she said.

He turned to meet her gaze. 'Then why do you look so miserable?'

'It's not Rufus who's making me miserable, it's you.'

'Is there nothing I can do to make you see sense?'

'What have you got against him? You're not still angry about him asking for a car, are you?'

Her father snatched his gaze away from her and gripped the steering wheel. 'I don't trust him. I never have. I once caught him snooping through my desk.'

'Perhaps he'd lost something and thought it might have got caught up with your things?'

He snorted. 'The worst part is, I blame myself entirely. And don't think for a single moment that the irony of my actions is lost on me.'

'What do you mean?'

'That by marrying Julia I as good as invited a pernicious cuckoo into our nest here at Cuckoo House. I'm scared he'll push you out of it, Alice. That . . . that you'll be lost to me. Swear you'll never tell him about the house, that as of yesterday you now own it.' He whipped his head round. 'You haven't told him already, have you?'

'No, Dad, I haven't.'

They sat in silence again.

Until her father said, 'If you won't heed my warnings, you will be careful, won't you? I'm talking about contraception. You've got your whole life ahead of you. A baby would screw it up.'

She reached out and touched the hand that was nearest to her. 'I'll be careful. I promise.'

He stared at her hand. 'Have I been such a

poor father to you?' His voice was low and unbearably forlorn.

'Why would you think that?'

He shrugged. 'If he ever hurts you, in any way, I'll make damned sure he pays for it.'

21

Not surprisingly, things were never the same again after that weekend.

Alice and Tasha returned to school for their final year, but not as friends. Tasha made that very clear. Bad enough that Alice and Rufus had been carrying on behind her back, but then, in Tasha's own words, to flaunt their relationship by shagging themselves senseless and for all to hear, was 'just plain disgusting'.

A fortnight after the party, with an essay on Andrew Marvell to do, Alice was working in one of the study cubicles in the school library when the door opened at the far end of the room. Knowing she was alone, she leaned out of the cubicle to see who had come in and spotted Tasha with Freya Maynard; they scarcely left each other's side these days. 'Alice is nothing but a two-faced slut,' she heard Tasha say. Her cheeks burning, Alice rocketed forward in her seat to try and conceal herself. The words of Marvell's poem, 'To His Coy Mistress', rose up before her from the book of the desk. *'then worms shall try that long-preserved virginity, and your quaint honour turn to dust, and into ashes all my lust.'*

She snapped the book shut.

Footsteps approached. 'Oh, it's *her*.'

Never had so much contempt been poured into so few words. Alice turned round as casually as she could. It was time for yet another performance of sparkling indifference. Anything but let Tasha think she was rattling her. 'Oh, it's *you*,' she said in return. She picked up a pencil and twirled it for extra nonchalance. 'And for your information, Tasha, I am not a slut.'

'Then why do you behave like one?'

'What is your problem? No, really. What exactly *is* your problem? Why does it bother you so much that your brother loves me?'

'Love? Oh, come off it, Rufus doesn't love you.'

'I'd say I'm in a better position to know that than you.'

'What position would that be? Flat on your back with your legs wide open?'

Freya laughed. She was playing her part of subordinate sidekick well. Alice leaned forward and tapped Tasha on the arm with the pencil. 'Careful what you say, Tasha. If you make me out to be such a slut, what does it make Rufus?'

Tasha recoiled from the pencil. 'I don't know how you've done it, but you've blinded my brother and trapped him. I know what you're up to. You want to be one of us, a Raphael, and you think by having Rufus you'll achieve that. Well, it won't work. You're not one of us. And you never will be. You're just a nobody. A weirdo Barrett. I'm embarrassed to be associated with you.' She linked an arm through Freya's. 'Come on, Freya, let's find somewhere more conducive to study.'

The door closed after them with a wheezing mechanical shoosh, followed by a soft, decisive thud.

Silence.

Exhausted from the strain of her performance, Alice slumped forward and rested her head against her forearms on the desk. Not only was she a slut for loving Rufus, but she was a nobody. What was that all about? And what the hell was so special about being a Raphael? Anyone would think Tasha was a member of the royal family the way she carried on. Alice didn't know which of them was the more self-deluded — Tasha, or herself for believing this was just a small glitch in their friendship, that once Tasha had got things into perspective they would be best friends again.

Now, though, she was wondering if she wanted to be best friends with someone who could be such a vicious bitch.

Alice had always known that Tasha idolized her brother but now she understood that it was an exclusive right to idolize him. Probably in Tasha's eyes no one else was good enough for Rufus. Well, tough luck girl! Rufus thought she was more than good enough. Hadn't he claimed her? Her heart lurched at the memory of him saying, *You're mine now.*

The day after the party and before he'd left Cuckoo House to return to London, Rufus had asked Alice to go for a walk with him. 'While you were talking to your father, I spoke to my mother,' he'd said. 'She seems to think that for the time being it would be better all round if we don't make too much of a big thing about our relationship. She doesn't want your father to be any more antagonized. As she rightly pointed out, there are your exams this summer to think about. Mine, too.'

'You don't regret telling them about us, do you?' she had asked him.

'Of course not. But last night I got carried away with the excitement of it all. With hindsight, maybe it's a situation that needs careful handling. You are my stepsister, after all. Not that that worries me. What's more important to me is that your father needs to know that he can't go on controlling you in the way he does. You have to stand up to him. We have to stand up to him. We're not children any more.'

'He doesn't control me,' she'd said indignantly.

'No?' Rufus had given a little shrug. 'Well, whatever you say. Now I don't want you to worry over the coming weeks and months. I'm being assigned to a hospital as of next week, so I won't be easy to get hold of.'

'Can I write to you?'

'Of course. I'll do my best to write back, but as you've no doubt worked out for yourself, I'm not much of a letter writer. But keep yours coming. Who knows, I might get some time off and surprise you with a visit if I get the chance.'

It was only after he had left for London that Tasha revealed the true extent of her disgust for Alice's behaviour. Later that evening, Alice's father had driven them back to school. No one had spoken for the duration of the two-hour drive and Alice had felt nauseous the whole way. It hadn't been from car-sickness.

Thinking now of Rufus's rock-sure certainty, Alice decided to write to him. She would tell him how awful Tasha was being; he would sort everything out. He would tell Tasha not to be so stupid. If Tasha was going to listen to anyone, it would be Rufus.

How wrong could she have been?

Not about Tasha, but about Rufus.

★　★　★

A month after Alice posted her letter — a long, worrying month during which she didn't hear from Rufus — she received a reply. She and Tasha were at home for half term when his letter arrived.

Dear Alice,

I've always been honest with you and so I'll come straight to the point. I've met somebody else and being with her makes me realize that you and I were kidding ourselves when we thought we were in love with each other. Your father would never have accepted me, so this is best all round. I hope you can see the sense of what I'm saying and won't make any trouble. When all is said and done, you are my sister and we have to get along.

Regards,
Rufus.

P.S. At Mum's request, I'm planning on being at Cuckoo House for Christmas.

Somebody else.

Alice couldn't believe it. Or the offhand way she had been dumped.

Somebody else.

It wasn't possible. How could he have done it? How could he have tossed her aside so easily?

She read the letter over and over. If she didn't know his hand-writing so well, she might have convinced herself the letter was a malicious hoax on Tasha's part. But there was no denying who had written it. No denying, either, that in one sweep of his pen, he had broken her heart.

With each reading of the letter, she began to doubt everything he'd ever said to her since that day when he'd first kissed her in this very room. Had he ever cared for her? To end things so abruptly — to allow himself to 'meet' somebody else — had there ever been anything of a genuine feeling in his entire body for her? What had he been thinking when he'd 'met' this somebody else? Had she bedazzled him to the point where he lost all memory of Alice? Or had Alice never really featured in his conscious mind? She thought of the many letters she had written to him, of the desperately lonely weeks when she didn't hear from him. She thought of how she had given herself to him the night of her birthday. Only now to be discarded so cruelly.

Apart from her father, who was upstairs in his darkroom, Alice was alone in the house — Julia and Tasha had gone shopping — and safe in the knowledge that no one would hear her, she lay on her bed and cried herself out. Never had she cried so much in all her life.

There seemed no end to her tears. Each time she thought she might be nearing the end of them, she would remember a conversation with Rufus, a look from him, a smile, or a gesture, and she would be consumed by a fresh wave of desolation. The memory that hurt her the most was the night of her party, when he'd turned up to surprise her. That had to have been real, surely? He couldn't have gone to so much trouble if he hadn't cared about her, could he?

Or had Dad been right? Had it been nothing but a carefully constructed plan on Rufus's part to get at her father, to torment him in the worst possible way? Alice had to concede that given the circumstances — her having sex with Rufus virtually under his nose — her father had acted with extraordinary and uncharacteristic restraint.

A knock at the door had her lifting her head from the pillow. 'Go away!' she croaked. She'd lost track of the time and supposed Tasha and Julia were back from shopping. To have Tasha gloat over what Rufus had done to her would be more than she could bear.

The door opened. 'Alice?'

At the sound of her father's voice, she said, 'Haven't you learned yet not to burst in on me?'

Frowning, he came over to the bed. He sat on the edge of it. 'What's wrong, love?'

She thrust Rufus's letter at him. 'See for yourself. Just don't be too happy about it.'

She watched him read the letter, his eyes flickering along each line; some of the words were smudged from her tears. When he'd finished, he carefully folded it in half, then in half again. He put it on her bedside table. Next to the framed photograph she had of Rufus. The framed photograph she had kissed goodnight every time she switched off the light. 'I'm sorry,' her father said. 'I'm sorry I allowed him to hurt you. But I warned you. I warned you he was a little shit. Didn't I say that I didn't trust him?'

'It's not him, Dad!' she wailed. 'It's you. You made him do this! He would have loved me if it hadn't been for you!' She didn't really believe what she was saying but she needed to blame someone and her father hadn't exactly helped the situation, had he?

'Oh, Alice, don't let him do this to you. He's not worth it.'

'Don't keep going on about how awful he is. I loved him, don't you understand that? He was everything to me. *Everything*!'

'For two seconds in your life, he was everything. But not any more. Now he's nothing. And don't think I've forgotten the promise I made to you. I said that if he ever hurt you, I'd make him pay.'

★ ★ ★

Things went even further downhill from then on. Alice and Tasha returned to school but a week later Alice was diagnosed as having glandular fever and because her father was away in Norway on an assignment, Julia had to come and fetch her home.

Alice had always considered Julia's presence at Cuckoo House as being little more than that of a shadow. She was a vacuous woman who rarely held an opinion that wasn't a cliché. Alice's mother would have hated her; she would have condemned her in an instant as being a neurotic, wishy-washy bore. Doctor Barbara Barrett had been very keen on backbone and ambition. The only task Julia had carried out with any real purpose was when she had arrived at Cuckoo House with Tasha and Rufus and had organized people to cook, clean and maintain the house for her. Since then her input had been minimal. Certainly this was the first time she had tackled the drive to school on her own.

It was also the first time that Alice had spent more than ten minutes in her company alone. Alice had absolutely no idea what to say to her during the journey and so she feigned sleep.

Which would have worked had Julia not been in the mood to talk. 'Do you feel very poorly?' she asked Alice.

'Yes,' Alice replied, her eyes closed. She couldn't recall ever feeling this ill before. She felt leaden, her head too heavy for her neck to support, her throat scratchy and raw, her every nerve zinging. The doctor had said it was unlikely she would return before school started again in January. Even then, he'd warned her she might not feel up to it.

'You'll probably want to go straight to bed when we get home,' Julia said.

'Yes,' Alice replied again.

'Have you heard from Rufus?'

Alice said nothing.

'Does it still hurt?'

What was this, state the obvious time?

'Love's a fickle thing, Alice.'

Shut up!

'I can understand why you would have fallen for him.'

Shut up. Shut up. SHUT UP!

'But really, when you look at it objectively, what you imagined you felt for Rufus was nothing more than a teenage crush. You'll soon get over it. Just remind yourself that a childhood without a crush wouldn't be a childhood.'

'Could you not talk about it, please?' Alice said hoarsely.

'It's easy to get confused when our emotions are involved,' Julia said as if Alice hadn't spoken. 'We all make mistakes.'

Yes, thought Alice. My father definitely did when he married you.

'We all do things we regret.'

Yeah, tell me about it.

'Things have recently become very difficult between your father and me. He's not an easy man to live with.'

Alice opened her eyes and turned to regard her stepmother. 'I don't think he's at all difficult.'

Julia shot her a sideways look. 'How do you put up with him?'

'There's nothing to put up with. He's my father.'

Again as if Alice hadn't spoken, she said, 'God knows I've tried, but I just don't seem to be able to make him . . . ' Julia's voice faded away and she started to cry.

Oh great, thought Alice. Just what she needed; a feeble, weepy Julia. 'If you're going to cry perhaps it would be safer if we pulled over,' she said wearily.

They pulled over into a layby. Cars and lorries thundered by, shaking the Range Rover Dad had bought Julia last year. 'I thought you'd be able to help me,' Julia sniffled, her pale face spotted with ugly red blotches. 'Bruce never loses his temper with you.'

'That's because I don't annoy him.'

'You think I do?'

'Yes.'

Julia cried even harder. 'I don't think I can take much more.'

'Then go. Just leave him.'

'It's not as easy as that.'

No, thought, Alice, it isn't, is it? 'My father is nothing more than financial security to you, isn't he?' she said coldly.

Julia blew her nose and glanced nervously at Alice. 'Why do you say that?'

Alice looked her stepmother dead in the eye. 'I know,' she said. 'I *know* why you married him. So does my father.'

Julia's lips trembled. 'I don't think we should continue with this conversation.'

'Why not? It's the first time we've ever had anything that remotely resembles an honest conversation. And if you want the truth, you're not a patch on my mother and that's probably what drives my father mad. He despises you. He despises the fact that you're so weak and can't stand up to him.'

More tears spilled down Julia's face. 'You hate me, don't you? You hate me nearly as much as your father hates me.'

'I don't, actually. You're nothing to me. Just as Rufus is nothing to me. Just as Tasha means nothing to me. Do you know what she's put me through at school? She's telling everyone I'm a slut for loving your precious son. I may be a fool, but I'm not what she says I am.'

Julia sniffed loudly and rummaged for a tissue in her bag. 'Tasha's very attached to Rufus. She . . . ever since her father died, she's worshipped the ground he walks on.'

'And you think that's healthy?'

'I don't really see anything wrong in it. But I'll tell you what is wrong, and that's how Bruce treats me. Have you ever wondered about the way your mother died?'

Alice stiffened. 'It was an accident.'

'Not suicide, then? You don't think she finally snapped, that she woke up one morning and realized she couldn't go on living with a mad man?'

22

Alice wasn't proud of herself. But then these days she hardly knew herself. Nor did she seem able to control her anger.

She had said that Julia meant nothing to her, but this turned out not to be true. Alice was consumed with loathing towards the woman, spewing toxic hatred at her for the slightest of reasons. Often for no reason at all. If she couldn't exact revenge on Rufus, she would settle for making his mother's life even more wretched than it already was. Every time she laid eyes on Julia or heard her thin, pleading voice, the coil of revulsion inside Alice tightened. Whenever Julia made yet another attempt to placate or reach out to her, or excused Alice's behaviour on the grounds that she wasn't well, Alice upped her game. When her throat allowed it, she screamed foul-mouthed abuse at her stepmother. One day she hurled a book at her. Who would have thought she would prove to be so thoroughly her mother and father's daughter?

After weeks of taking whatever insults and spite Alice threw at her, Julia finally showed a hint of spirit and came close to fighting back.

It was three days before Christmas — Tasha hadn't yet come home from school; she had gone to stay with Freya — and Alice was in the kitchen rolling out pastry for mince pies whilst her father sat at the table reading aloud to her from P.G. Wodehouse's *The Code of the Woosters*. Story time, late afternoon when the light had gone from the day, the two of them companionably alone in the kitchen, had become a regular event and was the highlight of Alice's day. It was a comforting reminder of when she'd been little and her father had read to her at bedtime.

'That was Tasha on the phone,' Julia said, breezing into the kitchen and instantly destroying the cosy, tranquil atmosphere. 'She and Rufus will be arriving tomorrow afternoon.' She looked directly at Alice, an unexpectedly brave, challenging look of score-settling in her eye. 'Rufus is bringing his girlfriend with him. I trust you don't have a problem with that?'

Alice tightened her hold on the rolling pin.

'You don't think it would have been polite to have checked first?' her father asked without looking up.

'Polite, in the sense of tiptoeing around Alice's feelings? Is that what you mean?'

Bruce carefully marked his page, closed the book and faced Julia. 'You know damned well that's exactly what I mean.'

Julia laughed bitterly. 'Whoever considers my feelings? Whoever wonders how I feel about something?'

'Oh, do put a sock in it, Julia! Why should anyone else contribute to the stockpile of your self-absorption when you do such a fine job of it yourself?'

What little fight Julia had mustered was gone. 'Is that what this Christmas is going to be like?'

she asked, her voice tight and over-wrought. 'Am I to be nothing but the butt of your cruelly barbed comments?'

'We wouldn't be having this tedious discussion if you hadn't been so high-handed and encouraged your son to flaunt his new girlfriend under Alice's nose. But thanks to you, I think it's safe to say that we're now set for a real old Rice Krispie Christmas. And by that, I mean there'll be plenty of snap, crackle and pop. Really, Julia, you have only yourself to blame.' He turned his back on her dismissively and returned his attention to P.G. Wodehouse. He flicked through the pages. 'Now then, Alice, where were we?'

'Do not treat me this way,' Julia said. Her words were spoken slowly and a little breathlessly.

He said nothing.

Alice resumed rolling out the pastry.

'I said do not treat me this way.'

''*I am a shy man, Bertie.*'' Bruce read aloud, ''*Diffidence is the price I pay for having a hyper-sensitive nature.*''

A stifled squawking sound came from Julia's direction and then the door crashed shut. For several moments, both Alice and her father carried on as if nothing had happened. When the tense atmosphere in the kitchen had stopped reverberating, he raised his head from the book.

'You OK?' he asked.

Alice blinked. 'I can't believe Rufus could be so crass. Couldn't he have waited?'

'I could put my foot down and say he can't bring her with him, but that would be exactly

215

what he'd want me to do. That way he gets to play the hard-done-by stepson. By letting him bring his girlfriend with him, you and I are going to prove just how meaningless he is to you now.'

Alice put a finger to her lip. Her father was right. But he was also wrong. Horribly wrong. This was the first time since she had blamed him for Rufus finishing with her that they had openly discussed him again. She knew though that he had had plenty to say on the subject with Julia. She had heard him shouting at her, describing Rufus's behaviour as manipulative and cold-hearted, devious and callous. Julia's response had been to say that Alice had known perfectly well what she was getting into, that in actual fact, it had been Alice who had cleverly manipulated Rufus into a relationship with her.

With her father so certain that Rufus now meant nothing to her, how could she tell him that she had secretly been hoping that when he returned to Cuckoo House for Christmas and spent some time alone with her, Rufus would see what a terrible mistake he had made? How could that happen now, now that he was bringing his new girlfriend home with him?

'Carry on reading, Dad,' she said as she pressed a crinkled-edged metal cutter into the pastry.

*   *   *

The following afternoon, in a state of high agitation, Julia set off to the station.

From the moment Isabel Canning stepped

216

over the threshold of Cuckoo House, she swept into their lives like a breath of fresh air. In Alice's mind this unknown quantity had been cast in the role of Public Enemy Number One. Meeting her face to face made Alice realize that her cause to win back Rufus was lost. There wasn't a chance in hell of Alice competing with this incredible creature. Blonde, blue-eyed, and beautiful beyond belief, she looked older than Alice had expected. She was charmingly jolly and she greeted Alice and her father like long-lost friends. Either Rufus hadn't explained the situation to her, or she was a better actress than Alice could ever hope to be.

Within an hour of being in Isabel's company, Alice could quite understand how Rufus had fallen under her spell. She had a knack for showing great interest — whether it was genuine or fake — in her surroundings or whatever somebody was telling her. She enthusiastically admired the criminally expensive curtains and sofa Julia had recently had made for the sitting room, she raved ecstatically over the Christmas tree Alice had decorated, declaring it the most perfect she had ever seen, and she was particularly interested in Bruce's work, professing to dabble in photography herself — a remark that would normally elicit a snort of derision from him. She somehow managed to extract a promise from him to show her his darkroom before she left.

So much for Public Enemy Number One.

All the while, Rufus looked on with pride and adoration shining in his eyes. Never once did he look directly at Alice. Why would he when he had this wondrous and enchanting goddess to gaze upon? He was completely captivated.

However, Tasha was not so captivated. Maybe that was because she knew Isabel was a genuine threat. This was no teenage crush; this was a fully formed woman who had stolen her brother's heart. It explained to Alice why Tasha appeared to have returned to Cuckoo House with a shyly extended hand of friendship towards Alice: she needed an ally. Who better than the girl whose heart had been broken by her brother? That was why she had been all smiles since arriving home. That was why she had asked how Alice was feeling. That was why she had said what an awful time she'd had whilst staying with Freya and how brilliant it was to be back and how much she had missed Alice. By anyone's standards, it was an audacious U-turn. Did she really think Alice was so desperate for their friendship to be restored that she would conveniently forget all that had passed between them?

* * *

The running of Cuckoo House was not as efficient as it had once been. A sullen, greasy-haired woman with a nose stud and a habitual sniff came in once a week to clean half-heartedly and after suffering a heart attack, Mrs Randall had abandoned their kitchen. Seeing as her father couldn't really be trusted to cook without setting fire to anything and rarely could Julia handle anything more complex than an omelette without a panic attack, Alice had

218

assumed responsibility for cooking over the Christmas holiday. Whilst stuck at home, and since she had been well enough, she had been teaching herself to cook to relieve the boredom. Stupidly she had planned to astound Rufus with her newly acquired culinary skills. Tonight she was going to cook roast duck with an orange and cranberry sauce.

But Isabel wouldn't hear of it. 'We can't have you slaving away in the kitchen on your own,' she insisted, 'not when you've been so ill. Tasha and I will help you.'

'What about me?' Rufus asked, 'I could help as well.' He looked and sounded as if he didn't appreciate being left out. He had a hand placed around Isabel's waist; a hand Alice was trying hard not to look at.

Laughing, Isabel shook him off. 'Away with you! Go and spend some time with your mother. It's ages since you last saw her.'

When he pouted like a small child denied his favourite toy, she laughed again. 'Go on, *shoo!* This is girl time. I'm going to find out from your lovely sisters everything about you that you've tried to hide from me, and I don't want you butting in.'

Rufus exchanged his first direct glance with Alice and visibly paled. Oh, my God, she thought, Isabel didn't know anything, did she?

★ ★ ★

Public Enemy Number One. Alice had to keep reminding herself. But it was useless. How could

219

she hate Isabel? How could she hate anyone who was such fun and who was showering such warmth, kindness and encouragement on her? They were standing together at the sink, peeling potatoes, and Isabel was promising that when the time came, she would put in a good word for Alice and Tasha with an old family friend who was a theatrical agent in London.

'I don't believe in nepotism,' Tasha said sulkily. She was sitting on the worktop, banging her heels against the cupboard below. She was twisting a length of silver tinsel in her hands and the glowering expression on her face suggested that any minute she might take Isabel from behind and garrotte her with the tinsel. 'I want to know I made it to the top through my own merit,' she added, 'otherwise why bother?'

Isabel had to be aware of Tasha's brooding hostility towards her but nothing in her conduct betrayed how she felt about it. Her manners were impeccable. 'Gosh, Tasha, you're so right,' she said cheerfully. 'I applaud your conviction. I'm afraid I don't have half your talent, so am quite shameless in asking for a teensy leg up when necessary.'

'What kind of work do you do?' asked Alice, curious. She couldn't imagine Isabel doing any kind of boring nine-to-five job or anything remotely practical. She couldn't peel potatoes properly, that much was obvious. Alice had surreptitiously redone the ones she'd hacked at.

'What do I do? Oh Alice, I wish I knew sometimes. Well, officially I'm an events organizer, you know, organizing parties, conferences, charity balls, that sort of thing. Hopelessly superficial.'

'And unofficially?'

Isabel laughed. 'Unofficially I'm a free spirit looking for a sense of purpose to my life. I dabble here and there. One minute I want to be an artist, the next I want to be a photographer. That's why I'm so fascinated by your father. I'm so in awe of him. I've come across his work time and time again. He really does take amazing pictures. But then you know that, don't you? You must have the most incredible photo albums of you growing up. I'd love to see them.'

Tasha's heels had taken up a faster and more vigorous beat against the cupboard door. 'That's the funny thing about Alice's father,' she said, 'I can't recall him taking a single photograph of us as a family.'

Alice smiled awkwardly. 'It's true. Dad's always preferred taking pictures of wildlife or landscapes.'

'I don't blame him,' Isabel said. 'People can be enormously tiresome the moment you point a camera at them. Not that you'd be tiresome,' she added quickly before Alice had had time to register any kind of a slight.

'Exactly how old are you, Isabel?' Tasha said. 'You seem so much older than Rufus.'

'Oh, I'm positively ancient.' She laughed. 'Call the police, I've cradle-snatched your brother!'

'I reckon you're thirty,' Tasha persisted.

'Thirty,' Isabel repeated with a raise of her elegant eyebrows. 'Well, I've always been told I look older than I am, but you're out by five years.'

'You're twenty-five?' Alice intervened, keen for some strange reason to repair the damage Tasha was doing. 'You look much younger than that.'

'That still makes you quite a few years older than Rufus, doesn't it?' Tasha continued relentlessly. 'What's it like going out with a toy boy?'

'It can be a terrible pain sometimes,' Isabel said with a weary sigh. 'I can't tell you how often I've forgotten to blow his nose for him or make sure he's home in time for bed.'

Alice smirked, but knowing she'd been made fun of, Tasha looked furious. She jumped down from the workshop. 'I'm bored,' she said. 'I'm going to go and talk to Rufus.'

When they were alone, Isabel said, 'Would I be right in thinking Tasha doesn't like me very much?'

'She's very protective of her brother.'

'What about you, Alice? Are you very protective of Rufus?'

'Are you asking me if I like you?'

Isabel smiled. 'That's exactly what I'm asking you.'

To her amazement, Alice replied, 'I didn't think I would at first, but yes I do.'

'Thank you. Now tell me everything you think I should know about Rufus. No holding anything back. I want to know all his nasty habits. Apart from the fact he hates it when he can't get his own way.'

★ ★ ★

During dinner, Rufus was displaying this very same trait. Tasha had laid the table in the dining room and had decided where they would all sit — she must have devised the seating plan with malicious pleasure. She had put her mother and Bruce at each end of the table with Rufus between his mother and Alice and Isabel between Bruce and herself. Rufus was far from happy with the arrangement. Especially as Isabel was asking Bruce so many questions about his work and was hanging on to his every word. Alice hadn't seen her father so animated in a long while. He was happily playing the part of generous and affable host, pouring wine, cracking jokes and heaping endless praise on the cooks who had produced the meal. He was enjoying himself, Alice realized.

Unlike Rufus, who, stuck with his lacklustre mother and Alice for conversation, was clearly having a miserable time. Alice had tried to engage him in conversation, but no matter what she said — and given the circumstances, she thought she was being remarkably big-hearted — he wasn't interested. His attention was focused entirely on Isabel. Every now and then she would slide a glance in his direction and beam a dazzling smile at him.

They had moved onto dessert when Rufus clinked his spoon against his glass. 'I have an announcement,' he said. They all turned and looked at him. 'I was going to wait until Christmas Day, but I've never been known for my patience, so here goes. Isabel and I are going to be married.'

There was a momentary silence. Not one of them had seen that coming. Not even Isabel, from the startled expression on her face.

'Well, isn't anyone going to congratulate us?' Rufus demanded.

'Of course, darling,' Julia said quickly. 'We're all absolutely delighted for you; it's just that it's ... it's so sudden. You've taken us completely by surprise.'

At the other end of the table, Bruce laughed raucously. He reached out to Isabel and placed a hand on her forearm. 'Isabel, do you have any idea what you're letting yourself in for by marrying Rufus? If I were you, I'd start running. Oh, take that look off your face, Rufus, I'm only joking. You can take a joke, can't you?'

23

At breakfast the next morning, Tasha said, 'I know a good joke. Would you like to hear it, Isabel? It's about Alice and Rufus.'

Alice froze.

As did Rufus. 'Shut up, Tasha,' he said.

'That's no way to speak to me, Rufus. Not on Christmas Eve. It is supposed to be the season of good will, after all. Honestly, Isabel, you'll love my joke. Take no notice of Rufus. Actually, Alice knows the joke better than me; she should tell it to you really. Alice?'

'I think I'll pass on breakfast,' Alice murmured. She pushed back her chair and stood up. She was halfway to the door when her father came in. 'Dad,' she said, 'why don't you show Isabel your darkroom?' She fixed him with a wildly frantic look, praying that he'd catch on, that he was entering a potential war zone and needed to get out fast, preferably taking Isabel with him to avoid an almighty showdown.

'You must be telepathic, Alice,' he said brightly, 'I was just going to ask Isabel if she'd like to take a look.'

For once Rufus was in agreement and practically hustled Isabel out of her seat. The perfect guest, Isabel merely frowned prettily and went along with what was being suggested. When she was safely out of ear shot, Rufus said, 'Alice, don't go. We need to talk.' He closed the door,

225

blocking her escape.

'Oh, well if you two are going to have a cosy tête-à-tête,' Tasha said offhandedly, 'I'll leave you to it.'

Her brother turned on her. 'The fuck you will! Now sit down and tell me what the hell you thought you were playing at?'

Tasha's mouth dropped. She couldn't have looked more shocked if Rufus had physically struck her. She quickly rallied, though. 'I just think your future wife should be aware that you screwed her future sister-in-law then dumped her. Don't you?'

'Why, Tasha?' Rufus replied. 'Why would you think that was a good idea?' He turned to Alice. 'Is this your doing? Have you put her up to this as an act of revenge?'

'No! The last thing I want is for anyone else knowing how you humiliated me.'

His eyes narrowed. 'I didn't humiliate you, Alice. You and I had a bit of a thing for a while and then I came to my senses and finished it with you. End of story.'

'If that's all it amounted to, why don't you tell Isabel that?'

'Oh, don't be obtuse! From the outside looking in, it looks a darn sight worse than it really is, you being my stepsister.'

Alice tried not to flinch at his casual dismissal for her love for him. 'It doesn't look so good from the inside looking out, if you want my opinion.'

Rufus started furiously pacing the length of the kitchen. 'Is this what you're going to do for the rest of my life? Hold me accountable for a moment of madness?'

'I'm not doing anything!' Alice had to stop herself from screaming the words in his face. 'If I could take a pill to make me forget what we did, then I'd take it right now. I'd take a whole bloody bottle of pills if it meant I could wipe you completely from my memory! And in case you've forgotten, it was Tasha who wanted to reveal our dirty little secret, not me.'

He swung his gaze round to his sister. She stared back at him with a determined and defiant expression. 'I just think you should be honest with the woman you're going to marry, Rufus,' she said. 'How would you feel if Isabel concealed something like this from you?'

He went over to her. 'Tasha,' he said, his tone suddenly soft. He rested his hands on her shoulders. 'I'll give you anything you want, I'll *do* anything you want, so long as you never breathe a word of this to Isabel. I don't want to lose her. She means the world to me and I don't want anything to spoil my happiness. Do you understand that?'

'But how can you be sure that you love her, or that she loves you? You've known her for no more than a few months. Why do you — ' Tasha's voice cracked. 'Why do you always have to go and change things?'

He took her in his arms. 'Oh, Tash, it doesn't matter how long you've known someone when it's the real deal.'

She tilted her head back to look up at him. 'But wasn't that how you felt about Alice?'

Wishing she was invisible, Alice moved quietly towards the door to escape. She didn't want to hear Rufus's reply. Hadn't she been put through enough already? But she was too slow.

'What I feel for Isabel couldn't be more different from what I felt for Alice,' he said. He glanced over to Alice. 'And that's the truth.'

'Fine,' she said. She opened the door and fled. Her eyes brimming with tears, she ran upstairs, passed Julia on the landing and nearly knocked her flying. She locked herself in her room and lay on the bed, exhausted. Dr Whittaker had warned her that she shouldn't overdo it, that it took a long time to fully recover from glandular fever. How about a broken heart? How long did that take?

She fell into a deep, dreamless sleep and two hours later she awoke to an eye-opening revelation. It was no longer her heart that needed mending; it was her pride. She sat up and explored this thought further. She didn't love Rufus any more. She didn't know when it had happened, but her feelings for him had changed. They must have changed because how else would she have been able to cope with the last twenty-four hours if she'd still been in love with him? No, what was hurting now was her pride. It was the shame of knowing she had allowed herself to be treated so shabbily that hurt. Well, it was time to hold her head up high again. Because if she didn't, the alternative was to turn into an emotional wreck like Julia. She would rather die than do that.

Buoyed up with a new inner strength, she slid

off the bed and went over to the turret. Staring out of the window, she took in the grey half-light of the day. The end of the garden and the surrounding moorland was hidden by thick freezing fog. There was no sign of the sun. It was by far the gloomiest Christmas Eve Alice had known. Snow was predicted for tomorrow. A white Christmas. Would that cheer them all up?

She thought of Rufus's shock announcement last night at dinner. From the expression of surprise on Isabel's face, Alice didn't think they had agreed to break the news that evening. Maybe Isabel had wanted to tell her parents first.

As a result of the announcement, they had learned a lot more about Isabel. Like Alice, she was an only child and her mother lived in America with her third husband — she had been widowed twice before. Isabel had grown up in Norfolk in a house that sounded straight out of a Bertie Wooster story with its house parties and grouse shoots. Two years ago Isabel's mother had met a New York financier, eighteen years older than her, and had moved to live in a place called the Hamptons. Alice had never heard of it but Rufus clearly had because he said he was really looking forward to going there with Isabel. Isabel described her mother's new home as being excessively overstated, but infinitely more civilized than the freezing cold mausoleum in Norfolk where she had grown up.

Alice's breath had formed a patch of condensation on the window. She wiped the pane of glass and below her in the garden she saw two figures emerge from the fog: her father and Isabel. In his hands was a camera and he was pointing it at Isabel. Dressed in a thick scarf wound loosely around her neck and what Alice recognized as her father's tattered duffel coat, Isabel was striking a series of comical poses. Bruce moved slowly about her, capturing her every pose, her every angle. Walking backwards, he beckoned her towards him, all the while the camera placed firmly to his eye. Recalling how only last night Alice had said that her father rarely took photographs of people, preferring penguins and snow-capped mountains to human beings any day, she felt a shadow of unease settle on her. She shivered and took a step back from the window. But not before a kaleidoscope of faded memories flashed before her.

She pressed a finger to her top lip and tapped it. He wouldn't. Oh, dear God, he absolutely wouldn't.

Would he?

★ ★ ★

Seldom did Alice's father encourage guests to visit Cuckoo House, but for the last three years, much to Julia's horror, as well as Tasha and Rufus's disgust, he had invited George to join them for Christmas lunch. She always turned up late, tricked out in an actual dress and with a bottle of her famously noxious home brew. Today was no exception. She was introduced to Isabel and Alice could see Rufus cringing that his precious wife-to-be was being forced to rub shoulders with such a fright. But Isabel took

George in her elegant stride and was as charmingly interested in her as she had been in the rest of them. 'You keep chickens? How wonderful! That's what I intend to do one day. How many do you have? And what about foxes? Do you have much of a problem with them?'

'I shoot the blighters. I hope you're not one of those lily-livered types who objects to such things.'

'Good Lord, no! My stepfather taught me to shoot when I was ten years old.'

'I think shooting's barbaric,' remarked Tasha.

'You wouldn't think that if you'd found your henhouse had been massacred by some mangy, flea-ridden fox. Bruce, haven't you taught this girl anything about living in the country?'

Bruce held up his hands. 'Not my bailiwick, George. Any complaints should be directed to her mother.'

* * *

It was after lunch, during present-giving time, when everyone was groaning from having eaten too much and flinging wrapping paper in all directions, that they took their places for the opening scene of the final act of the drama they were caught up in. Alice had always wondered just how much of what followed could have been avoided had it not been for those bloody cherry liqueurs.

With his customary air of indifference, Alice's father handed Julia a present. He didn't wish her a Happy Christmas, nor did she utter a word of thanks. Alice watched her picking uninterestedly at the sticky tape. When Julia finally had the paper off, she looked over to where Bruce was sitting next to Alice. 'Why?' she asked. 'Why have you given me a box of cherry liqueurs when you know I hate them?'

'Do you?' he said with exaggerated astonishment. 'Since when?'

'Since forever. Since before the very first time you gave me a box and all the times since.' Her voice had spiralled to an embarrassing high-pitched whine.

Bruce shrugged his shoulders. 'Oh, well, I'll see if I can do better next year. But why don't you try one? Who knows, you might find you like them. People do change.'

'Some people will never change and that's the greatest disappointment of my life!' She flung the box across the room at him. It caught him on the chest then dropped to the floor at his feet. She ran from the room.

'Bruce Barrett, you are such a bastard,' Rufus said. He rose slowly from the sofa where he was sitting with Isabel. 'Chocolates. Is that all you think my mother's worth? A box of chocolates you know perfectly well she doesn't like?' He moved towards the offending box. He lifted a foot and they all knew what he was going to do next.

'I wouldn't do that if I were you,' Bruce said quietly.

Rufus brought his foot down with a vicious stamp and crushed the box. He then turned to Isabel. 'I want you to know here and now, Isabel, you will not be subjected to this vile man's company ever again. This will be the last time we come here.'

'Oh, don't talk such rubbish, young man.'

It was George who had spoken. Rufus glared at her with contempt. 'No one asked you for your opinion, you filthy, mad old hag.'

'Rufus!' This was from Isabel. She looked genuinely horrified. 'You can't speak to a guest like that.'

'She isn't a guest,' he responded hotly. 'She's a hanger-on. The local crazy woman.'

George smiled happily at the description but Alice was incensed. 'Rufus,' she said, 'apologize to George immediately.'

Rufus laughed. 'You have to be out of your mind. Hell will freeze over before I apologize to her.'

'Then I suggest you leave.'

'Isabel and I will leave when we're good and ready.'

Alice got to her feet. She squared up to Rufus. 'Isabel is perfectly welcome to stay as long as she wants, but you,' she pointed a finger at him 'are not.'

He laughed. He actually laughed. 'Oh, do us all a favour and shut up, Alice.'

'Don't tell me what to do in my own house.'

Tasha joined in. 'It isn't your house, Alice, so stop telling Rufus what to do.'

Alice managed a wan smile. 'Actually, Tasha, this house does belong to me, so I'm perfectly entitled to say who is welcome and who is not. And right now, your brother isn't.'

Both Tasha and Rufus stared at her.

'Yes, you did hear me correctly. Cuckoo House became mine when I turned eighteen. So if I were you, I'd start behaving yourselves.' She turned to Isabel. 'I'm sorry you've had to witness this ugly scene, but as my father warned you, you really ought to know what kind of a family you're marrying into. Oh, and by the way, Rufus and I slept together on my eighteenth birthday. Ask him about it. He'll tell you it was all very casual and meaningless. Well, it was on his part. I made the same mistake as you; I fell in love with him. Hard to fathom how or why now.'

Isabel's eyes grew wide and she stared at Rufus.

'You bitch!' He shouted at Alice. 'You total sodding bitch!'

'I'm warning you, Rufus, speak to my daughter like that again and you'll regret it.'

As if heeding the warning from Alice's father, Rufus took a moment to compose himself. 'Tasha, Isabel,' he said, 'come on, let's leave them to it.'

Tasha was immediately at her brother's side, but as Rufus grabbed her hand and pulled her from the sofa, Isabel appeared less sure. At the door, she hesitated. Alice smiled at her, hoping to convey a look of understanding, that she knew Isabel was caught between a rock and a hard place.

'Are you coming, Isabel?' Rufus was glowering furiously.

'Yes,' she said.

'Bravo, Alice!' her father said when they were alone.

234

Alice sighed. 'Thanks, Dad. Sorry I had to pull rank on you. You know, telling them about the house.'

'Think nothing of it. It was time it was said.'

Alice picked up the crushed box of chocolates.

'How about a drink?' Bruce offered. 'George, I expect you'd like something after all that, wouldn't you? I know I do.'

'Dad? What's this?' In Alice's hands, the flattened lid had slipped off the box and instead of smashed chocolates inside, there was a necklace; a delicate gold chain with a solitaire diamond. She held it up and the diamond sparkled in the firelight. 'Oh, Dad, why didn't you tell Julia what you'd really given her?'

'What does it matter? What does any of it matter?' He went over to the tray of drinks on the table behind the sofa. 'George, what do you fancy?'

'Give me something stiff with plenty of kick.'

★ ★ ★

It was three thirty in the morning and Alice couldn't sleep. Some Christmas it had turned out to be.

Rufus hadn't left immediately as he'd threatened. The weather forecasters had got it right about the snow. It had started falling shortly after George's departure; slowly at first then quickly, gathering momentum until it was a full-blown blizzard. Only a fool would have set off in such treacherous conditions. Rufus was many things, but he wasn't a fool.

It was still snowing; Alice could see and hear it pattering softly against the window. It was years since they'd been snowed in, but if it kept up like this, in all likelihood no one would be going anywhere for the next twenty-four hours.

Rufus had apologized in a desultory fashion for losing his temper and Alice suspected that Isabel had had something to do with that. Alice had wanted her father to give Julia the necklace he had bought her, if only to make peace over Christmas, but he'd shaken his head and said enough was enough. Alice wasn't entirely sure what he had meant, but she hadn't pressed him. Having locked herself in her sanctuary after the cherry liqueurs fiasco, Julia had childishly refused to come out. If it had fitted, Alice would have been tempted to slide the necklace under the door with a note telling her to stop acting like a sulky teenager.

Resigned to a sleepless few hours ahead of her, Alice decided to go downstairs to make herself a drink. Rather than risk disturbing anyone, she didn't switch on her bedside lamp but carefully made her way to the door, then out onto the landing. She had reached the bottom step when she heard noises coming from the direction of the sitting room. The door was open a crack, letting a faint glowing light from inside spill out in the darkness of the hallway.

Alice went to investigate. Maybe it was her father and like her he'd been unable to sleep. She suddenly thought how nice it would be to have his company, to mull over the day's events together.

At the door, she hesitated before peering through the tiny gap. What if it wasn't her father? What if it was Rufus and Isabel?

The first thing she saw was the Christmas tree with the lights switched on. Then she saw the log fire burning in the grate and the two naked bodies directly in front of it. There was no mistaking what they were doing. Or that it was Isabel with her head of silvery-blonde hair cascading around her shoulders, her skin radiant in the firelight, who was lying on her back with Alice's father moving languidly on top of her. They were gazing deeply into each other's eyes, wholly immersed in each other, their expressions intense.

Neither of them was aware of Alice or that she had crept away.

24

Most people would agree that Boxing Day could not be anything other than a forgettable anticlimax to the main event. But Boxing Day at Cuckoo House that year proved to be the exception to the rule and became a day no one would ever forget.

When Alice had finally managed to sleep she had fallen into a profoundly deep, dead-to-the-world kind of sleep. As she surfaced, heavy-headed and befuddled, she recalled a disturbing dream she'd had of her father and Isabel. But then her head cleared. It hadn't been a dream. It had been real. All too real. It had really happened.

She threw on the first clothes to hand and hurried downstairs. If her father and Isabel had fallen asleep in the sitting room, there would be all hell to pay if anyone else discovered them. Or was that what her father had planned all along: to be discovered? Was this his way of paying Rufus back? To destroy his relationship with Isabel? Oh, God, was her father really capable of such a thing? Had he planned this from the moment Isabel had set foot in the house and he'd understood the extent of Rufus's feelings for her?

The sitting room was empty. The Christmas tree lights were still switched on but the fire had burned out. There was no sign that anything untoward had taken place here. Even so, Alice checked for any damning evidence; stray items of underwear would be sure to set alarm bells ringing.

Alice didn't know what to do next, other than go upstairs and wake her father and demand to know what the hell he had thought he'd been doing. But how would she react if he was to say he had done nothing but fulfil his promise to her?

She took refuge in the kitchen and while she busied herself with making a pot of tea, she stared out of the window. Beneath an unwaveringly crystalline sky and a brightly shining sun, the snow was already melting, dripping off tree branches and exposing patches of grass. A blackbird was pecking intently in a small circle of exposed earth. It eventually found what it was looking for: a worm.

The sound of raised voices from upstairs and running feet broke the still quiet. What now? Had Rufus discovered what his fiancée had done? Alice went to find out.

Julia was on the landing. She looked dreadful, as though she had aged a hundred years overnight. Her face was deathly pale, her eyes were bloodshot and tears were streaming down her face. Next to her was Rufus and wearing only a pair of boxer shorts, he was reading something. A letter? 'No!' he cried. '*No!*' He dropped the piece of paper to the floor, turned on his heel and shot off towards his room.

'What is it?' Alice forced herself to ask. 'What's happened?'

Julia's answer was to lean against the wall behind her and slowly slide down it until she was crouched on the floor. She drew her knees up to her chest and wrapped her arms around them. She started to cry. 'How could he?' she wailed, more to herself than Alice. 'How could he do this?' Her hand flew to her mouth, stifling a scream.

Her heart racing, Alice picked up the discarded piece of paper. Her father's handwriting was instantly distinguishable. She had read no more than a few words when Rufus reappeared. He was wearing a pair of jeans now and a T-shirt. 'Her clothes and case have gone,' he said. His voice was unlike Alice had ever heard it before. It had lost all of its potent clarity.

Dreading the answer, Alice said, 'Do you know where my father is?' She was hoping against all hope that her worst fear wasn't about to be realized.

Julia suddenly let out a manic scream. 'He's gone as well!' she screeched. 'Read the letter for yourself.'

'But he can't have. Not without saying goodbye.'

'It seems your father's capable of anything,' Rufus seethed. 'Go on, read the letter. It's all there.'

So it was. Bruce Barrett and Isabel Canning had run off together. There were no words of apology. No remorse. No regret. Just a few lines about living life to the full and seizing the day. There was no mention of when he might be back. With or without Isabel.

'What's all the noise about?' It was Tasha, emerging from her bedroom like the bleary-eyed dormouse at the Mad Hatter's Tea Party. 'Oh God, Mum, you're not still crying over those bloody cherry liqueurs, are you?'

Alice left Rufus and Julia to explain. She ran downstairs to the kitchen, unlocked the back door, and raced round the side of the house to the garage. Her father's Jaguar was still there but Julia's Range Rover was gone. There was a single set of tyre tacks in the snow that led inexorably away from the house. 'Oh, Dad,' she murmured. 'What have you done?'

* * *

She was held personally responsible, as if it had been her job to control her father. The sad truth was, she *was* responsible. Her father had done this entirely for her benefit. He had exacted his revenge on Rufus in the cruellest way imaginable. Having made their feelings clear, no one wanted to talk to Alice now. Julia had shut herself in her sanctuary and downstairs in the sitting room, after Alice had made a fire, Tasha and Rufus had holed themselves up in there, making it obvious she wasn't welcome to join them. Not really knowing why she was doing it, other than needing to be busy, Alice put a tray of coffee, mince pies and sandwiches together for Rufus and Tasha. She didn't bother knocking, just went straight in.

Standing by the fireplace, his knuckles white with the force of his grip on the poker, Rufus

241

was jabbing a log into place. 'I thought she loved me,' he was saying. 'I really did. But she couldn't have felt anything for me, not when she could go off with a man old enough to be her father.' He shook his head, gave the log another vicious jab.

Now you know what it feels like, Alice thought nastily.

'I suppose you're quietly cheering to yourself,' Tasha said as Alice put the tray down on the table in front of her. 'And you can take that away,' she added, pointing at the tray. 'We don't want anything from you. If we want anything to eat, I'll make it myself.'

'Tasha, don't be such an idiot.' With great effort, Alice kept her voice level.

'Don't call me an idiot. Not when your father has broken my brother's heart, not to mention what he's done to our mother. She's up there in her room, inconsolable. I doubt she'll ever get over the shame of what that disgusting man has done.'

'I'm sorry,' was all Alice could say. Although part of her wasn't.

'I bet you were in on it, weren't you?' Tasha continued. 'Your father probably told you what he was going to do. I wouldn't put it past you to have helped the pair of them slip away in the night.'

Rufus whipped round from the fire. 'Did you, Alice? Did you help them?'

'No! I'm as shocked as you are.' Well, that wasn't totally true, was it? She'd had a warning. She'd seen them in the garden. And then last night. Could she have stopped them? If she had spoken to her father, would he have listened?

Something in Rufus's face made her think he didn't believe her. 'Our situation here is now untenable,' he said. 'Just as soon as our mother is feeling better, we'll leave. You can stay here all on your own, Alice. I certainly don't intend to be around when your father returns. I wouldn't give him the satisfaction of ever setting eyes on me again.' How pompous he sounded. 'Now if you'd kindly leave us alone, Tasha and I have things to discuss.'

Untenable, repeated Alice silently as she left them to it. What did Rufus think this was, a Victorian melodrama?

For days, weeks and months afterwards, Alice looked back on that day and wondered if Rufus ever blamed himself for what happened next. Certainly she blamed herself often enough. Had Rufus taken a different line, if he had been more of a support to his mother or forced her to pull herself together, would the worst have been avoided? But he did neither of these things. Instead he indulged her weeping and wailing and added to her hysteria by insisting they had to leave, saying Alice couldn't wait to be rid of them. The tension and ill-feeling escalated until, in the end, Alice did shout at him and his mother that she would be glad to see the back of them.

★   ★   ★

An excruciating twenty-four hours later, during which time there was no word from her father, Alice went out to the garage to sit in his car. She thought she might find some kind of solace there. Despite what he'd done, and despite the appalling mess he'd left her to cope with, she wanted to feel his presence. Where better than his beloved old Jag?

When she opened the garage, she found that his car had been trashed. The tyres had been slashed and the paintwork had been scratched; there were places where it had been gouged quite deeply. When she approached the driver's seat, she saw Julia slumped over the steering wheel. At first Alice thought her stepmother was asleep, sleeping off her petty act of revenge.

But Julia wasn't asleep. When Alice tried to shake her awake, her body was stone cold. On the passenger seat beside her was an empty bottle of sloe gin liqueur, along with a selection of empty pill bottles.

25

The silence was abrupt and long.

Clayton waited patiently for Alice to continue, but she didn't. He wasn't very good with silences — he always felt uncomfortable around them, like he was with police officers and tax inspectors — but in this instance he was determined to keep his mouth shut. There would be no putting his great, big clumsy foot in it.

After taking a lengthy, steadying breath, Alice spoke again. 'I've never forgotten that moment,' she said, 'when it hit me that Julia was dead, that she had taken her own life. She had hinted that she might do as much, that day in the car when she came to fetch me home from school. She had said she didn't know how much more she could take. She had even questioned whether my mother had killed herself for the same reason. But I didn't think she meant it. I simply never took anything she did or said seriously. I should have done more for her.'

'You don't really think you were responsible for her death, do you?' Clayton said.

Alice shrugged and turned to look at the glowing embers in the grate. 'I was very cruel to her at times. My father and I were so dismissive of her.'

'She could have left any time she wanted. She chose to stay. Whatever her reasons for doing so.'

'Only because she was weak. A stronger

woman would have walked away. She wasn't that woman. Aren't the weak supposed to be helped by the strong?'

Clayton didn't respond. Another moment of silence passed between them. 'Dare I ask what happened next?' he said quietly.

Alice turned to look at him. 'Ah, the writer in you wanting all the ends tied up?'

'Something like that.'

'Well, I'll give you the shortened version. A post-mortem was carried out and Julia's death was officially recorded as a suicide. There was talk of her having been under a lot of stress recently, of her being unhappy. Both Rufus and Tasha went as far as to say that my father was to blame, that he had as good as tipped those pills down her throat. Naturally that had everyone wondering for a while. Was it possible? Had Bruce Barrett murdered his wife? Then, of course, my mother's death was raked over again. The gossip machine was churning like mad by this stage. The local newspaper played its part and then a couple of the nationals picked up on it. The combination of my father's reputation as a photographer of some repute, and his first wife having had a public persona for a number of years was too tempting a story to pass up. Not to mention that he had scooted off with a woman so much younger than himself.'

'Where was your father when all this was going on?'

'He'd disappeared. No one could track him down. The police knew that at the time Julia had been sitting in his car swallowing handfuls of pills he and Isabel were on a flight to Chile, but from then on there was no trace of the pair of them. I remember him saying after my mother's death that he had been glad he was out of the country when she had died as then no one could point the finger in his direction. He must have been relieved it happened again in the same way.'

Clayton knew he was probing unashamedly, but he couldn't stop himself. 'Did you ever seriously wonder about your mother's death?' he asked.

'For no more than a blink of an eye. My mother was not the suicidal type. If she was unhappy she would have sooner killed my father than herself.'

'And when did your father finally surface?'

'A week after Julia's funeral. He telephoned to say sorry for having gone off without leaving a note for me. He said he'd felt badly about that but knew I'd understand in the end. I told him about Julia. He went very quiet but when I asked him to come home, he said he couldn't do that. I begged him. 'Do this one thing for me,' I pleaded. But he wouldn't budge. Not even when I threatened never to speak to him again if he wouldn't come back when I needed him most. He told me I'd be fine, that I didn't need him any more. I yelled at him that he was wrong. I ranted. I cried. I called him a selfish bastard for only thinking of himself. He said he was being anything but selfish, that he was thinking only of me. 'You don't deserve the shame of having me around,' he said. 'If people want to think I drove Julia to suicide, it's better for you if I'm not there.' He went on to say that he was starting a new life with Isabel. I told him he had to be out of his mind. He said that maybe he was, but he didn't care because Isabel made him happy, happier and more alive than he'd felt in years. He went on about life being for living and that he hoped if a chance of happiness came my way I'd have the sense to take it. I reminded him that I'd thought I'd be happy with Rufus and look where that had got me. And then I told him that as of that moment, since he obviously cared so little about me, he no longer had a daughter. My last words to him were to say that I would never speak to him again. Ever.' She sighed deeply, closed her eyes and when she opened them she pressed a finger to her top lip and stared into the fire. She looked so solemn, so very sad.

'Do you think your father really did plan to use Isabel to get back at Rufus?' Clayton said as he watched her reach for a log and toss it into the embers of the fire, sending sparks flying. 'Or do you think the attraction between them was real from the word go?'

Without looking at him, she nodded. 'It wasn't until some time later that I came to the conclusion that the attraction was genuine. I thought about the way I'd seen him photographing her in the garden and I knew there had been a powerful intimacy to what they were doing, as if he was already making love to her through the lens of his camera.'

Clayton could picture the scene all too well. 'And what of Rufus and Tasha?' he asked. 'What happened to them?'

'They left the day after the funeral. I never saw or spoke to them again. Tasha didn't return to school. I asked the headmistress if she knew where Tasha had gone to finish her A-levels, but she didn't know. Rufus's last words to me were to say he hoped I was satisfied now, now that my father had destroyed his family.'

'He had a highly tuned sense of drama, that young man,' Clayton said.

'Could you blame him? His mother was dead and he'd lost his fiancée.'

'He could have done a lot more himself to avert the disaster. I get the feeling his every word and action was carefully orchestrated. Please don't take this the wrong way, but do you think he ever really cared about you?'

'I think my father was right: Rufus had been playing a game. He hated my father and used me to get at him. He knew, or thought he knew, that I was the only thing my father cared about. In the end, he was proved wrong on that score. Bruce Barrett only ever cared about himself.'

'I'm sure that wasn't true,' Clayton said. 'Your father lost his head over a beautiful woman; he wouldn't be the first man to do that.'

'That may well be true and I know this is going to sound like I'm wallowing in self-pity, but he never came back. That hurt. He wrote to me, but I couldn't bring myself to read his letters. I threw them away. Every single one of them. I didn't want to read what a great time he was having, I just wanted him to come home. Then I made sure he couldn't. I completed my A-levels, sold Cuckoo House — it was mine after all — and took a gap year. I left no forwarding address. I cut all ties with the place. The only person who knew where I was, was the solicitor I used in Derby to handle the sale of the house, and he was under orders not to pass on my new address to anyone. I used the same solicitor to change my name by deed poll. A year later than planned, I took up my place at university — not my first choice, just in case I could be traced, and I pretended I was somebody completely different. I gave myself a whole new back story. Just as my father had embarked on a new beginning, so did I.'

'You were very thorough.'

'Anger and rejection can do that to a person. Also, I didn't want anyone to associate me with what had happened. I wanted a clean slate. I saw myself as the Queen of New Beginnings.'

'Do you have any idea if your father tried to find you?'

She shook her head.

'Do you ever regret that?'

Frowning, she said, 'This is starting to sound like one of those awful daytime programmes when the host keeps asking probing questions and then a curtain swings back and a mystery guest, in this case my father, is wheeled on.'

'Sorry. I didn't mean to sound so tactless.'

'Oh, blunder away. The truth is, yes, I do regret what I did. Especially when I read of his death. It wasn't his obituary, just a reference to the fact that Bruce Barrett, the naturalist photographer, had died some five years earlier. In some ways, that was really what forced me to leave behind my life in London. The knowledge of his death seemed to compound the sense I had of having reached a dead end. The acting roles just weren't coming my way. Have you any idea how humiliating it is to audition for a blink-and-you-miss-it-walk-on part and not get the part? Too animated, I was once told.'

'I've been on the receiving end of far worse rejections, I can assure you. A commissioning editor at the BBC once thanked me profusely for the script I'd submitted. He said he'd run out of newspaper to line his son's hamster cage and my pages of mind-numbing effluent had arrived in the nick of time.'

She smiled faintly. 'You had the last laugh, though.'

'Sometimes I wonder.'

After another prolonged silence, Clayton said, 'I know this is going to sound tactless again, but when you learned of your father's death, did you find out anything about his life after he left here?'

She shook her head. 'All I know is that he died in Argentina about seven years ago. And before you ask, no, I've never felt the need to go there and find his grave so I can pay my belated respects. What would be the point, when I've always felt the spirit of him never really left this house?'

She yawned hugely and looked at her watch. Clayton glanced at his: it was nearly midnight. 'I must go,' she said. 'It's late and the neighbours will start to talk.'

'George has this place watched, does she?'

'No, not George. I was thinking of my neighbours, Ronnetta and her son, Bob. Bob tends to keep rather a close eye on me.'

'In a good way? Or a bad way?'

'In a habitually tedious kind of way.'

She was on her feet now. As was Clayton. 'You'll come back, won't you?' he said.

'Of course. We had a deal; my story then yours.'

★ ★ ★

Clayton saw Alice to the door, then watched the red tail lights of her car slowly disappear into the night. He locked up, but instead of turning out all the lights and going upstairs to bed, he returned to the room where they had spent the evening. He threw another couple of logs on the fire and reflected on all that Alice had shared with him. He could only wonder at the effect that being back here must be having on her. Whatever her feelings were, she hid them well. But then he guessed that was a skill she had learned at a very young age. For him, one of the most interesting things she had said was that she believed the spirit of her father had never really left Cuckoo House. Was it fanciful of him to think that she was right? How else could he explain the feeling he now had that any minute the door could swing open and, large as life, in would stride Bruce Barrett?

With his back to the fire, Clayton closed his eyes and listened to the silence of the house.

Only a matter of seconds passed before the silence was crowded out with voices. He could hear laughter as well. And tears. There was no doubt about it, the Armstrongs — and any other owners before them — may have stripped the place of its superficial trappings, but nothing could erase Alice's childhood from the house. He could feel it as acutely as he could feel the warmth of the fire on him. He opened his eyes and took a deep breath. He went and settled himself at the desk, took another deep breath and switched on his laptop.

A writer has an inexhaustible supply of excuses for why he cannot get down to the job in hand. It's too early. It's too late. Too noisy. Too quiet. Not enough caffeine in the bloodstream. The light is wrong. The paper isn't the right sort. The bookshelves need re-arranging. Venus and Jupiter are entering Uranus. Oh, the list is endless. However, for the poor devil suffering from writer's block, there is only one reason for not being able to write and that is debilitating fear; the fear that the brain is no longer wired in the way that it once was. The consequence of this is that with each failed attempt, the fear grows and grows until one day life simply doesn't seem worth living any more.

Clayton had come terrifyingly close to that low point. He had known what it was like to sit alone, late at night, at his desk contemplating his demise.

But now, with the kind of assurance he so rarely experienced, he knew he was free of the crippling fear he'd lived with these last few years.

The wires had reconnected inside his head and it felt good. It felt bloody good! He was zinging with creative energy.

He hadn't felt like this since working on that first magical script for *Joking Aside*.

26

With no work booked for the next day, Alice treated herself to the luxury of a lie-in. She stayed in bed until nearly eleven o'clock and the only reason she dragged herself from the warmth of duvet heaven was because there was an insistent ring at the door. She had ignored the first ring. And the second ring. But whoever was down there hammering the bejesus out of the bell was plainly on a mission to spoil her day. Maybe it was important. Like the world was about to be hit by a meteorite.

She was wearing her warmest and thickest flannelette pyjamas — they were practically bulletproof, who knows, maybe even meteorite proof — so she didn't bother with a dressing gown, but at the sight of Bob leering at her when she opened the door, she felt as good as naked. 'Nice togs,' he said, leaning nonchalantly against the door frame and looking her up and down.

'Not working today?' she said.

'I'm having a day off.' His gaze travelled the length of her again.

'Is that for me?' she asked pointedly.

He tore his eyes away from the apparent allure of her flannelette body armour and looked at the parcel in his large, shovel-like hands. 'The postman left it with us when he couldn't get a response from you earlier.' He grinned. 'Looks like I succeeded where he failed.'

'It must be your superior technique.'

The grin widened. 'I've certainly had no complaints over the years.' He gave her a wink, just in case she'd failed to catch the double entendre. 'So what's with the sleeping in till nearly lunchtime?' he asked. 'Recovering from a hangover after your late night out?'

'And what were you doing up past your bedtime spying on me?'

'Just keeping an eye on things. Somebody's got to look out for you, Alice.'

'Any particular reason why?'

When he didn't reply but seemed to be working up to say something else, she jogged his memory about the parcel: it looked like the manuscript she had been expecting. 'I'll take that then, shall I?'

He hesitated. 'If I give it to you will you have a drink with me tonight?'

'If that's how you usually ask a girl out, Bob, you might want to work on it. In my experience blackmail isn't the best approach.'

'But I've used all my best chat-up lines on you and they haven't worked. What else is left for me?'

Oh, what the heck, she thought. Why not put him out of his misery and have a drink with him? What would it cost her? And who else was asking her out for a drink these days? 'OK,' she said, 'what time tonight?'

'You're serious?' He looked like he couldn't believe his luck.

'I'm only saying yes to a drink, Bob.'

'Eight o'clock suit you?'

'That'll be perfect.'

'And you'll wear something nice? Something hot and tight?'

'Don't push your luck, Bob, or you'll feel something hot and tight wrapped around your neck, like my hands.'

His masculine pride firmly reinstated, he gave her the parcel and sauntered away. 'See you at eight. Don't be late.'

She closed the door and wondered if she had done the right thing. Was having a drink with Bob tantamount to handing him a condom with her name written on it? Probably. She blamed her rashness on last night. Too much rattling around in the past had addled her brain.

★ ★ ★

Showered and dressed and sitting at the kitchen table while eating a late breakfast of porridge and flicking through the newly delivered manuscript, she thought of the incongruity of having shared so much of her life story with a stranger. OK, not a complete stranger, but even so, it was still odd that she had confided in Clayton when she had never so much as breathed a word of her upbringing to anyone else. But then really, whom would she have wanted to tell? Certainly not any previous boyfriends. Not when they'd all borne an uncanny resemblance to Rufus. That would have really freaked them out. It would also have freaked her out to admit it.

She had never consciously chosen to date men

that were carbon copies of Rufus — nothing could have been further from her mind when she'd taken the plunge at university and started dating — but that was the way it had gone. It was as if she had approached a pick'n'mix counter for boyfriends and asked for a quarter of dark, floppy-fringed hair, a quarter of olive skin, a quarter of penetrating blue eyes and a quarter of fatal charm. Oh, and if a sprinkling of arrogant bastard could be added, so much the better. They hadn't always had that last quality, but many had. Whilst James Montgomery could in no way be described as a boyfriend, he had fitted the profile, just minus the arrogance.

Nobody needed to tell her that it wasn't healthy to be drawn to Rufus clones. It wasn't good. She really had to stop it. Yet how could she stop something she wasn't conscious of doing until it was too late? Perhaps her evening out tonight with Bob would help to broaden her horizons. An evening in his company might make her consider a different sort of man. Just not Bob!

Breakfast dealt with, she decided it was time to tackle something that was long overdue.

★　★　★

She arrived at Well House late afternoon; the light was already fading. A lamp shone from one of the downstairs windows and the dented and rusting boot of a familiar car peeped out from the side of the house. Two clues that suggested the mistress of the house was at home.

The house looked just as it always had: in need of urgent repair. Alice thought how sad it would be when the inevitable happened — when George's death would bring about the sale of Well House. The new owners would doubtless take the stone-built property by the scruff of its neck and transform it into a lavish country residence, stripping away all trace of its previous eccentric owner.

As she had always done, Alice went round to the back door. She was pleased to see that the same tarnished brass bell was hanging in the same place in the porch. The porch resembled an untidy potting shed more than a form of entrance; there were gardening implements propped against the walls, clay pots stacked into teetering towers, and parts of a dismantled hose surrounded a galvanized metal bucket. The bucket contained some murky water and when Alice looked up, she saw why; there was a hole in the porch roof.

She gave the bell rope a firm tug and waited. She suddenly felt nervous. George was the only living person who had known her since the day she was born and there was going to be some explaining to do.

'And about time too,' George said when she opened the door. 'If I didn't know better I'd say you've been avoiding me. Come in.'

The same George. No standing on ceremony. A wave of regret swept over Alice. New beginnings were all very well, but here was a very poignant reminder of what Alice had so decisively put behind her. Of what she had lost.

Ushered into the kitchen, Alice felt as though she had truly stepped back in time. Nothing had changed; it was as if she had been here only yesterday. A large, brutish rooster eyed Alice from the hearth rug in front of the Rayburn. He scratched at the rug, puffed out his chest, stretched his neck and strutted towards her. It was far from a flattering thought, but Alice was immediately reminded of Bob.

'Away with you, Percy!' George shouted. 'Another step and I'll take a broom to you.'

As if understanding every word, the rooster deflated himself and went back to loitering with menacing intent on the hearth rug.

'He's full of hot air,' George said to Alice. 'Take no notice of him. So what'll it be? Tea, coffee or something stronger?'

'Since I'm driving I'll take the safe option; tea, please.'

'Well then, don't stand there like a spare part, grab a chair and sit yourself down by the stove while I do the honours.'

Alice did as she was told and carried a heavy wooden chair from the table over to one side of the Rayburn. Percy didn't look at all happy with the arrangement and again raised himself up to his full adversarial height.

'Just give him a firm boot to his tail feathers and he'll soon get out of your way,' George instructed. 'Like most men, he's all cluck and no peck.'

The tea made, George eased herself stiffly into the armchair opposite Alice. Alice had naively hoped that George would have defied the passing of the years, but she was unquestionably older. Not exactly frail, but certainly not as robust as Alice had remembered her.

'Right then,' George said with an unnervingly direct stare over the rim of her mug, 'tell me all you know about my new neighbour at Cuckoo House.'

This was not the opening line of conversation she had been expecting and Alice took a moment to recalibrate her thoughts. She also felt just a tiny bit slighted. Didn't George want to know what she had been doing all this time and what she was doing back here?

'And you can drop the charade about his name being Shannon,' George said. 'I know as well as you do what his real name is. The day I gave him a lift to the shops, I saw a picture of him in a newspaper. That beard wasn't fooling me.'

A promise was a promise in Alice's book. 'I'm sorry,' she said with her best innocent face firmly in place, 'you've lost me entirely.'

George looked stern. 'His name's Clayton Miller, as in rhymes with Baby Killer, as posted on the Internet. It's really quite disgusting what people can get away with writing these days. Did you know that there are people out there in cyberspace playing *Where's Miller?* You know, like *Where's Wally?* People with nothing better to do are sending in photographs of sightings of him all over the world. He's everywhere: Swindon, Paris, Belfast, Mozambique. There's any number of sightings of him in Bruges, supposedly following in Stephen Fry's footsteps.'

Alice suddenly burst out laughing. 'George, what in the world are you doing with the Internet? You never even used to have a telly. I remember you thinking a pop-up toaster was the last word in decadence.'

George bristled. 'If I can find a proper use for something, I'm quite prepared to use it. I'm choosy, that's all. And if you must know, I've joined an online bridge circle. Those chat rooms are interesting, aren't they?'

Unbelievable, thought Alice. 'You be careful,' she said. 'You never know who you're chatting to.'

'It works both ways,' George said with a sly smile. 'So, and now that we've established we both know exactly who he is, how did our interesting visitor at Cuckoo House end up here? Did you have something to do with that?'

'George, I really can't comment on — '

'Baloney, maloney! Is he a friend of yours? Is that it?'

Alice could see she had no choice but to concede. 'Look, I made a promise to him. Please don't ask me anything else.'

The old woman slurped her tea noisily. 'Fair enough. I can respect that.' Another noisy slurp. 'He seems nice. I like him. Needs taking in hand, don't you think? Is that what you're doing?'

'I'm not really doing anything. And he's not a friend either. I've only just met him.' Alice explained briefly about Ronnetta and the cleaning agency, which in turn provoked a line of questioning Alice had been expecting when she arrived. She told George everything about her life after leaving Cuckoo House.

'Well, that's all that neatly clarified,' George said when she had finished. 'Apart from the one glaring omission of why you didn't come and see me when you moved back up here. Or did you think I'd long since shuffled off this mortal coil?'

'You'll never die, George. You'll outlive us all. But to answer your question, I think you were a connection too far. If I'm really honest, I was worried you'd tell me something I didn't want to hear.'

'Such as?'

'Such as my father might have been in contact with you at some point and . . . ' Alice faltered. This was something she had steadfastly refused to let herself think about, that her father had tried looking for her, that he really had cared.

'And asked if I knew where you were?' George finished off for her. 'Is that what was worrying you?'

Alice swallowed. 'Yes. Did he?'

★ ★ ★

Clayton had been up all night. Once he'd got started, the words had poured out of him with an unstoppable force. It had been one of the best nights of his life. He'd written for most of the day as well. But now he could barely keep his eyes open and no matter how much coffee he drank, he simply could not stay awake a minute longer.

He decided to take a nap. He kicked off his shoes and lay on the sofa. He closed his eyes.

Oh, that felt good. He wriggled a bit to get comfortable, adjusted the cushion under his head and then felt himself drifting. Drifting . . . drifting . . . drifting.

He was in a hot-air balloon, looking down on Cuckoo House. He could see Alice staring at him from the garden. She was waving and he was waving back at her. 'Don't go,' she called out. 'Don't leave me behind.' He floated away until finally he was hovering over the rooftops of London. The skyline looked like it did from that Mary Poppins film. He'd always loved the film as a boy; he'd secretly had a crush on Julie Andrews. He floated on, passing Trafalgar Square, Big Ben and then he was above Notting Hill, and oh, look, there was Stacey. And Barry. They were waving to him. 'I've got something for you,' he shouted down to them. He leaned over the side of the basket to throw it to them. 'This is yours,' he called out. 'You left it behind.' 'No!' they shouted. '*No!*' But it was too late. The bundle was tumbling through the air; faster and faster it went. It was unravelling. First a tiny pink leg appeared and then another followed by a head and two hands. It was a baby. '*No!*' he screamed. 'That wasn't what I meant.'

He woke with a massive jolt; his heart was thumping hard. He lay very still, waiting for his heartbeat to slow down. It almost had when his mobile rang. He leapt from the sofa and instantly regretted his haste. Light-headed, he snatched up the phone from where he'd left it on the desk next to his laptop.

'Greetings!'

'This had better be good, Glen,' Clayton snarled.

'Love and kisses to you, sweetheart. How's it going?'

'You really want to know?'

'No, I'm just calling because I have nothing better to do. Of course I want to know.'

'I've started writing.'

Silence from the other end of the phone.

'Glen? You still there?'

'I'm in shock. I've just picked myself up from the floor. Did I hear you right? You've started writing?'

'Hey, less of the sarcasm and more of the support for which I pay you so handsomely.'

'Tell me all. What have you got?'

'A bit of a departure from anything I've written before.'

'I like the sound of it so far.'

'What do you mean? Are you saying you didn't like what I've written before?'

'Just when exactly did you get to be so needy?'

'Oh, go blow smoke up your gigantically oversized ego! Now shut up and listen. I think I've got something. Something that's going to go the distance. It's about a family. A gold carat, all the way to the top, screwed up family.'

'Mm . . . remind me, has that ever been done before?'

'Of course it's been done before, but whoever got tired of watching other people mess up? Schadenfreude's never going to go out of fashion.'

'Good point. Talking of which, according to a

site on the Internet, you're currently languishing on a beach in Mexico. There's even a photograph of you. Although I'm inclined to think that showing you wearing nothing but a thong was an unnecessary touch.'

Clayton groaned. 'Will it never end?'

'That, my friend, is something we need to discuss. I've been wondering whether you should come back to London and deal with things. Just get it all over and done with. It'll be bloody, I'll warn you, but I'll be there for you. I'll hold your dainty little hand every step of the way.'

'As tempting as the idea is of you holding my hand, the answer is no. I'm not going anywhere. I'm staying here.'

'I thought you hated it there?'

'But I can write here. This place is working for me. I'm not leaving and that's flat.'

27

The point of Glen's call, other than to wind Clayton up, had been to let him know that Bazza and Stacey would be on the Stevie McKean show. Forget Brad and Angelina or the Beckhams, Bazza and Stacey were the new Golden Couple on the block. What the hell were they up to now? What latest promotional trick had they devised for themselves? Could it be yet more charity work? Perhaps they were campaigning to help the deprived credit-crunched kiddies of Notting Hill whose parents couldn't afford violin lessons any more? Or better still, were they there fundraising for a donkey sanctuary in Darfur?

Whatever the cause, Clayton was under no delusion that his name wouldn't be further besmirched during their television appearance — what chat show host could resist raising the subject? The last time he'd forced himself to watch them it hadn't ended well.

But it wouldn't happen now, would it? He was over that madness, surely? He could be trusted not to react and do something silly again? Couldn't he?

Don't watch the programme, Captain Sensible whispered in his ear. *Avoid it at all costs.*

Yeah right, like that was going to happen. This was classic road crash stuff. You could tell yourself all you wanted not to turn and stare, but

267

there wasn't a power in the world that could stop you from twisting round in your seat to have a jolly good gawp.

Well, if you must, Captain Sensible said priggishly, *but be it on your own head. However, I strongly advise against watching it alone.*

'Don't watch it alone?' Clayton said aloud with disbelief. Just whom was he supposed to invite to watch it with him?

No sooner had he articulated the thought than it came to him whom he could, and *would* invite. OK, it was pretty weird, but then what wasn't weird about the set-up here? Besides, she'd given him her mobile number and the instruction that if he needed anything he had only to ring her. Admittedly she had probably had something a little more mundane in mind when she'd offered her help. Keeping him company while he watched his two exes giving another tearfully brave performance on the teatime telly slot would not have been her first thought. Question was, should he insist that Alice restrain him if it all got too much? Should he warn her that on no account was he to be allowed to make a phone call?

OK, that was probably going too far. Having somebody with him, as Captain Sensible wouldn't hesitate to point out, was the ideal precautionary measure. He'd be on his best behaviour with Alice. It would also provide a convenient segue to giving her his story. A deal was a deal, after all. Originally he'd had no intention of sticking to this supposed deal of you-show-me-yours-and-I'll-you-mine, but he felt he owed her something. For one thing she had proved to be pleasantly agreeable to be around, interesting and fun, and had very likely saved him from dying of boredom here. There was also the small matter of what he was writing to broach with her. It was only polite that he ask her permission to go ahead with it. Naturally, he'd abandon the project if she objected. No question. There were lines that should never be crossed. This was one of them. What kind of a man would he be to go against her wishes?

Hmmm . . . observed Captain Sensible with his arms folded in front of him.

★　★　★

Alice had intended to read through the manuscript of *Liar, Liar, Pants on Fire* one more time in preparation for going into the studio next week, but Clayton's phone call had made her change her good intentions. She hadn't needed much persuading; the chance for some company was a welcome diversion. Her visit to Well House had been a lot more distressing than she had expected. She had been so deeply upset she had called off her evening out with Bob, much to his disappointment. She had claimed a headache. She didn't think for one moment he had believed her.

What George had told her had left her feeling more alone and isolated than she had ever felt in her whole life. What hurt most was that she had to accept that she had made a terrible mistake and there was no way of righting it. How would she ever come to terms with that?

* * *

'You OK?' Clayton greeted her when she arrived at Cuckoo House.

Surprised that he should notice there was anything wrong with her, she shook off his concern. 'I'm fine,' she lied offhandedly. She placed her coat over the back of a chair in the kitchen and noticed the tray of tea things on the table. There was a plate of biscuits and a Mr Kipling fruit cake which she remembered seeing in amongst Clayton's bags of shopping the other day. Over on the work top, it was action stations with the teapot and a box of teabags all set to go.

With his back to her as he put the kettle on the hob, Clayton said, 'You mentioned on the phone earlier that you'd been to see George yesterday. Did she scold you very badly for not visiting her before?'

'She was remarkably lenient with her scolding,' Alice replied, 'but I ought to warn you, she knows who you are.'

Clayton turned round. 'You told her?'

'I didn't need to.' Alice explained about George seeing a newspaper and then checking him out on the Internet.

'She uses the Internet?'

Alice nodded. 'I know; it's too incredible for words. It's like suddenly discovering the world really is flat. And don't worry about her telling anyone about you being here. She would never do that.'

'My agent seems to think that I should go

home and face the music.'

Alice felt a pang of disappointment. She would miss her visits here to see him. Or was it, she wondered, the house she would miss visiting? 'When will you go?'

Clayton shook his head. 'I've told Glen I'm not going. Not yet, anyway.'

'I'm glad,' she blurted out.

He looked at her hard. 'Are you? Why?'

Embarrassed at her admission and worried that he might misinterpret it, she said, 'Well, you don't want to go back to London until the dust has properly settled, do you? And the longer you stay away from London, the more chance there is of those journalists finding someone else to get their teeth into. That's all I meant. Kettle's boiling,' she said helpfully.

With his back to her once again as he dropped two teabags into the pot, he said, 'I also have another reason why I want to stay on. The thing is, I've started to — ' He broke off and turned to face her. 'Is that your mobile?'

'Not guilty; it must be yours.'

He put down the teapot, looked about him, then eventually located his phone on the other side of the kitchen beneath a hand towel. While he took the call, Alice finished the job of making the tea.

'No, Glen,' Clayton said wearily, 'I haven't forgotten. Yes, I'm well aware that it starts in ten minutes. I'm even more aware that you'll make me miss it if you don't get off the line. Yeah, it's great that you care so much. Love you, too.' He ended the call and caught Alice's eye. 'I hope

271

your agent doesn't treat you like an idiot the way mine does.'

'What starts in ten minutes?'

He put his mobile on the table and picked up the completed tray. 'The Stevie McKean Show. I thought you could watch it with me.'

'Any particular reason why?'

'To save me from doing something silly.'

★　★　★

'Why exactly are you putting yourself through the ordeal of watching Barry and Stacey being interviewed?'

'When I could have my teeth extracted without anaesthetic, you mean? Good question.'

'And the answer?'

Clayton passed Alice a biscuit. She was sitting on the floor just a few feet away from where he was fidgeting anxiously on the sofa. The first guest was banging on about a forthcoming come-back tour and album. He was a knuckle-dragging moron from a long-forgotten boy band with a drugs-to-hell-and-back biography to flog. He had yet to purchase his return ticket, by the looks of his glittering eyes. He was beyond dull. He was mind-numbingly, stultifyingly boring. He would make a baboon with a speech impediment sound articulate. 'There'll be a tour, right . . . an album, of course . . . it'll be the comeback of all comebacks, man . . . it'll make Take That's comeback look like . . . like shit, man. Sorry, dude. Are we cool about swearing?'

'Still waiting for that answer,' Alice said.

'Sorry, I got sidetracked by the sparkling quality of this guy's riveting banter. I've decided it's time to see how I'll react. Or rather, I want to know whether I'm overreacting.'

'OK, but here's the deal. If you go psycho on me, I'm out of here.'

Finally, having exhausted the moron's supply of misplaced bravado and shifted him from the sofa, Stevie McKean was now introducing his next two guests. The audience began their dutiful burst of enthusiastic applause. His body thrumming with nervous energy, Clayton slid off the sofa and joined Alice on the floor. His shoulder touched hers.

She turned and looked at him. Their eyes met and for the craziest of nanoseconds he contemplated kissing her. Anything to distract himself.

Erm . . . not a good idea, Captain Sensible cautioned from the back row of the cheap seats inside his head.

The applause reached its crescendo as Lucky Bazza and Stacey took their positions on the sofa. Stacey's expression, as she acknowledged Stevie and the audience, was loaded with sugary Hallmark card sincerity. She even had the Princess Di head tilt going on.

'Well,' said Stevie when the applause had ebbed away, 'you've had a busy time of it recently. I don't seem to be able to open a magazine or a newspaper without seeing the pair of you in it.'

'I'll second that,' Clayton muttered.

Lucky Bazza gave a coy little shrug as if to say,

what's a guy to do, can we help being so damned popular? 'Yes, Stevie,' Stacey said gravely, 'we're hoping it's all going to calm down before too long.'

'Like hell you do!' Clayton muttered.

'Are you going to mutter like that throughout the entire interview?' Alice asked.

'Probably.'

'I hear congratulations are in order,' Stevie said with a twinkling, meaningful look. 'I hope there's an invitation in the post for me.'

Stacey reached for Lucky Bazza's hand and they gazed sickeningly into each other's eyes. After an eternity had passed, Stacey said, 'You're more than welcome to the wedding, Stevie, but I have to tell you, it won't be anything grand. It's going to be very low-key.'

'Oh, in that case I won't come,' Stevie quipped. 'I only do grand these days.' The audience tittered, as did the Golden Couple.

'We don't want to do anything overly lavish,' Lucky Bazza said earnestly and speaking for the first time, 'not when there's so much human suffering in the world. It would seem obscene.'

'So no delicious photos in *Hello!* for us to enjoy?'

If it were possible, Lucky Bazza adopted an even more earnest tone. 'There will be pictures in *Hello!*' he said, 'but we won't be touching a penny of the fee; we're donating it to an orphanage in Malawi.'

There was a collective *aah* from the audience.

'Would that be the same orphanage where the world's most notorious child-snatcher stole a baby?'

274

The audience snickered, but there was a perceptible slip to Stacey's sugary Hallmark card expression. 'Now, Stevie,' she rebuked him, 'you know that's not true. Madonna went through all the proper channels. Why only the other day, she was telling me that — '

'I don't believe it!' Clayton shouted at the television. 'They're hobnobbing with Madonna these days!'

'Ssh!' Alice said.

'You're pals with dear old Madge, are you?' Stevie said with an exaggerated look of awe.

'We've spoken a few times on the telephone,' Stacey said. 'I decided to get in touch with her about the orphanage so we could make a donation.'

'It's what everybody does, isn't it?' muttered Clayton. 'It's the first thing that would enter my mind if I had some cash to give away. I'd call Madonna.'

'So you're getting a right old wodge of cash for your wedding snaps, are you?'

'As Barry explained,' Stacey said with a steely tone that belied the saintly expression on her face, 'we won't be receiving a penny. It will all go to the orphanage. After we lost our — ' she paused for unmistakable dramatic effect — 'after we lost our baby — ' another pause as she and Lucky Bazza exchanged doe-eyed glances — 'we just felt this was the right thing to do. Something positive.'

'Oh, shit, here we go.'

'*Ssh!*'

'The loss of your baby has been well-documented

275

in the press, and I know how painful that must have been for you, so perhaps it's better if we don't — '

'That's all right, Stevie,' Stacey said hurriedly, as if she were terrified she might be denied the chance to lay out her stall of well-publicized emotions. 'We don't mind talking about it. Especially if it will help other couples who have had to face the trauma of a miscarriage.'

'You're very brave.'

'I wouldn't say that,' she said. 'But if Clayton is watching this . . . ' she snapped her head round to find the camera and stared directly into it like a real chat-show pro. 'I'd just like to tell him that we no longer bear him any malice.'

'Really?'

'Really, Stevie. In my opinion he needs help. You know, professional help. Barry feels the same way. Isn't that right, Barry?'

The camera zoomed in on Lucky Bazza's face: his forehead was shiny with perspiration. 'Clayton had more than his fair share of problems and bad luck,' he said, 'and I want him to know that I wish him nothing but the best.'

The camera stayed on Barry for an unnaturally long time, then slowly panned to the show's host. 'Ladies and gentlemen, I think we should give this extraordinary couple a round of applause and wish them well for the future. And Clayton,' he added when the clapping was over, 'if you are listening out there, let me tell you, you look a right slapper in a thong!'

'It wasn't me in the thong!' Clayton shouted back at the TV.

276

'That's all we've got time for today, folks,' beamed Stevie. 'Catch us tomorrow when I'll be chatting to a medium who's regularly in touch with a whole host of stars, including Marilyn Monroe, Frank Sinatra and Elvis. Don't miss it!'

Clayton zapped the television with the remote control. 'It wasn't me in the thong,' he repeated as the screen went blank and he stared at it in stunned silence.

'That was pure Tate and Lyle,' Alice said. 'Any sweeter and our teeth would be falling out. As an antidote, do I get to hear your side of the story now?'

28

'You have to understand that I never meant for things to turn out the way they did,' Clayton said.

'I'd decided that had to be the case,' Alice said. 'You don't strike me as being a viciously vindictive man.'

'It just got out of hand. I couldn't stand to see them constantly parading their smug happiness. Everywhere I looked, there they were, grinning like a couple of idiots. Bazza had never been into all that celebrity crap. The Cult of the Jackass, we used to call it. But with Stacey at his side he changed; he bought into what we'd always despised and he and Stacey became an obscene parody of a Showbiz Couple. Don't get me wrong, Bazza isn't stupid, he has talent, but Stacey's the literary equivalent of a footballer's WAG. She's so in there for the main chance.'

'So how did it get out of hand? What was the trigger that caused you to make the phone call?'

'If you know about the phone call, then you know they were on *This Morning*. Bazza was promoting a new film that was about to premiere in the States and saying how much he and Stacey were looking forward to flying out to LA the next day. They just looked so infuriatingly pleased with themselves, coyly laughing off the suggestion that they were now part of the Hollywood glitterati. To cap it all, Stacey then leaned forward to the two hosts, dear old Philip Schofield and whoever his sidekick was that particular week, and asked if it would be all right if she could share something important with them and the nation. She actually said, 'the nation'. Who did she think she was, the Queen?'

'What did she say?'

'She announced that she and Bazza were expecting a child. The first of many, she added with a wink in Bazza's direction, as if to say, you'd better pull your finger out, mate. She even said that maybe they would adopt as well, that the world was full of babies in need of a loving home.'

'But why did that matter so much to you?'

He shuffled awkwardly. 'I'd wanted children but she'd been dead against it. She'd said she couldn't think of anything worse than a screaming brat puking over her precious carpets and Italian bed linen. And suddenly, there she was flaunting herself as a nauseating celebrity mother-to-be.'

'So the red mist descended?'

'They were doing a phone-in, you know the kind of thing: members of the public call to have their quid a minute's worth of air time, or whatever the going rate is, so they can chat with a celebrity as if they're old buddies. Right, I thought, I'll call in. I'll have my quid's worth. I'll wipe the smirk off their self-satisfied faces.'

'Ooh,' Alice cringed, 'with or without the benefit of hindsight, that doesn't sound like a smart move.'

Clayton pushed his hand through his hair.

'Believe me, from then on, nothing I did was smart. I gave a false name to whoever it was operating the phone lines and when they put me through, I congratulated Bazza and Stacey on an outstandingly phoney performance. It was Bazza who sussed my voice first and the look of horror on his face was all I needed to drive home my point.'

'Hang on, aren't you supposed to be in a different room from the telly or radio when you take part in these call-ins? I thought there were feedback problems.'

'You think a little detail like that was uppermost in my mind when I was totally fired up to let them have it?'

'Fair point.'

'And I did let them have it. I gave it to them with both barrels. I didn't hold back. I told them, and ironically the *nation*, exactly what I thought of them, how Stacey had been sneaking round my back seeing Bazza, how they'd both lied and cheated. And did they really think they'd make such good parents when Stacey had all the maternal instincts of Shannon Matthews' mother and Bazza was nothing but a social climbing twat.'

Alice smiled. 'You got all that out before you were cut off?'

'I can only imagine that somebody in the control room had a sadistic streak running through him or her and must have thought, 'Hey, this is a bit of a lark, let's see how far we can go with it.''

'What happened next?'

'I put the phone down before Bazza and Stacey could respond, then sat back and watched them, along with Phil and his sidekick, try to compose themselves. Inevitably, an advert break followed but they still had to resume the conversation, or so I thought. But Bazza and Stacey had legged it by the time the programme returned. Phil apologized and said that owing to being terribly upset by my outburst, Bazza and Stacey were unable to continue. So what did I do? I called in again and said that in future they should choose guests who had more guts and backbone, preferably with a bit of decency.'

'You were one angry man, weren't you?'

Clayton nodded. 'But think about it, if you had been presented with the chance to do the same thing to Rufus, wouldn't you have done so? Wouldn't there have been a part of you that wanted to get even by publicly humiliating him?'

'Oh, don't get me wrong,' she said. 'I'm not judging you. I'd have done something like that in an instant, given the opportunity.' She rubbed at a small faded patch of denim on the knee of her jeans. 'But I've learned the hard way that revenge leaves a nasty taste in the mouth.' Frowning, she gazed at her knee with studied interest. 'Tell me the rest of your story,' she said quietly.

'I will, but first I need a drink. Something with an alcoholic content. How about you?'

'What are you offering?'

'Wine. That's all I have. Other than George's grog.'

'A glass of wine will be fine. Thank you.'

Out in the kitchen, Clayton let out his breath.

OK, so far, so good. He hadn't lost it. That was a good sign.

Behind him, on the table, his mobile rang.

'Yes, Glen,' he said.

'You watched the programme?'

'Every heart-tugging second.'

'Quite a performance, I thought.'

'It's as if they were born to it.'

'But you're OK?'

'My God, Glen, is that a lump of concern I can hear in your voice?'

'No, it's a Custard Cream.'

'Well, bugger off and leave me alone. I'm sure you must have far more important clients than me to deal with.'

'All my clients are more important than you, Clay. I forgot to ask earlier, done any writing today?'

'This morning, yes.'

'Progressing OK?'

'Ah, I get it. Your newfound concern for me hangs on my writing again and the thought of yet more filthy lucre coming your way.'

'I have two ex-wives to take care of.'

'No you don't! You've never even been married. You don't even have a girlfriend.'

'But who knows what's around the corner for me? How does that song go? Marriage and divorce go together like a horse and carriage?'

'I think you'll find it's love and marriage. And no way is any sane woman going to marry you.'

'You're a hurtful swine.'

'As I've told you before, sweetkins, it's what keeps our relationship so fresh. Now if you don't mind, I'm busy. I have company.'

'Oh? Tell me more.'

Clayton rang off.

From the last of the bottles of wine he'd bought, he poured out two glasses of Merlot and made a mental note to himself: *another shopping expedition now a matter of extreme urgency.*

He rejoined Alice and found her standing at the window, looking out over the front garden. He wondered how much she could actually see, given that it was dark outside. Perhaps it was the past she was really looking at. On the desk, to her left, was his laptop. Thankfully it was closed. Safe from accidental prying eyes.

She turned, probably at the sight of his reflection in the glass. Shocked, he saw an expression of intense sadness on her face. If he didn't know better, he'd say she was close to tears. 'You all right?' he asked.

She did that jerky head-wobbling thing that people always did when they were far from all right.

He put down the glasses on the coffee table. 'I'm no expert in these matters, but I don't think you're all right. What's wrong?'

'I'm fine,' she snapped. 'I'm absolutely — ' Her voice cracked and she coughed, as if trying to hold something back. Then she burst into tears and turned away from him.

Oo-kay, tears. Right. And the best course of action would be? 'Um . . . can I get you anything?' he said.

She shook her head.

'Tissues?'

This time her head moved in an affirmative direction.

He returned as fast as he could with a box of Kleenex from the kitchen. 'Man strength,' he said, holding the box out to her. 'Guaranteed to let you down.'

She responded with a choky sob and plucked several tissues from the box. She wiped her eyes, blew her nose and started crying all over again. Only louder this time.

Ooo-kay. Obviously something more than tissues was required. Reassurance of some kind. He put the tissue box down on the desk. Right. What if he touched her? Would she jump a mile high? He didn't want to make her feel any worse. On the other hand, if she objected violently, it would at least distract her. But on the other hand — how many hands was he up to now? — what if she thought he was trying something on?

Meanwhile, her sobs and shaking were growing in intensity. He had to do something. He cautiously touched her shoulder. She didn't react. Not even a flinch. He braced himself for a shove and a slap and slowly turned her towards him, his arms encircling her. She leaned against him awkwardly at first and then sank into him, her head resting on his shoulder. Nice shampoo, he found himself thinking as he breathed in the scent of her hair. Probably not the time or place, he then thought. Say something soothing. But he couldn't think of anything remotely soothing to say. He'd never been good coping with tears. Stacey used to say it was because he was so repressed and he ignored other people's emotions so that his own wouldn't become infected.

With no ready words at his disposal, he started to rub Alice's back, moving his hands in slow, self-conscious circles. He then held her a little closer. He could feel the softness of her breasts pressed against his chest. That feels nice, he suddenly thought.

It also felt bad. Should he be enjoying himself this much when she was clearly so upset? His hands moved from her back to her shoulders. He noticed she had stopped crying now. Was that his cue to let go? Was his work done? Perhaps just a little longer. Just to be sure.

One of his hands now seemed to be working of its own accord and had somehow found its way to the nape of her neck. He cradled her head gently, stroked her hair. Now the whole of his body seemed to be working of its own accord; he was holding her closer still and his other hand was now heading towards the smooth, warm skin of her neck. He tilted her face up to his and placed his lips very lightly over hers.

He snapped his eyes open. How had that happened? And when had his eyes closed? His mouth still hovering over hers, he found himself staring into the dark, dark depths of her gaze.

'Are you going to kiss me?' she asked. 'Or just leave me dangling here?'

'I must confess, a mad, crazy part of me was planning on kissing you. What do you think? Good or bad idea?'

'Let's see how it goes, shall we?'

He closed the tiny space between them and

kissed her. And kept on kissing her. 'Verdict?' he said, when he finally broke away. 'Good or bad idea?'

'I haven't made up my mind yet. Can you kiss me again, please?'

He smiled. 'With pleasure. But I have to warn you, I don't take criticism well.'

'Don't worry; I think you'll pass with flying colours.'

29

There was a split second of awkwardness when they at last pulled apart and after some lowering of eyes, some disentangling of limbs and some throat clearing, Clayton took matters into his own hands. Their kissing might have been a brief and pleasant distraction — it certainly had been for him — but he could see that Alice was still upset. About what exactly, he had yet to discover, although he had his suspicions. 'You sit here and have an obscenely large glug of wine while I organize a fire,' he said.

'I'll do the curtains,' she countered.

'No you won't. I'll do them.'

He led her to one of the sofas. 'Do as you're told and sit down and relax.'

She looked at him curiously, her head tilted. 'Did you have a shot of double-strength testosterone with your breakfast this morning? This newfound manly forcefulness is very unnerving.'

'Is that what's wrong with me? I thought there was something; I just couldn't put my finger on it.'

She smiled and he felt a flicker of warmth spread through him. She really did have the most charming and heart-warming of smiles. Why hadn't he noticed that before?

When he had the fire lit and the curtains drawn, effectively shutting out the outside world, he went and joined her on the sofa. He didn't put an arm around her. He'd taken one liberty when she wasn't feeling herself; two would be exceedingly unchivalrous.

'Stacey always accused me of being insensitive,' he said, 'but you know, I don't think that was entirely fair of her. For instance, I did happen to notice that you were ever so slightly upset over something a few moments ago. You hid it well, though. To the untrained eye it could have gone unnoticed. Do you want to tell me what it is?'

Again the smile. A little sadder than the previous one, but it still had the same effect on him: a flickering, tender warmth.

'It was what George told me about my father,' she said.

'I wondered if it was that.'

She looked at him over the top of her wine glass. 'For an insensitive man, you're pretty sensitive, aren't you?'

They were sitting about a foot apart and he was strongly tempted to kiss her once more. On his case again, Captain Sensible roared through a megaphone at him: *Liberties!*

'What did George tell you?' he asked.

'She said that my father came back to look for me. According to George he tried really hard. When she told him the name of the estate agent who had sold the house, he went to them to see if they knew where I was. All they could do was pass him on to the firm of solicitors I'd used, but of course they were under strict instructions not to give out any information

288

about my whereabouts. Apparently he gave them a letter to forward to me, but by this time I was in London and I'd moved so many times in the space of two years there was no way anything could have reached me.' She sighed. 'He tried to find me, Clayton, and that hurts. More than I ever thought it would.' She wiped away two small tears. 'He was a crazy father, a wildly unpredictable and passionate man, but I loved him. Maybe that was why I was so hard on him; I wanted to do something wild and irrational myself to hurt him in the way he'd hurt me. Why do we do that, hurt the ones we love?' She sighed again. 'God, what a family we were! You couldn't make it up, could you?'

Clayton shifted uncomfortably. 'Truth is always stranger than fiction,' he said quietly. He took a sip of his wine and in the silence that followed he listened to the sound of logs on the fire popping and spitting. A gust of wind rattled down the chimney and a whoosh of sparks flared. 'Did George know whether your father and Isabel stayed together?' he asked.

'No, she didn't know that. But the fact that my father came here alone probably means they didn't. It was highly unlikely that they would. She was so much younger than him. It had to have been nothing but a stupid fling.'

'If that's all it was, he paid a high price for it, losing his daughter. Especially as you were his only daughter.' It was the wrong thing to say. Alice's eyes filled and she reached for another tissue. 'Sorry,' he said, 'big mouth syndrome. I'm told there is treatment for it. It's a tricky procedure, involves having my head removed.'

She blew her nose. 'You're really quite a nice man, aren't you?'

'That's not what the newspapers would have you believe.'

'I've only read the one piece about you. I didn't want to read any more; it didn't feel right. It seemed too much of an invasion of your privacy. I'd hate for anyone to do that to me.'

Having earlier planned to tell Alice that he had started writing, and more to the point, *what* he'd been writing, Clayton knew that now wasn't the time to share this turn of events with her. That's right, Mr Sensitivity strikes again.

'Take my mind off things by telling me what really happened with Stacey and Barry,' she said, surprising him.

'You're sure it would help?'

She nodded. 'It might not be as effective a distraction as your kiss, but I'll take my chances.' She then leaned into him, inviting him to put an arm around her.

Who was he to refuse?

★   ★   ★

The morning after his telephone outburst on national television, and nursing a fearsome hangover, Clayton felt ashamed of his conduct. He'd gone too far. Having only just heard about his behaviour by reading about it in the newspapers, Glen phoned him. 'Had you been drinking beforehand?'

'I might have been,' he'd admitted.

'Is it starting to be a regular thing with you? The drinking?'

'That's the one thing you can rely upon me for, Glen,' he'd replied. 'Drinking to excess on a regular basis is not my thing.' It was the truth; he was a veritable lightweight when it came to alcohol. It was the first thing he and Barry had discovered they had in common when they'd met at university.

He had known in advance that the Golden Couple was due to appear on *This Morning* and so — just to help him get through the ordeal — he had prepared himself accordingly with a few breakfast bevvies while watching *The Jeremy Kyle Show*. Common sense would have dictated that watching another channel might have been a better way to handle their appearance. Or not to have switched the television on in the first place.

'Perhaps you could find a way to make amends,' Glen had suggested on the phone. 'The public is capricious. They loved it when you outed that tosser and his highly entertaining proclivities, but one look at the papers this morning tells me they're siding with Bazza and Stacey in this instance. It's the baby thing. Don't ask me why, but everyone loves a baby. Perhaps you could make a gesture of deep regret, a touching display of contrition. As abject as you can manage.'

The next day Clayton came up with the perfect apology. He would surprise the Golden Couple with baby presents galore. He would buy up Baby Gap and have everything installed in the house ready for their return from LA.

But why stop at Baby Gap? he'd asked himself. There was Mothercare, there was John Lewis, there were any number of shops he could use. Moreover, there was the Internet.

That was when it got out of hand, when his imagination took over and all coherent and rational thought fled from his head. All he needed to pull off his apology was access to Bazza's house.

When they'd been riding high on the success of *Joking Aside*, Bazza had bought an astonishingly expensive four-storey property in Notting Hill. In those days Clayton had been a frequent visitor and had been entrusted with the code for the alarm system — Bazza's mother's birth date. Unfortunately he'd never been entrusted with a key, but a little thing like that wasn't going to stop him.

From reading the papers he knew that the Golden Couple would be returning late the following evening, in readiness for yet another television appearance the next morning so they could bore the pants off everyone about their amazing time in LA — and so he had everything planned with military precision. He gained entry to the house in the dead of night by smashing a pane of glass in the French doors at the back. He stumbled through the house in the dark to the hall where he knew the control panel was situated for the alarm system. He also knew that there would be a brief delay before the system would route a call through to the police station, should he not be able to switch the thing off. He was banking on Lucky Bazza not having changed the system, or the number. He tapped in the code and at once the red warning light on the panel stopped flashing. He was in! Operation Baby was all set to go.

He passed the night on the sofa and woke early in the morning. He actually felt excited at the prospect of the next part of his plan. He poured himself a bowl of Coco Pops — Bazza's favourite cereal — then opened the fridge for some milk. There wasn't any. Well, of course there wouldn't be. The Golden Couple wouldn't have left a pint of milk to go sour in their absence, would they? He made do with a cup of black coffee and patiently waited for the first of the deliveries to arrive.

The van for Baby Gap arrived first. Clayton donned his disguise of a baseball cap and sunglasses and helpfully instructed the delivery driver where to put everything.

Next followed suit.

Then John Lewis, and at the same time as Mothercare, a man came to fix the broken panel of glass in the French doors.

Clayton was no expert when it came to babies and their requirements, but he was quietly impressed with his selection. He reckoned the ground floor of the house was full of everything that a couple could possibly want for their forthcoming offspring to take them from birth through to about four years old. There were clothes galore, a pram, a pushchair, bathing equipment, sit and ride toys, a torturous-looking device to extract breastmilk, bottles, a sterilizing unit, a highchair, box loads of toys, a playpen, a miniature table and chair set, a Moses basket, a cot and a lot more besides.

Throughout the busy day of activity Clayton had noticed a few passers-by taking interested glances at what was going on. One of the neighbours actually knocked on the door in the middle of the afternoon and, disinclined to show himself, Clayton persuaded the delivery driver from Mothercare to explain to the nosy old biddy that it was a surprise being organized. Hardly a lie, was it?

He was beginning to get a bit twitchy by five o'clock that the last of the deliveries wasn't going to arrive, but then ten minutes later, the van arrived. Except it wasn't a van-about-town kind of van, it was more like a removal truck. A stonking great lorry that was in danger of blocking the street. Oh, shit, Clayton thought when the two enormous delivery men opened up the back of it. He could see now why the two men were so large. They'd have to be to lug these things about.

'I think there's been some kind of mistake,' he said.

'No mistake, mate,' the larger of the two hulks replied. 'Got it all down here on paper.' He thrust the paper at Clayton. 'Right then, where do you want them?'

'You don't understand . . . I thought they'd be — '

'Come on, pal,' said Hulk Number Two with more than a hint of impatience to his voice. He had a skull and crossbones tattooed around his neck; it was a helpful clue to Clayton not to mess

294

with him. 'We ain't got all day, you know. We've got to be in Leamington Spa by eight.'

And with that, they began to unload the delivery. It was as well that the house was positioned at the end of the row and that there was plenty of access round to the back garden. As the two Incredible Hulks manoeuvred the items and put them into place, Clayton tried to convince himself that what he'd ordered didn't look half as terrifying as it did. The final touch was for Hulk Number One to install the timer device Clayton had ordered. 'Unless you're a qualified electrician, mate,' he was informed, 'don't even think about messing with the electrics. We'll be back to collect the gear in four days' time as it says on the paperwork.'

Once again, the neighbour next door was keeping a close eye on matters by pressing her nose up against one of her bedroom windows. She was probably already penning a furious letter to the authorities checking to see whether planning permission had been granted for these monstrous eyesores.

The Incredible Hulks finally drove off, leaving Clayton to review the situation. He wished now that he'd stuck to balloons. Balloons wouldn't have been so terrifying.

Back inside the house, he sat down at the kitchen table and wrote a carefully worded letter to Bazza and Stacey. Well, 'letter' was pushing it. A ten-word note was nearer the mark.

I hope you like my present to you both,
    Clayton.

He simply didn't know what else to say. And anyway, suffering from writer's block as he was, they were lucky to get that much from him.

A sudden dazzling light from outside made him go and stand at the window. It was so bright out there in the garden he half expected to see a spacecraft not unlike the one in *ET* to be hovering above Notting Hill.

Ohshitohshitohoshit! What in hell's name had he done?

Crammed into the garden, ablaze and each measuring approximately ten feet in diameter, was the grisliest sight he'd seen in the whole of his miserable life.

Online they had looked cartoon-cuddly-cute. They'd also looked small, not much bigger than your average garden gnome. He'd thought at the time they seemed an expensive novelty to hire, but Holy Moses, how had he missed the measurements? How had he cocked up so comprehensively? These monsters were huge. They were massive. They'd seemed scarily large in their unlit state, but now that the timer had switched on and they were illuminated, they seemed to have doubled in size and hideousness. They stared back at him like a gruesome collection of chilling decapitated heads from a Halloween horror movie. Their nightmarish, manic expressions suggested that any minute, if he so much as looked away, they'd start creeping towards the house to come and get him. There was a pale-blue elephant head, a russet squirrel head, a pink rabbit head, a yellow duck head and a purple pig head, all grotesque and demonically oversized. He wondered if they'd ever had bodies attached. If so, how big would that have made them? And what had been their original purpose? Fairground illuminations, perhaps.

But it was too late to do anything about them. He just had to hope that Bazza and Stacey wouldn't be too freaked out, that they would see the funny side of what he'd done.

He left the note on the kitchen table, reset the burglar alarm, and using a key he'd found hanging in the cupboard under the stairs, he locked the back door, posted the key through the letterbox and slunk away into the night.

He had apologized, he told himself as he made his way across London to his own home in Fulham. He had made good his public attack on them. What could possibly go wrong?

★   ★   ★

He soon found out exactly just how badly his plan had gone wrong. A little after five o'clock the next morning his telephone by the side of the bed rang. 'You psychopathic wanker!' Bazza yelled at him. 'What kind of a sick joke did you think you were playing on us?'

'OK,' he apologized, 'the heads were a mistake. I accept that. But the rest of it, surely you like the rest of the stuff? The toys? You like those, don't you?' He could hear himself pleading with Bazza.

But Bazza wasn't hearing him. 'Stacey's lost the baby because of you,' he shouted down the phone. 'It was the shock.'

'Oh, my God! What, the shock of seeing those heads?'

'No, it was the electricity!'

It turned out that Stacey had gone outside to switch off the power and had received an electric shock that had thrown her off her feet. Two hours later she had started to miscarry and Bazza had driven her to the hospital.

Appalled at what had happened, Clayton had gone to Notting Hill two days later to apologize, but his visit had only made things worse. Bazza had taken a swing at him and the next thing they were brawling in the street with Bazza shouting that he would personally see to it that he would become the most hated man in the country. Somebody — probably the nosy neighbour — called the police and at the sound of a siren fast approaching, Clayton decided his best option was to leg it.

In the days that followed he kept expecting a heavily armed unit to crash through his front door in the middle of the night and arrest him. He'd been responsible for the death of a four-month-old foetus; could he go to prison for that?

But prison wasn't what Bazza had in mind for him. His revenge wasn't to press charges for breaking and entry or causing Stacey to miscarry, but to hound Clayton through the press. With seemingly every journalist on his side, he painstakingly set about his task. Reporters and photographers set up camp outside Clayton's house, forcing him to draw the curtains and stay inside. It could have been worse. He could have had a mob of angry village folk wielding pitchforks and flaming torches on his doorstep.

The newspapers vilified him as a psychotic monster who had caused an innocent woman to lose her baby. *How Low Can a Man Get? . . . What New Low Now for Unfunniest Funny Man? . . . Funny No More . . . Funny Man Out of Control . . .* was the general theme when it came to the headlines. The sickest headlines were to be found on the Internet: *Clayton Miller the Child Terminator* was one of the least offensive things written about him online. Every minuscule aspect of his character was dredged up and dissected. Lists were compiled of all the questionable things he had publicly said or done. People he had apparently wronged in the past came out of the woodwork with a barrage of grievances to air. He discovered he had false friends aplenty; he was officially persona non grata. Even his cleaner abandoned him to tell her story to the *Sun*, sharing with the world earth-shattering stuff such as how he liked to eat his breakfast in the bath, how he sometimes left his toenail clippings on the bedroom floor, and shock horror, how some days he didn't bother getting dressed, just lounged about in his pyjamas with his hair uncombed whilst sitting at his desk not writing a single word. Clearly all signs of a mind seriously on the tilt.

In the end, Glen, the only one to stand by him, put out a statement to the press, stating very clearly just how sorry his client was and that Clayton had had no intention of causing anyone any harm; it had all been a terrible mistake.

Then in the early hours of a particularly cold, wet night, when not even the hardiest photographer was keeping an eye on the house, Glen spirited Clayton away and dispatched him to a place no one would find him.

30

As she switched off the light and slid beneath the duvet, Alice couldn't help but think it was just the sort of outlandish thing her father would have done. On the Richter scale of bad ideas it was certainly up there with the cherry liqueurs.

Unquestionably Clayton's heart had been in the right place when he'd planned his surprise for Barry and Stacey, and if the outcome hadn't been as it was, surely they would have seen the funny side of what he'd done. How Alice would have loved to have witnessed the shock on Clayton's face when he'd seen the gigantic animal heads emerging from the back of the truck. Even funnier would have been his reaction when he'd seen them illuminated in all their eerie glory. If it had been a scene from a film or a TV programme the audience would have laughed out loud. Moreover, Clayton would have come across as a hapless yet wholly likeable and sympathetic character. Not for a single second would he have been viewed as the evil monster the press had since portrayed him as being.

Alice had briefly thought that the best way for Clayton to defend himself, as well as repair the damage made to his reputation, was to go to the media with his side of the story. But Clayton was convinced that he couldn't trust a journalist to print what he actually told them. He maintained that anything he said would be deliberately misconstrued and twisted into something altogether different. He was probably right.

She recalled the day when she had first met Clayton, when he'd been Mr Shannon. The man he'd been then — the dishevelled, ill-tempered curmudgeon — was hardly recognizable to her now. She would no more have kissed that man than she would have kissed a toad in the belief it would change into a handsome prince.

Mmm . . . interesting analogy, she reflected.

She rolled over and her thoughts turned to her father. His memory was now more powerfully real to her than it had ever been. The tears she had cried for him at Cuckoo House this evening had come from a place deep inside her. A place she hadn't known existed.

She had been fine until Clayton had left her alone. Then, when she'd been on her own in the very room in which she had last seen her father, when he'd been making love to Isabel, the loss of him had hit her with a force so potent she had felt as if she had just heard of his death for the first time. She suspected, having never truly grieved for him, just as she hadn't for her mother, that it was some kind of delayed shock she had experienced.

But how could she ever make up for what she had done? The calculated act of wilfully wiping her father out of her life had never seemed more cold-hearted or brutal than it did to her now. Only two days ago she could have justified her actions to herself and to anyone who dared to question her motives, but now she couldn't.

The Queen of New Beginnings had got it

wrong. There was no such thing as a new beginning when you were devising it for the worst reason of all: revenge.

Acknowledging the sad truth of this had plunged her into a state of remorseful torment. Was that why she had turned to Clayton? Had he merely been a convenient shoulder to cry on? A case of any port would do if the storm was bad enough?

She replayed inside her head the moment he had taken her unawares and kissed her. Despite how upset she had been she had experienced a jolt of pleasant surprise pass through her and had willingly kissed him back. She had liked the way he had held her, very close but unexpectedly gentle, almost as if he'd been afraid to hurt her.

Where had this new man come from? This kind, thoughtful, perceptive and curiously attractive man? She tried to think when exactly he had changed and what could have caused the transformation, but she could come up with nothing more definitive than that the change must have been gradual. Perhaps it was merely that he felt more relaxed around her. More trusting as well. Yes, that was probably it. He had decided to trust her, just as she had trusted him when she had decided to share her childhood with him.

When it had been time for her to leave Cuckoo House, he had walked her to her car and kissed her one last time; it had been no more than a light brush of his lips against her cheek. Driving home, she had wished he had kissed her as he'd done before. Had he chosen the safe option to be polite, or had he regretted the way he'd kissed her earlier? Was he, she wondered, as impulsive as she was? And if so, was that a good thing? The combined force of two impulsive people could get themselves into an awful lot of trouble.

Just as her father and Isabel had done.

★　★　★

At Cuckoo House, Clayton was flying. Man, oh man, was he ever flying! The words were coming so fast his fingers couldn't keep up with his brain; they were thrashing the keyboard of his laptop with a frustrating lack of accuracy. But never mind. Throwing the story down was all he cared about. Errors could be dealt with later.

It is a well-known fact amongst writers that until that first word of a new piece of work is written, the writer believes utterly that what he is about to start writing is going to be THE BIG ONE. Invariably, once the first page is written, the belief begins to waver. OK, maybe not THE BIG ONE, but still something that will be considered a stupendous achievement and garner national, if not international, acclaim. By the end of the chapter, or the first scene, the writer knows full well that what he or she is writing is not going to tilt the world on its axis. In fact, it's not even going to tilt his own ego. It may prove to be as good a piece of writing as he has produced to date, but acceptance is there: this is just the same old dross kitted out in a new pair of Y-fronts.

But in this instance, Clayton believed whole-heartedly this was THE BIG ONE. He had written pages and pages of dialogue and knew, just absolutely *knew*, this was destined to be something he would be proud of. There wasn't a flicker of doubt in his mind; this had Major Success written all over it. He had felt exactly the same when he and Bazza had started playing with ideas for the script that went on to become *Joking Aside*. They'd been sitting opposite one another in the kitchen of their grungy flat, bouncing ideas off each other. As the exchange grew and their ideas and scraps of scribbled-on paper gathered momentum, they both began to get excited. 'This is better than our usual crap, isn't it?' Bazza had said.

'You betcha,' Clayton replied. 'If I'm not mistaken, we've reached the quality end of the colon.'

Clayton's instinct then had been bang on the money. Which was why he didn't doubt himself now. He hadn't suffered the debilitating horror of writer's block for as long as he had — all those times he'd started on an idea only to stall — to know when it just wasn't happening. He reckoned writer's block wasn't unlike erectile dysfunction: all-consumingly shaming, the sort of thing a man just can't bring himself to discuss openly. Not that he'd actually experienced the latter. But then when was the last time he'd had the chance to put the equipment to the test anyway? For all he knew he could have acquired any number of problems in that department since it had last been on an outing. A sex life;

now there was an interesting concept.

He immediately thought of Alice.

As forays into the unknown went, he wouldn't remind a repeat performance of this evening's activities. He'd been tempted to try his luck again when she was leaving but Mr Sensitive must have been cosying up with Captain Sensible, because he'd reined himself in and settled for a gentlemanly kiss on her cheek.

He let his mind linger on the pleasurable memory of kissing Alice, then with great effort, he shifted gear and dragged his thoughts away from her as an attractive woman and back to when she'd been a young girl shortly before her mother had died. Not once during her chats with him had Alice referred to how she'd felt about her mother's death. Was that deliberate? Or was she a natural storyteller, moving the narrative along to what she deemed the next important part of the story?

But Clayton wanted to write more about Barbara Barrett. Could he use some artistic licence and flesh out her character himself? Or would that be insensitive of him?

Bit late for that, Captain Sensible butted in.

All right, all right, he snapped back at Captain Sensible. Just as soon as Alice seemed less upset about her father, he would broach the subject with her. He would also tackle the tricky matter of telling her what he was writing. His timing would have to be right. He couldn't just wade in. He would have to use all his powers of gentle persuasion. He could do that, couldn't he?

He scrolled through what he'd just written and

as he tried to picture Alice and her mother together, it occurred to him that maybe he could talk to George about Barbara Barrett. He wouldn't be at all surprised if the crafty old girl was a mine of information. He'd have to tread warily, though. He couldn't let on to George what he was doing without having first OK-ed things with Alice. Speaking with her would be his next priority. Well, he'd leave it a few more days. Just to be on the safe side. No point in rushing in when she might still be troubled by her father.

See, he could be sensitive when it was required.

31

'You haven't brought any more of your gut-dissolving, diabolical brew, have you?'

'That, if you don't mind me saying, Mr Shannon, is not the most gracious way to greet a well-intentioned neighbour.'

Clayton stood back and let George in with a blast of corrosive cold air. It was uncanny that she had come knocking on his door so soon after he had decided he wanted to talk to her. What was she, some kind of mind reader? More likely a witch. 'Alice told me that you know who I am,' he said, 'so I suggest we bury Mr Shannon.'

'Shame, I was becoming rather attached to him. And fear not,' she mimed a zip being pulled across her mouth, 'I shan't be blabbing to anyone that you're here.'

'Thank you. So what can I do for you?' He knew exactly what she could do for him, but he needed to bide his time before strapping her to a chair and flashing a bright light into those beady little eyes of hers in order to carry out his interrogation regarding Alice's mother.

'No, it's more a case of what I can do for you, Mr Miller.'

'Please, call me Clayton.'

Her eyes twinkled mischievously. 'Goodness, you're not flirting with me, are you?'

He slapped his forehead. 'You've seen right through me.'

'Come on, Clayton,' she said with a chuckle, 'fetch your coat; you're coming out with me.'

'Only if you promise not to drag me back to your cave and have your wicked way with me. I have to warn you, I never have sex on a first date.'

'I'll do my best to control myself. Oh, and you'd better bring that ridiculously large-brimmed hat I saw you wearing when we first met; we don't want anyone cottoning on to who you are, do we?'

★ ★ ★

They were in the car, destination downtown Stonebridge and its myriad heady delights when, above the noise of the engine and gears screaming in blood-curdling distress, George shouted at him, 'You're looking a lot better than the last time I saw you. What's changed?'

'Perception as well as charm,' he yelled back.

'You seem different, and not just because you've shaved off the beard. Never been a fan of whiskers myself. You could almost pass for handsome now.'

'And the charm just gets better and better. Carry on like this and you'll have me wrapped around your little finger in no time at all.'

'You're already there, my friend. Are you going to answer my question? If not, I have a theory.'

'This I have to hear.'

'I think the sudden improvement in your wellbeing may have something to do with our sweet Alice. Am I right?'

'How in hell's name did you reach that conclusion?'

'No need to shout,' she said as his yelled and startled reply coincided with an unexpected lull of quiet in the car. 'But it stands to reason. You're all alone in that great big house with only Alice to keep you occasional company. What red-blooded man's thoughts wouldn't turn towards her? She's grown into a very attractive young woman.'

'I really think you ought to get your overly active imagination under control. Nothing has passed between Alice and me.' As he said this, he had a vision of George standing guard in a watchtower observing his every move through a pair of hi-tech, super-strength binoculars. His kissing Alice had probably been written up in a log book.

She shot him a sideways glance. 'Very well, if that's how you want to play it. I can respect that. But you're not a bad catch. I doubt many women would run screaming from the room when you walked in. Alice could do a lot worse than hook up with you.'

'George,' he said, 'whilst I'm inordinately grateful for you taking me shopping and showing such a sensitive and tender-hearted interest in my personal life, do you think there's the remotest chance that you might just shut the hell up?'

'No chance at all. And anyway, I'm not just taking you shopping; you're treating me to afternoon tea at the Penny-Farthing. I've decided you need a change of scene. We don't

310

want you going stale, do we?'

'I knew today would turn out to be my lucky day.'

* * *

The cafe had been designed to appeal to those with a discerning eye for an overload of kitsch. Moderation had not been *le mot juste* when its decor had been conceived. A heavy hand had been given free rein to all things Victoriana. There were black and white photographs in abundance, mostly portraying ridiculously dressed men staring death in the face whilst sitting astride penny-farthings. There were copper kettles galore, racks of lace and doilies, a rocking horse, masses of crockery on display as well as a row of bed warmers. What Health and Safety would have to say about the porcelain potties that were liberally dotted about the place was anybody's guess. Laden down with large wooden trays and gliding between the tables as if on castors, were waitresses dressed in mob caps and long black dresses with frilly white pinnies. Clayton felt as if he was an extra in a bonnet drama; he kept expecting Dame Judi to drop a breathless curtsey at their table.

Instead of Dame Judi, a flame-haired, rosy-cheeked woman arrived to take their order. She held a small pad of paper and a pen, behind which was an expanse of wobbling cleavage. 'Afternoon, George,' she said. 'What's it to be today?'

'My usual for me, Theresa.'

'And you, sir?'

'I'll have the same,' Clayton said, from beneath the brim of his hat and avoiding eye contact at all costs, which unfortunately meant he was eyeballing the woman's ample bosom.

When they were alone, George said, 'You have no idea what my usual is; how do you know you'll like it?'

'It's crossed my mind that maybe this place offers the answer to your immortality. No way could you have cheated death for so long without consuming some kind of secret elixir of life. I thought I'd try it for myself.'

She let rip with a deep-throated cackle, drawing attention from a nearby table. 'You're a ballsy mutt, I'll give you that.'

'Steady; that sounds worryingly like a compliment.'

'Make the most of it; you won't be on the receiving end of many more.'

'I'm glad to hear it. I don't think I could take the strain.'

'Tell me,' she said, her voice lowered and her elbows firmly planted on the table, 'why Shannon? Why choose that as an alias?'

'Does there have to be a reason? Sometimes life is nothing more meaningful than a series of random choices plucked out of the ether.'

She tutted. 'Random choices be damned! An intelligent man like you coming up with a wishy-washy hypothesis like that; I'm disappointed in you.'

'As with many people before, you've made the mistake of overestimating me.'

'Poppycock! I have the perfect measure of you.

Besides, I've done my homework on you; Ralph was your father's middle name and Shannon was your mother's maiden name.'

He stared at her. 'Then why ask the question?'

'I only ever ask questions to which I already know the answer.'

'I suppose there's some curious logic to that approach.'

With surprising speed and efficiency, their waitress reappeared with a large tray of what turned out to be a selection of dainty, crustless sandwiches. There were oversized scones, too, with jam and cream, along with a china teapot, a milk jug and two sets of cups and saucers.

'A sweet tooth, George?' Clayton queried when once again they were alone. 'I'd never have guessed. I had you down as more of a hemlock-with-a-side-order-of-cyanide kind of person.'

'Goodness, how Alice must love your pillow talk!'

He offered her the plate of sandwiches. 'You first. I want to make sure they're not poisoned. Just out of interest, why do you keep going on about Alice and me? Has she said something to you?'

'It's what she hasn't said that interests me more. I've given the matter a lot of thought and I think you would be good for each other.'

'What on earth has given you reason to think that?'

'It's knowing Alice as well as I do.'

'But you haven't seen her in years. She can't be the same person you knew from way back when.'

'In my experience people rarely change. Yes, there'll be some superficial changes I'll grant you, but the fundamentals, the essence of a person's character, that's carved in stone. Are you going to let that tea stew for the rest of the day or are you going to pour it?'

'That's an intriguing theory,' he said, dutifully lifting the teapot over one of the cups, 'and I'm inclined to — '

'Here in the civilized world we like the milk first,' she interrupted him.

He reached for the milk jug. ' — agree with you.'

'Not too much.'

Seizing the opportunity George had given him, he said, with his voice at a discreet level, 'Alice has told me the whole story about Rufus, and about Isabel running off with her father and then Julia committing suicide, but I'm curious about her mother, Barbara Barrett. Alice doesn't talk about her in the same way she does about her father. Were they not very close?'

'Oh, I think they were close enough, but girls and their fathers often have a different bond, don't they? Alice may not care to admit to it, but she idolized her father. He was a real larger-than-life character. Not an easy man to live with, it has to be said, but who wants a boring straightforward man in their life? That's why I think Alice could well be attracted to you. You're complex, with many tantalizing layers to you. You're also a fair bit older than she is, and better still, you don't conform to the usual niceties. In short, you remind her of her father.'

Clayton choked on his tea. Spluttering painfully, his eyes watering, he rammed his paper napkin against his mouth. 'I'm not sure I like the sound of that,' he croaked.

'Oh, don't look so shocked. There's nothing new in a girl replacing her father with a younger version. Lots of girls do it.'

'I think you're wrong. Reading between the lines, my guess is that Alice is more likely to go for men who resemble Rufus.'

'That may well have been the case in the past. But have they made her happy? No, take it from me, the man she really falls in love with will be nothing like that dreadful so and so, Rufus. You'll do very nicely for her.'

'Why is it, George, that after any time I spend with you, I always end up feeling mentally eviscerated?'

★ ★ ★

At the sound of tapping at the kitchen window, Alice looked up from the manuscript she was reading. 'The door isn't locked,' she said, not needing to check who it was. Ronnetta's nails tapping against glass had a unique sound all of their own.

Ronnetta let herself in. 'It's freezing out there,' she said with an exaggerated shiver.

'Yes,' said Alice, 'anyone would think it was winter the way the weather's carrying on.'

'What happened to global warming, that's what I want to know? They told us to plant nothing but grasses and cacti in our gardens a

315

few years back and what happened to them? They got swept away in the floods, that's what!' She pulled out a chair and sat down. 'You look glum. What's wrong?'

'Nothing. I'm fine. I'll put the kettle on, shall I?'

'And there's a diversionary tactic if ever I heard one. So what are you up to?'

'Work, believe it or not.' Alice inclined her head towards the half-read manuscript on the table. She had hoped that absorbing herself in it would help lift her mood. She had woken that morning after dreaming of her father; he'd been calling for her from his darkroom at Cuckoo House but whenever she had tried to answer him, to tell him where she was, she couldn't make herself heard.

'Any good, what you're reading?'

'Very good. I'm looking forward to going into the studio next week to record it. It should be fun, this one.'

'Oh, well that answers my next question. I was hoping you could help me out again.'

'Sorry, next week is pretty busy for me. I've got that book to do and then I'm down in London on Friday for a voiceover.'

'Something for the telly?'

In common with so many people, Ronnetta viewed television as the Holy Grail in Alice's line of work. In a way it was, but the bread and butter work, the work that came in on a regular basis and could be relied upon to pay the bills, was rarely television work. 'It's for a budget airline,' she explained. 'The usual kind of thing:

safety drills, flagging up the duty free, thanking people for flying with them and giving advice about car hire.'

'All the way down to London for a few lines of blah, blah? I could do that.'

Alice laughed and the kettle clicked off. 'I'm sure you could. Tea or coffee?'

'Coffee please.'

'It'll have to be instant; it's all I have at the moment.'

'That's fine. So how come you bailed out of your date with Bob the other night?'

'It wasn't a date.'

'Wasn't it?'

Their drinks made, Alice carried the mugs over to the table. 'Bob's very nice, Ronnetta,' she said, choosing her words with care, 'but — '

'He's mad about you; you do know that, don't you?' Ronnetta said.

Alice's heart sank. 'I'm extremely fond of Bob,' she tried, 'but he's . . . he's simply not — ' She faltered. How could she tell her friend and neighbour that her son just wasn't her type, and never in a million years would he be? 'Look, the thing is, I've met someone else,' she said with a flash of inspiration.

Ronnetta's face dropped. She really was so very proud of her only son. She was probably thinking how on earth could Alice have chosen someone else — *anyone* else — over her precious boy. 'So why did you agree to go out with him the other night?' Ronnetta asked. There was a trace of the tigress protecting her cub in her voice.

'It was just a drink I agreed to have with him,' Alice replied. 'Nothing more. Bob may have thought there was more to it than that, but I didn't. I'm not the sort of girl who leads men on, Ronnetta. I would never do that. Least of all to your son.'

The other woman picked up her mug of coffee and sighed. 'Oh, well, that's that then. Pity, I'd like to have you as a daughter-in-law.'

Alice smiled. 'Better still, you have me as a friend.'

Diplomatic relations once again reinstated, Ronnetta said, 'So who's this man you've met? Some clever schmuck you've met through your work down in London?'

Alice had two choices. She could tell an all-out lie. Or she could tell a partial lie — one that encompassed elements of truth that she was willing to impart. She chose the latter option. 'It's the man staying at Cuckoo House,' she said.

Ronnetta sat up straighter. 'But I thought you said he was weird.'

'He is.'

'I don't understand. Why would you choose weird when you could have Bob?'

'When Cupid fires that arrow, it falls where it falls.' Alice winced. Did she really just say that?

Ronnetta pulled a face and looked about her. 'Am I imagining things, or have you bought one of those plug-in air fresheners? The sort that now and then squirts an embarrassing sickly pong into the air?'

Alice laughed. 'I'm sorry; it was a shocker of a thing to say. I have no idea where it came from.'

318

Smiling, Ronnetta said, 'Any more comments like that, you keep them firmly to yourself. What shall I tell Bob? He's going to be shattered.'

'He'll be fine.'

They sipped their coffee in silence, until Ronnetta said, 'I still think you look glum. What is it? Is it the weird bloke? Does he not feel the same way about you as you do for him?'

Again Alice was faced with a choice: pretend she was perfectly all right, or go some way in being honest. 'It has nothing to do with him,' she said.

'What then? Is it something I can help you with?'

Touched that Ronnetta should want to help her, and knowing she had disappointed her over Bob, Alice felt the need to make amends in some way. 'I haven't been entirely honest with you,' she said. She then explained about growing up at Cuckoo House and how she had promised herself when she sold it never to set foot in it ever again. Too many bad memories, was as far as her sketchy explanation went — memories, she said, that had stirred things up for her. There was no need to go into all the details, was there?

'Well I never,' said Ronnetta when Alice had finished. 'You think you know a person, and then out of the blue they completely throw you. You're a strange one and no mistake.'

'Bet you're now thinking Bob's had a lucky escape. Who in their right mind would want to be involved with me?'

'You mean, other than the weird bloke?'

32

It was the first week of December and Clayton
didn't think he had ever experienced such bitter
coldness. It bit deep. Right through to his
marrow. Alice didn't seem to be aware of the
cold. But as she had reminded him several times
already, she was made of tougher stuff than him.

They were taking a walk across the moors. So
far they hadn't encountered anyone else mad
enough to be out. Surrounded by a landscape
that was lunar in scale, vast and desolate, it was
as if they had the world to themselves. He stood
for a moment to adjust his scarf and to catch his
breath. Alice was a fast walker and he was
becoming increasingly aware that he wasn't as fit
as he could be. 'It's going to snow later,' she said
matter of factly, tipping her head back to look at
the sky; it was ominously grey and pendulous.

'A man could die up here all alone and no one
would ever know,' he remarked. 'He would be
forgotten entirely. All trace of him gone for ever.'

She turned and smiled. 'But at least the
coyotes and grizzly bears would remember him
fondly.'

'You wouldn't be teasing me, would you?'

'Perish the thought.'

'Perish is exactly what will happen to me out
here in this cold. How do you stand it?'

She laughed. 'I love it when you're so positive.'

He smiled back at her and on an impulse

reached for one of her gloved hands. 'Should we encounter any grizzly bears, you will protect me, won't you?'

'You have my word.'

They walked on, hand in hand. A week had passed since they had last seen each other. Clayton had been surprised how disappointed he'd been when Alice had explained that she had a lot on and wouldn't be able to call in and see him. It had felt like a long week since he had kissed her. He'd thought about her a lot in those days. It was hard not to, given that he was secretly writing about her on a daily basis. He'd also thought about George's theory that he reminded Alice of her father. He still didn't know what to make of that. He could think of worse men to be likened to, but he wasn't at all convinced that George knew what she was talking about. He still thought charming bastards — men like Rufus — were Alice's type. And charming was something he had never been described as. Only one way to find out where he stood in her estimation.

'Alice, can I ask you something?' he said as they stopped to climb over a stile.

'Yes,' she said, hopping over the wooden step and turning to face him.

He followed her over the stile, but with less elegance and agility. 'Does James Montgomery bear any resemblance to Rufus?' he asked.

'Wow,' she said, her eyebrows raised. 'What put that thought in your head?'

'Oh, you know, an inquisitive mind casually mulling things over.'

A fierce gust of wind blew at the hair that had worked itself loose from beneath her woolly hat. She removed one of her gloves, tucked the hair back into place and looked at him. They were standing very close, their bulky coats almost touching. 'I think you've given this more than a casual mulling over,' she said.

'Does that bother you?'

'I think that my answer bothers me more, because you're right, almost every man I've been attracted to bore some kind of resemblance to Rufus. You'd think I would have gone out of my way to avoid reminding myself of him, wouldn't you?'

'Logic doesn't always play fair. Um . . . would it be impertinent of me to suggest you try a different type of man?'

The corners of her mouth lifted. 'Do you have a particular type of man in mind?'

'Well, there is this chap I know. He's a complete idiot and can be relied upon at all times to do or say the wrong thing.'

The corners of her mouth lifted further. 'So much for his good points. What about his bad points?'

'Ah, much too numerous to go into.' He bent his head and kissed her very slowly, very lightly. Her lips were icy cold against his own cold mouth, but he soon felt a warmth spring between them. He drew her closer to him, suddenly wanting to touch her in a way their coats simply wouldn't allow. He wanted to feel the warmth of her skin, the smooth softness of it. Just imagining how it might feel made his heart beat faster and a powerful, all-consuming surge of desire made him want only one thing: to get Alice back to Cuckoo House as fast as possible. 'Have we walked far enough?' he whispered in her ear. 'Can we go home, please?'

'Any reason why?'

'Plenty. And all of them guaranteed to make us both feel a lot warmer.'

'Then what are we waiting for? Let's go.'

★ ★ ★

After a frantic search, Clayton found what he was looking for in the master bedroom. The gods were looking down on him kindly for once. He shut the drawer and hurried back to where he'd left Alice in his bed. 'We're in luck!' he said, putting the box on the bedside table. 'What's more, it's a full box.'

She smiled and flipped back the duvet, inviting him to get in. He didn't need inviting twice. He stripped off what remained of his clothes and slid in alongside her. He lay on his side and ran a hand the full stunning length of her naked body. She sighed at his touch. He did it again and she closed her eyes and sighed louder still. He stopped what he was doing. 'Now what do we do?' he asked.

Laughing, she rolled on top of him. He held her face in his hands, took in the happiness of her expression and kissed her. He then stared into her eyes and felt himself falling. Falling deep into the dark depths of her gaze. Nobody had ever told him falling could feel this good. She kissed him on the mouth, brushing her lips lightly over his, before working her way down to his neck, to his shoulders, and then to his chest. 'Feeling any warmer now?' she murmured.

* * *

When they looked out of the window later, it was snowing. 'You were right,' he said as they stood and watched the plump flakes falling from the sky. She was wearing his shirt — and nothing else — and Clayton could honestly say it had never looked better. Her legs were amazing and had no business being covered by jeans, which until today were all he'd ever seen her wearing. In fact, her body had been a revelation to him. It was unimaginably perfect. In every way. Having discovered the wonder of it, he was drawn to it like a magnet and he couldn't stop touching her. He was touching her now, his hands around her waist.

'You do know that I can't possibly let you leave here today,' he said. 'Not in this weather.'

She turned and looked at him. 'You'd like me to stay?'

'You don't want to?' His heart plummeted. Had he presumed too much?

She smiled and wrapped herself around him. 'I'd love to stay.'

'Excellent. How about something to eat? I need to build up my strength; you're an exhausting woman to hang out with.'

As tightly wrapped around him as she was, she managed to press in closer still to him. He liked the feeling. He liked it a lot.

It must have snowed persistently throughout the night.

Sculptured by the wind, bulging drifts of perfectly white snow had transformed the garden and the surrounding moorland into a landscape of exquisite beauty. The sky was grey and low with the threat of yet another snowfall and, uncomfortably reminded of the very last time she had witnessed snow to this extent at Cuckoo House, Alice sat at the kitchen table watching Clayton get breakfast ready in his amusingly haphazard way. Humming to himself, he was repeatedly tracking back and forth to the fridge and cupboards because he kept forgetting something.

By rights they should both be exhausted after the night they'd had — sleep had not exactly been on either of their minds — but Clayton looked as alert and bright-eyed as she'd ever seen him. He broke off from humming. 'How many eggs would you like?'

'Just the one, please.'

'And sausages?'

'Two, please.'

'Rashers of bacon?'

'Two again.'

'Have you ever thought of the word rasher?' he said as he began loading up the grill pan.

'Rasher?'

'Yes, rasher. Such a simple word, but the more you say it, the funnier it becomes. It's what we in the trade call a comedy word. Hedge is another

325

one. Go on, say hedge.'

'Hedge.'

'There you go. It's a ridiculous word.'

'I must be missing something.'

'You don't find it funny? My God, Alice, what's wrong with you?'

She laughed. 'It's not me. It's you. You're barmy.'

'Bingo! You've hit upon another gem. The word mad isn't the least bit funny, but barmy is bang on the money.'

'If you say so.'

'I *do* say so. The same goes for weasel. Rascal. Stout. Scuttle. Perky. Scoundrel.' He slid the pan under the grill and went over to the sink to wash his hands. 'Tomatoes or beans?'

'Are they comedy words?'

'No, they're options for breakfast.'

'In that case, tomatoes. You're much too full of beans as it is.'

He came over and kissed her. 'A man can't be happy?'

She put her arms around his neck and pulled him down to her. 'How shall we spend the day?'

He stroked her hair. 'Here's the plan. After we've eaten breakfast, I'll make a fire in the sitting room and we'll spend the day in there. And later, I might even do some more writing.'

She looked up at him. 'Writing? *More* writing? When did you start?'

His hands stopped moving. 'Um . . . just recently,' he said quietly.

'Why didn't you say anything?'

'I . . . I was — ' He straightened up.

She took holds of his hands. 'It's OK,' she

326

said, 'I understand. It was too soon, wasn't it? You didn't want to jinx things. But how brilliant for you. You must be so pleased.'

He sat in the chair next to her. His expression was unexpectedly serious. 'I am pleased,' he said slowly. 'But the thing is, it's . . . it's all down to you.'

'Me?'

'I couldn't have got going again if it wasn't for you. You'll never know how grateful I am.'

'Don't be silly, I haven't done anything.'

'Yes you have. You've . . . ' He broke off.

'I've done what?'

He swallowed and squeezed her hands gently. 'You've inspired me. You've inspired me to write something with more depth and gravitas than I've ever written before. Hey, if Bazza can move on, so can I.'

'Of course you can. But how did I help you?'

'By . . . ' Again his voice fell away. 'The thing is, Alice, what I've started is — '

Her gaze flickered away from his. 'Sorry to interrupt you,' she said, 'but I think we have what we call in the trade a grill-pan situation.'

'Oh hell!' He leapt to his feet and went to deal with the smoke that was billowing from the grill. 'It's not as bad as it looks,' he said, flapping a tea towel at the pan.

Alice watched him with a growing sense of affection. He was such a one-off. And fancy her being responsible for helping him to start writing again. Life was full of surprises.

★　★　★

327

It's not as bad as it looks.

The words were yet another damning indictment of his behaviour; they would be chiselled on his gravestone, along with all the other less-than-flattering home truths. At the rate he was going he would need a stone the size of a skip to accommodate all his wrongdoings. Better still, why not toss his miserable remains in a skip and do away with a gravestone?

He hadn't meant to open his great big gob; the admission that he had started writing had slipped out in a moment of unaccustomed elation. And, of course, he should have told Alice. He should have grabbed the moment and had the courage to explain exactly what he was writing. The longer he kept quiet, the worse it would appear.

But the thing was, he couldn't tell her. He was terrified that if he did, two things could happen. One: the script, along with his newfound ability and confidence to write, would be jinxed just as Alice had suggested. And two: she would freak out and ban him from writing another word. She would accuse him of being exploitative. Of being untrustworthy. Of sneaking around behind her back. All of which was true.

The net result would be that he would lose the best script he had ever written. He would also, despite it being early days between them, lose Alice, who was surely the best thing to have come into his life in a long while. He was surprised by how much losing her bothered him.

Whichever way he viewed matters, the situation had disaster written all over it if he opened his mouth. He'd come this far; he simply couldn't let this opportunity slip through his hands. If he could hold his nerve, he could finish the script, own up, and then somehow convince Alice that it really wasn't as bad as it looked.

33

'I've got bad news.'

'In that case, Glen, give me the good news first.'

'Did I say there was any good news?'

'OK, invariably it's debatable as to how good the good news is with you, but it's what agents do. You soften the blow of the bad with what you perceive as being good, even if you have to make something up. It's in Chapter Two of the *How to be an Agent* handbook.'

'What's in Chapter One?'

'Avoidance Tactics, subheaded, Beating About the Bush and How Never to Answer a Direct Question.'

'Clay, there is no good news.'

'Did you not read Chapter One?'

'There is no good news.'

'What? None at all?'

'Other than I managed to talk my way out of a parking ticket this morning.'

'Well, that is good news.'

'I thought so, too. Now about this bad news.'

'Do you have to? I was enjoying that rare and beautiful moment between us when it was all love, peace and harmony.'

'Sorry, I'm a busy man; I don't have time for love, peace and harmony. Especially not with you.'

'There you go again, making me feel so special.'

'It's a gift. But if you don't mind me saying, you're sounding remarkably chipper.'

'Am I?'

'Does that mean you're still writing?'

'Like a demon.'

'Really?'

'Really. What's more, I'm prepared to stake my life on you thinking this is easily the best thing I've ever written.'

'You don't have to be modest with me, you know. Try a more upbeat pitch. Give it a touch more confidence.'

'I'm being serious.'

'All right then, when do I get to read this magnum opus, this stupendous work of genius?'

'Give me another week. Then I'll email you some pages.'

'That'll take us to the middle of December. The week before Christmas.'

'Is that a problem for you? Don't tell me you're forcing yourself to endure yet another five-star holiday in some unbearably luxurious location for the festive season?'

'Of course I am. What else would I be doing for Christmas? Sticking around here in the damp and cold? I don't think so.'

'Silly me, I was forgetting Chapter Three of the *How to be an Agent* handbook, the part that teaches the importance of impressing your clients with your dedication to the noble cause of spending the money they earn for you.'

'So how am I doing?'

'Oh, you're right up there. You're impressing the pants off me.'

'Well, put them back on because here comes the bad news. Craig and Anthea are coming home for Christmas. Some relic of a relation has died and, as we speak, they're on their way back for the funeral.'

'And what would that have to do with me precisely?'

'It has everything to do with you, you moron! You're staying in their house. You have to leave pronto.'

'But I can't!'

'Sorry, you have to. Craig and Anthea will be arriving in Derbyshire the day after tomorrow.'

'But I can't leave. It's not as simple as that.'

'It's going to have to be. This was never a permanent arrangement.'

'But I'm writing here. It's working for me. For the first time in more than three years, it's happening for me again.'

'I'm sure you'll continue to write when you come back to London.'

'LONDON! Are you mad? I can't possibly return there. It's the last place on the planet I want to be.'

'It'll be fine. You're no longer the focus of the nation's thoughts. Christmas and what to give smelly old Uncle Sidney is on everyone's minds right now. You're way down their list of concerns.'

'I don't give a damn about that. I just know I won't be able to write if I leave. I have to stay here at Cuckoo House.'

'Clay, we've established that isn't possible. If you don't want to come back to London and the area up there is providing the necessary ambience for you, why don't you check into the nearest hotel? Meanwhile, you'd better make a start on your packing. I'll ring the cleaning agency and organize for someone to give the place the once over before Craig and Anthea arrive. I'll give you a ring in the morning.'

The line went dead. Clayton stared at the mobile in his hand. He could not have looked at it with more abhorrence if it were a dead rat he'd just found in his trouser pocket. He was all set to ring Glen back, to say heaven only knew what, when a flash of car headlights in the dark caught his attention at the end of the drive. With half an eye on the car as it approached the house, he scrolled through that day's work on his laptop, saved and closed it. He went to let Alice in.

He hadn't seen her for ages. Absolutely ages. Practically a lifetime.

Well, not since breakfast that morning.

For the last week, while she was commuting each day to the recording studio in Nottingham she had, at his suggestion, moved in with him. Every evening when she set off from the studio, she would text him to say she was on her way and during the time it would take for her to complete the journey, he would battle to concentrate on the scene he was writing. If he didn't focus hard, he was in serious danger of frittering away the time imagining the awesome pleasure of making love to her that evening.

He had admitted to her last night in bed that he couldn't remember when he'd been happier. 'What about winning all those awards?' she'd asked. 'Surely that must have been better?'

'Not even close,' he'd said. He had been speaking the truth. Awards, as he'd come to know, meant nothing. Any old fool could win an award. You only had to see the so-called award-winning rubbish on the television right now to know the truth of that. Too often it was nothing more than make-up and prosthetics, costumes and canned laughter. Where was the writing? Where was the talent? The craftsmanship? These people spent ten hours in make-up and about ten seconds stringing a few lines of lousy dialogue together to produce a sketch that your average smutty-minded schoolboy could write.

But happiness, as he'd learned, was as fleeting as an English summer. He'd been on top of the world lately, and indeed, only minutes earlier, he'd been happily looking forward to Alice arriving back and how they might entertain themselves for the evening. He'd even been thinking how lucky he was — he was writing better than he ever had and against all the odds he was in a relationship with someone he genuinely cared about. More amazing than that, she cared about him.

Of course there was still the issue of his confession to Alice hanging over him, but he'd managed to shove that down the back of the sofa cushions, so to speak. Out of sight, out of mind.

But now Glen's phone call had ruined the happy equilibrium he'd been experiencing. Where the hell was he going to go? And wherever he ended up, would he still be able to write?

334

Much as it pained him to consider it, was Glen right? Was it time to return to London? After all, he couldn't stay here in Derbyshire indefinitely. He had to go home some time. That had always been on the cards.

★ ★ ★

'I stopped off at the Indian takeaway,' Alice said, putting a large brown carrier bag on the table. 'I'll put it in the oven, just to make sure it's really hot. I hope you like what I've chosen. Clayton? What's wrong? Did the writing not go well today?'

Without answering her, he helped her out of her coat. It was funny how he liked doing the smallest things for her. He removed her hat, smoothed out her hair and unwound her scarf. Then he kissed her, very slowly, very surely, one hand at the nape of her neck, the other resting on her ribcage, his thumb just grazing her breast. He was tempted to go on undressing her, but he knew he'd be doing it for the wrong reason: as a way to put off answering her question.

'I have to leave Cuckoo House,' he said, releasing his hold on her. 'Tomorrow. The owners are coming back. Glen's suggesting I go home to London. He seems to think I'm old news now and that all the hoo-ha has died down.'

'Oh,' she said. Her voice was flat. 'London. Right. Well, yes, I suppose you do have to leave, don't you?' She moved away from him and opened the oven.

He helped her load the foil dishes inside. 'I don't want to go back to London,' he said, when she'd closed the door.

She turned and looked at him and he could see she was trying to hide how upset she was. 'I don't want to go back to London,' he repeated. 'I don't think I'll be able to work there.'

'Is that the only reason you don't want to go back?'

'No,' he said simply.

She swallowed. 'Then don't go back.'

'I'll have to find somewhere else to stay. Do you know of a good hotel nearby?'

She put a finger to her top lip as he'd frequently seen her do when she was concentrating or was uncertain about something. 'What kind of hotel were you thinking of?' she asked quietly. A small frown had appeared on her forehead. She tapped her lip with her finger. For some reason the gesture seemed intensely erotic to him; it made him want to take hold of her and carry her upstairs to bed. 'Because I'll be honest with you,' she went on, 'there are only B&Bs round here, and a lot of them will be closed for Christmas.'

'That doesn't sound very promising.'

'I don't think a B&B would suit you that well anyway.'

'I'm inclined to agree with you.'

She took a step towards him. She tapped her lip again. His desire for her increased. 'There is one place I know of which might suit you,' she said. 'It's not at all grand. Nothing like here.'

'Go on.'

She moved closer still, then placed the palms of her hands on his chest. She looked up into his face and he felt his pulse quicken. 'The trouble is, the landlady is a stickler for rules,' she said.

'What, such as no guests after ten o'clock at night? That wouldn't be a problem.'

'She also has a ban on muddy boots. Oh, and she's not at all keen on hairs left in the plughole, shower, bath or basin. And she's a total Nazi when it comes to toothpaste etiquette; if you squeeze from the middle you'll be out on your ear. The same goes for touching the remote control for the television.'

He began to smile. 'And the bedroom arrangements?'

'Ah, now that's where things get interesting. It would be obligatory for you to keep her company at night.'

'You know, at a pinch I think I could manage that.'

'In exchange, she'll leave you in peace to write to your heart's content.'

'It sounds perfect. But are you sure the arrangements would work? I would hate to intrude. More importantly, I'd hate to — '

She raised one of her hands from his chest and placed the tips of her fingers over his mouth. Again he felt an erotic charge. 'You wouldn't be intruding,' she said softly. 'Far from it.'

He kissed the tips of her fingers, then moved her hand aside and kissed her briefly on the lips. 'So when do we tell George I'm moving in with her?' he said.

She laughed. 'Now I'd pay good money to see that.'

He kissed her again. 'How about we switch off the oven and go upstairs for a while? I need to show you just how grateful I am.'

34

It was a long time since Alice had let anyone live with her. The two occasions she had tried it had not been a success. Disastrous was nearer the mark. The close proximity of another person on a permanent basis had hastened the end of both relationships. So letting Clayton move in with her was a huge risk. But she had done it because the thought of him leaving had seemed infinitely worse.

In the split second when he had broken the news that he had to move out of Cuckoo House, and that his agent was suggesting he return to London, she had felt as if the air had been knocked out of her. To her surprise, she had been close to tears. It was then that she realized how strongly she felt about him and how upset she would be if things ended between them so abruptly. In a knee-jerk reaction to this insight she had invited him to stay with her.

So far, a week into the new arrangement, things were going well. Better than well, in fact. There was a natural ease to their being together. He seemed to fit in at Dragonfly Cottage quite comfortably. There were no wet towels lying on the bathroom or bedroom floor; no scrunched up socks left to find their own way to the linen basket; and no coffee mugs or beer cans lurking in obscure places. He even understood that there was no such thing as a dishwasher fairy who visited in the night and had readily taken on that particular duty, having previously memorized where she kept everything in the cupboards. What's more, the toothpaste was handled in the correct manner. Perhaps more unbelievable still was that this morning she had found him standing in front of the airing cupboard hunting for a toilet roll to replace the empty one in the bathroom.

There was a sense of rightness about his presence in the cottage with her. It was something she had never experienced before. It was something that also scared her. This was a man to whom she could become deeply attached and with a track record for not holding onto a man for longer than a few months — six months was her record — she was in the daunting position of having found someone she didn't want to lose. All her previous relationships had been disposable; this one she wanted to keep for as long as she could.

Initially she had been frightened to trust her feelings for Clayton, seeing the relationship as too good to be true. But the more time she spent with him, the more real it felt to her. And the more secure she felt. She loved it when she discovered something new about him, such as the ease with which he could rattle off a cryptic crossword. Then there was his talent for juggling. OK, juggling wasn't exactly the most useful of talents, but given how cack-handed he often appeared to be, he really was rather good at it. She had also discovered that he had never learned to drive and that he'd had a boyhood crush on Julie Andrews when she'd played the part of Mary Poppins. He said she was the first person he'd ever admitted this to.

Clayton's appearance at Dragonfly Cottage had not gone unnoticed by Ronnetta and less than two hours after his arrival, she was tapping on the kitchen window under the guise of calling round for a cup of coffee. Introductions were duly made — Clayton having reverted to his alias of Ralph Shannon — a full investigation carried out, and after she'd left, Clayton said, 'Is it my imagination, but would I be right in thinking your neighbour didn't approve of me?'

'She was measuring you against her precious son.'

'And found me wanting?'

'I'm afraid so. But don't take it to heart; no one could measure up to Bob in her eyes.'

Now as Alice weighed out the dried fruit for the Christmas pudding she was making, she could hear Clayton speaking on his mobile in the sitting room. She knew he had been waiting for a call from his agent ever since yesterday morning when he had emailed some of his script to him. She would have loved to read what he'd sent, and curiosity had very nearly made her ask him if she could, but because he'd seemed a little on edge she had held her tongue, deciding there would be plenty of time yet to read what he had written. It gave her a thrill knowing that she had unwittingly been a part of curing his writer's block. He had called her his muse. 'I hope you're going to credit me,' she'd responded. 'Muses don't come cheap, you know.'

341

'I'll do better than that,' he'd replied. 'I'll dedicate the whole thing to you.'

The one thing that she felt sad about since Clayton had moved in with her was that her visits to Cuckoo House had come to an end. She missed going there. She missed the newfound connection with her mother and father.

She stirred the Christmas pudding mix, reminded of how her father had once tried to make one. Taking over the kitchen, he had insisted that he needed an audience while he created his culinary masterpiece, claiming that any great maestro needed an appreciative audience. Alice was summoned to watch him work, except her role proved to be participatory rather than that of an observer, and she was despatched to the larder to fetch the ingredients and to weigh them out. Only when all was to hand, was she allowed to sit at the table. As to be expected her father didn't actually follow the recipe faithfully. He added or substituted ingredients for no real good reason, saying, as he tossed in a handful of Liquorice Allsorts, that adaptability was the name of the game. 'Never be afraid to take a risk or try something different, Alice,' he told her. He had decided to cook the pudding in the pressure cooker and succeeded in smashing a window in the kitchen when the whole thing exploded. Undeterred, he declared he would have another crack at making a pudding the following Christmas, saying he wanted to create a tradition of him making one every year. 'Do that and I'll leave you,' Alice's mother had threatened him.

The threat wasn't ever put to the test as Alice's mother didn't live to see another Christmas. Following Julia's arrival at Cuckoo House and her subsequent appointment of someone who knew what they were doing in the kitchen, Mrs Randall made it clear that she would no more let her employer loose in her domain than she would serve Pot Noodles for Christmas lunch.

This Christmas Alice was hoping for a blend of the old with the new. She would be spending it with Clayton but intended to invite George to join them. Last year Ronnetta had had Alice round for Christmas lunch and had things been otherwise, Alice wouldn't have hesitated to reciprocate the invitation, but given the circumstances she didn't think Bob would appreciate being forced to sit across the table from Clayton.

★ ★ ★

On the phone with Glen, Clayton was punching the air and turning cartwheels. OK, the last bit was a lie. Cartwheels were beyond him, but the air was definitely being punched.

'I don't know how you've pulled this out of the bag,' Glen said, 'but I'm picturing you at the BAFTAs. Hell, this is Emmy stuff! Who do you think should play the character of Abigail? I've got Bill Nighy down as the father; he'd be perfect. I've got to hand it to you, Clay: you've done it. You really have. It was a long time in coming, but the wait was worth it. In the words of Hughie Green, I mean that most sincerely.'

'Hey, go easy on the sincerity; it's dangerous

stuff when you're not used to it. If you're not careful one of us will end up choking on it.'

'How long before you've finished the entire script?'

'Not sure. Another month perhaps.'

'Well, what are you doing wasting time talking to me? Get back to your laptop and write! Meanwhile, I'm going to start talking to people this end.'

'I thought you had a holiday to get on with?'

'That's tomorrow. As soon as you've got off the line I'm going to make some calls.'

'Um . . . would you mind if we waited until I've finished the script?'

'Are you mad? I'm so excited about this I could kiss you!'

'Oh, God, not one of your big wet kisses. Anything but that. But seriously, Glen, and tell me the truth, do you think we should hold back from putting my name on the script?'

'No. I think sufficient time has passed for us to cash in on your infamy. Now get on with the rest of it and I'll be in touch when I get back from Mauritius. You're going to be the Comeback Kid of all Comeback Kids! Have a good Christmas. By the way, how's that hotel shaping up?'

'It's fine,' Clayton replied. He hadn't told Glen that he'd moved in with Alice. He wanted certain things in his life to be private. Even from his agent.

He ended the call and stared out of the window at Alice's small courtyard garden. He should have been feeling euphoric. He had been only moments earlier. But the feeling had

344

passed. For the simple reason that, now that Glen was going to start pitching his script, he had to tell Alice what he'd done.

He rubbed his hands over his face, dragging the skin down roughly, à la Edvard Munch's *The Scream*. He felt a bit like having a damned good scream himself. And not a silent scream. Way down in his guts, he knew he'd messed up. He should have gained Alice's approval and consent weeks ago. He shouldn't have put it off. But in his heart of hearts he'd known all along that she would be horrified at what he'd done. She would see it as a betrayal, a betrayal of her trust. Hadn't she told him that he was the first person with whom she had shared her story? And what did he go and do? Yeah, that's right, pinch it with the full intention of selling her innermost secrets to the highest bidder.

By God, he was a class act!

But he was consistent, if nothing else. He would keep quiet a little longer, until after Christmas. A revelation like he had up his sleeve could well ruin Alice's Christmas and with a trickle of integrity still flowing through his system he didn't want to do that to her.

35

In the end Alice did invite Ronnetta and Bob for Christmas lunch and amazingly they accepted her invitation.

They came bearing gifts: two carrier bags clinking with bottles of beer, gin, tonic, vodka and Bailey's. Combined with what Alice already had and the bottle of deadly vintage brew George had brought with her, they had a dangerously well-stocked bar. In the fifty minutes since he and Ronnetta had arrived, Bob had applied himself with serious intent to what was available, and after Clayton had declined to drink any of George's brew, joking that he was unaccountably attached to his internal organs, Bob had taken up the challenge of a large glassful. Alice had a horrible feeling that it was his way of proving himself more of a man than Clayton. He'd just tossed back the contents of his glass and with his eyes watering and his voice rasping, he was gamely holding out his glass for a top up from George. Just like a real man would.

Five minutes later and a second glassful consumed, he was red in the face and as playful as a Labrador puppy. Jabbing Clayton on the shoulder with a meaty fist, he was now offering him advice on how to get in shape. 'No offence, Ralph, but I can see you've let your body go. You're not exactly honed, are you? More like boned — there's nothing of you!' He aimed

346

another jabbing fist at Clayton's shoulder. While Clayton smiled grimly back at Bob, Alice hoped the level of alcohol induced merriment Bob was displaying wouldn't go too far and turn the Labrador puppy into a spurned, snarling pit bull terrier.

She also hoped that she could keep up the subterfuge of calling Clayton by his alias. She had warned George to remember that he was Ralph and not Clayton, although if she was honest, Alice couldn't quite see the point in it. If their relationship was going to continue, Clayton would have to dispense with the deception at some stage.

'Mistletoe moment!'

Alice looked up from where she was laying the table for lunch with Ronnetta's help. Before she had a chance to react, Bob had her in his grasp and was dangling a sprig of mistletoe inches above her head. 'Gotcha!' he said with a wide grin. He then clamped his mouth over hers. When she felt his tongue slide into her mouth, she wriggled with horror-struck disgust. After she'd shaken him off and had mentally disinfected her mouth, she saw Clayton looking on with a tight expression of disbelief on his face.

'Aren't you going to kiss me, young man?' asked George with a roguish twinkle in her eye. Bob couldn't have looked more terrified. He backed away, almost knocking over the Christmas tree and threw the sprig of mistletoe into the fire.

Just as she always used to, George had

smartened herself up for the occasion. She was decked out in a tweedy dogtooth-check dress that Alice could have sworn she recognized from the old days. Perhaps it had fitted her better then; now it gaped at her scrawny neck and emphasized her small, desiccated body. Alice felt a pang of sadness, acknowledging just how frail the old woman really was.

★ ★ ★

By the time they were midway through lunch everyone seemed less tense. Or maybe it was just Alice who was feeling less tense.

Despite having consumed so much alcohol, Bob was at least behaving himself, and with plates refilled, wine glasses topped up, cracker jokes read out, paper hats worn, the conversation around the table was relaxed and friendly. George was mostly responsible for that, regaling them with amusing tales about the inhabitants of Stonebridge — the hill folk, as she referred to them. Alice's favourite story was the one about the farmer who, back in the seventies when wife-swapping was supposedly all the rage in certain circles, had got entirely the wrong end of the stick and had placed an advertisement in the local paper with the hope of swapping his wife for a tractor trailer. He was later seen in the newsagent's with two black eyes.

'So what sort of work is it you do down in London, Ralph?' Ronnetta asked.

'Oh, this and that,' Clayton replied evenly.

'This and that?' repeated Bob, nodding his

head like that irritating bulldog from the insurance advert on television. 'What's that supposed to mean?'

'It means I'm a lucky sod and can do as I please.'

'Loaded, are you? I might have guessed.' Bob stared at Alice accusingly, as if to say, so that's the reason you've hooked up with him instead of me.

'And what's your line of work, young man?' asked George. Alice had noticed that George hadn't once called Bob by his name. She doubted it was because the old lady couldn't remember it.

'He's a telephone engineer for BT,' Ronnetta said proudly.

George narrowed her eyes. 'I hope you're not the engineer for whom I waited in all day and who never came. Let me tell you, I wrote a very strongly worded letter to British Telecom that evening.'

'Not my area,' Bob said. 'My patch is north of here.' He downed his glass of Merlot in one long gulp, then belched. He thumped his chest. 'Pardon me,' he said, 'better out than in.'

As Ronnetta mildly admonished her son, Alice risked a glance in Clayton's direction. As their eyes met, the corners of his mouth lifted into the smallest of smiles.

★ ★ ★

They were onto the Christmas pudding course when the shaky balance that had so far been in place collapsed entirely.

Alice had just poured a dash of brandy over the pudding and reached for the matches, when Bob rose unsteadily from his seat and took the box out of her hands. 'Stand aside, Alice,' he said, 'this is a job for Superman.' He clumsily scraped a match along the side of the box, then tossed it vaguely in the direction of the pudding. When nothing happened, he reached for the bottle of brandy.

'Could he be any more stupid?' Alice heard Clayton mutter under his breath. And then, when Bob poured the remains of the brandy over the pudding and struck three matches against the box at once and threw them at the pudding, Clayton said, 'Ooh, I stand corrected.'

It all happened so fast. There was a loud *whoomph* followed by a ball of fire shooting high into the air. It made instant contact with the lampshade that was hanging directly above the table.

Clayton reacted first. With lightning speed, he smothered the Christmas pudding with a plate then grabbed the oven gloves Alice had left on the sideboard. He climbed onto his chair and wrapped his hands around the lampshade. In as much time as it had taken Bob to create it, the near-disaster was averted.

'Clayton Miller, you are my all-time hero!' George cheered with a beaming smile. 'And you, young man,' she added, turning her attention to Bob, 'are an idiot of the first order.'

'Don't you call my Bob an idiot!' Ronnetta responded indignantly. The look she gave George could have vaporized her.

Alice wasn't interested in the potential spat breaking out amongst the rest of her guests; she was more concerned with Clayton. He'd pulled off the scorched oven gloves and was shaking his hands and blowing on them. 'Clayton,' she said, 'are you all right?'

'I think so.' He blew on his fingers and winced.

'Come with me,' she said.

Out in the kitchen, she ran the cold tap and made him put his hands under the gushing water. She could smell the unmistakable tang of singed hair. 'How bad does it feel?' she asked.

'I'll be fine. I'm just attention seeking.'

'Keep your hands under the water,' she said, when he tried to move them.

'He's quite a guy, isn't he?'

'Who?'

'Yonder Romeo, your neighbourly paramour. I could almost be jealous.'

'Don't be.' She touched his cheek and kissed him.

'Mm . . . do that again; that's definitely making me feel better. Any chance we could lose the guests and go upstairs?'

'There's nothing I'd like more. But until I'm sure your hands are going to be all right, we're not moving from this tap. How do they feel now?'

'I can't feel them; they're numb.'

The sound of raised voices, followed by a loud exclamation and footsteps had them both turning. Bob was standing in the doorway.

351

'So let me get this straight,' Bob said, swaying slightly but doing his best to look directly at Clayton and focus on him. 'Your name isn't Ralph Shannon, is it? George called you Clayton Miller. And Alice called you Clayton as well. You're that bloke off the telly and in the papers, aren't you? I've read a ton about you. And not one word of it good. I thought there was something familiar about your untrustworthy mug the second I laid eyes on you.'

'Who'd have thought it,' muttered Clayton. 'The dumb-ass can read as well.'

Bob's expression darkened. He came over and squared up to Clayton. 'What did you call me?'

Clayton turned away from the tap, his hands dripping water down his front. 'I think you heard exactly what I said, Tinkerbell. Unless you're going to claim deafness as an additional disability to your already extensive list of flaws, the most apparent being your crippling stupidity.'

'Oh, a smart mouth? Well, we'll see how smart you are when I've finished with you. Outside. You and me. Let's get this sorted.'

Alice intervened. She switched off the tap that was still running and put a hand on Bob's forearm. 'Come on Bob, that's enough. You're both saying things you'll regret tomorrow.'

'I'm not going to regret anything I say,' Bob blustered, pushing out his enormous chest and towering over Clayton.

'Only because you have the attention span of a goldfish and won't be able to remember anything ten minutes from now,' Clayton retaliated.

Alice tried to look stern. 'OK, that's enough from the pair of you. Any more of this playground squabbling and I'll be forced to put the two of you in the naughty corner.'

Bob swung his head from Clayton to Alice. For a moment he seemed at a loss as to what to say. 'What's he got that I haven't? That's what I want to know. I mean, come on Alice, you and me, we have a history.' There was real bewilderment in his face. His shoulders had even sagged a little. He suddenly looked so pathetic standing there in his paper hat that had slipped to one side of his head. 'Oh, hang on,' he said, 'I forgot. He's loaded, isn't he?'

Seeing that Ronnetta was now standing in the doorway, Alice appealed to her with an anxious glance, hoping she would step in and save her son from embarrassing himself further. Or from doing something stupid.

Luckily Ronnetta took the hint. She stepped towards her son. 'Bob, let it go, love. Just accept there's no accounting for taste.' She turned to Alice. 'I think we should probably go, don't you?'

To Alice's great relief, there was no animosity in Ronnetta's voice.

'You don't have to,' Alice said.

'I think it's best if we do.' She glanced at Clayton with concern. 'I've got some bandages if you need them. Oh, and I think you ought to check on the old girl; she's fallen asleep at the table. The excitement must have been too much for her.'

36

It was another Christmas to remember.

Not quite up there with the worst one in living memory for Alice, but a serious contender all the same and bad enough to make her wish she had spent the day alone with Clayton. They would have had much more fun, just the two of them. But no, she had to go and ruin everything by thinking it would have been rude not to invite Ronnetta and Bob to join them for lunch. As a consequence, poor Clayton had burned his hands — thankfully not badly — and heaven only knew how she was going to face Bob again. There was also the worry that Clayton's identity would soon be common knowledge in the village. The second Bob set foot in the pub, he'd be telling everyone just who was staying at Dragonfly Cottage.

When she had finally surfaced from her snooze at the dining table, George had been mortified by her slip of the tongue in calling Clayton by his real name. 'I was so impressed with your quick thinking the words just slipped out,' she had admitted to him. 'I'm so sorry. I hope I haven't caused you any problems.' Alice had never encountered George in apologetic mode before and she had found it almost as unsettling as the old woman's dress that was so poignantly too large for her. Clayton had played down the potential consequences of people knowing who he was, even saying that it was going to come out sooner or later, so why not now? Alice had been taken aback by the effect this one small, casual remark of his had had on her. Until he had uttered those words, she hadn't dared acknowledge, not even to herself, the doubt she had been secretly harbouring, the worry that perhaps the reason Clayton had wanted to continue with the deception was because she didn't really matter that much to him. Very quietly in the back of her mind, where she stored all her uncertainties and insecurities, she had subconsciously logged in this new doubt and it had got on with the job of steadily multiplying itself into the certainty that when it was time for Clayton to return to London, he would do so without a backwards glance in her direction and she would be merely chalked up as a pleasant and distracting fling, never to be thought of again. But as a result of this exchange with George, the doubt had been squashed in an instant and Alice's confidence had returned.

She had added her voice to reassuring George that no harm had been done in revealing Clayton's real identity. 'Didn't I make the same slip myself?' she had said to the old woman. 'It was a heat of the moment thing.'

'But you only did it because I'd opened my great big mouth,' George had responded. 'I hope this isn't the first sign of me turning into a dotty old dear. You must shoot me, Alice, if that's the case.' She had insisted then that it was time for her to go home. 'No, no,' she had said when Alice had tried to dissuade her, 'you two don't need a third party here playing gooseberry. I can see you're itching to be alone. Clayton's got that look in his eye but I don't know how much use he'll be to you Alice, what with those bandages on his hands.' She had then whispered something to Clayton in a way that Alice could only describe as collusive; it was as if they both knew something she didn't.

Now, as she sprawled on the sofa with Clayton whilst trying to decide what to watch on the television, she was intrigued to know what it was George had said to him. 'I feel it only fair to warn you,' she said, 'secrets are all very well when they're *my* secrets, but I draw the line at others withholding anything from me.'

Clayton looked up from the rumpled copy of the bumper Christmas edition of the *Radio Times* he was reading. 'Secrets?' he said. 'What makes you say that?'

She assumed a mock-serious expression. 'I'm just wondering what it is that you're keeping from me.'

'Why do you think I'm keeping anything from you? Why would I do that?' He was frowning now. Which made it harder for her to keep a straight face.

'You can't fool me, Clayton,' she said. 'I know there's something. You've got guilty as charged written all over you.'

'I have?'

'I can hear it in your voice, too. Better just to come clean and tell me what it is. You know you'll feel better for making a full confession.'

He slowly put aside the *Radio Times*. She

noticed that the frown on his face had deepened. He suddenly seemed tense. He wasn't looking at her either. Instead, he was concentrating hard on his left hand, smoothing out a wrinkle in the crêpe bandage she'd applied for him. The change in him caused a small alarm bell to start ringing inside her head. Something was wrong. What had she unwittingly stumbled upon? Whatever it was, she didn't want to hear it. If it was bad news, as she was sure it was, judging from the dramatic transformation in him, she didn't want him to share it with her. Having salvaged what was left of the day, she didn't want anything to spoil it. She wanted everything to be as it was this morning when they'd woken up and merrily wished each other a Happy Christmas. He had surprised her with a present — a heavenly Nicole Farhi cardigan that he'd bought online — and then they had made love. Afterwards they had shared a bath together and then she had given him the first of the presents she had bought for him, a leatherbound notebook. It was the best Christmas morning she had ever experienced. There had been nothing whatsoever in his manner to suggest that he had been hiding something from her. Something that was now making him unable to look her in the eye.

'What is it, Clayton?' she asked, dispensing with her childish reaction of not wanting to hear anything bad. 'Why do you look so serious?'

He swallowed. 'Because you're right. I do feel guilty. I knew it was wrong but I couldn't stop myself. I've done something you're not going to like.' He still wasn't looking at her.

'You're leaving? Is that it? You've decided to go back to London?'

He shook his head.

Right now there didn't seem anything worse than him leaving, so with the worst of her anxieties dealt with, she said more confidently, 'What then?'

'I've . . . I've been doing something behind your back,' he said. 'Something for which I should have asked your permission. You're going to be furious with me. And I can't say I blame you.'

She didn't have a clue what he was talking about, but trying for a note of levity, she said, 'You haven't been carrying on with George behind my back, have you?'

For the first time he looked at her. 'If only that was all I had done.' His gaze faltered and he looked down and fiddled with his bandages again. 'What made you suspect I was hiding something from you? Did you hear me talking on the phone to Glen?'

'Glen? What's he got to do with it?'

Leaving her question unanswered, he stood up. 'I think the best thing is for me to show you what I've done. Then you can decide for yourself just how morally bankrupt I am.'

★　★　★

While he waited for the hangman's noose to be placed around his neck, Clayton left Alice on her own with his laptop. He stood outside by the back door, as if punishing himself by being in the

358

freezing cold. He had never dreaded a response to something he'd written as much as he did now. The harshest and bitterest critics could not have instilled more fear in him than Alice's impending condemnation. The chance was a slim one, but he hung onto it all the same; he had to hope that Alice cared for him sufficiently to forgive him.

When he could no longer bear the cold, he went back inside the house. He crept quietly through the kitchen towards the sitting room. He hovered anxiously outside the door, then went in to hear his fate.

She looked up from the laptop. 'You were right,' she said, 'you are morally bankrupt. How could you do this to me? How could you have thought this was a good thing to do?'

'I don't choose what to write,' he said. 'It chooses me.'

'That's bullshit. You stole this. You stole my life story. How do you think that makes me feel?'

'Put yourself in my shoes. I haven't been able to write in over three years, then out of the blue I meet you and you banish the fear that had crippled me for so long.' He went and knelt on the floor in front of her. 'Alice, you have to believe me; if I could have stopped myself from grabbing hold of the lifeline you'd thrown me, I would have. But I couldn't. OK, I was motivated by narcissism and the desperate need to write again, to feel I could still cut it. Call that rampant self-absorption if you want, but after the crap I'd gone through with Bazza and Stacey, life suddenly felt good again. Better than good.

So much better. These last few weeks have been the best I've known in years. And that's all down to you.'

She pushed the laptop at him. 'A fine speech from a fine writer. But it won't do. You lied. You betrayed me. With every word you've written, you've betrayed me. And I'll never forgive you for that. Never.'

'Please don't say that. Think about it.'

'I already have. Did George know about this? Was she in on it? Was that why she whispered to you earlier when she was leaving?'

'George knows nothing about it. She was — ' he broke off. In the circumstances, he could hardly tell Alice what George had whispered to him, that she had been congratulating herself on knowing that he and Alice would be good together. 'She was merely saying goodbye in her own inimitable fashion,' he said.

'Well, in my own inimitable fashion I'm saying goodbye to you. I never want to see you again. I want you out of my house.'

'I understand that you're angry. But please, Alice, take a moment to consider what I've said.'

'I've done all the considering I'm ever going to do. You clearly don't understand the first thing about me. If you did, you wouldn't have done this. If you'd ever really cared about me or my feelings, you wouldn't have done it.'

'I do care about you. More than you'll ever know.'

'Then prove it to me. If you delete what's on your laptop, you can stay. But if you don't delete it, you have to leave. The choice is yours.'

He swallowed. 'That's not fair.'

'Fair? You want to talk fair? How about we discuss how you continually cross-examined me about my family just so that you could make sure you got the details right for your script? Does that sound fair to you? Does it sound fair that I opened my heart and soul to you, imagining for one stupid moment you were interested because you cared about me? Does it sound fair to you that I kept my promise not to tell anyone who you were, while all the time you were preparing to tell the world the most intimate details of my life? My God, I've done some stupid things in my time, but thinking that we had something special going on between us was the dumbest thing I ever did.' She shook her head. 'I believed in you, Clayton. I think that's what hurts the most.'

37

'You know who that is, don't you?'

Clayton casually tipped his head to see whom Glen was referring to. It was the third time during their lunch that his attention had been drawn to the occupants of another table in the smart restaurant which, according to Glen, was now his favourite watering hole in Soho. Although at the laughable price being charged for a bottle of lightly carbonated water, a glass of it was the last thing any sensible person would consider drinking here. Presumably it was from the foothills of the Andes and sanctified by the Vatican.

'Got me again, Glen,' he said. 'Who am I supposed to have spotted this time?'

'It's one of the Cheeky Girls.'

'You're kidding me? A Cheeky Girl here? Why didn't you say? Point her out to me.'

Glen rolled his eyes. 'Facetiousness is not an attractive trait, Clay.'

'Nor is fawning over a half-starved Eastern European bird.'

'You've got to admit she is attractive. I mean, look at those legs. They go all the way up.'

'Eyes on me, Glen. Come on, concentrate. Keep the focus. You can do it.'

'You know what your trouble is?'

'Surprise me.'

'You've been out of civilized society for too long.'

'Wrong, my friend. I've been out of *uncivilized* society and am all the better for it. You should give it a try.'

'Whatever. Oh, and over there, two o'clock; it's that girl from Babe-a-Rama.'

'Babe-a-Rama? Don't tell me; a porn site you visit on a regular basis?'

'Oh, please, don't you know anything? Babe-a-Rama's the latest red-hot girl band and she's just started dating a rap star from the States. You know the guy, the one with all the gold teeth.'

'Rapping the hippety-hop is hardly my thing, Glen. And it shouldn't be yours either; you're way too old.'

Glen tore off a piece of focaccia bread and dipped it into a ceramic pot of olive oil; the oil was a rich golden colour and reminded Clayton of that old Castrol motor oil advert back in the seventies. The one with the spanner. Or was it later than the seventies? He tried to remember what music had been used for the advertisement. It had been something big and stirring. Something noble and magnificent that made you want to rush out and do the decent thing and pamper your car by changing its engine oil.

Noble and magnificent — those were two words he couldn't apply to himself. Two and a half months had passed since he had left Derbyshire — two and a half months since he had last seen Alice. Their parting had not been a theatrical, tearful, door-slamming event, which had made it seem so very much worse. After Alice had finished saying exactly how she felt about him, she had calmly explained that she was going to spend the night with George, leaving him at Dragonfly Cottage on his own. 'When I return tomorrow, I want you gone,' she had said. 'Along with every sign that you were ever here.'

He couldn't blame her for reacting in the way she had. He had treated her appallingly. He had done everything she had accused him of. And a whole lot more. Oh, so much more. The worst was yet to come, he was sure of it.

At eight o'clock on Boxing Day morning, he had found a taxi firm willing to take him to the station and after a two-hour wait on a freezing cold platform, he had caught the only train to London that day. Never had London appeared more bleak or depressing. Nor had his house ever felt less inviting. It had smelled stale and slightly damp and had been as cold as a morgue — the heating hadn't been switched on in months — and there was nothing to eat. It had been a stark reminder of his arrival at Cuckoo House. He had trudged wearily to the local shop in the hope that he would find it open. It was and he had gratefully scored himself some supplies. Mrs Patel had looked at him as if he had three heads when she saw him. 'You're back, then,' she'd said, while a hugely overweight, doughy-faced adolescent tapped in the price of a packet of Jaffa Cakes on the cash register. Bar codes were still a thing of the future for the Patels. In front of the till there had been a coffee mug sporting the princes William and Harry. A piece of paper next to it bore the words: STAFF

TIPS FOR XMAS. Yeah, Clayton had thought as he handed over his money to the fat kid, I'll give you a tip, sunshine: lose some weight! And here's another, don't ever abbreviate the word Christmas in my presence again. Xmas was a loathsome word in Clayton's opinion and he had always had an aversion to it.

'Yes,' he'd pointedly replied to Mrs Patel's undeniable statement of fact. 'I'm back. Happy Christmas.'

She had stared at him as though he'd uttered some kind of foul obscenity while at the same time exposing himself. But what was one more filthy disapproving look when he'd been on the receiving end of enough to be almost inured to them?

Alice's parting look would stay with him for a long time yet. He had felt utterly shamed by the intense disappointment in her face. Her expression had cut him to the quick, knowing that he had wilfully hurt the one person he had come to think actually meant something to him.

But the bottom line was, he clearly hadn't cared enough about her. Had his feelings been strong enough, he would have hit the delete button on his laptop, just as she had requested. But she had given him an impossible task, like asking a mother which of her two children she would save if they were both drowning. How could she have expected him to choose between her or resurrecting his writing career, the one thing that he had craved above all else these last few miserable years? Being able to write again had been akin to a blind man suddenly having his sight restored. Had she really expected him to be capable of throwing that away?

He had considered writing a letter of apology and justification to Alice, but had decided against it when he recalled the letters her father had sent her and which she had never read. Instead he had tried to convince himself that it was Alice who was in the wrong, that she had overreacted and like all reactionaries who go off at the deep end, she needed time to cool down and maybe even come to her senses. OK, that was pushing it, he knew, but a desperate man will think anything he wants to believe in the hope it will save him.

He had even kidded himself that if Alice watched *The Queen of New Beginnings* when it was shown on television, it would help her realize that what he'd written wasn't exploitative. Those who had been involved in the production process were all saying the same thing — that he had written with great sensitivity, not just when it came to Alice's character — or rather, Abigail's character — but in regard to all the other characters who had been a part of her childhood. Well, all of them except for Rufus, aka Lucius. That would have been pushing the bounds of disbelief. Everybody agreed that the two stars of the script were Abigail and her father. Clayton was pleased about that, not only because their relationship was pivotal to the story, but because he had genuinely wanted Alice to be happy with what he'd written and portraying her father, who he'd renamed as Ralph, in an empathetic light had been crucial to gaining her approval.

Once he'd arrived back in London, with no wish to be out and about, he had got his head down and finished the script. He had worked day and night and had it done within a fortnight. Not only had Glen been right about him no longer being of interest to anyone in Tabloid La-La Land, but true to his word, Glen had found a production company eager to take on his script. Things had moved fast and before he knew it, he was on set for most of the filming — poking his oar in as Glen called his input. The bulk of the filming had been done in North Yorkshire. A location scout had found the perfect house double for Cuckoo House — a Gothic pile called Long View on a windswept moor.

The scene that he was most proud of was the one when Alice joins her father in his car and he tries to make her understand the extent of Rufus's manipulative duplicity. Bill Nighy had agreed to take on the part of Bruce Barrett — miraculously he'd been available at such short notice — and he had played the role and that particular scene brilliantly, capturing every eccentric and affectionate nuance of the character. Clayton had felt the backs of his eyes prickle at the end of the scene. He wasn't the only one to be moved. A subdued hush had fallen on the set and then, as if embarrassed, everyone had begun talking at once.

An unknown twenty-two-year-old actress called Anna Burns had been chosen to play Alice as a teenager, and for when she was a young child, a girl who bore an uncanny resemblance to Anna was chosen. While she was terrific when she was being filmed, the moment the camera was off her, she morphed into a precocious bratlet with delusions of starlet grandeur, demanding organic sushi and Jelly Babies with the yellow ones removed. Apparently they brought her bad luck. Everyone had breathed a huge sigh of relief when Abigail's early years had been filmed and they could wave goodbye to the little monster. The general consensus was that they had all been living in fear that one of them would take the girl by the neck and squeeze very hard, or at least force her to eat her own weight in yellow Jelly Babies.

Whilst Clayton liked to think the green light had been given to his script because it was a work of pure genius and therefore forgiveness had been a natural consequence, he had to accept that a far more important factor had been at work in his being welcomed back into the fold.

Two factors to be precise: Bazza and Stacey.

As Glen had assured him, the public can be replied upon to be fickle, but the merry band of souls who make up the country's great unbiased press can also be just as fickle. And so it came to pass that the sun began to go down on the Golden Couple. Their mistake, as Glen pointed out to Clayton, was that like so many people before them they had assumed their reign was unassailable. Their PR people wildly miscalculated the public's appetite for Saint Bazza and Mother Stacey when they let loose a press release announcing that Stacey had just signed a contract to write a book entitled *How to Forgive and Forget*. It had major stinker written all over it. The savagely barbed Christy Rickshaw at the *Mirror* — who had recently had yet another of her novels rejected by every publisher in London — led the attack. Whilst the venting of her spleen might have been intended for those incompetent publishers who didn't know talent when it was right under their noses, Stacey was the one who copped the searingly vicious invective:

> When will it ever end, this obsession amongst publishers to print anything a D-rated celebrity has had ghosted for them? Who gives a stuff for what a nobody like Stacey Cook thinks? And who, by the way, is this woman? Other than being Barry Osbourne's latest squeeze? Okay, she lost a baby, but millions of women have had a miscarriage. What makes her so special?

Her dander up, Ms Rickshaw went on to ask whether she was the only one to wonder if Stacey might have lost the baby anyway? That, maybe, Clayton Miller had had nothing to do with bringing on her miscarriage.

The next day a piece appeared in the *Mail* picking up on the theme.

> Am I alone in reaching for a sick bag whenever I hear the names Barry Osbourne and Stacey Cook mentioned? If I have to stomach another good cause or publicity stunt that they've involved themselves with, I swear I will not be responsible for my actions.

And let's not beat about the bush: Barry Osbourne used to be defined by his talent as one of our best writers; now he's defined by his participation in a showbiz relationship that displays all the gravitas of a *High School Musical* plot. Could he have reduced himself to anything more woeful or feeble?

From then on the tide turned and Glen suggested the time was right for Clayton to surface, to tell his side of the story. 'Bazza and Stacey's downfall ensures your reinstatement,' Glen promised him. Clayton agreed that perhaps he could now start to show his face around town, but on the strict understanding that no PR company was involved. 'There's to be zero spin,' he told Glen.

'Tell it as it is,' Glen said, 'I hear you.'

Clayton doubted Glen ever heard anything other than the sound of money dropping through his letterbox.

'It'll give us a brilliant hook for *The Queen of New Beginnings*,' Glen went on.

'It needs a hook?'

'Don't be naive.'

Three days later, Glen set Clayton up with a journalist from the *Sunday Times* and the paper ran the interview the following Sunday. A few days later Glen received a call for Clayton to appear on the Jonathan Ross show. Glen was delighted. 'Couldn't be a better interview for you to do,' he crowed. 'Two much-maligned characters on the screen at the same time. It'll be TV magic!'

He didn't know about magic, but Clayton had given it his best shot in getting across his side of the story — how he'd tried to apologize to Stacey and Barry and how it had all gone hopelessly wrong. When he admitted how shocked he'd been at the size of the heads as they'd emerged from the truck, expecting them to be cute and adorable and no bigger than a garden gnome, whereas they'd proved to be practically Tyrannosaurus in scale, the audience had laughed and he'd known then that the worst was over.

Over for that particular cock-up maybe. Given his track record, he was an odds-on favourite for another cock-up before too long. But then as he'd always believed, one crisis at a time.

'Are you listening to a word I'm saying, or would I be better off trying my luck on the Cheeky Girl's table?'

Snapping to, Clayton said, 'Knowing her name might stand you in better stead.'

'Really? I've never bothered with names before.'

To say that Glen treated women as sex objects was overstating his commitment.

'So what was I missing? What pearls of wisdom were you offering up?'

'I was paying you a compliment, if you must know.'

'Good God! I missed the event of the century. Re-run it for me.'

'It wasn't much. Just that I knew you'd come good for me in the end.'

'I expect it sounded better first time round.'

371

'Ungrateful sod. I'm baring my heart and soul here and you're making fun of me.'

Agents, thought Clayton. Sensitive souls. Cut them and unbelievably they bled just like a normal human being. Amazing.

38

'Aaah . . . Oooh . . . Yes . . . do that again . . . '

'Sorry, Alice, could we give that another go? Only you really didn't sound like you were enjoying it.'

That's because I'm not, Alice thought crossly. She adjusted her headphones, folded her arms in front of her and stared back at the group of people the other side of the glass. They all looked about fourteen years old, making her feel about a hundred and ten. A man-child was speaking into her ear. 'Remember what we said, Alice: lots of sex. Really bring it home. You're being hit on by a sex god. You're powerless against him. But you're loving it. This is the most fun you've ever had in the bathroom. What's more, you're trying to convince the punters this is the most fun *they'll* ever have in a bathroom. We're selling them the dream. The fantasy. Life will never be the same again for them after this. I know it's a big ask, but can you do that?'

Alice nodded. She'd give him a big ask in a moment. Right up his backside! 'Yes,' she said, ever the professional, 'let's give it another go, shall we?'

Sex to sell a toiler cleaner? Where would it all end? What she couldn't understand was why Johnny Phoenix had agreed to voice-over the product. He certainly didn't need the money — his career was going from strength to strength. Having made a name for himself on the small screen he was now wooing them in Hollywood, for pity's sake. Was it simply too much of a temptation for him to turn down the opportunity to say, 'I don't only go round the bend, but I reach right under the rim . . . '? Heaven only knew how much he was being paid to front the campaign in its bid to challenge the other market leaders when it came to limescale and stains of an unmentionable nature. Well, good luck to him. And good luck to her too; she was being paid more money today than she had received in a long while for a job. Now, if she could just get into character — that of a toilet — and pretend she was enjoying the experience of Johnny Phoenix tackling her stubborn build-up in one easy squirt, she would be home and dry.

The hours dragged by, until mercifully the session was over and she was putting on her coat to leave. It had been a tiring job and she was eager to get away. In her experience it was always a mistake to have too many bright young things from the ad agency in the studio during recording; they all felt compelled and uniquely qualified to have their say on proceedings. Mostly because each and every one of them hoped to make their mark and couldn't bear the thought of anyone else coming up with a better idea and stealing a march on them. She wondered how the earlier studio session with Johnny Phoenix had gone. Had they been as inclined to interrupt and direct him as they had with her? Or had his star status been sufficient to ensure they'd kept their traps shut?

Hazel had been overjoyed to nail this job for Alice. 'It'll become a series of ads, no doubt about it,' she had enthused. 'You and Johnny will be like the Nescafé couple back in the eighties. Or was it Maxwell House? No matter, what's important is that this could be the beginning of something big for you, Alice.'

Alice had heard it all before. What's more, she had believed it all before. Every single word. Now she didn't. She didn't believe a word anyone said to her. Clayton had seen to that. He had robbed her of the belief that there would always be something better around the next corner. Once that was taken away from a person, what was left? Only the resounding conviction that life was pretty shitty. So how apt was it that she was providing the voice for a talking toilet about to be seduced by a squeeze of pungent green liquid? What next for her? What further lows could she achieve? Plenty, she was sure of it. The world was her oyster when it came to screw-ups. There was no one to touch her for it. She was too trusting, that was her trouble. Wasn't that why she had spent so many years forcing herself not to get close to another person? All those failed relationships because she refused to trust anyone. And look what happened when she did lower her guard! Was she just a bad picker, or were all men the same?

She had read several articles in the newspapers about Clayton, including an interview in the *Sunday Times* in which he appeared to be at his most candid. Yeah right; she could tell them a thing or two about his candidness.

It was Bob who had brought the first of the articles to Alice's attention. Alice had told Ronnetta everything, about Clayton stealing her childhood to write a script, and naturally, Ronnetta had kept Bob informed. As to be expected, Bob had not wasted any time in voicing his opinion, that he had known straight away that Clayton was a poncey-arsed shyster. He'd been all for taking Clayton apart by telling the local newspaper what he had done to her, but Alice had made him promise he wouldn't. 'I couldn't take the shame of everyone here knowing what a fool I've been,' she had explained to him. To her relief, Bob had respected her wishes and backed off. He'd offered to take her out several times, 'just to take her mind off things' and now it had become a regular thing; every Friday evening he took her for a curry. 'I know you don't fancy me,' he said the last time they were dining at the Bombay Mix. 'Not now, but give it time and who knows, you might just change your mind. You've got to admit, I'm not a bad-looking bloke. It's not as if I've got a face on me like a red arse of one of them baboons. And I'd always be straight with you. Not like some folk I could mention. What did you ever see in him, Alice?'

Good question. What had she seen in Clayton? It was hard now to remember. Had it been nothing more than getting caught up in the heat of what could only be described as a very strange moment?

George had been annoyingly bullish on the subject. If anything, she had taken Clayton's side. 'All I'm saying is that the man should have been given the opportunity to explain himself fully,' she had said to Alice.

'There was nothing he could say to explain or justify his actions,' Alice had retorted. 'He conned me.'

'And you can't think of a single good reason why he didn't tell you what he was doing?'

Without answering her, Alice had said, 'George, he wrote about you as well.'

'I should hope so. And I hope he wrote about me warts and all. I'd hate to think he sanitized me into an insipid old dear.'

'He certainly didn't sanitize you. He made you appear very eccentric. Positively off your trolley.'

'Excellent! I think Eileen Atkins would play me rather well, don't you?'

'Forget about Eileen Atkins!' Alice had said, exasperated. 'It's not excellent what he did. It's awful. It's an infringement of our rights. He came here and in the face of our good will he exploited us.'

'Really? You honestly think that?'

'What would you call it?'

'I think he got drawn into a situation and found himself a changed man as a result. A happier man. You were mostly responsible for that. You enabled him to write again. Aren't you just a little bit flattered and proud that you were responsible for that and that he thought your childhood worth writing about?'

'He should have asked for my permission.'

'And you would have refused it. He couldn't take that risk. Any fool can see that.'

'You're saying I'm a fool?'

'Unquestionably so.'

Always nice to know where one stands, Alice thought now as she stepped out onto the street.

Soho: it was a world away from her life in Stonebridge. But not so very far from Clayton, she supposed. How easy it would be to call him on her mobile and suggest they meet for a drink and a chat. Would he come? Would she manage to be civil? After two and a half months, would she be able to refrain from telling him exactly what she thought of him?

Not a chance. And if she couldn't take him to task, what else would they talk about? Finished that script yet . . . had it commissioned . . . is my life about to be trivialized in the name of comedic drama?

Comedic drama. That was a laugh. Or rather it wasn't. She could see nothing remotely funny in what Clayton had written. It was pitiable and catastrophic from start to finish. Just as their all-too-brief relationship had been.

Why, she wondered, did happiness have to be so fleeting? And fragile. One little knock and it shattered and was gone. Why, when a relationship ended, could the happiness one had previously experienced not remain? After all, the past couldn't be changed. What she had experienced with Clayton had actually happened, so why couldn't she hang onto those precious good memories? Why could she no longer recall how happy she had been with him?

Because her happiness had been based on a falsehood. It hadn't happened the way she thought it had. It had all been a lie. Clayton had deceived her into being happy. And that was unforgivable.

A man in a suit with a rucksack slung over his shoulder barged rudely past her, waking her up to the fact that she had been drifting aimlessly. It was almost six thirty and the streets were heaving with people intent on their journey home. She ought to be heading towards the underground herself, then onto Euston for her train home, but she couldn't bring herself to join the mass of commuters yet. She stood for a moment to check out the window of a shop selling vintage clothes. She spied an interesting black lacy dress, and thinking about the money she would receive for today's work, she put a hand to the door to go inside.

'Alice? Is that you?'

She spun round at the sound of the voice. '*James!*' she exclaimed, unable to conceal her surprise.

'Well, of all the gin joints,' he said with a smile. 'What brings you here?'

'I've been in a studio all day recording an advert for the telly. With Johnny Phoenix,' she added, mustering some professional pride and stretching the truth accordingly. So what if she hadn't set eyes on the man himself? James wasn't to know that.

'Wow!' he said. 'Good for you. Hey, you don't fancy a drink do you?'

Why not? she thought.

There were no tables free, so they grabbed the last two stools at the crowded bar. The place was packed, and with its wood-panelled interior and French-style aproned waiters, it also had the feel of being extremely expensive. But that was OK because Alice had no intention of paying. This one was down to James. She reckoned he owed her.

With two glasses of wine in front of them, along with a selection of olives and macadamia nuts, she said, 'So what have you been up to since we last met? Finished another book? I miss Matilda.'

He pushed a hand through his dangling fringe. A gesture that reminded her all too uncomfortably of Rufus. 'I miss you reading Matilda,' he said, 'and if I'm honest, just between you and me, the new voice isn't half as good as you.'

'I'm delighted to hear it,' she said. 'Why didn't you tell me yourself that I was being dropped in favour of a big name?'

Another rueful push of his hand through his hair. 'God, Alice, I was all set to, but I lost my nerve. I'm sorry. But it sounds like you're going gangbusters. Working with Johnny Phoenix, no less. What's he like? As irresistible as just about every woman I know thinks he is?'

'He's OK, if you like that kind of man,' she lied easily. Changing the subject, she said, 'Tell me more about Matilda. What's her latest adventure?'

He smiled. 'If I tell you something, do you

380

promise not to tell anyone?'

'Of course.'

'I've just signed a contract for a TV adaptation to be made of the first book in the series. It'll go out next Christmas. A primetime slot on Boxing Day. If it goes well, others could follow.'

'Congratulations.'

'Thank you. I still can't quite believe it. What's more, my agent found me a brilliant production company. They've worked on some great projects in the past. Right now they're putting the finishing touches to Clayton Miller's new drama. Do you remember all that hoo-ha when he disappeared last year? Well, it transpires he was holed up somewhere in the frozen north working on a completely new project. The word is, this is his best work yet. A change of direction, too.'

'Is that so?' Alice said as calmly as she could. 'Any idea what it's about?'

'All I know is that it's called *The Queen of New Beginnings*. Good title, don't you think?'

39

There was only one person Alice could talk to with regards to what she had just learned and that was George. George was the only person who knew the whole story. The silly old woman was also in need of a reality check and Alice was in the perfect frame of mind to give it to her. All that talk about Eileen Atkins playing her. What rubbish! What vanity! What self-inflated nonsense! And who would have thought that George, of all people, could be seduced by the thought of fifteen minutes of television fame? Unbelievable. Well, she wouldn't be so cock-a-hoop when she saw herself on the screen.

She parked behind George's Morris Minor and went round to the back door. She didn't bother knocking or ringing the bell. She was in no mood for social niceties. Ever since she had arrived home from London last night, she had had a foul temper on her.

There was no sign of George in the kitchen. Standing guard over a couple of hens who were pecking optimistically at the hearth rug, Percy eyeballed Alice with ferocious hostility. He thrust out his chest and pulled himself up to his full height. 'Oh, put a sock in it, Percy,' she said, 'I'm not in the mood.'

She called out to George. 'George, it's me, Alice.'

No reply.

'George?' she tried again, now moving beyond the kitchen. In the hallway she poked her head round several doors. Nothing. Only the sound of a grandfather clock ticking. Deciding George was either upstairs or in the garden, Alice climbed the stairs to rule out the first possibility. Taking care on the threadbare stair runner that was dangerously loose in places, she looked back the way she had come and saw Percy a few steps behind her. He was acting his socks off, giving her the kind of manic stare Jack Nicholson had won awards for. 'You missed your calling, Percy,' she muttered. 'You should have gone to drama school.'

He cocked his head, giving her yet more attitude, then hopped up onto the next step, which had the effect of propelling her towards the landing. He continued after her. 'George,' she called out. 'It's me, Alice.'

Still no reply. Perhaps she was in the garden, Alice decided. Percy was now on the landing with her. Still eyeballing her with plenty of attitude, he came right up close and pecked at one of her shoes. She took a step back. He advanced and pecked again. Another step. Another peck. Their two-step continued until he had manoeuvred her along the landing and had her jammed up against a door that was half open. 'Am I being daft, or are you trying to tell me something, Percy?' she said.

He ignored the question with a baleful look and strutted past her into what was George's bedroom. The most obvious thing to do seemed to be to follow him.

The room was in semi-darkness, the curtains drawn. But not so dark that Alice couldn't make out the shape of a body on the floor by the side of the bed. She rushed forward and dropped to her knees. 'George!' she cried out. Lying on her back, her head turned to one side, her mouth open at an unnatural angle, the old lady looked like a small, discarded doll dressed in oversized pyjamas. Her eyes were wide open and were darting over Alice's face as if trying to take it in. There was fear in her eyes. Relief too. And then tears. Huge tears spilled over and rolled down her crumpled cheeks.

'It's all right,' Alice said, choking back her own tears. 'Everything's going to be all right. You're not to worry.' She grabbed the eiderdown off the bed, covered George with it to keep her warm, then took out her mobile. She tried to stay calm, tried not to shake. She spoke slowly and clearly to the woman at the other end of the line, giving precise directions on how to find Well House and when that was done, she went over to the window and yanked back the curtains. Daylight flooded in. When she looked back at George, the old lady had screwed up her eyes.

'I'm sorry,' Alice said, 'is it too bright for you?'

George didn't answer.

Percy stared reproachfully at Alice as if to say, 'What the hell do you think?'

★ ★ ★

The doctor explained things to Alice with brutal detachment. George had had a stroke. A massive

384

stroke. There was no question of her going home. Hospital was where she would be staying for the foreseeable future. 'It's possible that she might regain some movement,' he said, 'maybe even some speech, but right now, given her age and frailty, I think that's unlikely. In all honesty, the end will probably come sooner rather than later.'

Alice could have cheerfully pushed a knife between his ribs. How dare he dismiss George so offhandedly. Didn't he know what an incredible woman George had been? What a tour de force she had been all her life? How dare this young whippersnapper, barely out of medical school, pronounce her life over?

'She can still see, hear and feel, can't she?' Alice said pointedly.

'To a degree, yes,' the doctor said.

'Well then, let's not write her off just yet, shall we?'

'I understand your desire to hope for the best, but the reality is your aunt is gravely ill and I think it only right to prepare you for the worst.'

'Thank you for your concern. May I see her now?'

'Visiting hours are — '

Alice quelled him with a look that Percy would have been proud of.

'All right. But not for long.'

★　★　★

The ward smelled of institutional cleaning fluid and the lingering and unappetizing odour of what had been served for lunch several hours earlier, or so Alice presumed. Maybe the ward always smelled of canteen food.

With the curtain drawn around them, Alice sat by the side of the bed, on the right side so George could see her. She held the old lady's hand. 'I go down to London for a day,' she said softly so as not to disturb the other patients, 'and look what happens while my back is turned. You really can't be trusted, can you?'

George stared at Alice, pale and glassy-eyed.

Alice swallowed back the painful lump in her throat. She couldn't bear to see George so debilitated. She dabbed at the old woman's distorted mouth, wiped away a small amount of dribble. 'We need to devise some form of communication,' she said. 'One blink is yes. Two blinks, no. Can you manage that?'

George blinked.

'Good.' Alice fought against the constriction in her throat, determined to maintain an air of hopeful optimism. 'I'm going to help you get well, George,' she said. 'Together we'll soon have you up and about.'

George blinked twice.

'Wrong answer,' Alice said. Her chest tightened.

George blinked once.

'You think it's the right answer?'

Another single blink.

'You're just going to give up?'

One blink.

George's eyes slowly fluttered as if alternating between yes and no and then stayed shut.

Alice gently squeezed her hand. There was no response. But then there wouldn't be. Just as the doctor had explained. She dabbed at George's mouth once more. A swish of movement had her turning round. A nurse, about the same age as Alice, appeared in the gap in the curtain. 'I think your aunt needs to sleep now. And don't worry, she'll be in safe hands here with us.' The girl was softly spoken and had a gentle manner about her. Alice felt inclined to believe her.

'You'll call me if there's any change, won't you?' she said, reluctantly rising from the chair and finding it hard to let go of George's gnarled and callused old hand.

'Of course.'

★ ★ ★

Alice drove home tired and depressed. Poor George. How long had she been lying on the floor of her bedroom alone and terrified? If only Percy could talk. She almost smiled at the thought of Percy, who was clearly as smart a rooster that had ever lived. If only he'd been able to channel his intelligence into using a phone and calling for an ambulance. George would worry about Percy and his harem; Alice knew that she would have to take on their care herself. In the short term it wouldn't be a problem, but what if the doctor was right and George was never going to get better and return home?

In her heart, Alice knew that this was the reality of the situation: unless a miracle happened, George would never return home to

Well House. Her days as an independent woman were over. No wonder she had communicated to Alice that she wanted to give up. Who wouldn't, in her shoes?

The word 'reality' resonated inside Alice's head. It had cropped up several times today. The doctor had used it to describe the severity of George's situation, as had Alice in her thoughts when she had gone to see George that morning and had been all steamed up in her desire to ram home what James had shared with her. 'See!' she had wanted to say to George, 'this is no longer a joke. This is really going to happen. The reality is we're going to be portrayed on national television as laughing stocks!'

Now none of that seemed important. Let Clayton Miller have his great comeback moment. So what if it was at the expense of anyone else? Yes, she could try to take out an injunction, or whatever it was called, to stop him going ahead with what he'd written, but there was always the danger that that would attract even more attention to herself. The one thing she had to hang on to was that at least he'd had the decency to change all the names in his script and its setting. She had to hope that if she kept her mouth shut, no one would ever know that it was her family he had written about.

But there were others involved; others who would know as clearly as day followed night that they had been written about.

Rufus and Natasha.

And not forgetting Isabel.

What if they saw the programme and tracked

Alice down? What if they started screaming defamation of character? What if they wanted to sue Clayton? She couldn't imagine Rufus wanting anything less than revenge in its purest form.

But there was nothing she could do about it. It was beyond her control. Besides, she had more pressing matters on her mind now. She had to do all she could to help George over the coming days and weeks. At the hospital she hadn't hesitated to fill in the necessary forms describing herself as a niece and therefore next of kin. No one had questioned her. Just let them try.

★ ★ ★

As the days slipped slowly by George showed no sign of getting any better. She had completely lost the ability to swallow and so a nasogastric tube had been fitted to get fluids into her, along with what passed for food. The sight of the tube, along with a drip attached to her arm, had initially alarmed Alice but she had quickly grown used to both things, seeing them as something positive, a means to build up George's strength.

Their method of communication had been extended; as well as yes and no, they now had established that a glance to the right meant that George agreed with Alice; a glance to the left meant she thought something was funny and a roll of her eyes meant what it always had — that she thought Alice was being an idiot and that she was to cut the bullshit.

There had been a good deal of eye rolling

389

during this afternoon's visit. Alice had told George about her meeting with James Montgomery in London and the latest news on Clayton and how his script was soon to be put out as a two-hour feature-length drama and that it was called *The Queen of New Beginnings*.

'George, if you roll your eyes like that any more, they'll pop out,' Alice said. 'And I for one won't scrabble about on the floor looking for them.'

George glanced to her left.

'I'm glad you think I'm being funny. Because actually I'm being deadly serious.'

Two blinks.

'You don't think so, eh? Well, I tell you what I am serious about; I have no intention of watching that lying cheat's programme when it goes out. Oh, for heaven's sake, you're rolling your eyes again.'

Two blinks.

'Stop saying no to everything.'

Two blinks again.

Alice wiped George's mouth. 'You're being very difficult today. I hope you're not trying to tell me that you want to watch his programme.'

One blink.

'I might have known. You're desperate to see how Clayton's portrayed you, aren't you? You're the vainest person I know.'

One blink. And a glance to the right.

Alice sat in silence for a moment. She stared off into the distance. On the other side of the ward, a group of people were gathered round the bed of a woman. She looked very ill, very tired. More than anything she looked as if she just wanted to be left alone. When Alice returned her attention to George, she found herself confronted with a gaze so intense she sat back a little. It was as if George was trying to tell her something. Something that their limited system of communication couldn't handle. 'What is it?' Alice asked.

Nothing from George.

'Do you need something? Do you want me to fetch a nurse?'

George blinked twice and rolled her eyes.

'You think I'm being an idiot?'

One blink.

Alice took a stab in the dark. 'I'm being an idiot with regards to what we were just discussing?'

One blink.

'Clayton and *The Queen of New Beginnings*?'

One blink.

'You wouldn't be trying to blackmail me emotionally?'

One blink.

'Just because you're ill, don't for one minute think you can make me do something I don't want to do.'

George's eyes remained open and fixed on Alice.

'Oh, for heaven's sake, if it's so important to you, I'll do you a deal. Stop nagging me and I'll try to arrange it so that we watch the wretched programme together. OK?'

One blink.

Alice could have sworn that if George had been able to, she would have smiled a smile of triumph.

40

A month after being admitted to hospital, George defied the experts and regained a limited amount of movement and the ability to speak. Now that she could swallow again, she no longer had the nasogastric tube fitted and had even put on a little weight.

As encouraging as it was that George could now talk, her speech wasn't at all easy to understand. More often than not, her words came out as fast as machine-gun fire and made little or no sense. It frustrated her immensely when yet again Alice failed to grasp what she was saying. The speech therapist explained to Alice that to George everything she said made perfect sense inside her head and so it was only natural that she would be upset with anyone else's apparent inability to understand her. George had never been one to suffer fools gladly so it was no wonder she lost her temper when Alice had to apologize for the nth time that she had no idea what George was talking about.

There were times when Alice didn't know whether to laugh or cry when she was having her ears verbally boxed as invariably the words George hurled at her weren't the right ones. Accused of being a jabbling wardrobe or a cucumber in chapamas was never going to hit its target in the way George thought it would.

Even so, it was a comfort to have more of the

old George back. It was a comfort also when George would reach for Alice's hand and gently squeeze it. There was little strength in her grip, but that didn't matter; it was the fact that she was able to reach out that mattered.

Most days George would greet Alice's arrival at her bedside with the same question: how were Percy and the girls? Alice's answer was always the same: they were fine; she was going to Well House twice a day to feed, clean and generally remonstrate with Percy. Denied access to Well House — Alice had locked it up for the sake of security — Percy's behaviour had grown worse. Like a surly, sulky teenager who had been denied access to his Xbox, he either completely ignored Alice or subjected her legs to an assault of vicious pecking. There was no reasoning with him. He didn't listen to a word she said when she tried to placate him by saying his mistress would soon be home, that he wasn't to worry. Why would he believe what she told him when in all honesty, Alice didn't believe it herself?

Today, when Alice took her usual seat by the side of her bed, George was in a particularly agitated mood. 'Slow down,' Alice said after George had bombarded her with a breathtaking stream of incoherency.

George ignored her and let loose with a furious look and another torrent of incoherency. Her tone and frantic demeanour suggested that she had just explained that there wasn't a moment to lose, the world was about to end and Alice hadn't understood the simplest of instructions on how to save mankind.

'Start again,' Alice said patiently. 'I didn't hear you properly.'

The furious look was exchanged for an equally familiar expression, the one that said, Don't-you-dare-patronize-me! 'The teapot,' George said. When Alice failed to make the appropriate response, George raised her voice. 'The teapot! *There!*' With great effort, she lifted her right hand and pointed vaguely towards her bedside locker. There was no teapot, only a plastic cup, a jug of water and a newspaper.

'You want a drink?' Alice asked.

George's eyes glinted.

'OK, you don't want a drink. You want me to read the newspaper to you, is that it?'

As if an unbearable weight had been lifted finally from her shoulders, George's whole body visibly relaxed.

But Alice's body did the opposite when she saw what it was that George had been so keen for her to read.

41

It was his big night and Clayton wasn't handling it well. With ten minutes to go until *The Queen of New Beginnings* started, Glen was schmoozing a new client on the phone in the room next door, leaving Clayton to sweat out his apprehension alone.

He had the television switched on with the sound turned down and with the remote control clamped in his hot, damp hand, he was like an actor with first-night nerves waiting in the wings to go on stage. He had always been nervous for what was the equivalent of an opening night performance for him. Before the pilot of *Joking Aside* had gone out, he had been so nervous he had actually thrown up. It didn't matter that he and Bazza had already watched a recording of the programme and knew that it more than hit its mark. What filled him with stomach-heaving, bowel-loosening, sick terror was knowing that a real audience would be watching and judging his work. He had never told anyone that he got so worked up in these situations, not even Bazza. He had always brazened it out. Or hidden himself in the toilet until the worst of his anxiety had passed.

He checked his watch.

Six minutes to go.

Was he too old to watch his programme whilst hiding behind the sofa as he had as a child with

Doctor Who? Without fail, it had been the Cybermen that had frightened him rigid. Something about those sinister featureless faces and the way their arms and legs moved. All credit to Russell T. Davies for resurrecting the show to such great effect, but those new Cybermen weren't a patch on the originals. They were too slick. A bit too camp, if he was honest. No real scare factor.

Four minutes to go.

Would Glen, the most unthinking agent in the universe, ever get off the phone?

It was worse than waiting to be taken to the gallows.

Not that he had ever waited to be taken to the gallows, but hyperbole had its place in situations like this.

In the old days he and Bazza had watched their work together. No matter where they were or what they were doing, they would set aside that particular evening when the show went out to watch it together. As soon as Clayton had discreetly dealt with his PST — Pre Show Tension — he would then be glued to the sofa with Bazza, the two of them analysing every line of dialogue they had written. Had they really got the timing of each joke right? Had the actor really nailed it?

Presumably Stacey now kept Bazza company on the sofa when he had something new to watch. Or maybe he didn't bother watching his work. Perhaps he was so cocksure these days he had only to glance casually with one eye at the studio recording and pat himself on the back.

Lately Clayton had almost begun to feel sorry for the Golden Couple. Their collective halo had definitely lost its shine and their TV appearances had more or less dried up. Rumour had it that Stacey had tried to get on *Loose Women* and had been turned down. As Glen said, how out of favour would you have to be not to get on that programme? The shots the paparazzi now snapped of them were less than kind. Only yesterday there had been a very unflattering series of pictures in a newspaper depicting a furious-looking Stacey emerging from a restaurant with Bazza; she appeared to be giving him hell over something. Clayton hadn't ever seen Bazza with such a hang-dog expression before. Last week one newspaper had suggested that Stacey had had a boob job and showed what they claimed were before and after shots. With the advantage of having once been her long-term partner, Clayton had to admit that her breasts did indeed look suspiciously larger. He doubted their size was attributable merely to being jacked up by a substantially padded bra.

Two minutes to go.

Come on Glen! Shift yourself! I can't face this alone.

It was an unavoidable thought — although being the coward he was, he had done his utmost to try and avoid it — but he wondered whether Alice was right now, this very minute, settled in front of her television at Dragonfly Cottage. Perhaps she was there with a hotshot lawyer by her side ready to take him to the cleaners. He had covered himself, though. He had changed all the names. He had changed the location. He had done everything to cover his back. He had done everything except the one thing Alice had asked of him.

The voice of Captain Sensible kept muttering ad nauseam that it might have been a good idea for Clayton to share his guilty secret with Glen. As his agent, Glen should have been made aware that there was a potential glitch on the horizon. He had a right to know just how close to the wind Clayton was sailing. Wrecking careers. Wrecking lives. By Jiminy, it was an impressive trick if you could pull it off.

But Captain Sensible wasn't having it all his own way. He now had to contend with the voice of Signor Ego. Signor Ego stubbornly maintained that he needed this success to be back in the game. And at any cost. So what if he was accused of stealing somebody's life story? So what if he had trampled on the feelings of a person who had shown him nothing but friendship and kindness? *And trust*, Captain Sensible piped up. *Let's not forget that.*

Clayton squeezed his eyes shut. Just how much rope did a man need to hang himself by?

* * *

For most of the evening they had had the television room to themselves. They had briefly had the company of an elderly man with an oxygen tank at his side but he had been taken away by a nurse halfway through the programme. Perhaps it had all been too much for him. There had also been a woman in a nearby chair who had fallen asleep during the last thirty minutes. Alice had been seized with the urge to jolt her awake and say, 'Don't you want to know how it ends?' The woman was snoring loudly now, oblivious to the credits rolling.

After the briefest of exchanges, both Alice and George kept their gaze on the screen. When Clayton's name passed before their eyes they again turned and looked at each other. But Alice couldn't speak. Her throat was tight and her eyes had filled with tears. From her wheelchair, George reached out to her and patted her arm. With great effort, she said, 'I was right. He did care about you.' The clarity of George's words, each one of them precisely and slowly enunciated, made Alice's heart clench.

Still unable to speak, she shook her head, then very gently laid it against George's shoulder. She needed to feel close to someone. She felt bereft, as if she had lost her parents all over again. Whilst it was true the actors hadn't looked anything like her parents, the way they spoke was uncannily reminiscent, especially Bill Nighy, who had played her father. She knew all too well that an actor is only as good as the lines that have been written for him, and it pained Alice that Clayton had so perfectly captured her father. How had he done that, and to such an incredible and insightful depth? All he'd had to go on was what she had told him. Surely she hadn't described her father to that extent?

In contrast, her mother had come across as a far more unknown quantity. Was that Clayton's interpretation? Or was that how Alice had depicted her mother to him? Maybe so. After all, her mother had died when she was still quite young and before her death she had been far more occupied with her work and her husband than with Alice. Not that Alice was criticizing her for that; it was just the way she had been. It hadn't been in Dr Barbara Barrett's DNA to be any other kind of a mother. Just as it had always been in Alice's DNA to be as close to her father as she had been. So it was only natural, after Barbara had died, that the special bond that already existed between Alice and her father would be strengthened yet further.

And what of Rufus and his family? Alice gave a little shudder as she thought how cruelly devious and manipulative Rufus had been portrayed. She pictured the scene when he had taken her to bed on her eighteenth birthday and her father had stormed in on them. How had her father borne it? Knowing Rufus better than she had, how had he stood by and let Rufus get away with what he had? But how could he have stopped Rufus? He had warned Alice and she had chosen not to believe him.

What were the chances that Rufus and his sister had watched the programme this evening and had seen themselves on their television screens? Oh, yes, Clayton had changed all their names and set the story in North Yorkshire, but there wasn't a hope in hell that Natasha and Rufus could be deceived into believing this wasn't a direct account of their time at Cuckoo House. Would they want revenge? She thanked

God that she had changed her name all those years ago — plucking the name Shoemaker out of the ether, just as Clayton had accused her of doing — and they wouldn't be able to track her down. Not easily, anyway.

And what of her feelings for the man who had put her through this?

As with so many things in life, the expectation had been worse than the actual event. There were times during the two-hour-long drama when she had watched herself on the screen and wanted to shout at the silly fool of a girl who was being taken in by Rufus. There were other times when she had cried. The scene when she was sitting in the car with her father, when he was trying to make her see sense, had been so intense she had held her breath. More light-hearted and whimsical had been the mystery trips they had shared together; seeing those moments brought to life so colourfully on the screen had reminded her all over again just how magical they had been to her.

A part of her wanted to thank Clayton for writing what he had. As a permanent record of her father, it was as authentic as she could have wanted. Even when he had run off with Isabel, Clayton had not shown her father in a bad light. Clayton could so easily have destroyed him; he could have turned him into a risible caricature, but he hadn't. On the contrary, he had written the whole thing with extraordinary sensitivity. He hadn't embellished, twisted, or exaggerated anything; he had simply written the story as faithfully as she had told it to him. As loath as she was to admit it, having read only a small part of his script back on Christmas Day, it was just possible she had misjudged Clayton.

It was the way he had ended the drama, and the inclusion of one character in particular, and the extra dimension it gave the story, that had been the greatest surprise of all. Clayton had written himself into the script. Under the guise of being a novelist suffering from writer's block, he arrives at Long View to try and cure himself. There he meets a young woman with a story to tell . . . they fall in love . . . they part . . . they get back together . . .

It made her wonder. Really wonder. Why had Clayton written the ending like that? Was it because, as George had just said, he had genuinely cared about her? Or had it had nothing to do with Clayton? Had he been instructed to tie up all the loose ends in a way that would leave the viewer with a warm rosy glow? Somehow Alice couldn't imagine Clayton allowing anyone to tell him how to write his script.

Something else that was making her wonder, was the hard-to-ignore fact that she was really in no position to judge Clayton as harshly as she had. To condemn him was to condemn herself. For hadn't she wilfully misled people all her life? Could she really excuse her behaviour on the grounds that she hadn't hurt anyone in the process of her deception, or gained financially from her half-truths? The word 'hypocrite' resounded in her ears.

She lifted her head from George's shoulder

and looked into her perfectly still face. The old lady was sound asleep.

* * *

Unable to sleep, Clayton lay in bed thinking about Alice. He was thinking about the ending he had written. Watching it play out had been weirdly unnerving. It had brought everything back to him. It had made him remember just how good his time with Alice had been.

What would she have made of it? Would it have been the final straw and had her throwing a very large, heavy object at the screen?

Or was he flattering himself that she had even bothered to watch the programme? What better insult to him than to refuse to watch it?

He turned over and tried to force himself to sleep.

Three hours later he was still trying to sleep. He couldn't stop thinking about Alice. The way she used to smile at him. The way she used to flash her dark eyes at him. The way she used to put a finger to her lip when she was concentrating hard or was unsure about something. The way she used to kiss him. And God help him, the way her body fitted perfectly against his when they were in bed together. He had particularly loved the way that, moments after she had climaxed, she would sigh and then laugh with undisguised pleasure. He had never before known a woman laugh in bed the way she did. Stacey had always treated sex very seriously. Everything had to be done by the book. No, not

403

there, you fool. Here! But with Alice sex had been refreshingly good-humoured and uncomplicated.

Fidgety with restless energy, he lay on his back. He shouldn't be feeling like this. He should be feeling immensely pleased with himself. He'd got what he wanted: a slot on primetime television and accolades aplenty. So why did it feel so pointless? Why did he feel like shit?

And why did he keep thinking that it wasn't until you lost something that you realized just how much you valued it?

Once more he turned over and this time buried his face in the pillow. Maybe suffocation was the answer.

42

It was almost like the old days. But without the cranks.

Joking Aside had regularly attracted a sizeable mail bag and Clayton and Barry had done their best during the first series to reply personally to the letters they had received, but by the time things had really taken off, they simply didn't have the time. They had been advised never, under any circumstances, to reply to the letters written by the obvious cranks. Their letters were easy to spot; they were postmarked from Looney-Tunes-Ville. One so-called fan had written to them every week with suggestions for their next series. Every outline was a variation on a theme, the theme being intergalactic warfare masterminded by a white toy poodle. Another person — they never knew whether the writer was male or female — would send reams of A4 paper covered in a scrawl so illegible they didn't have a clue what he or she was saying. During the whole of series two, Clayton was targeted with love poetry written by a woman claiming to have been married to him in a former life. The margins of her letters were childishly decorated with hearts drawn in red felt-tip pen. Glitter had occasionally been applied.

Clayton thought of those letters now as he flicked through the bundle of mail Glen had forwarded to him. It had arrived in the post that morning and it had been the first thing he'd opened. He'd put the rest of his mail to one side; it could wait. Signor Ego, on the other hand, could not; he needed to have his back patted.

He was a dozen letters into the pile and grateful that so far, in the nine days that had passed since *The Queen of New Beginnings* had aired, the programme hadn't drawn any crazies out of the woodwork. The letters were all complimentary, congratulating him on his comeback and saying they liked the change of direction he had taken. Brave and perceptive appeared to be the *mots juste*, along with 'explosively funny' and 'pitch-perfect'. Only one letter, the one he was reading now, referred to his recent 'troubles' and then only as a postscript. Whoever Joanna Philips of 3a Burnage Terrace, Basingstoke, was, she wished him well for the future and looked forward to more great drama from him.

He added her letter to the 'read' pile on the left-hand side of his desk and sat back in his chair. More great drama, he mused. Well, that remained to be seen. Like dealing with one crisis at a time, one success at a time was the way forward. Though where that next success was going to come from, he wasn't at all sure. Early days, he told himself. But he knew it wasn't. Glen had already been on at him for his next Big Idea. The production company behind *The Queen of New Beginnings* had also been making noises. There had been mutterings that he should write a sequel. Several of the letters he'd read this morning had suggested the same thing;

406

they wanted to know what would happen next. That was the thing with human nature: you gave people a happy ending but it was never enough. There had to be a what-happened-next stage. Which, of course, meant that the carefully orchestrated happy ending had to be destroyed for a new storyline to be created. And in all truth, he didn't have the heart to do that. He wanted to leave his fictionalized Alice in peace. He didn't want to put her through any more pain or disappointment. On paper or in real life.

He swivelled his chair restlessly, then stood up. Coffee. A caffeine fix to stop his mind wandering. A shot of the hard stuff to stop him obsessing over whether Alice had watched his programme. He'd do anything to know what she had thought of it. OK, that was blatantly untrue. He could, for instance, pick up the phone and ring her for her opinion. But he simply couldn't bring himself to do that.

While he waited for the kettle to boil in the kitchen, he glanced idly through the rest of his mail that had arrived that morning. There were credit card statements, a mobile phone offer, an invitation to a sofa sale and, tucked in between a communication from BT and another from British Gas, was a handwritten envelope. The writing was instantly familiar.

For several seconds he held the envelope in his hand and stared at it. This he hadn't expected. Behind him the kettle clicked off. He put the envelope down, made himself an extra-strong cup of instant coffee, grabbed the last packet of Jaffa Cakes from the cupboard, and with his hands full, he went back to his office, carrying the unexpected letter between his teeth.

He made a space on the desk, sat down and once again stared at the envelope. It now had a bite mark across the top of it. What to make of it? Only one way to find out.

Fortified with a few scalding sips of coffee and a Jaffa Cake, he opened the envelope with as much care as if it might contain a detonating device. In all likelihood, it probably did. Just not the kind that would take his limbs off or blind him. The pen was mightier than the sword, after all.

Dear Clayton,

I know this may come as a surprise to you, given everything that has happened, but I wanted to get in touch to congratulate you on *The Queen of New Beginnings*. You've really pulled it off with this one. Well done! You'll be doing the rounds of all the award ceremonies without a doubt.

At least now I know I did the right thing in splitting our partnership. I always knew I was holding you back. Remember I said you'd thank me one day? Hey, not that I'm expecting you to thank me!

Once again, congratulations.

Cheers,

Bazza

P.S. If you ever fancy meeting up for a drink, you know where I am.

Clayton read through the letter one more

time, absently eating another two Jaffa Cakes.

As he had thought before, what to make of it? The letter bore all the hallmarks of a man who wanted to let bygones be bygones. Congratulations and the offer of a drink. Whatever next?

Next came far sooner than he could have imagined.

Returning his attention to the pile of fan mail, he opened another letter and began reading it.

Dear Mr Miller,

He approved of the formality; there was too much familiarity in the world for his liking . . .

I watched with great interest The Queen of New Beginnings. *In fact I'd go so far as to say that I was spellbound by it.*

. . . Excellent. This was obviously someone who appreciated quality . . .

The programme was of particular interest to me because I strongly suspect that it was not a work of fiction.

. . . He sat up straighter . . .

Moreover, I would very much like the opportunity to discuss this matter further with you.

. . . His back was ramrod straight now and a feeling of unease was creeping over him like a cold shadow . . .

I'm intrigued to know how you came to write the piece. Of course, it could all be coincidence but I'm certain that this is not the case.

. . . His eyes flickered anxiously to the end of the letter . . .

Yours sincerely,
Isabel Blake.

Isabel.

Blake.

Isabel.

Rufus's girlfriend.

Rufus's girlfriend who ran off with Bruce Barrett.

Clayton racked his brains trying to remember the surname that particular Isabel had gone by. For some stupid reason he couldn't remember it. One thing he was absolutely sure of: it hadn't been Blake. But then it wouldn't be the same name if she had married.

And she hadn't married Bruce by the looks of things.

Or was he overreacting? Was this Isabel a completely different Isabel? Was she merely a curious viewer?

He read the letter again, this time taking in the contact addresses Isabel Blake had provided. There was an email address and a telephone number.

Canning!

Yes, that was the surname Isabel had gone by. Isabel Canning.

He drank his coffee, then chewed on another Jaffa Cake, hoping it would quell the queasy feeling in his stomach.

Whether or not it was the injection of caffeine into his system, the writer in him suddenly saw something positive that could come of this letter. If this Isabel proved to be *the* Isabel Canning, then she might just turn out to be an answer to a prayer.

A sequel . . .

Captain Sensible cleared his throat. *Just one itsy-bitsy, teensy-weensy little thing: will you tell Alice about Isabel getting in touch? No? You don't think she has a right to know?*

★ ★ ★

Clayton liked to think he wasn't as stupid as he looked, but he had to admit that recently his life had taken on all the prudence of a parent allowing a toddler to play with a box of hand grenades. But in this instance he prided himself on managing to retain at least a modicum of good sense.

Three days after receiving Isabel Blake's letter he had made contact with her. He had wisely decided against emailing her, for fear of her turning out to be a nut-job and inundating him with round the clock emails thereafter. No. He'd done the sensible thing and telephoned the number she had supplied — with him withholding his number, so she wouldn't be able to dial 1471 and retrieve his number and pester him, should things take a turn for the worse.

Oh, yes, he was thinking with a clear head, caution to the fore.

She had sounded both delighted and surprised to hear from him and they had arranged to meet up. He had suggested he would come to her and now as the train pulled into Haslemere Station, he took a moment to steel himself. No matter what, he had to seize control of their meeting. It was imperative that he sussed out the situation before committing himself to admitting anything. If she started making any unpleasant accusations, he would simply deny everything.

The taxi he had arranged to meet him was waiting on the road outside the station. He gave the driver the name of the restaurant he'd been given in Midhurst. It wasn't long before he was being dropped off.

When he spotted an attractive woman with shoulder-length blonde hair sitting at a table on her own with a glass of white wine in front of her, there was no doubt in Clayton's mind that she was *the* Isabel. She was just as he had pictured. Just as Alice had described her.

She knew him straight away, too, and rose from her seat. She was tall, slim and very elegant, simply dressed in a pair of white jeans and a pale-pink cardigan that was so fine it had to be made of cashmere. He clocked the absence of a wedding ring. The only jewellery she wore was a string of pearls at her throat and earrings to match. She had class act stamped all over her.

They shook hands. A firm handshake. Friendly as well. So far, so good. He cast a glance around the restaurant, checking for an army of lawyers to pounce on him. All he saw, he was pleased to note, were people eating their lunch and minding their own business.

'You made it,' she said. Her voice was light and friendly.

'Yes,' he responded. Oh, great, Mr Loquacious comes to town.

'Let me order you a drink,' she said. She waved to a young waiter who bounced over like an adoring puppy. 'What would you like?' she asked Clayton.

'The same as you,' he mumbled. So much for his intention to seize control of their meeting.

'Another glass of Chardonnay, Andrew,' she said to the puppy, rewarding his adoration with the kind of smile that would ensure he was her willing slave for the rest of his life.

'So,' she said when they were sitting down and the puppy had fulfilled his duty and left them two copies of the menu as well as drawing their attention to the specials on the chalkboard. 'Two words, Mr Miller,' she said. 'Cuckoo House.'

He drank from his glass of wine. 'Please, call me Clayton.' Make way for Mr Smooth.

She smiled a dazzling, white-toothed smile and flashed her blue eyes at him. 'Two words, *Clayton*: Cuckoo House.'

'Do you know if the grilled sole is any good here?' he asked, tapping the laminated menu with a finger.

She laughed. It was a light, tinkling laugh, guaranteed to have the strongest of men weaken. 'I can personally recommend it,' she said. 'The chef here cooks it to perfection.'

'Is this a regular haunt of yours?' He winced. Mr Cheese had now shown up.

'Yes,' she said. 'Shall we order? Or would you rather prevaricate for a little longer?'

'Under normal circumstances I'd prevaricate for as long as possible, but since these aren't normal circumstances, let's order.'

'A decisive man. Excellent.' She smiled at the puppy dog again and when he lolloped over to their table, notebook and pencil in hand, Clayton had a sudden image of Bruce Barrett and the decision he had taken that Boxing Day so long ago. Had it been a moment of decisiveness that Bruce had lived to regret? And would he himself regret coming here?

They both ordered the Dover sole with green beans and crushed potatoes. When had the humble mashed potato become elevated to crushed status? Clayton wondered. Was it when an incompetent chef had failed to bash out the lumps thoroughly?

Keep the focus, he warned himself. He suspected the elegant and supremely composed woman sitting opposite him was super smart and would crush him like a . . . like a potato given half the chance. 'So,' he said meaningfully and determined to take control, at the same time dispensing with his original plan. 'We both know exactly why I'm here.'

'Oh, yes,' she said happily. 'I knew there could be no coincidence in what you had written.'

Signor Ego tipped up the brim of his sombrero and peeped out. 'And what did you think of it?' Clayton asked.

'I thought it was very moving. I cried. For all sorts of reasons. Bruce loved Alice so very much, you know. I hope she never doubted that.'

'But he loved you more, didn't he? To have done what he did, he must have.'

'There are different kinds of love. A father can't possibly love a daughter in the way he would a lover.'

'Well, one certainly hopes not.'

She raised an elegant eyebrow. 'Do I detect a dig at the age difference between Bruce and me?'

'No. Absolutely not. You were undoubtedly very much a woman to him.'

'Not to mention a woman who apparently belonged to Rufus?'

'You switched horses very easily, if you don't mind me saying.'

'Have you never done that?'

'Excuse the mix of metaphors, but I have at least let the sheets cool down before switching horses mid-race.'

'Then I would suggest you've never lost your head. Or your heart.'

'Is that what you did with Bruce?'

She nodded 'And he with me. Nothing on this earth could have stopped us from doing what we did.' For the first time in their conversation, she lowered her eyes from his. For a moment she seemed lost in thought. It was as if the light had gone from her face. But then their waiter reappeared with their food and the smile and bewitching gaze were once more firmly reinstated.

When they were alone again, she said, 'Now it's time for you to tell me how you came to write *The Queen of New Beginnings*.'

'I met Alice,' he said simply.

'Alice,' she repeated. 'How is she?'

'All grown up,' was all he could think to say.

'Married?'

He shook his head.

'Where is she living? In London? Is that where you met?'

He shook his head again. 'She lives about five miles away from Cuckoo House. But for a time she did live in London.'

'Her father was devastated when she didn't reply to any of his letters. He wanted so very much to repair the damage he had done.'

'She was hurt by his apparent selfishness. She was left to cope with so much, not least the aftermath of a stepmother who committed suicide. She was only eighteen.'

Isabel put down her knife and fork and took a sip of her wine. Clayton felt the full force of her penetrating blue gaze. 'You sound protective of Alice,' she said. 'Are you involved with her?'

'I . . . I was.' It was the first time he had admitted this to anyone.

'Recently?'

'Why do you think that?'

She shrugged and ran her fingers up and down the stem of her wine glass. 'It makes sense. If you'd met her a long time ago you would have written *The Queen of New Beginnings* then. What does Alice think of it?'

He hesitated. He could so easily lie his head off. He could say that Alice had given it her full backing, that she thought it was a perfect portrayal of her family and her life. But there was something about the situation, about sitting here with Isabel — no longer was she a character from a page of dialogue he'd written; she was very much the real deal — that compelled him to speak the truth.

'Before I answer your question,' he said, 'can I ask you what you thought about the way your

416

character came across? Was there anything you disagreed with? Did I get anything wrong?'

She smiled. 'Are you asking if I was shocked by witnessing my behaviour?'

'No. I want to know if you think it was a faithful enactment of the events. These things are important to me.'

'I can only speak for the little that I took part in, but yes, I'd say you got it dead right. Which means you could only have done that with Alice's help.'

'But you're not angry with what I did? You don't feel a libel suit coming on?'

'Relax. I didn't write to you with anything like that in mind. Of course, if you'd upset me over the way you'd portrayed Bruce, I would be coming after you for sure. But tell me about Alice.'

He took a mental deep breath. 'I wrote it all without Alice's knowledge or permission after she had shared her story with me. She'd never told it to anyone else before and she had no idea what I was up to until I was more than halfway through it. When she discovered what I was doing, she was furious.' He explained in more detail how once he'd started writing he just couldn't stop. Despite the inevitable conse-quences.

'Heavens,' Isabel said quietly. 'You're a bit of a bastard beneath that engagingly winsome exterior, aren't you?'

'No argument there.'

43

'Does she hate me very much?'

Clayton pushed his empty plate to one side and took a moment to consider Isabel's question. 'I'm not sure. But she never said as much, so I'd be inclined to think she doesn't.'

'I'd like to meet her. Do you think she would agree?'

'You're asking the wrong person. We haven't spoken since Christmas. I have no idea what's currently passing through her mind. I would guess that if it's anything to do with me, it's not good.'

'Good Lord, what is it with that family and Christmas? Does it always have to be so dramatic for them?'

'Perhaps it's the fault of those who come into their orbit and cock things up for them?'

'Is that what you think I did?'

'Well, you didn't exactly help, did you? Sleeping with Bruce and then running off with him was hardly the best way to bring about family accord, was it? Don't get me wrong: I'm not making out my crime was any less serious. I flagrantly stole from Alice just as you stole from Julia.'

'Does love not get a mention? Don't you think that love sometimes justifies our actions?'

'You can gloss it up that way if you like; if it makes you feel better, but I know what I did was out of self-interest. I deliberately stole from Alice for my own reward. Was sleeping with Bruce an act of altruism? Or were you driven by your own needs?'

'You can play dirty, can't you?'

'I'm sorry, but there really doesn't seem any point in shirking the truth. I did that long enough with the woman with whom I was previously involved.'

'That would be Stacey Cook, wouldn't it? If you don't mind me saying, and if the tabloids are to be believed, that could not have been a happy relationship. What made you stay together for as long as you did? It strikes me that it was a very obvious mismatch.'

'Habit. That and a reluctance to change the status quo. Stupidly I'd thought it was better to have someone in my life rather than no one.' It was another thing he'd admitted aloud for the first time. Not even Glen had shoe-horned that admission out of him.

'And what if you had met Alice while you were still with Stacey? Would habit have stopped you from falling in love with her?'

'Who said anything about me falling in love with Alice?'

'Are you saying she meant nothing to you? That she was nothing but a handy shag whilst you sneakily robbed her of her life story?'

'No!' His voice rang out so loudly a couple at a nearby table turned and stared. 'Certainly not,' he denied more quietly.

Isabel's face broke into a slow smile. 'I didn't think so. You cared about her, didn't you?

Otherwise, you couldn't possibly have written what you did, not with so much sensitivity, especially when it came to her character.'

'And your point?'

'Oh, I'd have thought that was blindingly apparent. I'm just trying to say that nothing we do is as simple as it first appears. My running off with a man eighteen years older than me wasn't a mindless fling. As unbelievable as it sounds, it was love at first sight. And mutual love at that. Bruce and I were crazy about each other.'

'How long did you stay together?' This was something Clayton had been curious about for some time. Even more so now that he'd met Isabel.

'We were together right up until he died.'

'How did he die?'

'Pancreatic failure. There'd been no warning signs. Nothing. I woke up one morning and he was dead in the bed next to me.'

'Did you marry?'

She shook her head. 'We never felt the need to do so. He really was the love of my life, you know.'

'Yet you later married someone else?'

She looked him dead in the eye. 'And divorced him fifteen months after we married. It was a disaster, a ghastly mistake and something I should never have done. A bit like the mistake Bruce made with Julia. I was lonely; I thought I could replace Bruce.' Her gaze softened. 'How wrong could I have been? Bruce was irreplaceable. He was a genuine one-off. I still miss him.'

'So does Alice,' Clayton said. 'She cried when she found out that he'd persisted in trying to find her.' Clayton went on to explain about George telling Alice all that she'd known.

'George!' Isabel interrupted him. 'Is she still alive?'

'Alive and very much kicking. I swear that woman's indestructible.'

Their waiter reappeared to take away their plates and to offer them the dessert menu. They both declined. 'Just coffee, please,' Isabel said.

'The same for me,' Clayton added. 'And the bill.'

While they were waiting for their coffee to arrive, Clayton asked Isabel if she had ever heard from Rufus in the intervening years.

'No, we never spoke again. But then I never expected to.'

'What did you see in him?'

'A handsome, clever and charming man. Plus he was head over heels in love with me. What young woman would turn that down? I knew it would never last, though, that I would soon tire of being charmed by him. That was why I was so surprised when he suddenly announced our engagement in front of everyone. He'd previously dropped a few hints about us getting married before but I'd never said yes. I thought I'd made it clear to him that I believed we were far too young to consider such a thing.'

'By leaving him for Bruce you couldn't have squashed his enormous ego more effectively.'

'That wasn't ever my intention. I'm not a cruel woman.'

'I didn't say you were.'

'I did feel guilty about what we'd done, but

when Bruce told me just what kind of a man Rufus was, I felt I'd had a lucky escape. As did Alice.'

'What about Julia? She wasn't so lucky, was she?'

'Bruce told me that Julia had tried to kill herself before. It was a recurring threat of hers.'

'Really?' This was news to Clayton. Most probably it would be news to Alice as well.

'Oh yes. He came home late one night and found her unconscious in bed. She had taken an overdose of sleeping pills, not enough to kill her, but enough to make a point. Another time she locked herself in the bathroom and taunted Bruce by saying she was going to kill herself exactly the same way his first wife had. Even though he knew it was impossible for her to go through with what she was threatening because he'd had the electrics changed after Barbara's death, he broke the door down to ensure she couldn't harm herself in some other way.'

'Why didn't Alice or anyone else know about these suicide attempts?'

'She did it when the children were away at school. Bruce used to hate leaving her on her own. She blamed all her unhappiness on him. It was a nightmare for the poor man.'

'Being so unstable couldn't have been too much of a picnic for Julia. She only stuck it the way she did because she needed the security of his money to raise her children in the way she wanted.'

'Exactly right.'

Their coffee arrived, and after a moment's distraction of offering each other milk and sugar,

Isabel said, 'What about Alice? Was there ever any communication between her and Rufus? Or his sister?'

'Nothing. Not a word from either of them. Although there's every chance that could change now if either of them saw the programme and they choose to write to me as you did. I doubt they'll view things in quite the same open-minded way that you have.'

'If you'd really been worried about that you would never have gone ahead with the programme.'

That's what you think, Clayton thought with a stab of guilt. If Alice's heartfelt request for him to delete his script hadn't stopped him, the thought of any potential reprisals from a jumped-up twerp like Rufus certainly wasn't going to stop him.

'I meant what I said earlier,' Isabel said. 'I really would like to get in touch with Alice. Will you give me her address or perhaps her telephone number?'

When he hesitated — who was he to give out Alice's address? — Isabel backed him into a corner from which there was no escape. 'Better still,' she said, 'why don't you pass on my number to Alice?' She let loose one of her dazzling, white-toothed smiles. 'At least then you'll have the perfect excuse to get in touch with her yourself.'

'How do you know I want to?'

'Because it's written all over your face, you silly man.' The dazzling smile so effectively tightened its hold on him, Clayton felt helplessly lassoed to his chair.

44

Ronnetta swung open the doors of her drinks cabinet and started to mix Alice a cocktail. She rattled tops off bottles and swished and stirred, at the same time swinging her hips in time with Matt Monro singing 'From Russia With Love' on the CD player. 'This,' she said, 'will cheer you up better than anything else I know.'

'But will it render me a total wreck head in the morning?'

'Who cares about tomorrow? Let's get through today first, shall we? There. All done.' She turned around and handed Alice a tumbler of green liquid.

Alice took it doubtfully. 'And the key ingredient would be?'

'Crème de menthe. With a dash of pernod, ouzo, rum, amaretto, limoncello and a hotly guarded secret ingredient.'

It sounded as mad a way as any to use up an excess of duty free holiday booze.

'Here's mud in your eye!' Ronnetta said. Alice took a cautious sip and willed her liver to forgive her. As the liquid made contact with her taste buds, it was all she could do to stop herself from shuddering.

'What do you think?' Ronnetta asked, when she was sitting in the armchair alongside Alice. 'I invented it myself. I call it the Last Resort.'

'It's very sweet,' Alice murmured as an intense

but not unpleasant sensation began to take hold of her throat.

'Another few sips and you'll get beyond that. Now then, what's the latest on George?'

Alice had just arrived home after her day spent at the hospital when Ronnetta had knocked on her door. She had taken one look at her and ordered her to come round for a drink and a bite to eat. 'You look worn out, Alice,' she'd said. 'What you need is someone to pamper you.'

Alice risked another sip of her drink and brought Ronnetta up to date on the news that George had had another stroke in the night. What little strength and mobility she had gained since the first stroke had gone again. The only upside was that she hadn't lost what limited speech she'd been managing previously.

'I'm so sorry,' Ronnetta said when Alice finished explaining. 'You've become very close to the old girl since she's been ill, haven't you?'

'I'm all she has.'

'Well, I'm sure she appreciates everything that you're doing.'

'I'm doing nothing but spending time with her.'

'Never underestimate how much good that does. Just having you there must be an enormous comfort to her.'

'Oh but, Ronnetta, if you'd seen her today . . . I'm worried there isn't any fight left in her, that she'll simply give up. The nurses are wonderful, but for someone like George being helpless is so dehumanizing.' At the memory of how defeated and wretched poor George had looked today,

Alice felt tears prick at the back of her eyes. To chase the memory away, she took a large mouthful of Ronnetta's Last Resort. Then another. She held the glass up to the light. 'How extraordinary,' she said. 'You were right about this stuff: it does get better.'

'As if I'd lie to you. And talking of lying, have you heard anything from that dreadful man?'

'Clayton?'

'Well, of course, Clayton. Who else would I mean? Unless you have a secret army of dreadful men who regularly lie to you. Or perhaps you were thinking of that atrocious stepbrother of yours. What was his name again?'

'Rufus.'

It had come as no surprise to Alice that, three weeks ago, when she had been watching *The Queen of New Beginnings* with George at the hospital, Ronnetta and Bob had been at home watching it as well. The pair of them had inundated her with questions the next day. Ronnetta had wanted to know just how true the programme had been and after Alice had admitted that Clayton had done an excellent job of being faithful to what she had told him, Ronnetta had thrown her arms around Alice and hugged her tightly. 'You poor thing!' she had cried. 'You poor, poor thing! What a dreadful life you've had!' No matter how vociferously Alice had denied that this had been the case, Ronnetta hadn't let it go. Her eyes shiny with tears, she'd said, 'You've never really had anyone there for you, have you?' From then on, it was as if Ronnetta had assumed the role of surrogate mother to Alice.

Now, up on her feet and clattering around in her drinks cabinet again, she seemed intent on pitching Alice headlong into Last Resort oblivion with a refill. But Alice was beyond caring. She felt happily light-headed. Better than she'd felt in days. If not weeks. It was as if the cares of the world had been lifted from her shoulders. 'You know, I've always thought of myself as having been lucky,' she said when Ronnetta placed her replenished glass on the table in front of her.

'Lucky?' repeated Ronnetta with a dubious expression. 'How do you work that out? Your mother died when you were a kiddie, your stepbrother played you like a cheap violin, your stepmother was a basket case and topped herself, and your dad — '

Alice put up a hand to cut Ronnetta short. 'No need to catalogue events, Ronnetta; I was there, remember?'

'So how come you reckon you've been lucky? Oh, and let's not forget what that rogue Clayton Miller did to you. You call that lucky?'

Alice laughed. 'Ronnetta, give it a break, will you? If anyone should be keeping score, it's me. And I did enough of that before, when I refused to have anything more to do with my father. Trust me, score keeping isn't the answer.'

'You try telling Bob that. He's got a list of scalps he wants on your behalf.'

Alice laughed. 'Where is Bob, by the way?'

'He's helping a mate over in Matlock with some DIY work. You see, that's the kind of man he is — always willing to give up his free time to

427

help people. Honest too. You wouldn't get any wily business from him. Unlike some people I could mention.'

Smiling, Alice said, 'You're never going to forgive me for making the mistake of choosing Clayton over Bob, are you?'

Ronnetta waved a hand around in the air, causing her bangles to rattle and slide on her arm. 'He was attractive enough, I'll grant you, but he was a bit dull. No real pizzazz to him. You could do so much better.'

Alice thought about Clayton and whether or not he had pizzazz. Maybe not all-singing and all-dancing pizzazz, it had to be said, but he'd had something. A sort of understated, enigmatic quality. She had liked that about him. She had liked his sense of humour, too, and that he'd never taken himself too seriously. He'd also been impulsive and again she had liked that. Time spent with him had never been boring, that was for sure. She thought of the first time they met and how she had fooled him with Katya. That had been fun. The look on his face had been priceless when she'd been so mercilessly rude to him.

She sighed, suddenly overcome with a very real sense of regret. If only she hadn't been so quick to tell him about growing up at Cuckoo House. Who knew how things might have worked out for them if she hadn't presented him with such an obvious temptation?

'You've got a strange faraway look in your eyes,' Ronnetta said.

'It's this cocktail of yours,' Alice replied. 'It

would give anyone a strange faraway look.' She downed another mouthful, thinking with wry amusement that she was in danger of acquiring a taste for it. Not only that, in her happily mellowed state, she was in danger of losing her animosity towards Clayton. It pained her to admit it, even to herself, but she missed him. Many a time when she had been at the hospital with George she had experienced the urge to talk to him, to find out how he was, to share with him her concerns for George.

Before last night, when poor George had taken a dramatic turn for the worse, she had been annoyingly vocal in her opinion that Alice should get in touch with Clayton to congratulate him on his programme. Having made the mistake of confessing to George that she had been surprised and pleased by what he had written, and even that she might have judged him too hastily and too harshly — given her own propensity to hide things from people — George had urged her to get in touch with Clayton. George also wanted him to know how delighted she was with the way she had been portrayed, and that she had been especially pleased with the actress who had been cast in the role. 'Just don't start boasting to all and sundry about your moment of fame,' Alice had begged her. 'Do that and I'll tell people you're ga-ga and they mustn't believe a word you say.'

George had replied with just one word. 'Cruel.'

Alice's fear that suddenly everyone would know that the programme was about her had not proved to be the case. Either no one in the area had watched it or they simply hadn't made the connection.

★　★　★

Hours later, Alice stumbled home. Acutely aware that she needed to take preventative measures to ward off a stinker of a hangover, she filled the kettle for some coffee. While she waited for it to boil, she drank a glass of water. And another. That was when she noticed that the red light on her answer phone was winking. She pressed the play button and heard a voice that had the effect of instantly sobering her up.

'Hello Alice. I'm not sure which one of us will feel more awkward about this, although right now I reckon I might be out in front, but that might be presumptuous on my part as I'm pretty sure you'll still be furious with me. And for the record, I don't blame you for being angry. Anyway . . . um . . . oh hell, I've lost my thread. OK, right, yes, got it. Look, the thing is, you might not want to talk to me, but something's come up and if you could bear to return my call, I've got something important to tell you. And just in case you haven't got — '

The answer phone cut him off at this point. Alice could see there was another message waiting for her attention. She pressed play again. Once more Clayton's voice filled the kitchen.

'Sorry,' he said, 'I'm rambling on. Nerves. Well, fear actually. Maybe even terror. Not that I'm saying you're scary, Alice. Well, you were

430

when you were Katya. Oh, hell, I'm off again. Look, here's my number, just in case you threw it away.'

After he'd repeated the number for her, he said goodbye and the kitchen went quiet. There were no more messages.

The kettle clicked off in the silence. Alice made a cup of coffee and then made a decision. It was time to bring back an old friend.

★ ★ ★

The ringing of his mobile roused Clayton from a deep sleep in which he'd been dreaming he was working on the checkout in a supermarket. But the machine for reading the bar codes had gone wrong and people in the queue were getting restless. A big ugly guy had started pelting him with his shopping — eggs, tomatoes, rolls of toilet paper. Others had joined in. It was a full-scale mob attack. The manager had then appeared. Dressed in riot gear, he carried a transparent shield and a baton. He said it was always like this on a Monday night. Disorientated, his eyes barely open, Clayton fumbled for the phone in the dark.

'Hello,' he said groggily. He almost expected it to be the supermarket manager.

'Hello, mister.'

'Hello,' he repeated, trying to shake himself awake. He switched on the bedside lamp. He blinked at the brightness and when he was able to focus he checked to see what time it was: it was five minutes past midnight. 'Who is this?' he demanded. If it was some call centre in India hoping to sell him something or inform him that he or a member of his family had won the chance to go on a holiday of a lifetime they were in for a nasty shock.

'Don't tell me your memory is as bad as your manners.'

OK, so not a call centre. A wrong number. And from someone who wasn't English. 'Whoever you are,' he said, 'try concentrating on what you're doing and dial correctly next time.'

'Hey mister, you the big idiot! Not me. I dial very carefully. I always do things carefully. Not like you. You the most careless man I know.'

He sat up. His brain suddenly made itself half useful. *Katya?* 'Hey,' he said, 'you can't just ring up and hurl abuse at me like you used to.'

'No? Well, we see about that. I no lose my touch.'

'That much is clear. How have you been?'

'You really interested? You really want to know? Or you just being polite?'

'I think you established a long time ago that politeness is not one of my strong suits. So tell me, how have you been?'

'I've . . . I've been better.'

He was pushing his luck, but if he didn't say it, he knew he'd regret it. 'I've missed you,' he said.

The line went quiet.

'Are you there?'

Still nothing.

'Alice?' he said, concern making him dispense with playing along with Katya. He could hear something faint and muffled in his ear. 'Alice?'

he repeated. 'Are you all right?'

'No.'

'What's wrong?'

'I'm crying, you horrible, insensitive man!'

'Oh, Alice. I'm sorry. I'm sorry for what I did, that it upset you so much.'

'Who said it was anything to do with you? This may come as a surprise to you but the world doesn't revolve around Clayton Miller all of the time.'

'I'm sorry.'

'And stop saying you're sorry.'

'Sorry. Oh, hell, I can't stop saying it now.'

From the other end of the line came the sound of Alice blowing her nose. 'I've missed you,' he said again when she'd finished.

'I've missed you, too,' she said so softly he very nearly didn't hear her. 'Especially recently since — '

Clayton waited for her to continue. When the silence had gone on for longer than he could take, he said, as gently as he could, 'Since when, Alice?'

'Since George had a stroke.'

Shocked, it was now his turn to fall quiet.

'It happened several months ago,' Alice went on. 'She's been in hospital ever since. Then last night she had a second stroke. I . . . I don't think she's going to recover from this one.'

'Alice, I'm genuinely sorry. It doesn't seem possible. Not George. She seemed indestructible.'

There was another pause in the conversation while Alice blew her nose again. Then: 'She

433

wanted you to know that she thought you'd done a great job with *The Queen of New Beginnings*.'

'Really?'

'She was very pleased with her screen-self.'

'She was a gift. It took no effort at all to shape her character.'

'You did a wonderful job with my father. I was frightened you might have turned him into a figure of fun. Or worse, a man who had no real feelings for anyone.'

'I would never have done that, Alice. You watched it, then?'

'I had no choice. George insisted. We watched it together in the hospital.'

Clayton pictured the scene, the two of them sitting on plastic chairs in some cheerless hospital room. He suddenly knew there was something hugely important he should do. 'Would you mind if I came up there to visit George?' he asked. 'I'd like to see her. To thank her.'

'I'm sure she'd love to see you. She must be sick of seeing me every day; you'll make a welcome change for her.'

'What about you? Would . . . would you like to see me?'

'I can think of worse things to do.'

'In that case, I'll come up tomorrow. Which hospital is she in?'

He scribbled down the necessary details. When he'd got all the information he needed, Alice said, 'You mentioned in your message on my answer phone that you had something important to tell me. What is it?'

'It can wait until tomorrow. I'd rather tell you face to face.'

'That sounds ominous. Is it good or bad?'

'I'm . . . I'm really not qualified to say.'

'Won't you tell me now? I shan't sleep for wondering what it is.'

'Goodnight, Alice. I'll text you when I'm on the train and I know what time I'll be arriving.'

'Don't you dare hang up on me!'

'But you know better than anyone how I need my beauty sleep. Goodnight. Sleep well.'

45

Alice woke early the next morning. Relieved that Ronnetta's Last Resort hadn't inflicted too much damage, she showered and dressed, ate a hurried breakfast and got down to work at the kitchen table. She had the last hundred pages of a manuscript to read before going to the hospital to see George. The manuscript was a first for her; it was for a much-applauded debut novel. It was contemporary adult fiction and she was determined to make a good job of it as for some time now she had been hoping to break into the world of adult fiction. She would love to work on more books like this one.

She had read solidly for an hour when her mind began to wander from the text and she found she was rereading the same lines. Her concentration had gone and knowing from experience there was no point in bullying her brain to do something it didn't want to, she allowed herself a small distraction: to think of Clayton.

She was both anxious and excited about seeing him later today. It hadn't been her intention last night to admit that she had missed him, and she certainly hadn't intended to cry. When she had picked up the phone she had been full of feisty Katya, imagining with amusement the expression on Clayton's face at the other end of the phone. But the moment he had said he had missed her, something had cracked inside her. He'd made it worse by calling her Alice, compelling her to dispense with the act of Katya and to be herself. She had lost it then.

In bed afterwards she had realized that ringing Clayton while pretending to be Katya had been nothing but a means to speak to him without having to talk to him honestly. Katya had effectively been a carefully constructed cloak of invisibility. Except Clayton hadn't played by the rules; he'd snatched the cloak off her, leaving her emotions vulnerably exposed. With hindsight she should have waited until today before ringing him.

She looked at her watch and wondered if Clayton was already on the train and on his way. She had decided not to tell George that he was coming to see her. She knew that it would make the old woman's day and she wanted his arrival to be a surprise for her. Whatever criticisms Alice had of Clayton, it was good of him to go to so much effort.

What wasn't so good was his refusal to tell her last night what it was he had called her about in the first place. Why the mystery?

She made herself a cup of tea and got back to work.

★ ★ ★

Clayton blamed Signor Ego. If only he hadn't been so damned greedy for yet more back-patting affirmation, Clayton wouldn't have stuffed the letters Glen had forwarded to him in

437

his pocket to read on the train.

Captain Sensible rolled his eyes and muttered something about there being only one person who should shoulder the blame. It was Clayton who had set this particular ball rolling and it would be Clayton who would have to explain matters to Alice. How she would take this latest turn of events, he didn't know. Isabel surfacing from the past was one thing, but Natasha and her brother — even if the odds of it happening had to have been high — was an altogether different kettle of fish.

Alone in the first-class carriage as the changing landscape streamed past him, he read the letter again. How tempting it was to open the window and throw the piece of paper out onto the track.

Yet the decision wasn't his to take. Yes, he'd put Alice in this invidious position, but that didn't give him the right to interfere with her life under the pretext of trying to protect her. In all probability she would assert she didn't need protecting. And who knew, maybe this could lead to some sort of closure for her.

He tossed the letter aside with a flash of irritation. Since when had he started using words like closure? He'd be suggesting she try past-life regression therapy next.

He plugged himself into the Waterboys' *Book of Lightning* on his iPhone. He had started out the day thinking how much he was looking forward to seeing Alice again, but now he was dreading it. He had confidently imagined that he now had the situation in hand, at least on a level he felt he could deal with. But with the arrival of this letter, that confidence had gone to hell in a handcart.

He tried to sleep. But he was too agitated to nod off. When he reached the track 'Everybody Takes a Tumble', he gave up trying to sleep. How could he when Mike Scott was taunting him with lyrics like: *To break your heart into pieces is what I'm here to do . . . I've got nothing but trouble in store for you . . . and everything bad that you ever heard about little old me is true . . .*

A mortar attack of shame went off inside him. He had to make amends. He simply had to protect Alice. And there was only one way to do that, he realized with a bolt of clear thinking. Or manic certainty, depending on your viewpoint.

He neatly folded the letter that lay on the table in front of him, ripped it into four evenly sized pieces, checked he was still alone, then stood up and opened the window. He watched the bits of paper flutter away.

There.

Problem solved.

No decision required.

The letter had never existed.

Captain Sensible groaned. *Clayton Miller, how do you live with yourself?*

I'm protecting Alice, Clayton silently replied.

Yourself, more like it, Captain Sensible fired back with disgust.

★ ★ ★

The last time Clayton stepped foot inside a hospital had been when his mother had been dying. She had suffered a stroke, just like George. But unlike George, she hadn't lingered. Parted for a mere two months from the only man she had ever loved, she had seemed in a tearing hurry to catch up with him.

Clayton followed the directions Alice had given him on how to locate George's ward. After a few missed turns, he eventually found it. At the entrance, he mentally adjusted his tie and straightened his hair. A sign to his right informed him politely but firmly to clean his hands from the dispenser on the wall. He put down the bunch of flowers he'd brought from the shop downstairs and squirted a dollop of what smelled like an alcohol-based gel onto his hands. He rubbed it in.

That was when he saw Alice. She was sitting by the side of a bed, a book on her lap. He could see her lips moving, as if she was reading aloud. Even at this distance, the withered husk of a woman in the bed who was hooked up to God knew what in the way of life-saving machinery bore little resemblance to the spirited woman Clayton had last seen on Christmas Day. He hoped he would be able to mask his shock.

He approached the bed slowly, not wanting to disrupt what seemed such an intimate moment. But as Alice turned a page and raised her head slightly, she caught sight of him. She hesitated, glanced at George who had her eyes closed, then back at Clayton. She beckoned him nearer. When he was standing beside her, she smiled fleetingly then leaned closer to George and took her insubstantial hand in hers. 'Look who's come to see you, George,' she said.

The old woman's eyelids flickered open. First she focused on Alice, then she followed the direction of Alice's gaze. After what felt like an eternity had passed, her eyes finally settled on Clayton. Her expression didn't change; the mischievous face that he remembered was now devoid of all animation. But then he saw something; the dullness lifted from her eyes and was replaced by a sparkle of vibrant emotion. He moved in closer and bent to kiss her cheek, something he had never done before. 'George,' he said, 'it's got to be said, I've seen you looking better.' He showed her the flowers he'd brought. 'The best money could buy. I had them specially flown in this morning from the Channel Islands for you.'

'Li . . . ar.' Her voice was faint and strained.

'Yeah, I knew I wouldn't be able to fool you.'

'I'll see if I can find a vase,' Alice said.

Clayton handed her the bouquet and when she'd gone he sat in the chair next to the bed. George stared at him. Clayton stared back at her. 'If you could keep quiet for just a few moments,' he said, 'and let me get a word in edgeways, there's something I want to say, something important.'

Her eyes sparkled. 'Sur . . . sur . . . surprise,' she said after several attempts to get the word out. 'Nice.'

'Hey,' he said with a smile, 'what did I say about keeping quiet? Zip it old woman, it's my

441

turn to speak. OK? Good, because it's important what I have to say. I want to thank you for giving me a lift to the shops that day when we first met. If you hadn't done that, I would never have had the pleasure of getting to know you and that would have resulted in a massive gap in my script where you should have been. You really added something to it. I just want you to know that.'

'St . . . stopbing suss . . . sussentimental, you're making mesick. Youwer . . . youwer a beaky bastard fwhat you did.'

'You're right, George, I was a right beaky bastard, but you understand why I did it, don't you?'

'Dint intrupt me. You have to makebings right floliss.'

'Floliss?'

'For . . . Alice.'

'George, I'd love nothing more. But do you think there's any chance she'll ever forgive me?'

'Time. Give . . . her . . . time.'

'I hope you two aren't talking about me.'

Clayton started. 'Of course not,' he said much too quickly. He stood up and tried not to look guilty as Alice squeezed past him to put his flowers, now in a vase, on George's bedside locker.

'Hezlibing,' George said.

Clayton looked to Alice for help.

Alice smiled sweetly. 'She said you were lying.'

'Traitor,' Clayton hissed good-humouredly at George.

'You . . . need . . . to . . . talk.'

Again Clayton looked at Alice. 'She's right, we do.'

Alice nodded. 'We will, George,' she said. 'But not now. Clayton and I will talk later. For now, he's come to see *you*.'

'Or maybe the three of us could talk,' Clayton said, suddenly seeing a way to deliver his news to Alice with a safety net in place. 'I'll go and see if I can find another chair.' He hurried off before Alice could stop him.

When he returned, he positioned himself on the other side of the bed from Alice. *Nice going,* muttered Captain Sensible. *Using a dying old lady as a human shield; it gets better and better. I'm so proud of you.*

'So, Clayton,' Alice said, 'put me out of my misery. What was it you wanted to tell me face to face? Or are you going to say you'd rather not say anything in front of George?'

He swallowed and met her challenging gaze. 'No, no, this is fine. The thing is, since *The Queen of New Beginnings* went out, I've received a fair amount of mail about it. Including a letter from a woman called Isabel Blake.' He paused, seeing the look of two and two making four in Alice's face. 'And yes, she did indeed turn out to be Isabel Canning. I've met her and she says she would really like to meet you. But she quite understands that you might not be so keen to meet her.'

Alice frowned and put a finger to her top lip; she tapped it slowly.

'I didn't give her your address or telephone number,' Clayton added. God, he wished Alice would stop tapping her lip. It was such a small, insignificant gesture on her part, but he still found it strangely erotic. Right now it was proving to be a powerfully evocative reminder of their brief time together. It was something he had deliberately not written into his script when shaping Alice's physical characteristics for the screen; he had decided it was too intimate a detail to share with the rest of the world. 'I told her I'd pass on a message and her contact details,' he went on with the greatest of effort, trying and failing miserably to tear his gaze away from her face. 'It's entirely up to you what you do.'

Alice tapped her lip some more. He silently groaned. It was as if she was teasing him! Eventually she lowered her hand. 'What about Rufus and Natasha?' she asked quietly. 'Have you heard anything from them?'

'No,' Clayton lied without hesitation.

She stared at him hard.

'No,' he repeated, trying not to flinch.

And with that easy lie came the certain knowledge that he had just blown things for ever with Alice. He wasn't to be trusted. Even if what he had done had been to protect her. No, she deserved somebody decent. Somebody whom she could trust implicitly. Somebody who wouldn't look her right in the eye and lie so effortlessly.

He had left home this morning thinking that maybe, if she could forgive him for what he had done, there might be a chance to pick up where they had left off. But now he knew that could never happen. He cared too much for her to put her through the misery of being involved with him. He was an integrity-free zone. She really did deserve better.

The lyrics from the Waterboys' song 'Everybody Takes a Tumble' echoed inside his head — *I've got nothing but trouble in store for you* . . .

What more needed to be said on the matter?

46

They were in the hospital cafeteria; misleadingly it was called The Orchard Cafe. The name conjured up a place of elegant refinement, of chintz and cream teas and starched linen napkins. The reality was quite different: the smell of fried food was heavy on the air and the place was a tip, with stacks of abandoned trays of plates waiting to be removed. There were chips mashed into a floor that was as sticky as a roll of fly paper, and stains on the walls that looked like Jackson Pollock had had a hand in their creation. To describe it as grim was a gross understatement. It was probably the breeding ground for the NHS's next superbug.

But if their surroundings were grim, it was nothing compared to the gloomy expression on Clayton's face. Alice wanted to believe it was the awfulness of the oil-soaked sausage roll he was endeavouring to eat that was responsible for his expression, but she had her doubts. She sensed he wanted to tell her something. Something that he believed would upset her more than his earlier revelation about Isabel. Which actually didn't seem that bad to Alice. She was hardly going to throw herself at Isabel after all this time and scream, 'You stole my daddy!' A meeting with Isabel would be all right. She would be able to cope with that. What she wasn't so sure about, if it ever happened, was a meeting with Rufus and Natasha.

'Alice?'

Realizing that Clayton had been talking to her, she said, 'Sorry, I was thinking of Isabel. And then Rufus and Natasha. How long do you think it will be before we can rule out them getting in touch via your agent?'

Clayton put down his knife and fork and moved the stainless steel salt pot to the right of the pepper pot, then, as if not liking the arrangement, he switched it back. 'Um . . . I don't think it will work quite like that,' he said. 'There are things we script writers rather hope for, things like repeats and DVD sales.'

'You mean it'll go on for ever, that I'll never be able to stop worrying that they'll suddenly reappear in my life?' Some of her old anger resurfaced. In fact, damn near all of it resurfaced in one furious instant. And in that instant, gone was her apology, her intention to say that it had been hypocritical of her to condemn him for something she was also guilty of doing. 'Just what gave you the right to go sneaking around behind my back the way you did!' she threw at him. 'How the hell did I ever trust you? God, you were convincing!' Her voice was raised and people were looking at her, their curiosity undisguised. But she didn't care. Let them look. Let them know what kind of a man she'd been conned by.

'You're right,' Clayton said quietly, his head down, 'and on all counts. I'm not to be trusted.'

'And that doesn't bother you, admitting that

you're the lowest of the low?'

'Would it make you feel better if it did?'

The heat of her anger cooled. She sighed. 'I've lost the plot, if I'm honest, Clayton. I no longer know what would make me feel better any more. Other than George making a miraculous recovery or dying sooner rather than later so that her last days are still worth something to her.'

After fiddling with the sugar bowl, and with his head still down, Clayton said, 'I'm glad I came up to see George.'

His words further calmed the atmosphere between them. 'I'm glad, too,' Alice said.

'Will you keep me posted on her?' he asked.

'Yes.'

He finally raised his head. 'She seemed to think I made a reasonable fist of *The Queen of New Beginnings*,' he said, 'if that doesn't sound too much like I'm blowing my own trumpet.'

'You have every reason to be proud of it; it was good. The programme turned out better than I imagined it would.'

'Is that the nearest I'll get to an honest appraisal from you?'

'You want more? You want me to shower you with flattery? Is that it?'

He shook his head. 'I just want your honest opinion and then . . . ' His words fell away and he was back to playing chess with the salt and pepper pots on the table.

'And then what?' pressed Alice.

He looked at her. 'First give me your honest opinion. Whatever else, that's important to me.'

Whatever else . . . Alice thought, that sounded

ominous. 'OK,' she said, 'since it seems to matter to you so much, I thought you did a great job. For that reason alone I thought I could forgive you for what you did. You gave George a fantastic amount of pleasure, too. So that adds to your stock.'

After a lengthy silence, he said, 'I never set out to hurt you. I want you to know that. But I had to write your story. It was a lifeline to me; I had no choice but to grab hold of it. I'm just sorry it was at your expense. I'm also sorry for everything else that may happen as a consequence of what I did.'

Again his words had an ominous ring to them. 'Such as?' she asked.

'Such as Isabel wanting to meet you. I wasn't sure how you'd react to that.'

'Right now, I think it'll be OK. How did she seem? Has she changed?'

'You're asking the wrong person. I never met her before so I don't know how the years have treated her.'

'Of course,' Alice said absently. 'It's easy to forget that you weren't there with us all. When I was watching the programme I sometimes got the strangest feeling, as if you'd been there with us at Cuckoo House. It was because you'd captured the mood and feel of everyone involved so well.'

'I was only able to do that because you told me your story so well in the first place.'

'At last, I get some long overdue credit.' Her voice was heavy with scorn. He couldn't fail to hear it.

'I would have loved nothing more than to give you all the credit, Alice, but I didn't because I thought it would make everything worse for you.' He picked up his fork, speared a piece of sausage roll, then seemed to think better of it. Pushing the plate away from him, he glanced at his watch.

'In a hurry?' she asked.

'Just keeping an eye on the time; I don't want to miss my train. There isn't another for several hours.'

'Oh,' she said flatly. 'You're not stopping the night then?'

'No,' he said. 'Why? Did you think I would?'

'I thought maybe we could have had — ' She stopped herself short. How had she got it so wrong? How had she leapt to the ridiculous conclusion that Clayton might want to spend the evening with her? Stupidly, oh, so stupidly, she had imagined that because he had said he'd missed her he might want to make things right with her. As shaming fury with herself grew, she was forced to acknowledge how much she had hoped the outcome of today would be that Clayton would be back in her life. She knew exactly where that hope had sprung from. It had been because he'd given *The Queen of New Beginnings* a rose-tinted happy ending with her living happily ever after. Yeah right! Like that was ever going to happen to her!

She looked at him across the table. He was now fiddling with a paper napkin, meticulously folding it in half and in half again. He was midway folding it once more when he suddenly

450

screwed it into a tight little ball and tossed it onto his discarded plate. She had never seen him like this before. So distracted. So on edge. As though he were uncomfortable around her. One last vestige of hope roused itself: was he on edge because he didn't know how she felt about him? Was that what this was all about? If she told him, would that change things?

'Clayton?'

'Alice?'

They'd both spoken at the same moment.

'You first.'

'You first.'

They'd done it again.

'Great minds think alike,' Alice said with a nervous smile. 'You go first, I insist.'

If she had thought he looked edgy before, now he looked as though he were standing before a firing squad. Whatever he had to say, it was clearly causing him a lot of anxiety.

'I need you to understand something, Alice,' he said. 'I really enjoyed our time together. It meant a great deal to me. It still does. Not only that, you gave me something incalculably precious; you inspired me to write again. And with that came the confidence and belief I could do it. You'll never know just how grateful I'll always be to you for that.'

She sensed the but of all buts just seconds away.

'But . . . '

There it was!

' . . . despite all of that, despite what you mean to me, or more precisely *because* of what you mean to me, I have to be completely straight with you. I can never be the man you'd want me to be.'

'How do you know what kind of a man I'd want you to be?' she said indignantly. 'Or indeed if I want you to be anything at all?' Oh yes, present her with a but and she'd come out fighting, you could count on that.

'OK, admittedly I may have got that wrong, but perhaps that was because I was . . . Oh, well, whatever I was basing it on, you have to know that I can't give you what you deserve. Remember, I'm the one we both agreed is morally bankrupt. I probably always have been and always will be. I wish I weren't the man I am because then things could be different between us. But I can't change. I am who I am. If I've shafted you once, who's to say I wouldn't do it again?'

'Put like that, how could I possibly argue with you? I'd have to be mad to want to have anything to do with you. I appreciate your honesty.'

47

There was nothing like being made to feel stupid to strengthen one's resolve. That had to be a good thing in the long run. As was knowing exactly where one stood. Alice was grateful for that, at least.

But really. No, *really*. How could Clayton have tried that old it's-not-you-it's-me crock of shit on her? She would have expected better of him, something considerably more creative. Anything but some pathetic I'm-not-the-man-you-need number. Who was he to say what kind of man she needed? Who was he to say she even needed a man? Big mistake, mister!

Another anxious look out of the window.

Another anxious glance at her watch.

Alice had been doing this for the last twenty minutes. Isabel was due to arrive any time now. Alice had no way of knowing if Isabel was a punctual kind of person or the type who would bother to call if she knew she was going to be late, so she was prepared to be on tenterhooks for a while yet. When she thought about it, and despite this woman having played such a crucial part in Alice's life, she knew next to nothing about her. How could it be otherwise? They had met only the once.

After Clayton had left the hospital early yesterday evening, Alice had returned to George. Battling his rejection of her, and eschewing any references to Clayton that the old woman made, Alice had discussed with her what she should do about Isabel. They were in agreement; Alice should meet her as soon as possible.

When Alice got home, she had taken the contact details Clayton had given her and emailed Isabel. She had decided against telephoning — she didn't want to hear Isabel's voice; she didn't want any clues to the Isabel of the here and now. She wanted to wait until she could look her in the eye and assimilate her. Within half an hour of sending the email, she received a reply. Ten minutes later and it was all arranged: Isabel would drive up to meet Alice the next day.

Today.

The sound of a car engine had Alice hurrying to the window. In the process of being parked on the road behind Alice's car was a large, shiny black four-by-four. When she saw the driver's door open, Alice ducked away from the window. She went out to the hall and waited for the sound of the doorbell. The last thing she wanted was to appear too keen by flinging wide the front door and pouncing on Isabel. A strategy of cool, understated welcome was required. But even though she was anticipating it, the shrill ring of the bell when it came made her jump. She counted to ten, took a deep breath and opened the door.

The first thing Alice noticed was the enormous bunch of flowers Isabel was carrying. The second thing she noticed was just how beautiful Isabel was. And when she smiled, Alice felt as if it had been only yesterday when she had last been on the receiving end of its dazzling charm. 'Come in,' she said, inexplicably tempted to do away with her strategy of restraint and to hug her guest. It was an echo of all those years ago when Isabel had arrived at Cuckoo House as the enemy and yet Alice had still fallen helplessly under her spell. Whilst it was true that she had aged, Isabel was unquestionably as lovely as Alice remembered. She was possibly even more beautiful; maturity had intensified what had been there before and given her an enviable depth of grace and elegance. In comparison, and beneath Isabel's alarmingly direct gaze, Alice felt as polished as a warthog.

'What a lovely cottage,' Isabel exclaimed after Alice had led her through to the kitchen and had offered to make some coffee. The smell of freshly made bread greeted them. Seeing the plaited loaf on the table surrounded by plates of cheese, quiche, olives, and slices of chorizo, Isabel let out another exclamation. 'Oh, Alice, you've gone to so much trouble. Please don't tell me you made that bread. Although I just know you're going to say you did.'

Alice gave a little self-effacing shrug. 'When I have the time I like to cook.'

'I remember what a good cook you were. For someone so young, you were immensely capable. I was quite in awe of you.'

'I wasn't that capable. I just got on with things.'

'And you haven't changed, I suspect. I'm so glad you agreed to meet me. When I asked

Clayton to try and arrange it, I didn't hold out much hope. He's an interesting man, don't you think?'

'That's one way to describe him,' Alice said noncommittally as she poured their coffee.

'He mentioned that you had been involved for a while and that — '

'I don't know what he told you,' Alice interrupted, 'but if you don't mind, I'd rather not talk about him. Milk? Sugar?'

'Just milk, please. I'm sorry for appearing to pry. That wasn't my intention.'

'I'm sure it wasn't,' Alice said curtly. *Really!* Just what had that wretched Clayton been saying! Was there to be nothing private in her life now? 'I think it's warm enough to sit outside,' she said, her tone no less clipped.

When they were settled in the small courtyard garden, after Alice had felt her scrutinizing gaze sweeping over her once more, Isabel said, 'You have a lovely home, Alice.' The sun was shining brightly and for once the garden was looking its best. 'How long have you lived here?' she asked.

Alice provided her with a potted history of what had brought her here, the hows and the whys.

'You seem settled,' Isabel commented when she'd finished. 'I envy you that. My feet never stop itching; they're always looking for some-where new to go. Of course, it's not my feet that are the problem, it's what's inside me that's at fault. I've never been able to fill the gap your father left in my life after he died.'

At last, thought Alice, the elephant in the

room had been referred to. But she didn't say anything. She waited for Isabel to continue.

'Did Clayton tell you anything about the conversation he and I had?' Isabel asked.

'No,' Alice answered, 'only that you wanted to meet me.'

'Good, that means I can tell you the whole story without worrying that you've heard some of it before. Firstly, I want you to know that I really did love your father. It wasn't a mere passing fancy taking off with him the way I did. Never have I done anything so reckless or so impulsive and which felt so right. Since then, with one exception, I've never felt so sure about something as I did that Christmas. I hope you can believe me. Your father was genuinely the love of my life. I would have done anything for him.'

'Did he feel the same about you?'

'Yes.'

'You made each other happy?'

'Yes. Very happy.'

'Then it was all worth it then, wasn't it?'

'And that, if you'll forgive me, was said with great feeling. But then you've had a long time to wait before having the opportunity to say it.'

Alice took a sip of her coffee. 'I hope you're not going to be so annoyingly reasonable throughout this entire conversation.'

They stared at each other. Very slowly, they each began to smile, and then they laughed. Easily and companionably.

'You know, Alice, that's exactly the kind of thing your father might have said. Do you suppose he's looking down from on high and willing us to straighten this mess out on his behalf?'

'And wouldn't it be just like him to leave it to us to sort it out?'

'Well then, if nothing else, let's show him how it's done.' Isabel put her mug of coffee down on the table. 'I might be overstepping the mark, but can I do what I wanted to do when I first arrived?'

'What's that?'

'I'd like to give you a hug.'

They were just letting go of each other when Alice saw Bob's head appear over the garden wall. He whistled loudly. 'I hadn't got you pegged as being into girl-on-girl action, Alice, but now I see where I've been going wrong all this time.'

'Go away, Bob!'

'Aren't you going to introduce me?'

'No!'

'Spoilsport.' He waved at Isabel. 'Hi,' he said, 'I'm Bob.'

Isabel smiled. 'I'd got that bit.'

'So who might you be?'

'She's none of your business,' Alice cut in. 'Now go and pump some iron or whatever it is you do to prove what a man you are.'

'Why? Are you going to start hugging again?'

'If you must know, we're going to have some lunch. Now buzz off!'

Bob looked at Isabel. 'She gets like this when she's premenstrual. Very shirty. I'll be seeing you, then.'

458

His head disappeared from view but his voice could still be heard. 'Say nice things about me, Alice. I can still hear you.'

'Come on,' Alice said to Isabel, 'we'll have lunch indoors, away from Big Ears.'

'I heard that!'

'You were meant to!'

★ ★ ★

'You have some very interesting men in your life,' Isabel remarked when they were back inside the kitchen and Alice was slicing the loaf of bread. 'I take it Bob has a soft spot for you?'

'A soft spot in the head more like it. For some strange reason he refuses to give up on the idea that eventually I'll fall madly in love with him. He's actually been very kind to me recently. He — ' She stopped herself abruptly. She didn't want to go into all that business with Clayton. Her priority today was her father. 'Help yourself to some quiche,' she said as she put the bread knife down and sat opposite Isabel. 'Glass of wine?'

'Thank you. But only a small one. Finish what you were saying.'

'What was I saying?' Alice said, feigning absent-mindedness.

'About Bob being kind to you.'

'Oh, that. It was nothing. Olives?'

'Was it to do with Clayton?'

Alice put the dish of olives down. 'Now why would you say that?'

'Because I know he was upset about what

happened between the two of you.'

'Well, that's what you get when you prove yourself to be a duplicitous bastard. People get hurt and upset. He'll get over it. Besides, I don't believe he could have been that upset, not after his visit yesterday. He made his feelings very clear.'

'Are you sure about that?'

'Oh, yes. He gave me a very nicely prepared little speech about him not being good enough for me. Have you ever heard a more lame or more clichéd excuse for bailing out?'

'You don't think he was being sincere? Maybe he truly believes he isn't worthy of you after what he did. Mm . . . this bread is to die for, Alice. You must give me the recipe.'

'Do you always try to think well of everyone?' Alice asked after she'd considered what Isabel had said.

Isabel laughed. 'Certainly not. But there was something about Clayton that struck me . . . oh, let's just say he struck me as being quite a complex character. But a good man at heart. Which I know you won't agree with, given the way he went about writing *The Queen of New Beginnings* without your permission, but I can imagine how that happened for him. There he was, presented with a fantastic opportunity to cure himself of his writer's block — how could he not follow it through in the hope that, eventually, he would be able to convince you he wasn't betraying you or your father?'

'Yes, yes, yes!' Alice snapped impatiently. 'But you can't deceive or trample on other people's feelings without there being consequences.'

'You don't need to tell me that. If I hadn't given in to my feelings for Bruce, Julia might still be alive and you would never have been separated from your father. You don't think I've had to consider those consequences all these years? But you know, the truth is, if you were to rewind time and put me back at Cuckoo House that Christmas, I'd do exactly the same thing again. I wouldn't be able to stop myself. I think Clayton found himself in a similar situation with the golden opportunity your story gave him. He simply couldn't stop himself. Maybe he and I have something in common: we're both weak. Whereas you, Alice, are strong and able to resist such selfish temptation.'

Irritated that Clayton had found himself such a staunch defender in Isabel, Alice said, 'Look, can we leave Clayton out of the conversation, please? I want to know more about the life you and my father had together. Tell me what you did when you left Cuckoo House on Boxing Day.'

Isabel smiled and helped herself to some cheese. 'First let me say something I've always wanted to say. It's many, many years too late to make a real difference but I need to do it. I need to apologize to you. I'm sorry your father and I left in the way we did. It was wrong on just about every level you could possibly name, and I've always regretted that we never explained or said goodbye to you. Your father felt the same way, too. It was why he wrote all those letters to you. You did receive them, didn't you?'

461

'Whilst I was still living in Cuckoo House I received lots of letters, none of which I read.'

Isabel's expression changed. She suddenly looked profoundly sad. 'Oh, Alice, your father feared as much, but you must believe me when I say he never gave up.'

'I know. George told me about him going to see her.'

'Bruce knew and understood that you were angry and hurt by what we'd done but he believed that in time you'd forgive him. Have you forgiven him? Tell me that you have, Alice. If not for my benefit, for the sake of your half-sister.'

'For Natasha's sake? Why on earth would I do that?'

Isabel's expression changed again and a slow smile radiated back at Alice. 'Your father and I had a child, Alice. Her name is Grace and she's eleven years old.'

48

'A child? You have a daughter?'

Isabel's face shone with happy pride. 'Yes, what's more, she looks very like you, Alice. She has your father's blonde hair, mine too, but her eyes are dark just like yours and she has the very same smile. That's why I keep staring at you.'

'I can't believe it. My father had another child. All these years and I never knew. I'm . . . I'm stunned.'

'Would you like to meet her?'

Alice's eyes widened. 'You're not going to say she's been sitting in your car all this time while we've been chatting?'

Isabel laughed. 'Of course not! She's at school right now. Her best friend's mother is picking her up — ' Isabel looked at her watch, ' — in about an hour. She's staying the night with them so I don't have to rush back.'

'Eleven years old,' murmured Alice. 'I can't take it in. Does she know about me?'

'Most definitely. She wanted to come here with me today but I thought it would be better to wait before the two of you met. You do want to meet her, don't you?'

Alice nodded mutely. A sister. She had a sister. She had lost her father, but she had gained a sister. It was too much to take in. 'Do you have a photograph?' she asked.

Again Isabel smiled as she reached for her bag

and fished out a cream leather wallet about the size of a paperback. She gave it to Alice.

'She's lovely,' was all Alice could say after she had studied the two photographs.

'And why wouldn't she be when she looks so like you?'

Alice raised her head sharply. 'I'm not lovely. I'm the least lovely person alive. I deliberately pushed my father away. I . . . I hated him for leaving me the way he did. I wanted to punish him so much. And he must have hated me for what I did to him.' She put a hand over her mouth but it did nothing to stop her from breaking down and crying.

Isabel put her arms round Alice. 'Oh, Alice,' she said softly, 'he never hated you, not for a single moment. He loved you. He loved you unconditionally. Nothing you did could have ever changed that.'

* * *

Clayton was wondering how things were going up in Derbyshire. Late last night, Isabel had telephoned to explain that Alice had been in touch with her and that a meeting had been arranged. She had promised to ring him to let him know how it had gone. He hoped that the meeting would have a positive outcome. The last thing he needed was yet more blame hurled in his direction. In all probability, though, he had heard the last from Alice. Be it blame or otherwise.

After the way he had treated her yesterday at

the hospital, he considered himself fortunate not to have ended up in the A and E department. During the train journey home he had regretted his cruelly detached manner towards her and had wanted repeatedly to call her on his mobile to repair the damage. But that would have only muddied the waters. He had to stand firm and believe that cutting the tie with Alice, and thereby giving her a lucky break, was the one decent thing he was going to get right in his life.

Oh, very sporting of you, murmured Captain Sensible. *Very altruistic. A pity you didn't listen to me in the first place!*

Go to hell! Clayton fired back. He screwed up the piece of paper he'd been doodling on and chucked it at the wastepaper bin. As with all the other pieces of screwed up paper he'd thus far thrown, it fell wide of its target.

He was trying to write.

And he was failing miserably.

It was just like it used to be. No matter what he did, the words just wouldn't come. Not the way he needed them to. He had tried cheating his brain. I'm not writing, he'd told himself, I'm merely making notes.

Notes.

That was all.

Nothing creative.

Nothing to get excited about.

Nothing that was of any importance.

Except it was. It bloody well was important! It meant everything to him. Without it he was like a marathon runner who'd had both his legs chopped off at the knee. Or how about a pianist who'd lost both his hands in a saw mill accident?

He grimaced. He could do without the gruesome images, thank you very much. If that was the best he could manage creatively, then he should end it all now.

He sighed heavily, lifted his feet up onto his desk, tilted his head back and stared at the ceiling. There was a crack directly above him. He followed its trajectory towards the window. How long had that been there? Was it serious? Was it a sign of subsidence? Should he get someone in to take a look at it?

He sighed again and wondered what to do next by way of displacement activity. He could only sit here for so long pretending he was writing. He thought of the letters he had yet to reply to regarding *The Queen of New Beginnings* and tried to summon the enthusiasm to deal with them.

One letter in particular stuck in his mind. He snapped forward in his chair and rummaged through the overflowing in-tray. Eventually he found the letter he was looking for: the one from Bazza. He read through it and pondered his old friend's postscript. Had he meant it? Or had it been one of those superficial, show-bizzy, throw-away remarks made by the kind of people Bazza now hung out with? He forced his brain to remember Bazza from the old days; the Bazza who would no more have gone all luvvie on him than he would have . . . would have slept with a mate's long-term girlfriend.

He rubbed his unshaven chin and let out a long, deep noise that could have been mistaken for the growl of a bear suffering from chronic toothache and being prodded with a stick. What a colossal cock-up his life had turned out to be. Could he get nothing right?

How ironic it was that so many people had written to him after watching *The Queen of New Beginnings* and described him as being extraordinarily insightful and perceptive. What a joke that was when it came to understanding himself. He was a mess. A total screwball of contradictions and self-interest. He couldn't think of a single redeeming feature that he was in possession of.

Now that had to take some doing. That would go down well in his obituary.

And how long was it since he had thought about his obituary? He couldn't remember the last time. Feeling unexpectedly nostalgic for his old hobby, he lowered his feet from his desk, sat up and pulled his laptop towards him. If nothing else, writing the announcement of his own death never used to let him down.

Clayton Miller, one of the country's top comedy script writers —

No, delete that; after *The Queen of New Beginnings* he was no longer confined to comedy:

One of the country's foremost comedy drama script writers has sadly died at his home in London. His decomposing body was found slumped over his desk in his squalor-filled study three weeks after his death. It is thought that the ceiling had fallen in on him. The police were called when neighbours complained of a foul smell emanating from his dilapidated house. 'It was the filthy windows covered in blue-bottles on the inside that caught my attention,' claimed one neighbour. 'I didn't like the look of that at all.'

Clayton stopped writing.

What in hell's name was he doing? What new madness had he succumbed to? Was this how he now saw his demise? Alone and friendless; so marginalized from society that it would be weeks before anyone noticed his absence?

Was this colossal self-pity or a warning that he should get a grip?

The latter, he decided.

And that decided, he made another decision. He would ring Glen and suggest they have dinner. He would do it now.

But there was no answer from Glen. Kate, the latest in a long line of pretty assistants, who were becoming exponentially younger as Glen grew older, explained that he was tied up in meetings for the rest of the day. Picturing his decomposing body and all those bluebottles, Clayton was tempted to ask Kate out for dinner, but she rang off before he had the chance to prove what a desperate, gold-plated idiot he really was.

His gaze fell on Bazza's letter.

Moments passed.

Why not?

Why not have a reconciliatory drink with Bazza? What harm could it do?

★ ★ ★

Bazza had suggested a bar in Covent Garden and Clayton strongly suspected that an alcoholic beverage or two may have already passed Bazza's lips before Clayton arrived. He himself had considered knocking back a large quantity of Dutch courage before leaving the house and he regretted not having done so; being so wired he was in danger of doing or saying something very foolish.

Dressed in a hideous brown linen suit — the colour reminded Clayton of the lumps of clay he'd tried to turn into ashtrays and coil pots during pottery classes at school — Bazza rose unsteadily from his chair and stuck out his hand. 'S'brilliant that you made it,' he slurred. His hair was dishevelled as if he'd encountered a force-ten gale on the way from Notting Hill and his shirt was unbuttoned one button too low; a mat of grizzled chest hairs spilled out.

Clayton shook hands with him. It felt a very peculiar thing to do. He couldn't recall ever shaking hands with Bazza before. How could two people who had once been so close — they'd even shared a bed for a month in the first bed-sit they'd rented together — be reduced to acting so formally, like a couple of business associates?

More to the point, why was Bazza three sheets to the wind and looking such a mess?

'You look well, Clay,' Bazza said. 'What do you

fancy to drink? I've made a start on some wine.' He indicated the near-empty bottle of Sancerre on the table.

'I'll get us another,' Clayton said, thinking that apart from Glen, Bazza was the only other person who called him Clay. He attracted the attention of a waiter straight away, an almost unprecedented feat for him, and ordered a second bottle. Meanwhile, Bazza refilled his own glass and drank thirstily from it.

'S'how have you been?' he asked when he'd drained his glass.

'So, so,' Clayton replied. 'How about you?'

'Oh, me, I'm fine. I'm doin' just fine. Life is tippety-top. Never been better. Bloody fantastic. Got it all goin' on.'

'Right,' said Clayton awkwardly. 'I'm really pleased for you.'

Bazza looked over the top of Clayton's head towards the bar. 'That waiter is taking his time with the wine, isn't he?'

This, thought Clayton, is going to be an interesting evening.

Their waiter materialized, opened bottle and glass in hand. He poured their wine and left them alone.

'To old friends,' Bazza said, his glass already against his mouth.

'To old friends,' Clayton echoed quietly, not a little bemused. 'Thank you for your letter,' he said. 'It was good of you to bother.'

Bazza swatted the air with his hand. 'Meant every word of what I said. You wrote a bloody good script.' He leaned forward, placed his elbows on the table. 'Bloody good script, in fact. Better than anything I've ever written.'

'Oh, I wouldn't go that far. You've done some great work.'

'Crap! All crap. All meaningless crap. Yours had substance. It had a depth of integrity I can only ever dream of. Hats off to you, Clay. You did good. I'm proud of you.'

As much as Signor Ego could spend the entire evening and long into the night lapping up this kind of praise, Clayton had to put a stop to it. It was making him queasy. 'What's wrong, Bazza?'

Bazza leaned back heavily in his chair. 'Wrong? What could possibly be wrong with me? I've got it all.'

'So why do you look and sound so damned pissed off?'

Bazza shook his head. 'Don't know what you mean.'

'Come on, Bazza, I know you better than anyone. Something's up with you. You don't get drunk. You're like me, a lightweight when it comes to booze. A couple of Babychams and you'd be nodding off in the corner of the room. What's going on?'

'You really want to know? You care? After what I did to you?'

'As strange as this may seem, I do care.'

Bazza put down his glass. 'You promise you'll keep this to yourself? I really can't afford for this to get out.'

Clayton nodded. 'I promise.'

'My life has turned to shit. I've got writer's block and a bitch of a girlfriend who seems to think she can resolve the world's financial crisis by patronizing every sodding shop in town with my money. *My* money, Clay. *My* hard-earned money.'

Clayton blinked.

And blinked again. He didn't know how to react. Only a short while ago he would have been punching the air that Bazza had got his comeuppance.

But he'd never felt less like cheering. He felt nothing but pity for his old friend. He topped up their glasses. 'Bazza,' he said, 'welcome to my world.'

49

The wine flowed. As did Bazza's confessions.

Clayton listened to his old friend describing how his life with Stacey had become a waking nightmare.

She'd sucked every last ounce of creativity out of him.

She was bleeding him dry.

She was obsessed with sex.

He was a pathetic husk of the man he'd once been.

'All she cares about,' Bazza said, leaning in so close to Clayton their heads were touching like lovers, 'is fame and celebrity. She's hired her very own PR firm, got some woman working for her who's on a mission to make a name for herself. I don't think I can take much more of it.'

'Then don't,' Clayton said. 'End it. If I recall, you're rather good at ending partnerships.'

Bazza looked at him blearily. 'Ouch, man. That hurts.'

'The truth always does.'

'You're still cross with me?'

'Wouldn't you still be cross if you were me?'

'I'm sorry, Clay. I got it wrong. Horribly wrong.'

'So why not just tell her it's over?'

'Because I'm terrified how she'll make it play in the press if I back out of the wedding now.'

'You make her sound like Lady Macbeth.'

'Oh, dear God, believe me, she's far worse. How did you make things work with her for as long as you did?'

'I was too idle to do anything about it. I just let her get on with it. It seemed easier that way. Confrontation has never been my thing.'

'I'm beginning to realize I'm not much cop at it, either.'

'Better start learning if you want to keep your sanity.'

Bazza groaned. 'I can just see her PR machine swinging into gear. It'll be Heather and Macca all over again. I'll be accused of God knows what. Wife beater. Paedophile. Cross dresser. Tory voter. My career will be over.'

'Just like mine was.'

Again Bazza stared at him with bleary, bloodshot eyes. 'But you bounced back.'

'Yeah, that's right, I bounced back. Just like that. It was a piece of cake.'

'I'm sorry.'

'What are you actually sorry for, Bazza? For breaking up our partnership? Or for sleeping with Stacey behind my back?'

'For more than you'll ever know. C'mon, let's have another bottle of wine. This one's run dry on us.'

★ ★ ★

Clayton was a bottle of wine behind Bazza and was marginally the more capable of the two when they staggered outside to hail a cab. When they had one, Clayton helped Bazza into it. He

474

was just giving the cab driver Bazza's address when Bazza said, 'Clay, you're not leavin' me, are you? Please come back home with me.'

The cab driver winked at Clayton. 'Looks like it's your lucky night, mate, you've pulled.'

'I get it all the time,' Clayton said, 'it must be my sweet face.'

The cab driver laughed. Then he looked at Clayton more closely. 'Hang on, don't I know you?' He swivelled round to look at Bazza. 'Him too.'

'I doubt it. We're hardly likely to move in the same circles, are we? Now, are you going to drive my friend home or not?'

The cab driver's expression hardened. 'You people are all the same. You get yourself on the telly and you think you can treat the rest of us like dirt! Well, you can get your friend out of my cab. I ain't driving him nowhere!'

Swearing loudly, Clayton manhandled Bazza out of the back of the cab and propped him against a lamppost while he waited for another taxi to show. Just as one drew up and lowered its window, Bazza groaned and vomited messily just inches away from the vehicle. The driver cursed and drove off.

'And for your next party trick?' Clayton said with a sigh. He found a small packet of tissues in his pocket and tried his best to wipe Bazza down.

'Sorry,' Bazza murmured, 'I never could hold my drink.' He staggered and Clayton caught hold of him before he fell into the gutter. 'You will come home with me, won't you?'

'I'm not convinced that's one of your finest ideas, Bazza. Not with Stacey around.'

'She's away. C'mon, come back with me. We could pick up a curry on the way. It'll be like old times.'

Clayton winced at the thought of the putrid mess he'd have to clean up if Bazza was sick after a curry. 'OK,' he said, 'I'll come back with you, but let's skip the curry.'

Bazza put his arm around him. 'You're a good friend. The best.'

'Yeah, you'll be telling me next that you love me.'

Bazza patted Clayton's cheek clumsily. 'And I do. Really. That's why I regret what we did.'

'All water under the bridge.'

'But it's not. Not for me, anyway. Not until I tell — '

'Hey, we're in luck,' Clayton interrupted him, 'here's a taxi. Try not to look so drunk. And whatever you do, no throwing up now.'

★ ★ ★

They made it to Notting Hill without mishap and after Clayton had paid the driver, he helped Bazza up the steps to his front door. 'Is the alarm on?' he asked, taking the bunch of keys from Bazza's unsteady hand and inserting the right one into the lock.

'Always is.'

'I'll see to it.'

Bazza made no comment when they were inside and Clayton was tapping in the code;

instead he stumbled in the direction of the kitchen. Clayton caught up with him and watched him select a bottle of wine from the rack. Clayton took it from him. 'Maybe we should pass on that,' he said.

Bazza frowned. 'When did you get to be so boringly sensible and grown up?'

'Only in the last few hours. In any case, it's all relative; one man's sensible behaviour is another's wacky race. How about some coffee?'

'No. I don't want coffee. It'll sober me up and I don't want to be sober. I want to stay drunk for ever.'

'A genius plan if ever I heard one.'

'Don't mock me, Clayton. I'm on the edge here. One push and it'll all be over.'

'And since when did you get to be so melodramatic?'

'Since I started dancing with the devil.' Bazza suddenly slumped heavily against the nearest wall. He covered his head with his hands and started to moan as if he was in pain.

Concerned, Clayton said, 'Bazza, how about I get you upstairs to bed. You strike me as a man who's had a long day.'

'I told you, I'm a man on the edge.' He lowered his hands and tried to focus on Clayton's face. His eyes were wobbling all over the place. 'I have to confess something to you,' he said. 'If I don't, I might just lose what little reason I still have.'

'Fine. You do that; I'll be your father confessor. But first, let's get you upstairs.'

'OK, but you have to promise to listen to me.

And not judge me too harshly afterwards. OK? You promise?'

'Yeah, yeah, I promise.'

Like a dazed child being taken home after a particularly boisterous party, Bazza allowed Clayton to help him up the stairs. On the landing he seemed to have difficulty locating his bedroom and dithered between two closed doors. Clayton pushed one door open and Bazza recoiled from it as though the bogeyman himself was hiding inside the room. 'No!' he cried, 'don't make me sleep in there!'

Curious, Clayton peered round the white painted door. It looked very much like Bazza and Stacey's bedroom, going by the clothes strewn over the back of a chaise longue and the ton of make-up covering the dressing table. Behind him on the other side of the landing, Bazza was struggling to work the handle on the opposite door. 'I'll sleep in here,' he said.

'Allow me.' Clayton turned the handle and pushed the door open for Bazza to go inside. It bore all the hallmarks of a very plush spare room. The bed, complete with a pale peach canopy of silk, was made up with the kind of bedlinen, cushions and eiderdown Clayton would never have been trusted to come in contact with when Stacey had been in charge of running their house together. Magazines had been artfully placed on bedside tables, along with boxes of tissues and upside-down water glasses. With vases of silk flowers dotted about the room, it looked very much like a five-star hotel bedroom. Or worse, something artfully prepared for a photo shoot for *Hello!*. A copy of which just happened to be on one of the bedside tables. It was a very alien environment to Clayton and he thanked his lucky stars he'd never been subjected to such a hellish place.

Bazza shrugged off his jacket, let it drop to the floor and threw himself straight on to the bed. Lying on his back, his legs hanging off the side of the bed, the heels of his shoes bounced on the carpet. Clayton bent down and eased off his shoes. He then swung Bazza's legs up onto the bed. He spied an expensive-looking papier-mâché wastepaper bin next to a chest of drawers and placed it on the floor beside the bed. He drew Bazza's attention to it. 'Keep your aim true,' he said. 'We don't want Stacey ticking you off for puking on the carpet.'

Bazza groaned. 'Don't remind me of her!'

Anxious that Bazza might have got an important detail wrong, Clayton said, 'When do you expect Stacey back?'

'Tomorrow.' And then Bazza did something Clayton would never have dreamed possible; Bazza started to cry. Not a discreet little I'm-all-choked-up kind of cry, but an explosive all-out wail. It's the booze, thought Clayton.

Bazza turned onto his side. 'Clay!' he howled. 'Come closer.'

Clayton did.

'Closer,' Bazza implored him.

He reluctantly got down onto his knees so that his face was on the same level as Bazza's; the smell of vomit had him leaning away.

'Clay,' Bazza said, 'I've got to tell you

something. It's important.'

'Can it wait until you're feeling more like yourself?'

'No! I have to tell you now.' He sniffed loudly and very snottily. 'You weren't responsible for Stacey's miscarriage,' he said.

'What?'

'Losing the baby had nothing to do with you.'

'But you told me it was all my fault. You phoned me. You were furious. You told the press. You — '

'It wasn't Stacey who got the electric shock. It was me. And it wasn't that bad. Whatever caused Stacey to miscarry, it wasn't anything to do with you. Maybe it was the flight coming back from LA. Maybe it just wasn't meant to be. But her losing the baby was nothing but a coincidence.'

Clayton was struggling to make sense of what he was hearing. 'So why did you blame me?'

'It was Stacey's idea. I went along with it because I was as mad as hell with you for getting into our house and putting those bloody awful things in our garden. Then, when later that evening Stacey realized she was losing the baby, I was so upset I wasn't thinking straight. I really wanted that child and I needed someone to blame. When it was official that Stacey had miscarried, the first thing she said was that she blamed you. I just took it from there. Of course, once the story started to roll it gathered its own momentum and there was no going back.'

'You let the press hound me,' Clayton said quietly.

'It was Stacey. She made me swear that I

would stick to the story.'

'You publicly humiliated me every chance you got.' Clayton's voice was low. 'You as good as destroyed me. You could have stopped it. But you didn't. The pair of you sat back and let me suffer. Every opportunity you got, you drove home another nail in my coffin.'

Bazza nodded. 'It's all true. I'm sorry.'

'Sorry? Is that it?'

'What else can I do or say?'

Clayton got to his feet. He looked down at his old friend with disgust. 'If you don't know the answer to that, then I give up on you. And there was me thinking I was as low as it gets. Why, I'm a rank amateur compared to you.'

50

After a week of flitting about the country from one recording studio to another on a variety of jobs that ranged from sugar-coated customer care to corporate training videos, it was Saturday morning and Alice was once again behind the wheel of her car. She was driving south to Sussex, on her way to meet her sister. Or more accurately her half-sister: Grace.

She had never once considered the possibility that her father may have gone on to have another child. Just as she had never considered the likelihood that he and Isabel would have stayed together for as long as they had. She had told George all about this latest development and even she had been surprised. But she'd also been happy for Alice. 'It means you're not alone now,' she had said. 'You have a family again.' As true as this was, it was a bittersweet observation and filled Alice with a weight of melancholy regret. If only she hadn't been so pig-headed she would have known this young girl from the moment of her birth, would have been a part of her life. It would also have connected her to her father in a way nothing else could.

With the A3 now behind her, Alice followed the satnav directions given by a calm but firm woman — a woman who sounded like she'd never once taken a wrong turning in her life.

Squirrel's Patch was isolated, approached through a dense wood of beech trees and as Alice slowed her speed and saw the house ahead of her, she experienced the sensation of entering a fairytale-like world. Built of classic Sussex stone with a low sloping roof, the house was neatly placed in a clearing. There were two small chimneys at either end of the roof and with an off-centre door and porch draped in a rambling rose it looked as if it had originally been two cottages that had been joined together. There was a small front garden in full flower and with the sun shining down from a faultless blue sky, the scene was a tableau of idyllic enchantment. Strangely, Alice felt instantly at home.

She stepped out of her car and was greeted by a peaceful stillness. The only sound to be heard was birdsong. It really was another world. From inside the porch, the door opened and Isabel stepped out. Behind her a slightly built girl with shoulder-length blonde hair appeared. Alice recognized her at once from the photographs she had seen and while her mother came over and hugged Alice, she remained shyly where she was. Rendered shy herself, Alice offered the girl a small, tentative smile. She badly wanted Grace to like her and was anxious not to say or do the wrong thing by leaping in too fast.

Slipping a cool hand through Alice's, Isabel said, 'Come and meet Grace; she's been dying to meet you. She was up at six o'clock this morning, she was so excited. Isn't that right, Grace?'

'I've been dying to meet you, too,' Alice admitted. 'I couldn't sleep last night for my excitement.'

Grace smiled and Alice saw that Isabel hadn't been exaggerating when she'd said that her daughter had the same smile as Alice. 'I've made you some flapjacks,' Grace said. 'Do you like flapjacks?'

'I love them.'

Isabel put her arm around Grace's shoulders. 'She takes after you, Alice. She's a brilliant cook. Unlike me.'

'I'm not brilliant, Mum. Just better than you.'

Isabel laughed. 'Well, let's go in and put your expert baking to the test, shall we?'

Inside, the decor was pure country house with plenty of antiques, tasteful fabrics and delicate watercolours hanging on the walls. Nothing was overworked or in excess though, and Alice felt charmed and embraced by the warmth of its welcome. They were now in the kitchen, a large L-shaped room with two sets of French doors leading onto a terrace and a gorgeous cottage-style garden. 'Who has the amazing green fingers?' asked Alice.

'Believe it or not, it's Mum,' said Grace. 'Would you like me to show you round the garden? There's a small area that I'm allowed to grow things in. I've planted some lupins and some rhubarb.'

'Thank you, I'd like that.'

'That all right with you, Mum?'

'Of course,' Isabel answered with a smile. 'I'll make some tea and we'll have it outside.'

* * *

All trace of her earlier shyness now gone, Grace escorted Alice round the garden. First she showed Alice the raised beds devoted to herbs and salad vegetables, then the beds that seemed to be overflowing with colour and texture. The impression was that the flowers and shrubs had grown at random, giving a natural organic feel, but Alice suspected that chance had not been at work here; the garden had been carefully planned right down to the miniature clay pots that contained tealights and lined the curving herringbone brickwork path. Beyond a weathered summerhouse there was a hammock strung between two apple trees; lined with a tapestry throw and a large cushion it looked wonderfully inviting. As the sound of cooing doves drifted on the warm, still air, Alice could easily imagine herself happily dozing in the hammock.

'This is my bit of the garden,' Grace said proudly as she led Alice away from the hammock. 'Do you like it?'

'Very much.' Alice said as she took in a mostly bare patch of soil containing a crown of rhubarb and two orderly rows of lupins. Separating it from the surrounding area was a boundary made up of large seashells; they had been placed with great care. 'Did you do it all yourself?' Alice asked, trying not to sound patronizing.

'Oh yes. I'm going to sow some spring

cabbage tomorrow. And maybe some runner beans.'

'I remember growing radishes when I was about your age.'

'Really? What else did you grow?'

'Carrots. Except they didn't grow any bigger than my thumb.'

'That was probably because you didn't dig the soil enough before you put the seeds in.'

'Goodness, you know your stuff, don't you? I reckon your fingers must be as green as your mother's.'

She shrugged. 'Not really. I have a lot to learn.'

'Well, good for you. I've only got a tiny garden compared to yours. Perhaps you'd like to see it one day?'

'That would be great. I've never been to Derbyshire. Will I be able to see the house where Mum met my dad?'

Taken aback by the girl's directness, Alice said, 'We'd certainly be able to see it from the outside, but not inside. There are other people living in it now.'

'That's a pity. Never mind. It'll still be cool to see Cuckoo House. I've heard a lot about it. And about you. You're just as I pictured you.'

'Is that a good thing?'

'Oh, yes. Mum's never wrong. She said you were pretty and you are.'

'Now you're making me blush.'

'Why? I'm only telling the truth. Mum says I must always tell the truth, that it's really important.'

With a nasty stab of guilt, Alice said, 'Now I'm blushing even more.'

'Well, you shouldn't. I think it's going to be the coolest thing in all the world having you as my big sister.' She suddenly spun round on the spot and laughed gaily. There was such an air of vibrancy about her, an expressive joyful simplicity. She was as uncomplicated as a summer's day and just as lovely. 'My friends at school are all really jealous,' she said.

'Why?'

'Because you're famous.'

'I'm not famous.'

'You are. After Mum went to see you and found out what an amazing job you have, we bought one of your CDs.'

Flattered, Alice said, 'Which one?'

'*Matilda and the Grumpy Dragon*.'

'Did you enjoy it?'

'I thought you did the voices really well. I'd like to do that kind of job when I'm grown up. Is it difficult to do?'

Before Alice could answer, Isabel called to them from the terrace. 'Tea and flapjacks for anyone who's interested.'

Grace took hold of Alice's hand. 'Come on,' she said. 'Let's go.'

It was such a small gesture, such a casual instruction, but Alice felt her heart soar.

★ ★ ★

Late that evening, despite numerous ruses and pleas to stay up longer, Grace was finally

487

persuaded to go to bed. Isabel sat on the sofa next to Alice and placed a large photograph album on her lap. 'I wondered if you'd like to look at this,' she said.

'Pictures of my father?' Alice asked.

'Yes.'

Alice had already seen several framed photographs of her father around the house — Bruce and Isabel together, Bruce cradling a day-old Grace. She opened the album and turned to the first page, where an A4 black and white photograph had been placed. Wearing an open-necked shirt, the collar askew and slightly frayed at the corners, her father stared back at Alice, his gaze as penetrating as if he were in the room with her. He looked as if he was trying to decide whether to turn his head from the lens in annoyance or to laugh out loud. It was a look Alice remembered all too well. 'He hated having his picture taken,' she murmured. 'He never trusted anyone else to do a good job of it. Who took this picture?'

'I did.'

'Really? You've captured him perfectly.'

'Thank you. He did his best to teach me his craft; I like to think I occasionally got the 'money shot' as he called it. That's what I do these days. Portrait photography.'

'You work as a photographer?'

Isabel laughed. 'I have a small studio but honestly, Alice, I dabble. It's what I do in life: a dabble here, a dabble there. I'm one of life's great dabblers. It's probably because I inherited a stonking amount of money when I was young from a trust fund that my father had created for me. Then when my mother died, I inherited again. So you see, I've never had to do a proper job. I've been lucky. Or unlucky, depending on how you view these things.'

'I've been lucky as well,' Alice said thoughtfully. 'When I sold Cuckoo House, I hardly touched a penny of the money. Deep down I felt too guilty to do anything with it. Instead, I regarded it as a safety net for when work wasn't so easy to come by. I still do. I did use a small amount of it to buy Dragonfly Cottage, but the bulk of it remains untouched. And, of course, there was the money my great aunt Eliza had left for me in trust.'

'Bruce always hoped you'd be financially secure. I'm glad his hope wasn't in vain.'

Alice turned the page and looked at another picture of her father. In this one he was sitting in an armchair, engrossed in a book.

'I caught him unawares when I took that photograph,' Isabel said. 'He was so deep in concentration he had no idea I was even in the same room as him. It's a particular favourite of mine, that picture.'

Again, Alice had to admit that Isabel had captured her father perfectly. She turned the page and once more there was a striking black and white portrait of her father. 'I think you're being modest about your ability. This is more than mere dabbling. You must be very successful at what you do.'

'People seem to like what I do for them.'

'Do you only ever do black and white photography?'

'Yes. Colour seems too forced and clumsy for my eye when it comes to portraiture. It gives the sitter something to hide behind. Black and white is infinitely more revealing. I feel I can get to the heart and spirit of the person I'm photographing.'

'I seem to recall my father saying something similar, although of course he rarely took pictures of people.' She continued turning the pages of the album. She stopped at a photograph of her father with Grace; the little girl looked to be about two years old and was riding on his shoulders.

'That was taken in Buenos Aires,' Isabel said.

'Was that where you lived?'

'For a time. It was where Bruce did some of his best work. He did very little freelance work for magazines then and more gallery and exhibition work. He was in great demand. Being the silly man he was, he could never quite figure out whether that was a good thing or not. I used to accompany him on his trips. Even when Grace arrived, I still went with him, Grace as well. I think those trips were some of the happiest times of my life.'

'You mentioned earlier today that you'd lived in America. When was that?'

'After Bruce died. His death coincided with my mother's illness and so I went to be with her in Maine, where she was then living. She died a year after Bruce. I'd never been more miserable and that was when I stupidly made the mistake of marrying the first man who came along. The marriage only lasted fifteen months. I then decided to come back to England.' She laughed. 'I didn't want Grace picking up an American accent.'

Alice returned her attention to the photograph in front of her. 'He looks so happy,' she said wistfully.

'He was. But please don't think that Grace replaced you in any way. There wasn't a day when he didn't wish things could have been different with you. But he respected your right to punish him and so he left you alone.'

Alice looked up from the album. 'I feel awful that I behaved so badly. That I felt the need to punish him. It was cruel and needless.'

'Whatever guilt *you* may feel, think how bad I felt at times knowing that if I hadn't walked through the door of Cuckoo House, your father would never have left you. But neither of us can change the past so perhaps it's time to put that behind us. What do you think? Shall we give ourselves a break and look to the future? After all, Grace deserves the best of both of us, not two miseries hung up on guilt. Why not award ourselves a new beginning?'

Alice smiled. 'I think that's a great idea.'

'Excellent. And just in case you were wondering, Grace thinks you're the best big sister she could have.'

'That's good, because I think she's the best little sister I could have. I'm so pleased you got in touch with Clayton.'

'So am I. How is he, by the way?'

'I don't have a clue. I haven't heard from him since he came up to see George.'

'And in response to the steely tone in your voice, I shall back off and show you another album of photographs. That's if you're interested?'

The next album contained photographs that were even more of a surprise than the ones Alice had just looked at. They were the pictures she had witnessed her father taking of Isabel in the garden at Cuckoo House that foggy Christmas Eve. The intimacy Alice had guessed at was there in every photograph. Reminded so strongly of that day, she couldn't help but think of Rufus. 'Can I ask you something, Isabel?'

'Of course. Ask anything you want. I have nothing to hide from you.'

'Do you think Rufus really loved you?'

'Perhaps in his young and limited way. But I think what he was more in love with was the idea of me and in particular the lifestyle he thought I could offer him. You see, he knew about my trust fund and as we both came to know, Rufus had more than a passing interest in wealth and the status and security it could bring.'

'I think on one level my father was worried that Rufus was only interested in me because he hoped that I might come with a conveniently generous bank balance, but on the whole I think he was more concerned that Rufus was using me to get at him. I didn't believe it at the time, for the simple reason I didn't want to believe it. But I soon realized Dad was right. He was right about so many things.'

* * *

492

With promises made that they would get together soon, Alice left Squirrel's Patch after lunch the next day. It had been one of the most enjoyable weekends she had experienced in a long while and she headed north a lot happier than when she'd set off from home yesterday morning. She no longer felt any apprehension that Grace wouldn't like her. And best of all, she felt as though she had finally made peace with her father.

She was stuck in a long tailback of traffic on the M1, remembering how she had made Grace laugh with her impersonations of Lisa and Marge Simpson, when her mobile went off on the dashboard.

When she heard what the person on the other end of the line had to say, her happiness evaporated in an instant.

51

Stacey had once said that Clayton was a natural for attending funerals. Something about him being a miserable sod. Fair enough.

As far as he was concerned, funerals were meant to be sombre occasions. He had no time for those people who showed up wearing bright colours and a beaming smile and claimed that it was what Great Uncle Arnold would have wanted. Wrong! Great Uncle Arnold deserved a little respect. Not to mention a display of reverence. What he didn't deserve was a load of relatives or so-called friends who couldn't be arsed to do things properly. Was it any wonder society was going to hell in a handcart when basic social niceties were being flouted so flagrantly?

Which was why, when he had got the call from Alice, he had immediately taken his black suit to the dry cleaners and bought himself a new white shirt. He was wearing the suit and shirt now, complete with a black tie. Every now and then, when the train he was on passed through a tunnel, he caught sight of his reflection in the window and he had to admit the colour black suited him. OK, he looked like a character out of *Reservoir Dogs*, but there was no denying the severity and sharpness of what he was wearing was scoring highly in the gravitas stakes. Perhaps he should wear it more often.

The last funeral he had attended had been his mother's and he'd been adamant then that things would be done properly for her. Just as he had for his father. When his time came, he planned to have as sombre and mournful an occasion as possible. Plenty of long faces; that's what he wanted. The *pièce de résistance* would be his choice of music. He had that planned already: lots of stirring Russian funeral music. You couldn't beat it for top-quality gloom. There would be nothing light-hearted about his passing. Death was a serious matter and it should be treated with due deference.

He just hoped that George hadn't left any daft instructions for the way her funeral was to be conducted. All he knew at the moment was that she was to be buried in the cemetery of Stonebridge's Methodist Chapel and that she had picked out her plot many years ago, alongside her parents. Personally, he was all for burial, as opposed to cremation. There was something very unceremonious and cheapskate about being cremated.

He had spoken to Alice almost every day on the telephone since she had called to tell him about George. He was merely being a sympathetic shoulder on which she could lean during a difficult time, he had told himself every time he dialled her number and waited for her to answer. But when he had found himself looking forward to those times which he'd set aside to chat with her, he knew he was fooling himself. It had started when he had heard the tautness in her voice as she tried to hold back the tears while breaking the news. She had seemed so lost and vulnerable. So alone. It had made him want to be with her so he could offer more than a long-distance sympathetic shoulder.

He had contemplated telling her about Bazza and Stacey, by way of a distraction for her, but he had deemed it inappropriate, given that she had more important things on her mind right now.

When he'd told Glen about his night out with Bazza, Glen had been all for leaking Bazza's confession to the press, but Clayton had put a stop to that. Despite the depth of Bazza's duplicity, Clayton couldn't help but feel a degree of pity for his old friend. It had been a depressing experience witnessing Bazza drunk and pathetically weepy and he kept wondering if there wasn't a way to get him off the hook. Not completely — Bazza would have to face some kind of music — but he could quite understand the predicament in which the fool of a man had found himself: that of being under the thumb of a very determined woman.

He had no idea how to go about it, but what Clayton wanted was for Stacey to be forced into making a full confession, and the more public the better. He wanted her to feel just a fraction of the humiliation she had put him through. He wanted to wipe that pious, self-seeking, camera-hungry smile right off her face. He was sure that there would be those who would accuse him of being vindictive, but he'd challenge anyone not to react in a similar fashion if they had gone through what he had.

The morning after that revealing night out

with Bazza, Bazza had called Clayton. 'Um . . . I've woken up with the . . . with the vague recollection that something important took place last night,' he had said. The cautious anxiety in his voice had spoken volumes — all of Proust, Dickens and Shakespeare put together.

'What exactly do you remember?' Clayton had asked him. He hadn't reached the magnanimous stage of understanding the predicament his old friend had found himself in at this point. No, at that particular point, he'd felt nothing but furious contempt. It had been all he could do not to yell down the phone at Bazza and tell him just what he thought of him.

'I remember telling you something,' Bazza had replied.

'Can you remember what?'

'Oh, come on, Clay, don't do this to me. Help me out. Tell me what I said.'

'Nice one, Bazza. You screw me over, then ask me for my help. That really takes some doing.'

There had been a groan from the other end of the phone and then the unmistakable sound of Bazza being sick. Clayton had put the phone down. Ten minutes later Bazza was back on the line. 'Just tell me,' he said, 'what did I say?'

'Well, let me clue you in.' And Clayton had. Every incriminating word of Bazza's confession.

'What are you going to do?' Bazza had asked when Clayton had finished speaking.

'I haven't decided yet. I'm waiting until the urge to kill you has passed.'

★ ★ ★

His train arrived on time and as he stepped down onto the platform, Clayton looked for a familiar face. Isabel had telephoned him last night and offered to meet him at the station and then drive him to Stonebridge for the service. He felt glad for Alice that Isabel had gone to the trouble to come up to Derbyshire for the funeral. Isabel had only met George once, and a long time ago at that, but as she had explained to Clayton, apart from wanting to support Alice, she felt it was something Bruce would have wanted her to do.

Like Isabel, Clayton had two reasons for coming today: one, he wanted to be there for Alice, and secondly, he wanted to pay his respects to an extraordinary woman. It was funny how you could go through life moving casually from one acquaintance to another without a single one ever touching you, but then suddenly someone could appear out of the blue and stop you in your tracks. In George's case, that may well have been more to do with the fact she had been pointing a gun in his face.

He spotted Isabel before she saw him. She was dressed in a black trouser suit and a pale-grey silk blouse and she stood out effortlessly from those around her. As Clayton made his way across the platform towards her, he did a double take. Alice had told him about Grace, but seeing the young girl in the flesh, he was struck by her likeness to Alice. It was all in the eyes and the mouth. Amazing.

'Clayton!' Isabel greeted him as if he were a long-lost friend. 'Goodness, you look smart.

How was your journey? Are you hungry?'

'Yes, I agree I do look very smart. Yes, I had a reasonable journey. And no, I'm not hungry. I had a sandwich on the train.'

'Very comprehensively answered,' she replied with a playful smile. She turned to her daughter. 'Grace, this is Clayton.'

'Durr, Mum, I had worked that out for myself. Hello,' she said politely to Clayton.

'Hello to you, too.'

'Well then,' Isabel said, 'let's get out of here, shall we?'

★ ★ ★

They drove straight to Stonebridge. The area around the Methodist chapel was jam-packed with cars and enormous four-by-fours covered in dust, mud and goodness knows what else. George's funeral had clearly brought the world and his wife down from the hills. They managed to find themselves a space to park and walked the short distance back to the chapel. Inside, the place was full to overflowing. Isabel led the way to the front, where Alice had seats reserved for them. Clayton experienced a peculiar sensation as he took his seat in the pew with Isabel and her daughter. It took him a moment to establish precisely what he was feeling: it was a sense of belonging.

A tap on his shoulder made him start. He turned round and found himself face to face with Ronnetta and Bob the Body Builder. He smiled awkwardly. Ronnetta came close to

499

smiling back at him but Bob looked as if he might like to rip Clayton's head off and kick it into next week.

He was saved from this ignominy by the arrival of George's coffin. Borne aloft on the shoulders of six burly, ruddy-faced men, Clayton watched its progress. Behind it and looking pale but composed, was Alice. She was wearing a close-fitting black dress that stopped well below her knee and with the combination of high heels (something he'd never seen her wear) and her hair swept up on top of her head, Clayton thought she'd never looked lovelier. Was it weird of him to think that, given the circumstances? She slipped into the pew next to Isabel and leaned forward to give him the faintest of smiles. It felt good to be on the receiving end of a smile from her, even as fleeting and strained as this one was.

★ ★ ★

The general consensus was that George would have strongly approved. The service had been conducted in a simple but traditional manner and afterwards everyone had enjoyed drinks and sandwiches in the private room Alice had booked at The Hanging Gate, a pub conveniently placed just a short walk from the chapel. When the guests had finally drifted away, each taking the time and trouble to thank her, they had all said the same: 'It was just as George would have wanted.'

Now, as Alice kicked off her shoes and sank

gratefully into the softness of the cushions of her favourite armchair by the French door that looked into her garden, she listened to what was going on in the kitchen. Isabel, Grace and Clayton were putting some supper together.

She had been banned from helping. 'You've done quite enough,' Isabel had said firmly. 'Now do as you're told and sit down.' Alice hadn't put up any argument; she was exhausted. It had been ten days since she had got the call from the hospital to say that George had died, but it felt longer. She had been devastated that the old lady had died alone and it still bothered her now. She should have been with her. With no official next of kin on hand, the task of organizing George's funeral had fallen to Alice. She had done it willingly.

She closed her eyes and listened to the clatter of crockery and the soothing murmur of voices. Isabel and Grace were staying with her for a couple of days and she couldn't be happier about that. Clayton was stopping the night at The Hanging Gate and returning to London in the morning. No matter what had passed between them previously, she had known that she had to let Clayton know that George had died. She had also been very aware that George would have liked the idea of him coming to her funeral.

She didn't know how it had happened, but since that phone call, she and Clayton had slipped into a routine of him ringing her every evening. Knowing that he cared sufficiently to do that had meant a lot to her. Maybe it meant too much. It was proving impossible to stay angry with him. Despite some aspects of his behaviour, he was, she had to admit, a good man at heart. Isabel said that in some respects he was like Bruce, in that his decision-making process didn't work like most people's did. But there again, who was Alice to talk? Hadn't she made some off-the-wall decisions in the past? Such as pretending to be someone she wasn't. Such as deliberately misleading people. Perhaps she and Clayton had more in common than she had supposed.

'Are you asleep, Alice?'

She opened her eyes and found herself being stared at by Grace; she was standing just a few feet away from her. 'No, I was just thinking. How's it going in the kitchen?'

'That's why I'm here. Mum wanted to know what you wanted to drink with your supper. Red wine or white wine?'

Alice roused herself from the armchair. 'That's all right,' she said, 'I'll come and help now.' No sooner had she stood up and stretched the tiredness from her body, than Isabel's voice rang out loudly from the kitchen. '*No!* I don't believe it! How could they have done that to you?'

Alice looked at Grace. 'Any idea what they're talking about?'

'Clayton was telling Mum something I don't think I was supposed to hear. He was talking very quietly. I'm pretty sure Mum made me come and ask you what you wanted to drink just to get rid of me.'

'And did you hear anything?'

Grace's face lit up with a conspiratorial smile. 'Do you know someone called Bazza?'

'I know of him.'

'Well, Bazza drank too much wine and he got very drunk and then he was sick and — '

Isabel burst into the room. 'Alice! You'll never guess what Clayton's just told me!'

Following Isabel was Clayton; he didn't look happy. 'All things considered, I'd rather we discussed this later,' he said in a tone of voice that suggested no one dare argue with him. He cast a meaningful glance in Grace's direction.

★　★　★

'We need a plan,' Isabel said. 'A really good plan. We need to come up with something that will teach Stacey a lesson she won't forget in a hurry.'

'What's with the 'we'?' Clayton asked. 'Who said I needed any help?'

'Don't be silly, Clayton,' Isabel replied, 'of course you need help. Isn't that right, Alice?'

They were in the sitting room, Grace had gone to bed and finally Alice had been let in on the big secret. She was shocked that anyone could have been so publicly duplicitous, that Bazza and Stacey had not only blamed Clayton for something he hadn't done but they had gone out of their way to encourage the press to vilify him. Even that hadn't been enough for them. They, or maybe Stacey in particular, had then made it their business to take advantage of his downfall. 'If Clayton doesn't want us interfering, then I really think we should respect his wishes,' she said.

'Oh, don't be boring. Come on, everybody, think! There must be something we can come up with.'

Alice looked over to the sofa where Clayton was sitting. She thought of the first time he had kissed her when she had been upset about her father. It was after they'd been watching that awful chat show on television with Bazza and Stacey. How the two of them had had the nerve to be interviewed like that and to put on such a breathtakingly sanctimonious act she didn't know. She recalled Stacey's sugary platitudes, her sickening facial expressions, her artificial smiles and laughter. All faked. All designed to gain public sympathy. All carefully planned, right down to the irritating little tilt of her head. What a fraud the woman was.

If there was one thing Alice couldn't abide it was injustice; it was something she had learned the hard way. The more she thought of what Stacey had done to Clayton, the more she felt compelled to right the awful injustice he had suffered. But how? What could she — ? A thought skittered through her head. She looked away from Clayton and tried to grab hold of the thought, to stop it slipping away from her. She tapped her forefinger against her lip. Moments passed. She slowly returned her gaze to Clayton and was surprised to see him looking at her in a very odd way. There was an intensity in his gaze that she was sure hadn't been there before. 'Do I have your permission to suggest something?' she asked.

'Go ahead,' he replied almost inaudibly.

'It may sound a bit far-fetched,' she said, 'but I think I've come up with something, a way to exact a little revenge on Stacey. Actually, it's a way to exact quite a lot of revenge on her.'

52

The make-up girl was one of those hip-looking types kitted out in baggy low-waisted black jeans, a minuscule T-shirt that may well have fitted her better when she'd been ten years of age, a stud through her nose and silver rings on both thumbs. She dabbed Clayton's face one more time then declared him ready. He removed the paper bib from his neck and thanked her as profusely as if she had just announced that he'd won the lottery. Oh, yes, Mr Congenial was in town.

It was all preparation for his impending television appearance. Normally before he appeared in front of a camera he would be snapping and snarling like a caged animal — he'd been known to snap and snarl whilst actually in front of a camera — but today was different. Today he was sweetness personified, ready to give the performance of his life.

He was invited to wait in the green room, where a man he vaguely recognized was sitting on a leather sofa and talking into a mobile phone. Next to the man on the sofa was a girl flicking through the pages of a Filofax. She was in her late twenties with a fraught air about her; presumably she was the man's publicist. She looked up and smiled at Clayton when he sat in the chair opposite. There was no smile from the other man, just a look of reproach as if Clayton

506

had no right to be in the same room as him. Up yours, thought Clayton.

Glen had offered to come with him but had then discovered he was otherwise engaged with another client. 'I'll record the programme and watch it later,' he had assured Clayton. Glen had been delighted when Clayton had suggested he try to get him on a chat show for some extra publicity. 'I'll turn you into a media tart yet,' Glen had responded. 'What's our hook?' he'd asked. 'What are we selling? Have you started on that sequel?'

'We're selling my innate charm and affability,' Clayton had told him.

'You'd better come up with something else because I'll tell you right now, that won't get us a ten-second slot on hospital radio,' Glen had huffed.

Initially they didn't get any takers, just as Glen had warned, but then two days ago a call had come in from *The Stevie McKean Show* saying they'd been let down by a guest and could Clayton fill in?

From that moment, the first part of Alice's plan was up and running.

Next it was down to Bazza to play his part.

When Clayton had returned to London after George's funeral, Clayton had called Bazza and asked to meet him for a drink. 'You're not going to hit me or anything, are you?' Bazza had asked warily.

'No. But I am going to hit you with a plan of extraordinary brilliance.'

They had met for lunch in a small Greek

restaurant just around the corner from Clayton's house. After Clayton had outlined what was going to happen, Bazza very nearly turned all weepy on him again. 'But why?' he'd asked. 'Why would you do this for me?'

'Because I'm a soft-in-the-head bugger and old friendships mean something to me. I also want retribution.'

'I don't know what to say. I'm blown away. I promise I'll repay you somehow.'

'That won't be necessary. You just have to accept that you're going to look pretty stupid for a while.'

Bazza had scoffed at that. 'I can't look any more stupid than I have recently. At least this way, I'll get my life back.'

★ ★ ★

Across London, in Clayton's sitting room, Alice checked her watch. 'Time to give Isabel a call,' she said, 'then we'd better put the television on.'

Bazza nodded and also checked his watch. Alice smiled to herself: it was like a military operation. Operation Stitcheroo as she had nicknamed it.

Isabel eventually answered her mobile. 'Everything OK your end?' Alice asked.

'I said I didn't want to be disturbed,' Isabel replied haughtily. 'You know I don't like to be interrupted when I'm with a client. Especially one as important as this one.'

'Well done.'

'Whatever it was you wanted to discuss, I'm

sure it can wait until tomorrow when I'm back in the studio. Goodbye.'

Alice ended the call on the specially bought pay-as-you-go phone and turned to Bazza. 'Everything's going according to plan at your place.'

'I still can't believe we're going to get away with this,' Bazza said. He pointed the remote control at the television: *The Stevie McKean Show* had just started.

'I do hope you're not questioning my ability,' Alice said.

'Oh, no,' Bazza said quickly. 'Clayton's told me you're awesome. It's just that it seems too easy. Too simple.'

'The best plans are. You're sure you've got the recording stuff organized?'

'Yes. It's all set up. Don't worry.'

They sat on the sofa, both of them waiting for Clayton to make his appearance. They didn't have long to wait: he was Stevie's first guest.

He looked almost jaunty as he ambled down the steps to the interview area. Dressed in an open-necked navy-blue shirt, a cream jacket and a pair of faded jeans, sporting a trim new haircut, he looked good. While the audience clapped, he took his seat on the sofa that was placed at an angle to the host's desk; he leaned back and crossed one leg over the other. 'He looks so casual,' Alice remarks. 'So at ease.'

'It's an act,' Bazza said. 'He hates chat shows. He'd rather gnaw one of his hands off than do this.'

'I know; that's what makes it all the more

incredible.' She kept to herself that she thought Clayton had never looked better or more attractive. And that she suddenly felt massively distracted by the sight of him. Since George's funeral they had grown closer again, but only as friends — friends who were in league together, plotting revenge on a particularly unpleasant person. She wished it was otherwise, that Clayton would view her as he once had, but he clearly didn't. Sometimes she felt like opening up to him. But she couldn't. Not when she still felt the sting of his rejection that day in the hospital cafeteria. She had shared her feelings with Isabel, at the same time making her swear she wouldn't breathe a word of it to Clayton. Isabel had urged her to be brave, to take the risk of being hurt. 'What's the worst that could happen to you?' she had said. 'You'll feel silly, angry and tearful, but you'll get over it in time.'

Meanwhile, on the television screen Clayton was going through the motions of the interview, talking about *The Queen of New Beginnings* and how it had set him off in a new direction with his writing. Which was exactly what they'd planned for him to say. Then inevitably, Stevie turned his questions in the direction of ancient, well-trodden ground.

'So, tell me, Clayton, how are things between you and your old writing partner, Barry Osbourne? Any chance of a reconciliation between the two of you?'

Clayton uncrossed his legs, then recrossed them. He shuffled a bit. He fiddled with one of his cuffs. He smiled ruefully. He looked exactly like a man who had been put on the spot. Again, it was what they had planned. 'Are you working up to ask me how things are with Stacey?' he said. 'Is that what you really want to know?'

Stevie laughed lightly and exchanged a look with the audience. 'Well, since you've raised the matter, how are things? I'm sure everyone here, as well as the viewers at home, would love to know.'

There was a bit more shuffling from Clayton. A bit more cuff-fiddling. Another rueful look. 'Not good, if you want the honest answer,' he said. 'I still feel so guilty about Stacey losing the baby the way she did. I don't think I'll ever get over the guilt.' He suddenly snapped forward in his seat, rested his elbows on his knees. 'You know, Stevie, I'd give anything to hear Stacey say she forgives me. No, really, I mean it. And yes, I know that she's said it in interviews, indeed I believe she said it right here on this show with you. But, the thing is, she's never said the words directly to me.'

After lingering on Clayton's pained expression, the camera turned to Stevie. Stevie took his cue. 'Well, Clayton,' he said, 'who knows, maybe Stacey is watching us right now.' And in one of the cheesiest moments in television history, he said, 'Stacey, if you are watching us, why not get in touch with Clayton? Why not put the man out of his misery?'

There was a laugh from Clayton at this. The camera swung back to him, just in time to catch him say, 'You make it sound like an offer to have me put down, as if I were a dog.'

'Steady, Clayton,' murmured Alice anxiously, 'stick to the script. No ad-libbing.'

The host laughed too and announced they'd be right back after the break.

Bazza turned to Alice. 'Ready?'

'Yes.'

★ ★ ★

The make-up girl was dabbing at his face again, applying a dusting of powder to stop his skin from glistening under the glare of the cameras. He was tempted to ask for an extra-thick coating of the stuff to cover his blushes. How the hell he'd said what he just had without cracking up he didn't know.

His microphone was needlessly being readjusted when he heard Stevie replying to someone who was talking to him in his earpiece. 'You're kidding me? It's for real? Are you mad? Of course, we'll go with it. This could be television gold!' He smiled obsequiously at Clayton. 'I've got a surprise for you.'

'Really?' said Clayton, pretending he hadn't heard the one-sided conversation.

They were counted back in and once again Clayton assumed an air of nonchalance. Which was the last thing he was feeling.

Face to camera, Stevie was telling the audience about his next guest, some actor from *The Bill* who'd got an autobiography to flog — so that's who the bozo was in the green room. 'But first, girls and boys, we've got a surprise guest on the phone. Some of you might be thinking we've set this up, but hand on heart, this is one of those spontaneous television moments we all live for.' He turned to Clayton.

Clayton smiled nervously and sat up slightly straighter, for all the world a man fearing a trap about to be sprung on him. 'You're not going to present me with a red book and say *This is Your Life, Clayton Miller*, are you?'

'Better than that; we've got Stacey on the phone for you!'

'No!'

'Oh yes! She was watching the programme and felt compelled to call in.' Stevie swivelled his head and stared into the appropriate camera. 'Hi, Stacey,' he fawned. 'It's good to speak to you again. How are you?'

There was a silence and then what sounded very like the chink of glass against glass and liquid being poured.

'Err . . . Stacey, are you there?'

'Oh, hi Stevie, I'm sorry, I didn't think you were ready for me yet.'

'We're more than ready for you, my darling. How are you?'

'Can . . . can I be honest with you?'

'Of course.'

'Is Clayton still there with you?'

'He is. Is there anything you want to say to him?'

There was another silence, another chink of glass and the sound of more liquid being poured. A lot of liquid. Practically a bucket full.

'Stacey?'

'Sorry . . . I'm just in the most awful state here. You can't imagine how I'm feeling. I've done something awful. Something so, so bad.'

Probably at the instruction of the voice in his earpiece, Stevie adopted his extra-caring face. 'You do sound a bit upset, love. What's the problem?'

'There's something I have to say to Clayton. I can't go on any longer unless I do.'

Stevie turned his caring face to Clayton. 'Clayton, would you like to say something to Stacey?'

The camera fully on him, Clayton said, 'Hello, Stacey.'

There was a stifled gasp from Stacey.

'What is it, Stacey?' asked Clayton. 'You don't sound well.'

'I'm sorry,' she mumbled. 'I'm really sorry.'

'What are you sorry for?'

'For . . . for everything! I've treated you atrociously.' She started to cry.

Clayton exchanged a look with Stevie, as if getting his permission to go on. 'Is this about you sleeping with Barry behind my back?'

'*No!* Well, I am sorry about that, but not as sorry as I am about . . . Oh, God, I've spilled my drink now!'

'Stacey, what *exactly* are you drinking?'

'Um . . . just a little something to get me through the day. Don't we all need a little help now and then? I'm not an alcoholic, if that's what you're suggesting.'

'So long as you're sure it's helping,' Clayton said. He raised his eyebrows at Stevie.

514

'It's all there is in my life these days,' Stacey said with a loud and messy sniff. 'Oh, nothing's going right for me any more. My life's a sham. I should never have left you for Barry. He's not half the man you are. He's too weak. I need a man who can stand up to me.'

'Stacey, darling,' Stevie cut in with his ultra-caring voice, 'what about forgiving Clayton, can you do that? That's what we all want to know.'

'But you don't understand. It's . . . it's Clayton who has to forgive me. I lied about him causing my miscarriage. I made Barry lie, too. He didn't want to, but I forced him. I've forced him to do so many things. But you see, I wanted someone to blame for losing the baby and . . . and Clayton was perfect. Oh, this feels so liberating, finally to tell someone the truth. Oh, why didn't I do this before?'

Clayton turned to Stevie, his expression all wide-eyed shock. 'I don't believe I'm hearing this. My life was very nearly ruined. I was . . . I was cast as a monster. A child killer.'

For once, Stevie seemed lost for words. 'I'm as shocked as you,' he finally managed. But then he twitched, very likely in response to the voice that Clayton could hear bellowing in the man's ear. 'What we all want to know now, Clayton,' he said, 'is can you forgive Stacey for what she did?'

Milking the moment for as long as he could get away with, Clayton hummed and aahed and eventually he said, 'You know, I think I can. After all, harbouring a grudge never did anyone any good, did it?'

From down the line came a tearful howl. 'Thank you, Clayton. Thank you, thank you, *thank you*. You're a wonderful man.'

There was a click and then the line went dead.

'Well,' said Stevie, 'I don't know about everyone else, but I think we've all just been on an incredible journey together. What we need is a quick break. Be right back with you!'

53

With the kitchen table littered with newspapers, Alice, Bazza, Isabel and Clayton were studying the results of their handiwork.

All had covered Stacey's drunken confession on live television. Even the broadsheets had dipped their dainty toes into the murky waters of the unedifying story. Condemnation was sweeping and total. Not a single journalist had a good word for Stacey. No one had rushed to defend her. Bazza had also come in for criticism but he'd been portrayed as merely weak rather than a hard-nosed malevolent schemer. In some quarters there was a hint of sympathy for him, for having been under the thumb of such a vicious piece of work.

'I think we can safely say,' Clayton said, looking up from the copy of the *Express* he was reading, 'your fall from grace will be short-lived, Bazza. The press are effectively siding with you.'

Bazza looked doubtful. 'I still don't think I deserve to come out of this so well.'

'I agree,' said Alice.

Bazza's face turned red and he looked at her with discomfort. 'I should have stopped Stacey,' he said. 'I know that.'

'I agree again,' Alice said flatly.

Whilst Clayton had forgiven his old friend for what he'd done, he knew that Alice wasn't so easily inclined. It was understandable; she didn't know Bazza, and she didn't share the history that he and Bazza did. He was touched, however. Her censure meant that she cared about him. But then he'd known that already, as why else would she have gone to such lengths to help him? That night in her cottage, the day of George's funeral, when she'd been deep in thought, trying to think of a way to expose Stacey's deception, he had very nearly done away with his good intentions and given in to his ever-increasing desire for her. Had Isabel not been sitting in the room with them, he would have leapt from his chair and, well, suffice to say, the evening would have taken on a very different slant. He still hadn't figured out how something as insignificant as Alice touching her lip could cause such a strong reaction in him. He had only to imagine her doing it and he felt the unmistakable stirring of arousal for her. It was like a switch inside him. Weird. Bloody weird. But nice weird. Definitely nice.

Her voice light, Isabel broke into his thoughts. 'Alice,' she said, 'don't be so hard on Bazza. I spent only a few hours with the woman, but I swear I've never known a more vain, pretentious or demanding client; she spent the whole time telling me how to do my job. I think Bazza and Clayton deserve medals for putting up with her for as long as they both did.'

Finished with the *Express*, Clayton closed it and pushed it aside. 'Speaking for myself, I hardly think I deserve a medal for having a woefully ineffectual nature when it comes to that woman.'

'Never mind a medal, an Oscar more like it, after your performance with Stevie McKean. Don't you agree, Alice?'

Alice smiled. 'Isabel's right: you were utterly convincing, Clayton. Only once did you worry me when you veered off the script.'

He returned her smile. 'It's you who deserves all the credit. Not only did you come up with the entire plan but your impersonation of Stacey was scarily spot on. I was shaking inside at that voice. You were fantastic.'

'I was shaking as well,' said Bazza. He turned to Clayton. 'How about we form a new partnership and call it Wimps R Us?'

'Sounds like a winner to me.'

'Oh, stop it you two,' said Isabel. 'Neither one of you is a wimp. Barry?'

'Yes?'

'Tell us again how Stacey reacted when you arrived home. You told it so well earlier I don't think I shall ever tire of hearing it.'

Was it Clayton's imagination or was there a mutual admiration society taking shape between Bazza and Isabel? Clayton glanced at Alice and saw straight away by the way her lips had curved into the tilt of a small, ironic smile that she was thinking the exact same thing as he was. Well, well, well.

Bazza's response to Isabel's request was to grin like an idiot and say, 'Really? You really want me to go through it all again?' All that was missing from his words was a boyish oh-gee-shucks.

Amused, Clayton said, 'Tell you what, Bazza,

why don't you oblige the lady while I make us some more coffee.'

'I'll help you,' Alice said.

'Oh, well, if you're sure,' Bazza said, looking like a man who couldn't be happier to be left alone with such an appreciative audience.

When they were at the other end of the kitchen, Alice whispered to Clayton, 'You thinking what I'm thinking?'

'And some,' he whispered back.

'I didn't see that coming.'

'Me neither.'

'Do you think it could work?'

'You're asking the wrong person. I'm a total dud when it comes to understanding how relationships work.'

Alice frowned and looked away. Clayton immediately regretted his words; would he never connect his brain to his mouth? He plugged in the kettle and watched Alice run a finger through a trail of toast crumbs on the worktop. Toast crumbs he hadn't tidied up from breakfast.

While Bazza had been putting into effect the final part of the plan last night, Alice and Isabel had come back here to stay with Clayton, Isabel having arranged for her daughter to stop the night with a school friend. It had been an incredibly well-executed operation and Clayton had to admit he'd enjoyed the buzz it had given him. Getting one over on Stacey had meant a lot to him. Possibly too much. But hey, he could live with that.

He tuned into what Bazza was saying to Isabel. Bazza had always been a master storyteller; he had a real talent for capturing all the details and nuances of a story and bringing it to life. Right now he was describing how when he'd returned to Notting Hill, timing his arrival so that he missed Isabel's departure, he had suggested to Stacey that there was something on YouTube she might be interested to see. Downloading the recording he'd made onto the internet had been one of the tasks Alice had assigned to him, along with hiding Stacey's mobile and disconnecting the landline so that no one could ring her before he got back. According to Bazza, Stacey had watched the recording with her eyes and mouth wide open. It was the first time he had known her to be quiet for more than two minutes.

'But it's not me!' she had cried. 'That isn't me speaking on the phone. Why would I admit to those things? I've been here all afternoon. I swear it!'

'So you didn't pick up the phone and call in?' he'd asked her. 'You're sure your conscience didn't finally get the better of you?'

'Of course I'm sure!' she'd screamed back at him. 'Why would I ever want to confess to what we did?'

'Well, it sure as hell sounds like you.'

'But I can prove it isn't me!' she had screeched. 'The photographer will verify I never went near the phone.'

'What photographer?' Bazza had asked.

'What do you mean, what photographer? The one you arranged to come here, of course.'

'I did no such thing.'

'You did! The photographer who you said was going to take those special publicity shots of me. She called the other day to make the appointment. She said you'd been in touch with her.'

A few more denials from Bazza and apparently the penny had dropped and had clanked around at the bottom of an empty, echoing drum for Stacey. 'What's going on?' she had demanded.

'Since you ask, rather a lot. I've had it with you, Stacey. You may thrive on all the arguments we have, and you may also be able to live with the guilt of what we did to Clayton, but I can't. I want out. Or more accurately, I want *you* out. I want you out of my house and my life. I want the old me back. The me I can respect.'

'You can't mean that. What about our wedding?'

'It's not going to happen. I must have been crazy ever to think we could be happy together.'

She had then turned on him, just as Bazza had known she would, which was why he had needed a back-up plan. She had threatened to go to the press and tell the world what a vile man he was, that not only had it all been his idea to blame Clayton for the loss of their baby and that he'd then set her up to take the fall, but he did unspeakable things to her in bed. Humiliating things that no woman should ever have to endure.

That was when Bazza had slipped a CD into his laptop and said, 'I knew that's how you would react, so listen to this and see if you hear anything that might help you to reconsider.'

The CD had been made earlier in the week with Alice's help. It contained yet more confessions made by Stacey in an emotional, drunken state. She spoke of her relationship with Barry, how it was founded on nothing more substantial than her ambitious desire to be with someone who could offer her the lifestyle she craved. She spoke of her drink problem. How it had been fuelled by the shallowness of her existence and how increasingly difficult it was to keep it a secret. She spoke of the strain of living a life of lies, especially the one she had devised about Clayton.

'Blackmail,' Stacey had said when the CD came to an end. 'You're prepared to stoop to that?'

'Just as you are,' Barry had replied. 'And please, there's a lot more where that came from. I have access to an endless supply of your confessions. One wrong word to anyone from you and I'll leak this to the press. And a lot more besides.'

'I have no idea how you've managed this, but tell me, how could you do this? We were so happy together. We had it all.'

'No, Stacey, *you* had it all. Yes, I was happy with you for a time, but then I discovered the real you. It's what happens in every relationship. The layers are peeled back and the true self is exposed. And the fact that you've just threatened to lie to the press yet again in order to exact revenge on me proves what kind of a person you really are.'

'You hate me so much?'

'I hate what you've turned me into.'

Hearing Bazza repeat those words to Isabel now as he came to the end of his story, Clayton thought they made a pretty good punchline. Borderline cliché, admittedly, but no less effective.

The kettle clicked off and while Clayton spooned coffee into the row of mugs, he said, 'Alice, I meant what I said earlier about how fantastic you were. You were the brains behind it all. Without you, it wouldn't have been possible. God only knows how you had the patience to listen to those hideous chat show recordings Bazza got hold of.'

She shrugged. 'It's what I do; it's how I learn a new voice. To be honest, it didn't take that long to master Stacey's. I nailed it after only a few hours of studying it.'

'Well, you did it brilliantly. I want you to know how much I really appreciate everything you've done. Not just for me, but for helping Bazza to extricate himself from a nightmare of a situation.'

She gave him one of her flickering, tentative smiles. 'Be quiet and make the coffee,' she said, 'you're embarrassing me.'

He had just finished pouring water into the mugs when his phone rang. He stopped what he was doing and took the call.

It was Glen. Again. There had been dozens of calls that morning, all from Glen, all following up on *The Stevie McKean Show*. Journalists were in a frenzy of eagerness to interview Clayton. Similarly, Bazza's agent and publicist had been fielding a barrage of calls. Stacey's publicist had also been in touch with him to say she couldn't get hold of Stacey and to ask if he knew what the hell was going on. Bazza had wisely switched off his mobile. The minute he had heard about Stacey's confession, Glen had phoned Clayton last night. He had congratulated Clayton on finally being publicly declared an innocent man. Clayton didn't tell him how the confession had come about. Nor did he intend to. Well, not yet anyway. One day, maybe.

'Your life is turning into a soap opera, my friend,' Glen said to him on the phone now.

'How so?'

'I think you'd better get yourself over here. Right now. As in pronto. As in *NOW!*'

'Any reason why?'

'I currently have two people in my office claiming they're going to whip your ass with a libel suit.'

Clayton's hand tensed around the phone, and wishing he'd taken the call in his office, he turned his back on Alice and lowered his voice. 'Are they brother and sister by any chance?'

'As a matter of fact they are. And if you don't mind me saying, your reaction sounds worryingly like you were expecting this.'

'You know me; I always expect bad news.'

'Be that as it may, I'm working my butt off to keep them sweet and it's not working.'

'Just plead ignorance. You're good at that.'

'I don't earn enough from you to have to put up with this level of abuse, you know.'

'And there was me thinking you did it for love.

By the way, for the sake of clarification, tell me the names of the two people in your office.'

'Natasha and Rufus Raphael.'

Now that was what Clayton called a punchline.

54

Clayton's first thought was to pretend that nothing was amiss. However, the instant he came off the phone and registered the kitchen had fallen ominously quiet, he knew it wasn't going to be so simple. 'What?' he said as three expectant faces stared back at him.

'Who was that?' asked Alice. Her voice was casual and light, but it wasn't fooling him. 'Whoever it was,' she continued in the same relaxed tone, 'they've turned your face a whiter shade of pale. To coin a phrase. Anything you want to tell me?'

'How's your coffee?' he asked merrily.

'Forget the coffee,' Alice snapped. There was nothing nonchalant in her voice now. 'Just tell me what's going on. What's happened?'

Isabel and Bazza looked anxiously at Alice and then at him.

Clayton's pulse quickened. He raked his hands through his hair. Right, it was time to come clean. No more hiding anything. He swallowed and did his best to look Alice square in the eye. It wasn't easy. He cleared his throat. 'It's Rufus and Natasha,' he said. 'They're with Glen. In his office. And they're none too happy.'

* * *

It had to happen. Ever since *The Queen of New Beginnings* had been aired, Alice had known that

527

eventually, one way or another, Rufus and Natasha would reappear in her life.

The moment Clayton had turned his back on her to continue his conversation on the phone she had known he was trying to hide something. She had been right. Catching the words 'brother and sister' she had known that things were about to take a turn for the worse.

Once she had recovered from the initial shock, she had felt surprisingly calm. She still did. She didn't even feel angry with Clayton. Yes, he was responsible for creating the situation, but maybe it was time to face up to Rufus and Natasha. It was either that or go on hiding from them for the rest of her life, and that would make her a coward, which she wasn't. And what did she have to feel bad about? It wasn't as if the way they had been portrayed had been an exaggeration of their behaviour; they really had been as awful as that. If anyone needed to feel bad, it should be Rufus and Natasha.

She was now in the back of a cab with Clayton, on their way to his agent's office. They were both silent. Both staring intently out of the side windows as if they were seeing London for the first time. The triumphant mood of earlier — the bonhomie of a crack team getting one over the enemy — had evaporated. Clayton was drumming his fingers on his leg. He hadn't wanted her to come. He had said he wanted to handle this on his own, to keep Alice out of it. But she had refused to listen. 'You've caused enough trouble on your own already,' she had told him. Her words had come out with more hostility than she had intended and while Clayton was in the hall saying goodbye to Bazza as he prepared to go home, Isabel had taken Alice to one side. 'Let Clayton do this his way,' she had whispered. 'He wants to protect you from any trouble Rufus and Natasha may try to cause you. Why not let him do it? It's obviously important to him.'

'I don't need anyone to protect me,' she had answered. 'I never have and I'm not about to start now.'

'We all need someone to protect and help us at some stage in our lives, Alice. It's not a sign of weakness.'

The traffic was horrendous and they seemed to have been at a standstill for ever. How did people stick it? she thought. Come to that, how had she stuck it for as long as she had? Whenever she had a job to do in London, the intensity of the city always appalled her. The person she had been when she'd lived here — the person who had enjoyed London — now seemed a stranger to her.

'We might as well walk,' Clayton said. 'It'll be quicker. Do you mind?'

'No, whatever gets us there fastest. I'm keen to get this over and done with.'

Clayton passed some money through to the driver and they got out. They completed the rest of the journey in continued silence, Clayton leading the way. It was a sultry, blurry-skied early summer's day and the streets were crowded with people spilling out from shops, restaurants and bars. The air was viscous with car fumes and it was a relief to come across a deserted street. It was closed to all traffic due to a gushing burst water pipe. A gathering of men in high-visibility vests and hard hats looked on helplessly. Had it not been for the hard hats, Alice suspected they might have scratched their heads to show everyone just how tricky a problem it was to solve.

They had reached Soho now and it wasn't until Clayton drew to a stop in front of a small, unprepossessing door that he spoke. 'Is there anything I can say to you that would make you change your mind?' he asked.

'What about?'

'About me doing this alone.'

'Clayton, this is my battle. Let me sort it out my way.'

He shook his head slowly. 'The thing is, Alice, I can't do that. I've made many mistakes in my life, but this is one I have to rectify personally.'

'Why? Why does it matter to you so much?'

'Because . . . because I care about you. I care about you a lot.'

'You do?'

'Please don't look so surprised. I've never stopped caring about you.'

She frowned and looked down at the ground, poked at a discarded matchstick on the pavement with the toe of her shoe. 'Caring is such a vague word. People care about many things, like the cost of petrol or global warming.' She raised her head. 'What do you actually mean by it?'

He stared at her, his gaze unblinking. 'I'm

trying to tell you I made a mistake,' he said at length.

'I'm sorry, but you're going to have to be more specific. Which particular mistake? After all, there have been a few.'

'I'm talking about us. I should never have kidded myself I didn't want to be with you.'

'But you did. That day at the hospital, you couldn't have made your feelings for me clearer.'

'Another mistake in the long and depressing history of Clayton Miller mistakes. I thought I was doing the right thing, only to discover it was entirely the wrong thing. You're the most amazing person I know, Alice. I don't think I've ever known anyone like you. You're the first thing I think of when I wake up in the morning and the last thing when I go to bed at night. Tell me, is there anything I can do to make you think well of me again?'

'I . . . I don't know what to say. We're standing here in the middle of Soho and you choose now to tell me all this. Why? What's changed?'

He drew in his breath, then let it out. 'I don't know. Maybe it's got something to do with the thought of Rufus hurting you all over again. The very idea of it makes me want to tear him apart. You know, the whole limb from limb thing with my own bare hands. Very primeval, I admit.' He ran a hand over his face. Then rubbed at the back of his neck. 'Perhaps only love can make a person feel that way. What do you think?'

Stunned, she put a finger to her lip. She tapped it thoughtfully. *Love*. He'd used the word love. But did he mean it? Did he even know what it meant? She tapped her lip again.

Clayton suddenly groaned. 'Please don't do that.'

'Don't do what?' she asked.

His answer was to take her in his arms and kiss her. It was a kiss of immense passion.

'We're making a terrible spectacle of ourselves,' she said, when a crowd of drinkers outside a nearby bar started whistling and cheering.

'I've made a terrible spectacle of myself all my life,' he said, still holding her close. 'I'm beyond caring.' He tipped his head to kiss her again.

She gently pushed him away. 'Not so fast, mister. We have serious business to attend to.'

★ ★ ★

Glen shared the three-storey building with a firm of accountants whose services were readily and conveniently offered to his clients the moment they signed up with his agency; good rates were guaranteed. His office was on the ground floor.

Clayton led the way to an open-plan reception area where there was no sign of anyone behind the sleek, curving desk. He took Alice's hand. 'Please,' he said, 'will you let me try and smoothe the waters on my own? There's really no need for you to get involved. A few simple but adamant denials on my part and we'll soon have this wrapped up. They really don't have a leg to stand on when it comes to hurling accusations of libel around.'

'Sorry, Clayton, I'm afraid that's not good

enough for me. But I will meet you halfway. I won't come in with you, so long as you don't deny anything. Or smoothe the waters. You're to tell them the truth about how you came by the story. And if they want to meet me at a later date, tell them they can.'

'You're sure?'

She kissed him on the cheek. 'Whether they have a leg to stand on or not, I'm convinced Rufus and Natasha won't pursue a libel suit. The shame would kill them, they won't risk going public with it. For now, let's see what they've got to say for themselves, shall we? The more I think about it, the more I believe that it's me they want. And to get at me they have to go through you. They probably want my silence on any further revelations they're worried I might come out with.'

Clayton gave in. 'OK, but I want you out of sight for now. I don't want to give Rufus the opportunity to confront you today. There's another office just down the corridor. Why don't you go and sit in there?'

'Don't you worry about me. I'll make myself invisible.'

⋆ ⋆ ⋆

Clayton didn't bother knocking on Glen's door. He strolled in as casually as he had ambled down the steps of the set for *The Stevie McKean Show*. Plenty of smoke and mirrors, that's what was needed. 'Glen,' he said volubly, 'I hope you appreciate that you've probably ruined the best

533

day's writing of my life. But I'm sure you had your reasons.' He ignored the warning look on Glen's face — a harrowed face that looked like it had seen the future and it wasn't good — and turned his head to get his first sighting of Rufus Raphael. *Come on, you bastard, let's be having you! If it's a fight you're after, I'm your man!*

He almost jumped back in surprise. Holy shit! This was not what he had been expecting.

★ ★ ★

With her ear pressed against the door, Alice was straining to hear what was going on. So far only the introductions had been made. And by a voice she didn't recognize; presumably Glen's.

Next came some indistinct mutterings Alice couldn't make sense of and then came Clayton's voice. 'So what exactly is it you're accusing me of?' he asked.

Alice held her breath, waiting to hear who would answer his question: Rufus or Natasha?

'Please don't insult our intelligence with an attempt at obtuseness. Let's get straight to the point, shall we?'

It was Rufus. No question. Still the same patronizing and superior arrogance in his voice. Still the same dismissive drawling lilt to his words. She could picture him looking down his nose at Clayton. He probably hadn't changed at all. It made Alice think that an older version of the person she had once known would be an adversary of some magnitude. Had he become a doctor? She shuddered at the thought of what his bedside manner might be like. She certainly wouldn't want to be informed by him that she was dying. He'd be the first to pull the plug on her!

'And what point is it that you want to get straight to?' asked Clayton.

'That your grubby little script was not a work of fiction, as your abysmal and inefficient agent here has been claiming, but was based on a pack of lies told to you by a conniving bitch my sister and I once had the misfortune to know.'

Conniving bitch! Alice was ready to crash open the door and have her say. But hearing Clayton speak, she held back. 'Now listen, you ingrate,' he said in a commanding voice she had never heard him use before. 'Firstly, my agent is many things but he is neither abysmal nor inefficient, and secondly, the misfortune was entirely that young woman's.'

'You admit it then! Your script was based on what that wretched girl told you.'

Natasha had now joined in. There was no mistaking her voice. It was lower than Alice remembered it, but the contrived refinement and conceited self-importance were as they had always been. If not more so. For a bizarre moment, Alice found herself mimicking the voice in her head.

'And what if it was? What are you going to do about it? Sue me? Yeah, why don't you? Tell the world that it's you in the script in all your glory. But the truth is, the consequences will be far more damaging to you than they ever would be to me. I have first-hand experience of how the press will treat you when they get hold of this juicy little story. Your friends will all look at you anew and one by one they'll disown you. You'll be social pariahs. Meanwhile, I'll be riding high on a wave of free publicity that you'll have provided for the sequel I'm currently writing. Hey, you know what, give me your address and I'll slip an invitation in the post to you to attend a private showing of it. Glen? Any thoughts of your own to offer?'

Alice froze. *Sequel.* She didn't like the sound of that.

'I think you're dead right, Clayton. I'm all for getting as much free publicity as I can for my clients. Strikes me this is the perfect gift horse and I look forward to looking it right in the mouth. I apologize for mixing my metaphors, but this could be the cash cow of cash cows.'

There was silence then. It seemed that Clayton had outmanoeuvred them.

Rufus eventually spoke. 'We want to speak to her. We want to know why she did this to us. After all this time, why?'

'I'm sorry, to whom are you referring?'

'Don't push my patience; I warned you not to be obtuse earlier. I'm talking about Alice. Alice Barrett.'

Rufus uttered her name as if it was poison on his tongue.

'We want to know what she hoped to gain from this.'

'Not everyone does something in the hope of gain. Yet very likely that's a concept you don't understand. Given your behaviour towards Alice all those years ago, I think unrepentant self-interest is a way of life for you both.'

'And you're basing this view on what? On lies and exaggerations by a fool of a girl who threw herself at me? Because that's what really happened. From the word go, Alice was obsessed with me. She trailed round after me, day in, day out. She never gave me a moment's peace. She was a fantasist, imagining that I was in love with her. What's more, she was as unbalanced as her father. A man, I might add, who pushed two women to their death. The man was a dangerous lunatic. Clearly Alice inherited the crazy gene from him. And to think you believed a word of what she told you.'

The blood pounding in her ears, Alice had heard enough. She could countenance being branded a liar and not right in the head, but she would not stand here another second and hear the memory of her beloved father being disparaged.

She turned the handle and pushed open the door. Despite what she had said to Clayton, it was time for her big entrance.

Oh, it was more than time.

55

It was difficult to know just who was most shocked when Alice entered the room. Everyone fell instantly quiet. Everyone stared at her. But it was Alice who stared the most. She openly gaped, robbed in a flash of the murderous anger that had been bubbling up within her the other side of the door.

Rufus stared back at her, a sardonic glint darkening his eyes. 'Well, well, *well*,' he drawled. 'Here she is at last. The person everybody's talking about. What a stir you've caused.'

'What happened to you?' she asked.

'This?' he said, tapping the arm of the wheelchair he was sitting in. 'This old thing? Is that what you're enquiring after? How very rude of you to come right out with such a question. But of course, we couldn't really expect polite discretion from you, could we? Hardly your style, is it? Blabbing is more your forte.'

'Alice didn't blab,' Clayton said sharply from where he was standing in the corner of the room next to the window. 'She merely recounted her childhood to me.'

'That's all right, Clayton,' Alice said, 'I can handle this.'

'Handle what exactly, Alice?' asked Natasha. 'The fact that you've tried to destroy our reputations?'

'That was never her intention.'

'Clayton, please,' Alice said gently. She looked at Natasha, seeing her properly now for the first time, no longer a teenager but a young woman the same age as Alice. She seemed older, though. And tired. Very tired. There were lines at the corners of her eyes, and her mouth, turned down and creased either side, was marred by an expression of what Alice guessed was a permanent state of bitter resentment. There was no softness to her. She looked as if life had worn her down a long time ago.

Beside her, in his wheelchair, Rufus sat defiantly implacable. He was wearing a pair of dark-blue jeans and Alice could see by the way the fabric lay that beneath it his legs were withered and useless. The anger she had experienced earlier for him was now replaced with pity. How he would hate to know that. 'Perhaps it would be more appropriate for the three of us to talk about this in private,' she said, directing her words at Rufus.

'Why? Are you worried that we'll expose you for the lying bitch you are in front of these people?'

Clayton, who seemed to be coiled like a spring, lurched forward. 'Listen, you little shit! Just because you're in a wheelchair don't think for one moment it wouldn't give me the greatest of pleasure to kick your sorry arse out of here and onto the street.'

'Oh, oh! Fighting talk. Now that's more like it. Alice, would I be right in thinking you and this man are bedfellows? Because if I'm not mistaken, I'm hearing the sound of someone keen to protect your honour. Which means, of course, that he's blind to your many faults, namely that you're a born liar and given to fantasizing.' He tutted and shook his head in a display of exaggerated disdain. 'Really, Alice, hiding behind a man just as you once hid behind your father. Still not brave enough to fight your own battles? I'm disappointed.'

'Why are you taking this line, Rufus?' Alice asked quietly. 'Why can't you face up to the truth of what happened to us? Are you now going to deny that your mother killed herself? And that it wasn't the first time she'd tried it?'

'What are you talking about?'

'It's true,' Alice replied calmly. 'I recently found out that your mother tried or threatened to take her life on several occasions. If it hadn't been for my father she would have succeeded long before she died so tragically.'

Rufus gave her a contemptuous look. 'Yet more fantasy from you. But what else could we expect?' He turned to Clayton. 'You see, this is what she's like. One lie after the other. It's sad, really; she needs help.'

Clayton let out a bark of laughter. 'Newsflash, Chuckles! It's you who needs help in dealing with that chronic case of denial you're patently suffering from. Take it from me, every word Alice has just said is true.'

'And how the hell would you know?' Rufus's tone was barbed with sneering condescension.

Alice raised her hand to Clayton; this question was hers to answer. 'I have it on good authority,' she said, 'that my father had to take your mother

540

to hospital after one of her attempts to kill herself and another time he had to break down the bathroom door to stop her from doing anything stupid. What's more, he kept it quiet because he wanted to protect us from what was going on.'

'How did you come by this information?'

'From Isabel.'

At the mention of Isabel's name, Rufus visibly stiffened. His expression tightened. But he didn't speak. It was a satisfying reaction from him.

'After what Isabel did to Rufus I hardly think we're inclined to believe a word she has to say on the matter,' Natasha said. 'And anyway, if our mother was unhappy, there was a good reason for it. She was married to a monster. That man put her through hell. He was never sympathetic to her needs; he mocked her and belittled her. It was a shockingly abusive marriage from start to finish.'

'My sister's right,' Rufus rallied. 'Moreover, Isabel is as much to blame for what happened as is your father.'

'You think it was easy for my father, knowing that Julia's only reason for marrying him was financial security? Well, I'll tell you this; Isabel and my father stayed together for many years and she made him happier than your mother ever did. And I'm glad about that.'

'Oh, how lovely for them both. You'll be telling me next that love conquers all.'

'She'll be telling you to shut the hell up if she has any sense,' Clayton chipped in.

The earlier rush of adrenaline that had

coursed through Alice was fading fast and she began to feel drained by the effort of sparring with Rufus. 'If you're not going to accept the truth,' she said wearily, 'what is the point in any of this?'

'The point, Alice, is that you have trashed our family name and I won't stand for it.'

'Yeah, we can see that!' Clayton snapped.

Alice winced and behind his desk, where he was looking like a man who had gatecrashed the wrong party, Glen drew in his breath. Rufus glared at Clayton. 'A cheap shot if ever I heard one.'

'Trust me, Bambi, there's plenty more where that came from. I did warn you. The fact that you can't walk doesn't protect you from hearing the truth. Not from me, anyway. What did you do, fall off your high horse? Or trip over your bloody great ego?'

'How dare you talk to my brother like that? Just who do you think you are?'

'That's OK, Tash, let him have his sport if he so desires. If you must know, Mr Miller, the summer after my mother died, in a moment of maudlin inebriation, I dived into a pool of water that was shallower than I was expecting and surfaced with a broken back. I hope that satisfies your curiosity. Yours too, Alice. And in case you were wondering, as a consequence of that accident I didn't finish medical school and so never qualified.'

'I'm sorry, Rufus,' Alice said. 'That must have been awful for you.'

'Please don't insult me with your phoney

sympathy; I've managed perfectly well up to now without it.'

The sour acrimony of his words spoke of a life not lived to the full. Of grudges harboured. Of blame and hatred carefully nurtured. Maybe there was even a sense of deep regret. How often had he looked at himself in that chair and pondered how different his life might have been if he had never brought Isabel home that disastrous Christmas? Chances were he never had and never would blame himself. But now that he had Alice to hand, he could lay all the blame on her.

After glancing over to Clayton, and keeping her voice as level and reasonable as she could, Alice said, 'Natasha and Rufus, can you tell me what you hoped to achieve by coming here today? What is it you want?'

When they both stared at her blankly, she carried on speaking. 'Because as far as I can see, you've had a wasted trip. You don't have any kind of a case against Clayton and, whatever you believe, the past cannot be undone. Which includes *The Queen of New Beginnings*. If you can't accept that it was a fair representation of our lives at Cuckoo House then you have to take a good look at yourselves. Now, if you have anything further to say on the subject, I suggest you don't trouble Clayton and his agent any longer.' She opened her bag and pulled out a card. She handed it to Rufus. 'You can contact me via *my* agent.'

He looked at it and his mouth curved into a sneer. 'Alice Shoemaker, voiceover artist. That's quite a come-down from your lofty ambition of being an actress, isn't it?' He handed the card to Natasha. 'Is Shoemaker your professional name?'

Ignoring the insult, she said simply, 'Yes.' Why give him the pleasure of knowing the real reason why she had changed her name?

After Natasha had read the card, Rufus took it back from her. 'Here's what I have to say about getting in touch with you, Alice.' He ripped the card in half, then in half again. He threw the pieces at her. It was a nasty, petty little gesture, intended to make Alice feel as worthless as her business card. 'Come on, Tash,' he said, 'let's get out of here. I've had enough.'

As they watched Natasha carefully steer her brother out of Glen's office, Alice wondered if Natasha was solely responsible for taking care of Rufus. If so, it meant that she had got her wish; she had the brother she adored all to herself.

★   ★   ★

When they were left alone, Glen said, 'Would either of you two care to fill me in on what I've just witnessed?'

'Later,' said Clayton. 'I need to talk to Alice on her own.'

56

I have never needed to be forcibly restrained or sedated in order to review a programme, but last night I came as close to it as I have ever been. I knew it was going to be a Herculean task when I settled down to watch the preview tape of the first episode (please God let it be the last!) of *Racey Stacey*.

What bright spark dreamed up this piece of vomit-inducing horror? What am I talking about? I'm talking about an hour of watching Stacey Cook assuming the role of third-rate chat show host while inviting a selection of nonentity guests and members of the audience to discuss their sexual proclivities. Disturbingly there were too many who needed no encouragement at all to lay out their fetishes and sexual hang-ups in so public a way. Call me an old-fashioned prude, but I really don't need a freakishly earnest Stacey cosying up to some ugly-looking half-wit while plumbing the depths of his urge to urinate over his girlfriend.

As the agonizing minutes of this dire programme dragged on, I began to feel nostalgic for the days of Mary Whitehouse. I couldn't help wonder if she hadn't had a point all those years ago. I shudder now, as I shuddered last night, to think what future TV torments lie in wait for us. Please, citizens of this beautiful country, I urge you under no circumstances to watch this rubbish. Yet even as I type these words, I know that your curiosity will be piqued and you will want to know just how low this programme really is.

But answer this, my friends, before you sink into the vast wastelands of mindless titillation, is this what our sceptred isle has been reduced to? Is this really what passes for entertainment in our enlightened age? Can we not do better? Can we not raise the barricades of human decency and arm ourselves against such depravity?

Brendon Torrington — *The Times*.

Do yourselves an almighty favour: DO NOT WATCH *RACEY STACEY*. In fact, write to your MP and demand that this pernicious freak show be removed from our screens at once!

Estelle Baker — *Daily Mail*.

Yes, we're well aware that Barry Osborne's ex-squeeze Stacey Cook is trying valiantly to resurrect her public persona ever since her drunken confessions were aired on *The Stevie McKean Show* a year ago, but do her 'people' really believe sufficient time has passed for her to be forgiven?

With a book soon to be launched, it's obvious that her PR machine has swung into gear to maximize publicity on all fronts, but frankly the boundaries have been pushed too far in this instance. Never have I witnessed such a flagrant attempt at self-aggrandizement. It's not the so-called saucy late-night content of the programme that bothers me so much as the rapt seriousness with which Stacey takes herself. She seems to be utterly convinced that we, the audience, are taken in by her performance to get to the heart of the matter. I've got news for you, Stacey: you're about as profound as a roll-mop herring. Nothing personal, of course.

Andrew Tillen-Jones — *Independent*.

A cross between a motherly caring Fern Britton and a sexy plain-speaking Katie Price, Stacey hits exactly the right note when it comes to getting her guests and audience members to open up to her. *Racey Stacey* — definitely worth a punt!

Joe Reeves — *Sun*.

3 Abbey Court House,
Brayton,
Hertfordshire.

PLEASE FORWARD TO ALICE SHOE-MAKER.

Dear Alice,

It's a year since my brother and I met with you in London and in the intervening time I have given a lot of thought to that day and the sharp words we were all guilty of exchanging.

I would have written sooner, but it has taken me a while to track you down, or rather, to locate your agent's address — I managed this eventually after discovering your website on the internet. I do hope your agent forwards this letter to you.

You may be wondering why I am going to the trouble to get in touch and I must admit that this is not an easy letter for me to write. The sad and embarrassing truth is that Rufus and I find ourselves in financial difficulties. The recession has hit Rufus's IT consultancy work badly and to make things worse, I have just been made redundant from the hospital where I worked part time as a dietician. It seems that when times are hard, nobody is interested in nutrition. Of course, my main job is to take care of Rufus. He is as independent as any paraplegic can be but he relies on me heavily, which is why I can only work part time. We bought this house when he finally left Stoke Mandeville Hospital and have lived together ever since.

Rufus has no idea that I am writing to you — he is a very proud man — but in extreme situations one has to do away with pride and seek help where it may be available. Which brings me to the point of this letter. Alice, I am asking you as your half-sister — which must count for something — whether you could help Rufus and me. We could call it a loan, if you like; a loan to tide us over until this wretched recession has passed. I hesitate to bring up the matter, but I'm sure you must have benefited financially from *The Queen of New Beginnings* and since the story included the Raphael family, I don't think it's unreasonable for us to benefit in some way as well. I am sure you know in your heart that it would be the right thing to do.

With kind regards,
Natasha.

P.S. I've read about the many awards Clayton Miller has recently received, including a BAFTA and an Emmy. I also read how he says he owes the success of *The Queen of New Beginnings* to one person in particular; he didn't name you, but clearly he was referring to you. Has he started work on the sequel he mentioned during our meeting last year?

Dragonfly Cottage,
Stonebridge,
Derbyshire.

Dear Natasha,

I'm sorry to hear of your troubles. It must be a very distressing time for you and Rufus. The world is currently in a terrible state of flux.

This may surprise you but I did not benefit financially in any way from *The*

Queen of New Beginnings. I have, though, had a run of luck with a series of television adverts I've voiced in the last year and I am enclosing a cheque for you. I hope you will take it in the spirit it is given in, not as a loan, but as a gift.

I wish you and Rufus well.

Best wishes,

Alice.

P.S. Clayton has been working on a new project which has nothing to do with the events of Cuckoo House. I managed to talk him out of that!

3 Abbey Court House,
Brayton,
Hertfordshire.

Dear Alice,

Please find enclosed your unwanted crumbs of charity. Whatever has passed between you and Natasha, I want nothing to do with it. If you thought you could buy us off to assuage your guilt for what you did, you are very much mistaken.

Rufus.

If you like your how-to-turn-your-life-around books dripping with treacle, then Stacey Cook's book will be just the thing for you. It's full of useful tips such as never compromising on your appearance and how to be kind to yourself. Even if you feel like slashing your wrists (my words, not

Stacey's) apparently the answer is to treat yourself to a full body massage, a facial, a manicure and a hair do. If you can throw in the extra treat of a little shopping expedition or lunch with a girlfriend, so much the better. According to Stacey, it's amazing how positive such a small amount of effort will make you feel. She makes no comment as to how much the poorer your bank balance will be after this pick-me-up, but I guess this is something she doesn't need to concern herself with now that she's acquired herself a new boyfriend in the super-wealthy Boris Nikolaeva, the latest questionable visitor to our shores from the gas fields of Siberia. My honest opinion of this book? It's a dead cert for the remainder bin.

Lou Ashton, *Daily Mail*.

Viewers are in for a rare treat this evening. Lock the doors, switch on the answer machine and put your feet up for the television event of the year. Reconciled after a regrettable period of not speaking to each other, the great writing duo Clayton Miller and Barry Osbourne are back! And never has their writing power been more formidably comic. Whilst watching the preview tape of *Reasons to be Cheerful*, I had to keep hitting the pause button to wipe away the tears of laughter and to give my sides a rest. Side-splitting and eye-wateringly funny, this is a sure winner. The boys are back! Hallelujah!

Miranda Stevenson — *Radio Times*.

See page 43 for an in-depth interview with Clayton Miller and Barry Osbourne and discover what is making them so cheerful these days.

57

It had been a small wedding. A no-nonsense wedding. No unnecessary frills. No pretentious or cloying gimmicks. Just a gathering of close friends and family to share the special day. It had been a little perfunctory perhaps, but that had been the prerogative of the bride and groom. When exiting the church, never had a couple looked more thoroughly relieved to get things over and done with. And never, in Alice's opinion, had a groom looked more terrified throughout the proceedings. He was a lot more relaxed now, now that he had a plate of food in his hands and had a few drinks inside him. With the aid of a chicken drumstick he was adding extra emphasis to his words by jabbing at the air in front of Alice's face.

'I've got to tell you, Alice, I hardly knew you when you walked into the church. You've scrubbed up a treat. Nice dress.'

'Thank you, Bob.'

He winked and waved the drumstick just inches from her nose. 'And to think you went to so much trouble specially for me.'

'That poor new wife of yours; how is she ever going to put up with you?'

'Kim will manage well enough. She's a sensible woman and knows when she's onto a good thing.'

'How did I ever let a catch like you slip

through my hands?'

Bob laughed. 'It's not too late. We could cause a stir by running off together when the party's over.'

'I can't speak for Kim, but I think Clayton might not be too happy with that arrangement.'

'Where is that man of yours, then?'

Alice turned and pointed across the lawn to where Clayton was hunkered down beside Kim's five-year-old son, Jake. They were having a very in-depth conversation about something.

Eleven months ago Bob had met Kim through work. He had been sent to fix a fault on her phone line and had ended up being fixed himself. Well, that was the way he told the story. Ronnetta's version was that he had been smitten at first sight and had sent Kim a bunch of flowers the next day. Attached to the flowers was a note asking her out for a drink. Very smooth.

'You know what, that fella of yours is shaping up to be better than I thought he would,' Bob said.

Alice did an exaggerated double take. 'Good God, did I hear right? Did you just pay Clayton a compliment? Marriage must already be mellowing you. Or is it the thought of impending fatherhood that's making you be so nice?'

Simultaneously they both switched their gaze to where a hugely pregnant Kim was sitting on a bench sandwiched between her mother and Ronnetta. The bench was positioned in the shade of a gnarled old apple tree but the late August sunshine was oppressively hot and poor Kim, literally bursting at the seams in her wedding dress, was suffering badly. Her face was flushed and glistening with perspiration. She wiped her forehead with a paper napkin while the two women either side of her did their best to keep her cool by fanning her. Alice knew just how excited Ronnetta was at the prospect of becoming a grandmother in two months' time; she talked of little else. As much as she already doted on Kim's son from her first marriage, she couldn't wait for Bob's own baby to be born.

'Kim's looking well,' Alice said.

'You mean she looks like a beached whale. If this baby doesn't come early I'll have to get hold of some winching gear to heave her in and out of bed. I'm told all the women in her family balloon up something rotten when they're pregnant.'

'I hope you're treating her kindly.'

'No choice in the matter. With the hormones she's got ripping through her I'd be a dead man to behave any other way.'

'Good. And I just know that beneath that bluff exterior there lies a loving and considerate husband and father-to-be.'

'I'm doing my bit, don't you worry. I've been there at all the antenatal classes. I'm a black belt in back rubbing and breathing exercises. So when are you and Clayton going to get spliced? Or are you still unsure about him?'

Alice smiled. 'Oh, I'm as sure about him as I'll ever be.'

'So why not get married?'

'Why change things when we're both happy with how things are? I don't believe in change purely for the sake of change. Anyway, we're too busy right now to think about anything like getting married.'

'Busy with the house?'

Again, they redirected their gaze; this time they both stared up at the house behind them. 'We're hoping to start work on the kitchen and bathrooms next month,' Alice said. 'I can't say I'm looking forward to the upheaval.'

'I've said it before and I'm saying it again, Alice, it was good of you to let us have our wedding shindig here. Letting Kim's mum and my mum have free rein here was brave of you.'

Alice shrugged. 'Think nothing of it; it was my wedding present to you. No point in having a lovely garden like this and not sharing it with friends.'

Shortly after George's funeral, Alice had received a solicitor's letter saying that his client, a Miss Georgina Harrington-Smythe, had left Alice Well House. 'But she couldn't have,' Alice had said when she went to meet with the solicitor who had written to her. 'There must be some kind of mistake.'

Affronted that his professionalism was being called into question, the balding man had replied crisply, 'I can assure you, Miss Shoemaker, we are not in the business of making mistakes when it comes to wills. I personally drew up the last will and testament of Miss Harrington-Smythe.'

'But when?'

'I was summoned to visit my client when she was in hospital. She was very clear on her wishes, namely that she wanted you to have Well House. There is also a not inconsiderable amount of money that she has bequeathed to you.' He had lowered his eyes to the papers in front of him on his desk and said, 'There is just one condition, though. You only inherit if you promise to take care of Percy for the rest of his life, and his girlfriends. Do you know who Percy is? Does this make sense to you?'

Alice had roared with laughter in the car on her way home. Then she had cried. Dear old George; what a wonderful woman she had been.

Looking about her now, Alice took in the garden that she remembered so fondly from her childhood and thought of all the plans she had for it. She was going to follow George's example and grow lots of fruit and vegetables. She planned to change how things were laid out, though, and she even fancied the idea of keeping some bees. Clayton teased her that she was going to end up as eccentric as George.

They had only recently moved into Well House. Before either of them could contemplate doing so, they had undertaken the job of clearing the place and sending in a team of professional cleaners. It had been sad to see so much of George disappear, but common sense had to prevail. They kept a few of the better pieces of furniture, both Alice and Clayton admitting that the house wouldn't be the same if it was entirely devoid of anything of George's.

Alice had yet to decide what to do with Dragonfly Cottage, but with Clayton needing to be in London so often, it made sense for him to keep his house down there.

Much to Alice's amazement, Clayton had

proved himself to be remarkably capable and enthusiastic when it came to the work that needed doing on Well House and occasionally she would come home from a job and find him knocking through a wall, nailing down floorboards or taking a door off its hinges to strip. It was fun not knowing what she might come back to.

But not everything was perfect at Well House. Percy did not approve of having a man living on his patch and would frequently demonstrate his disapproval by chasing Clayton. One day Percy had sneaked into the house through an open ground-floor window, despite being banned from doing so, and had crept up behind Clayton as he sat at his desk writing and had pecked him hard on the back of his leg. Clayton had jumped out of his skin and sent a full cup of coffee flying. Alice had tried to be sympathetic but had failed miserably; she hadn't been able to stop laughing.

For the safety of the wedding guests today, Percy and his girls were securely under lock and key in the henhouse. Smiling to herself, Alice returned her attention to Bob. 'Why don't you go and talk to Kim? See if you can tempt her into eating something. We don't want her fainting from hunger on her big day.'

⋆   ⋆   ⋆

Two days later Alice and Clayton were woken by the sound of a clanging bell. Alice went to the bedroom window and peered down to see who it was: the postman smiled up at her. 'I'll leave it in the porch, shall I?' he called out.

Alice went downstairs. The package had the words PLEASE DO NOT BEND written on it. It was addressed to Alice and Clayton, and taking it upstairs with her, Alice got back into bed with Clayton. She opened the package knowing what was inside — photographs that Isabel had taken last weekend when she and Grace, along with Bazza, had come to stay at Well House. They had been celebrating the success of *Reasons to be Cheerful*. The reviews had been excellent, as had the viewing figures.

Having previously made the mistake of turning himself into a very public figure, Bazza wasn't making that mistake again and had spent the last year keeping his relationship with Isabel as much under wraps as he could. The press knew that there was someone new in his life, as they did with Clayton, but fortunately no one was hounding them over it.

'You're looking incredibly serious in this photo,' Alice remarked.

'Really?' Clayton leaned over to get a better look. 'Mmm ... I can't remember, was I suffering from brooding alpha male syndrome that day or constipation?'

Alice laughed and turned to the next photograph. It was a group shot, one that Alice remembered Isabel taking by using the timer device on her camera so that she could also be in the picture. 'I'm going to frame this one,' she said decisively.

'Any reason why?'

'A very important reason; this shows every-thing wonderful in my life. This is my new family: you, Isabel and Grace, and Bazza.'

Clayton put his arm around her. 'I'm glad you've forgiven Bazza for what he did. It means a lot to me.'

'I know. But how could I not forgive him when I know he's going to marry Isabel?'

'You really think they'll marry?'

'Without a shred of doubt. They're so right together, don't you agree?'

'Even though Bazza's completely different from Bruce?'

'Perhaps that's why they're perfect together. Bazza isn't a replacement for my father.'

They went through the rest of the photographs in silence. When they'd looked at them all, Clayton said, 'George once said to me that she thought I was right for you because I reminded you of your father. Would I be very foolish to ask if that's true?'

When Alice didn't answer, Clayton said, 'Don't worry, there's no right or wrong answer.'

'But if I say yes, then you're going to think there's something weird about me, that I have some form of Oedipus complex.'

'So I do remind you of him?'

'Only in that from time to time you make the same sort of wacky decisions he used to make. You're complex, too. There'll always be some-thing new to discover about you. And you can be wildly unpredictable, like the day we went to Glen's office to meet with Rufus and Natasha. I had absolutely no idea how you felt about me until then. And then afterwards you surprised me again when you bundled me into a taxi and whisked me off to the Ritz for cocktails.'

'Where better to convince you that I really did love you and didn't ever want to be parted from you?'

She smiled. 'Lucky for you the concierge was able to supply you with a tie or you would have been declaring your feelings out on the street again.'

'I like to do things spontaneously. I can't prepare for all contingencies.'

'And that's one of the many things I love about you. So don't ever think of changing.'

'You must be the only woman in the world who doesn't want the man in her life to change.'

'What can I say? I'm not like other women.'

Taking the photographs from her, Clayton sorted through them as if searching for one in particular. When he came to a photograph of him standing behind Alice with his arms around her, he studied it thoughtfully. Alice watched him closely. Eventually he looked up. 'Can I ask you something else?' he said.

'Of course.'

'What would you say if I asked you to marry me?'

She slowly put a finger to her lip. 'Is that a trick question?' she responded cautiously.

'It wasn't meant to be, but I take your point; my question was too ambiguous.' He suddenly pushed back the duvet, slipped out of the bed and came round to her side of it. 'OK, same question but with a hundred per cent clarity.' He got down on one knee. 'Alice Shoemaker, will you marry me?'

She stared at him in shock. Her heart hammered. 'I don't know what to say.'

He looked disappointed. 'That wasn't quite the answer I was hoping for.'

'I'm sorry,' she said, flustered. 'I just wasn't expecting this. I thought you weren't the marrying kind.'

'When did I ever say that?'

'I suppose I just . . . I just assumed. It's not something we've ever talked about.'

'Well, you assumed wrong. And we're talking about it now. I love you Alice, and want to spend the rest of my life with you.'

'You really want to get married? To *me*?'

'No Alice, I'm down here wrecking my knee on a whim, in the hope a passing stranger will want to marry me.'

'You've thought about this? I mean, you've really thought — '

'Geez, Alice! Stop dickering about and say yes before — '

'Before what?' she interrupted him. 'Before you change your mind?'

'No, before my knee gives out completely. These floorboards are killing me.'

Laughing, she threw her arms around him and pulled him back into bed. 'Clayton Miller, I absolutely love you! And I love it when you're so romantic.'

'I try, Alice. Honestly, I try.'

She kissed him but no sooner had her lips touched his than he pushed her away. 'Oh no you don't, no distractions. I want my answer.'

'The answer is an unequivocal yes,' she said.

'You're sure? I mean, it's a big commitment taking on someone like me. It won't be easy.'

'Oh, I reckon I'm more than capable of doing the job.'

He smiled. 'I reckon you are too.' He held her closely and kissed her for a very long time.

A rousing cheer sounded inside Alice's head. *Hurrah for the Queen of New Beginnings!* This was one beginning that wasn't going to end badly. She had finally cracked it.

We do hope that you have enjoyed reading
this large print book.

Did you know that all of our titles
are available for purchase?

We publish a wide range of high quality
large print books including:
Romances, Mysteries, Classics
General Fiction
Non Fiction and Westerns

Special interest titles available in
large print are:
The Little Oxford Dictionary
Music Book
Song Book
Hymn Book
Service Book

Also available from us courtesy of
Oxford University Press:
Young Readers' Dictionary
(large print edition)
Young Readers' Thesaurus
(large print edition)

For further information or a free
brochure, please contact us at:
Ulverscroft Large Print Books Ltd.,
The Green, Bradgate Road, Anstey,
Leicester, LE7 7FU, England.
Tel: (00 44) 0116 236 4325
Fax: (00 44) 0116 234 0205